'An absolute masterpiece. Twisty, turny and full
of surprises!'
Angela Marsons

'Mel Sherratt's books are as smart and edgy
as her heroines'
Cara Hunter

'Mel Sherratt is the new queen of gritty police procedurals'
C.L. Taylor

'Twists and turns and delivers a satisfying shot of tension'
Rachel Abbott

'Heart-stoppingly tense. I love Mel Sherratt's writing'
Angela Clarke

'Gripped me from the first page and didn't let go until
the heart-stopping conclusion!'
Robert Bryndza

'A writer to watch out for'
Mandasue Heller

'Uncompromising, powerful and very real –
an important new voice'
David Mark

'Mel's vivid imagination really brings her characters to life'
Kerry Wilkinson

'Mel Sherratt is a unique voice in detective fiction'
Mail on Sunday

Praise for Mel Sherratt:

HUSH HUSH

Mel Sherratt is the author of eleven novels, all of which have become bestsellers. In 2018, she was named as one of her home town of Stoke-on-Trent's top 100 influential people. She lives in Stoke-on-Trent, Staffordshire, with her husband and terrier, Dexter.

MEL SHERRATT

HUSH HUSH

avon.

Published by AVON
A division of HarperCollins*Publishers* Ltd
1 London Bridge Street
London SE1 9GF

www.harpercollins.co.uk

A Paperback Original 2018

1

A catalogue copy of this book is available from the British Library.

ISBN: 978-0-00-827104-6

This novel is entirely a work of fiction. The names, characters and
incidents portrayed in it are the work of the author's imagination.
Any resemblance to actual persons, living or dead, events or
localities is entirely coincidental.

Typeset in Minion by Palimpsest Book Production Ltd, Falkirk, Stirlingshire
Printed and bound in UK by CPI Group (UK) Ltd, Croydon CR0 4YY

This b

For

To Chris and Alison,
for always believing in me.

ACKNOWLEDGEMENTS

This book might have my name on the cover but there has been an awful lot of teamwork in the background making it happen. Thank you to my agent, Maddy Milburn, who has been with me on my journey for several years now. She and her team are just the best. She's my partner-in-crime and her enthusiasm and vigour for my work is second only to her friendship.

Thank you to everyone at HarperCollins and Avon who have taken me under their wing – Charlie, Kate, Oli, Anna, Sabah, Dominic, Elke and Molly. I am feeling incredibly lucky to work with you all. Special thanks to my editors extraordinaire, Helen Huthwaite and Rachel Faulkner-Willcocks, who not only loved the idea of the series I was creating, but then helped me to develop it into something I am so proud of. I've always said that editors add the sparkle to my words: you two sprinkled everything with glitter.

Thanks to my besties who share the journey with me – Alison Niebieszczanski, Caroline Mitchell, Talli Roland, Cally Taylor and Sharon Sant. You guys are always there for laughter, bubbles, writer chats and cake – a support group second to none! I really can't thank you enough and hope there is always more to come.

And to a certain group of CSers. Every day, I laugh with you. You all know who you are.

A huge thanks to everyone at my local newspaper, *The Sentinel* and StokeonTrentLive. You continually fly the Sherratt flag and I am so grateful to you all. Particular thanks to Martin Tideswell for all you do for the city through your passion and dedication. You rock, Mart.

Thank you to Laura Alcock for allowing me to use the fabulous name of your business, Posh Gloss. As well, a huge heartfelt thank you to Gareth Higgins, MBE, who bid a handsome sum of money in aid of local charity, The Donna Louise, to be named as a character in this book. When I contacted Gareth, he told me that he'd bid for the prize for his dad, Mick Higgins. Thanks for your kind donation, Gareth. I hope I did you proud, gentlemen.

Thank you to all the bloggers and reviewers who give up their time to help me. I can't mention everyone by name as there are far too many and I would be afraid to miss one out. But each and every minute you spend reading my books and spreading the word about them means so much more than I can ever put into words. As well, a huge thanks to my loyal readers, some of whom I now call friends, who have sent me messages of support. Whether it be via email, tweets or Facebook, each one makes me believe that little bit more.

Finally, to my husband, Chris. Thank you for your unwavering support, love and honesty. For raising me up when I'm feeling down – and for twisting my twists just that little bit further! And for not complaining too much at the amount of times I burn our meals. I could never do, and would never want to do, anything without you beside me. Love you to bits, fella.

March 2017

George Steele came out of The Potter's, leaving the noise of the rowdy party still going on behind him. Outside, it was fresh, the hint of warmer weather around the corner.

It was nearing midnight as he began to walk home. He had planned on only having one more for the road, but that was two hours ago, and now he was struggling to stand up.

He wondered if Kathleen had left him anything to eat. He could murder something hot inside him. If she hadn't, he would wake her. She could cook him something. He salivated at the thought of a bacon butty.

It was a short walk down a country lane and along a small path. Sober, it took him half as long as it did when he was legless. He snorted to himself as he stumbled to his right. It would take him all night, zigzagging the road as he was.

His phone beeped and he pulled it out of his pocket. He brought it near to his face, trying to see who was calling him, but he couldn't read the screen, so he let it ring out. At this time of night, it would only be someone looking to cause trouble. He was sick and tired of people after a piece of him. Always wanting to fight with him, anger him, disrespect him. He couldn't even rely on his useless sons to sort anything out. They just weren't up to his standard when it came to what he expected of his family. And as for his silly daughter . . . He didn't have the words for how pathetic she was.

He was at the path now, minutes from home. The house stood on four acres of land, the room he'd had so much fun with hidden away at the bottom of the garden. It had been passed down to him by his parents, the only thing they'd given him he'd ever been glad of. How he had hated his father and the time spent with him there, at the hands of a monster. Still, at least it meant he'd known how to get the best out of his own family too.

George didn't hear a sound as someone crept up behind him. A crack to the head made him stumble forward. Another and he dropped to his knees. He turned around and was greeted with a whack in the face. Unable to see who it was in the dark, he tried to crawl away on all fours, but a kick to the stomach had him coughing. He held up a hand – each hit was followed by a pause.

'Wait!' he cried, catching his breath, sitting up on his haunches. 'Whoever has sent you to do this, I'll double your money.' He winced in agony as pain pulsed through his body. 'Because when I find out, be prepared to get a lot worse than you're giving me now.'

A hit to the side of his face and colours exploded inside his head. He dropped to the floor again.

It took a few more blows before he realised his attacker wasn't going to stop.

ONE

August 2018

Grace Allendale climbed the restaurant stairs to the first floor and slipped back to her seat at the table.

'We've just placed our order,' DC Sam Markham said, beaming at her. 'Won't be long now.'

Grace smiled back. It was Friday evening and everyone in Spice World was in high spirits. The clientele were letting off steam, catching up with friends and family. Grace would rather have ordered a takeaway and eaten alone at home, but needs must.

The restaurant was situated in the lower part of Hanley, around the corner from Bethesda Police Station, Grace's new headquarters. From the outside the Victorian building looked weather-worn and, as they'd walked inside the curry house, she'd wondered what she was letting herself in for.

But it had been a pleasant surprise to find a warm and modern atmosphere. There were tables full of diners spread out over the ground floor, and a grand staircase leading upstairs to many more. The music playing in the background was modern rock, not too intrusive, yet loud enough to be heard over the friendly banter of people out enjoying themselves.

This was the first time Grace had met her work colleagues since she'd got her new job as detective sergeant, a promotion from her former role in Salford. Grace had lived there for the past twenty-three years. She'd joined the police force after leaving university and had worked as a police constable before transferring to Major Crimes as a detective. She'd been quite settled in that role for several years, but when things took a tumble in her private life, she'd decided that she needed a new goal to aim for.

Having taken her detective sergeant's exam last year, when a post had come up in her birthplace of Stoke-on-Trent, she decided to put in for it. She needed a change, somewhere she could start afresh, even though she wasn't quite sure it was a good decision to come back to the town from which she and her mum had fled all those years ago. But circumstances were different now. The man who had caused them so much pain was no longer around.

After she'd been offered the job, Grace had got an invite to join the team for a night out before her start date on Monday. There was only one officer who hadn't been able to make it, someone called Alex Challinor, who had a previous engagement he couldn't get out of, although no one had enlightened her as to what it was.

Around her, her new colleagues were sharing some in-joke. Then suddenly Nick Carter, their DI, stopped laughing and turned to her.

'Sorry, we're ignoring you. You say you lived in Stoke when you were younger, Grace?' he asked.

All eyes fell on her. 'Yes, until I was twelve,' she replied. 'Then my parents divorced and I moved to Salford with my mum.'

'So, you don't have many memories?' DC Perry Wright asked.

'I have a few,' Grace nodded. She could remember far more than she would ever share with them. The nights she'd heard

4

her mum screaming as her father laid into her. The times there was no money for food because he'd spent it all in the pub. The days when he would go missing and be brought home by the police after being locked up in a cell. The weeks he spent with other women before fighting his way back into their house again. The double life he led that she knew nothing of until she was old enough to understand : . . . 'But I expect so much has changed since then, anyway,' she added.

'Not much to write home about,' Sam giggled. 'But we still love it. And you'll soon know the place, and its people. Even the undesirables.'

Nick raised his glass in the air. 'Welcome to the Major Crimes Team.'

Everyone joined Nick in a toast. Only Perry, sitting opposite her, didn't lift his eyes to hers as well. He hadn't joined in the conversation much either, she'd noticed.

The door to the restaurant opened and several men came in at once. From her first-floor position, Grace looked down at the newcomers as their laughter filled the room, booming, loud and boisterous. She counted four of them, all casually dressed in shirts and jeans; lean, with biceps and quads looking fit to burst through their clothes. A waiter rushed across to them and they were quickly seated, despite the busyness of the room.

As she turned back to her group, Grace noticed the atmosphere at their table had changed.

'Seriously?' Perry sighed. 'Can't we have one night out without it being a busman's holiday?'

'They might not see us up here,' Nick said.

'What's wrong?' Grace asked, realising she had a bird's-eye view from her seat at the end of the table. Nick had his back to the group.

'Meet part of the Steele family and some of their cronies.'

Sam nodded her head in the direction of the men. 'They like to think they're untouchable.'

'They own Steele's Gym in Baddeley Green,' Nick informed her. 'It's got a boxing club attached to it as well.'

'So, it's a legit establishment?' Grace questioned, trying to keep her voice calm and professional.

'Let's say it isn't just a place where you can go for a workout,' Nick explained. 'The Steeles are one of our local crime families. Their father, George, was murdered last year; his killer's still at large.'

Grace dropped her eyes momentarily, feeling her cheeks burn at the mention of that name, but none of the others seemed to notice. She'd read that George Steele had last been seen leaving his local pub just before midnight on March fifteenth the previous year. His family had reported him missing the next day, and he'd been found a few hours later on a shortcut through to his home. He'd been beaten to death. A thorough investigation had given the police no leads. Now it had been assigned to Alex Challinor, her absent colleague, to work on if anything new came to light.

'There are two sons and a daughter.' Nick looked at Grace. 'Eddie is the one on the right. He's the eldest brother.'

Grace looked down through the glass balustrade to see a man of about thirty-seven reading a menu before slapping it on the table and glancing around the room. She dropped her eyes for a moment.

'The one sitting opposite him is Leon. He's a couple of years younger.'

Grace focused on Eddie's brother, an almost identical version of him. If she hadn't known better, she might have thought they were twins. Both had dark brown hair and were well groomed – attractive in their own rough-around-the-edges way.

'There's a sister, too. Jade. She runs a nail bar in the gym with their mother, Kathleen,' Perry added.

'Testosterone aplenty.' Sam let out a long sigh. 'Maybe they'll be fine once they get some food.'

Nick sat up straight as three waiters walked towards their table. 'Speaking of which, here comes our order.'

Grace placed her napkin on her lap. As she dished rice on to her plate, she heard a squeal and looked downstairs. Leon Steele had seized a waitress who was walking past, pulling her onto his knee.

'Hey,' the woman protested, trying to get back to her feet, but he held on to her. She squirmed as he whispered something in her ear. As the group burst into loud jeers again, all heads in the restaurant turned towards them. Grace groaned inwardly. She was hoping to have more time to get to know her work colleagues before this happened.

Perry removed his napkin from his lap and made to stand up. But Nick held him back.

'Let's just see if it calms down,' Nick said as restaurant staff rushed over. 'It's going to get a lot more troublesome and ruin many people's nights if we wade in.'

Grace watched as Leon released the woman and held up his arms in surrender. 'Only having a bit of fun,' he shouted to the room as the waitress scuttled off.

'I hate how they think they own the place.' Perry scowled as he looked down at his food. 'Meanwhile we sit back and let it happen.'

'This is a night out, not a team briefing,' Nick chided. 'And for now they haven't seen us, so let's just leave it like that.'

Eddie Steele's gaze rose up and Grace dropped her eyes immediately. When she looked again seconds later, he was staring her way. Their eyes locked for a moment, as if they were the only two people in the room, before Grace lowered hers once more.

She couldn't hold her tongue. It wasn't what she'd intended

but she might as well come clean now. Really, was there any other way than to tell her work colleagues the truth?

Grace turned to the group and put her glass down heavily on the table, enough to get everyone's attention but not to cause too much of a fuss so that everyone else looked their way.

'You wanted to know all about me?' She looked at each one of them in turn, knowing that, once she'd said the next few words, everything was going to become a whole lot harder.

'They already know!' Nick intervened.

Grace tried to stop a frown forming on her face.

'I told them about Matt.' Nick shook his head. 'I'm sorry; I thought it would make things easier for you. I know how much you need a fresh start.'

'Yeah, we're all here for you,' Sam said. 'It must be really hard to deal with.'

Grace gave a faint smile. Nick stared at her. She could almost sense his thoughts, telling her to stay silent.

She didn't want him to lie for her. She wanted to be honest upfront. But it was clear from the look in Nick's eye that she needed to keep quiet.

She couldn't tell anyone that Eddie and Leon Steele were her half-brothers. And George Steele, criminal, racketeer and murder victim, had been her father.

TWO

September 2018

TUESDAY – DAY 1

Josh Parker pushed up the weight with a long and loud groan. His shift had finished half an hour ago, the same time Steele's Gym had closed, but he liked to stay behind to do his own workout.

It was half past ten in the evening and no one else was around. The clank of the hand weights as he put them back into the stand seemed to echo round the large room.

He'd worked at Steele's Gym since it had opened in 2006. On the outside, it was a standard gym, with a boxing club and a nail bar that was more often than not manned by Clara, the receptionist. The establishment purposely had no airs and graces, which suited most of their clients.

On the inside, behind the scenes, money was the tool. Cash was loaned to anyone who was desperate and couldn't get it elsewhere, and paid back with crippling percentage rates. Beatings were rife if money wasn't delivered on time and had to be collected. The monthly parties that they'd recently set up were working a treat to bring in extra too. It was something that Eddie Steele didn't like, but the money they were raking in each time was not to be sniffed at.

Josh knew the police were keeping an eye on him and the Steeles, as were the family they were rivals with, the Woodmans. They too were watching their enemies. Eddie had asked Josh in particular to pay attention to what was going on, even though Leon thought *he* was looking after the gym.

He clasped his hands together in front of his body and flexed his biceps. They almost seemed to pop out of his skin and he smiled at himself in the mirror.

'Looking good,' he said quietly. 'Looking good.'

A noise made him turn his head. He thought he'd heard a door open and he listened for a moment. But there was nothing else, so he went back to admiring himself.

Peace and quiet meant that he could pay attention during his workout. Music blaring through the day, the thump of the treadmills, the whining of the rowers, plus the banter from the clients all faded away once he was on his own. There were mirrors all around that he could look at without fear of being called narcissistic. He was vain, he admitted freely, but in this job it paid to look good. Working for Eddie Steele, it was expected.

He pushed the barbell above his head, glancing at a photo beside him on the wall. He and Eddie were fourteen and wearing boxing gloves, arms around each other's shoulders after fighting in the ring. Eddie had always been victorious in everything he did. He had a vicious streak Josh couldn't match, no matter how hard he tried.

Josh had known the Steele family since he was at junior school. He and Eddie had been in the same class and had gelled during a PE session when Eddie had legged someone over for tackling the football from him. A fight had ensued and Josh managed to break it up after the teacher had blown his whistle. As he pulled the boy up, a swift thump in the stomach when the teacher wasn't looking ensured that he and Eddie clicked.

And it wasn't just he and Eddie who had got close. Eddie's sister, Jade, had been the local sleep-around for years beyond school. At thirty-two now, she was the youngest of the three Steeles. Josh had spent a year with her himself in his early twenties, before realising his anger and temper would be better served to superior uses. Jade knew exactly how to wind him up. It was as if she goaded him deliberately. And because she was a Steele, the fact that he couldn't slap her around if she proved a threat to anything he was doing didn't sit well with him. He and Eddie had their fingers in lots of pies back then, long before the gym opened, and he wasn't up to losing that.

If it weren't for Josh Parker, Leon would be second-in-command. Josh knew that Leon hated this and there was no love lost between them. Much to Josh's annoyance, Eddie had always bailed Leon out of trouble, and since they were teens, Leon had wanted in with everything they did. Josh hadn't liked it, yet he'd put up with it, biding his time over the years before Leon could be taken out of the equation altogether. But now, Leon was stronger than ever, even though he was still only the younger brother.

Josh had tried on many occasions to land Leon in trouble with the law so that he'd be booted off to prison for a few years, allowing Josh to get his claws into the family business. There was so much up for grabs, and he wanted it. He'd earned it. And it was time he got what he was owed.

After a post-workout shower, Josh switched off the lights and locked up the building. Walking around to the back of the car park, he clicked off the alarm as he drew level with his car. The lights flashed yellow and he opened the boot and put in his gym bag. But as he closed it, he jumped as a figure appeared at the side of the car.

'What do you want?' he asked, rolling his eyes.

Out of nowhere, something was sprayed in his face. He squeezed his eyes shut as they began to burn.

'What the . . .?'

Josh put his hands to his face and staggered. More liquid was thrown on him. Then the smell of burning flesh was all around him as he dropped to his knees.

Crying out, he writhed on the ground. Some bastard had thrown acid at him. It was going to ruin his face! Fear coursed through him, tears were too painful to form. In desperation, he rolled over, trying to dampen his hands on the tarmac, wet from a recent thunderstorm.

He could hear nothing but his own screams as his skin fell from the backs of his hands. Breathing heavily, he tried to listen, to see if his attacker was still there. Was there anyone near him now? He pulled a hand away from his face, but pain ripped through him again and he cried out. It was as if his skin had shrunk, stretching like torn cling film.

Time seemed to slow as the burns went deeper. Then, he felt a hand on his shoulder and he was pulled over onto his back. Someone straddled him.

He couldn't open his eyes. He couldn't even hold out a hand in defence. All he could do was shout.

In silence, his attacker raised a knife high in the air.

THREE

Grace slowed down to catch her breath, and her run became a jog.

The house she was renting was around five miles from Bethesda Police Station, depending on which road you took, in a part of the city called Weston Coyney. Caverswall Avenue was just through a set of busy traffic lights and near to Park Hall Country Park.

The house was a pre-war semi, tucked away at the top of a cul-de-sac. Phil and Becky Armstrong, who lived next door, had been relieved to see her moving in, telling her in much detail about the rowdy family who had been evicted. It explained why it was clean and recently decorated, with a newly fitted kitchen and bathroom. Everything had been trashed before the last tenants had left.

Making sure the sound of the machine couldn't be heard through the walls of the adjoining house was the first thing Grace had checked with her neighbours. There was nothing worse than the drone and pounding of a treadmill, especially in the early hours of the morning. Luckily, she had space for it at the back of the house in the small conservatory, and the couple told her they couldn't hear anything. They said they didn't mind a bit of noise here and there after what they'd had to live with for the past six months.

She glanced at her watch: 5.35 a.m. Today's date had played heavily on her mind for the past few days. It was surprising she'd got any sleep really. But she had forced herself to read on her Kindle until she'd drifted off.

It was in the early hours that she'd woken up covered in a layer of sweat and sat up in bed. She could feel tears on her face; she hadn't cried in her sleep for a long time. She'd reached for the pillow on the empty side of the bed and let her tears continue.

The day had hardly begun and yet she was already dreading seeing the date on any paperwork she'd have to complete. September twelfth. Five years to the day that her life had changed forever.

In early 2013 she'd had a healthy husband who loved running with her and playing football every weekend. But shortly after his birthday in July, his weight began to drop a little, and it became difficult for him to shake off any minor bugs. His energy levels plummeted and, after a blood test at the doctor's, he'd been fast-tracked to the hospital as a matter of urgency.

Five years ago to the day, they had found out he had acute myeloid leukaemia. The consultant had spent an hour with them going through what could be done. It was curable and correctable with chemotherapy, but there was no possible way of knowing whether, even if they cleared it this time, it wouldn't come back. It had – three times in total – and he'd lost his fight in 2016.

Grace ran faster to stop images pushing themselves to the forefront of her mind. Matt had been thirty-two when he was diagnosed; she had recently turned thirty; and they were both in the prime of their lives. It had been heartbreaking to see her soulmate waste away.

She recalled the night he'd frightened them when he'd started to throw up and all this black stuff had come up, making Grace retch too. She could clearly remember the time he'd punched the wall in anger and then wept in her arms at the injustice of having to leave her behind. The times she'd administered his drugs because he'd been too tired to get out of bed. And that one moment when he had begged her to kill him, to put him out of his misery, would be forever etched on her heart.

She'd never had herself down as a nurse, but that's what she'd become during his last few months, until he was unable to be cared for at home and was admitted to a local hospice. She hadn't told anyone, but it had made it better for her. She had someone to watch over him all the time she wasn't there. She didn't want to be his carer – she wanted to be his wife.

Now, she hated not having to think for two people any more. Holidays, get-togethers, even the food shopping – when she did any – was all for her. It still took a lot of getting used to. Losing her mum as well, less than twelve months after, had *almost* taken her over the edge.

After a few more seconds, she switched the speed up on the machine. She pushed herself further and further, faster and faster, until eventually she had no choice but to stop.

In the kitchen, Matt's smile stared back at her as she grabbed a bottle of water from the fridge. She closed the door and ran a finger over his image. The photo had been taken before the disease had made him into a skeleton with no hair. Here he was healthy, eyes shining with no bags underneath them, glowing skin and a ferocious appetite for life. After two years, the memories of him at the height of his debilitation had faded and this was how she remembered him now.

She moved to the kitchen window. It looked like another

nice day ahead, clear blue skies and warmer-than-average temperatures. How she wished there weren't dark clouds hanging over her. You shouldn't dwell on the past, her mum used to say to her, but it was far easier said than done when the past had taken away a planned future.

Two hours later, showered and energised but still feeling emotional, she closed the door to the side of her that she didn't want people to see and headed to work.

FOUR

Bethesda Police Station was situated in the street of the same name, at the bottom of the city centre. Before 1910, Stoke-on-Trent was made up of six towns. It became a federated city with a merger in that year, Hanley then becoming the main shopping centre of the Potteries.

Grace had already been told by several disgruntled members of the public that Hanley was not, and never would be, Stoke-on-Trent's city centre as it was known on signposts. *Stoke* was the centre, it was where the railway station was situated and where the civic centre had been until recently. But to her, Stoke was a drive-through town with a few roads. It seemed that most of the money and resources were focused on Hanley, which was great for where she was based. Some areas had been pedestrianised, making them feel safer and a pleasure to walk around, perhaps sit in to have a sandwich during a work break. At night, like most cities of its size, it had its problems with the homeless and drunk and disorderly. Violence was often rife at kicking-out times, but for the most part it boasted a good vibe.

Coming back had been quite an eye-opener for her. Of course, she didn't remember much of the city at the age of

17

twelve, but after working for such a large force as Greater Manchester, policing areas in Stoke was a far easier way to learn of the local goings-on. Even after just a few weeks, Grace already had the lay of the land. And she had the previous detective sergeant, Allie Shenton, at her disposal. The woman was a fount of all knowledge, having already helped her out quite a few times with intel.

Filling her shoes was a big ask. She'd met with Allie the week after starting her position. Allie had recently taken up a new role as Community Inspector, heading up six community neigh-bourhood teams, one in each region of the city. During the meeting, Allie had told Grace about her work colleagues, some of the people she'd meet on her patch and some of the ones she'd want to avoid.

It had been an easy meet, lots of polite chat, but Grace had been thankful for an insight into what she had let herself in for. She had thought long and hard about returning to Stoke and Allie had made it a little better for her. Secretly, Grace realised that Allie was keeping an eye on what was going on at the station. It must be hard to let go after so long working in the same place. But equally, Grace had begun to look at her as a mentor. Allie hadn't minded when she'd questioned her further about a number of subjects and people.

Grace's first month in the role had been a quiet one spent with her team of three detective constables, getting to know the community and feel of the areas and also some of its inhabitants. The team were on the first of three floors of the station, along with several soft interview suites and also an area where civvy staff worked. Back in Manchester, Grace had been in a building that was in desperate need of refurbishment, both inside and out. Its layout had meant that she'd been in a room not even big enough to call a cupboard, with a team of four other officers. Here it was open-plan, with about thirty desks, all new, swanky even – although the kitchen was still a health risk with all the leftover food and dirty dishes lying around.

She smiled her thanks when a mug of coffee was plonked down on her desk, her 'Wonder Woman' mug a joke present from Matt just before he'd died. Across from her on the opposite desk, Sam Markham sat down with her own drink and clicked her mouse to wake up her computer. Grace now knew she was thirty-seven, living with her partner, Craig, and her six-year-old daughter, Emily, from a previous marriage. Sam was small in build with dimples in her cheeks and wore her long blonde hair mostly tied up in a ponytail, making her look even more baby-faced. But Allie had told her, 'Don't let Sam fool you. She's more than capable of holding her own when necessary.'

Down the room, she could just about see Nick squashed into his tiny partitioned office. An active man in his mid-fifties, he'd mentioned in small talk as he'd got to know her that his wife, Sharon, was begging him to take early retirement. But he enjoyed his job as detective inspector and wanted to stay working for the force because it kept his mind active. He was six foot three and ran several times a week to keep his middle-age spread at bay.

On her first day, as he'd shown her around the building, Nick had mentioned that the DCI thought it best Grace kept quiet about her connection to the Steele family for now. She had asked why but they had been interrupted when a man had walked past who he wanted to introduce her to. Nick hadn't picked up the conversation again afterwards. She'd wondered why, reasoned perhaps he had his own motives, which she would find out in time.

Nick's phone rang, and a rush of adrenaline flowed through Grace as she watched him stand up, beckoning her over quickly before putting it down with a bang.

'I thought you might want a heads-up. Call's just come in about a body found at Steele's Gym,' Nick told her.

Grace groaned inwardly.

'Someone's been attacked with acid and then stabbed in the car park. Josh Parker's car is there.'

'Josh Parker?'

'He's Eddie Steele's right-hand man.'

'Ah.' Grace watched him leave the room.

When she stayed where she was, Nick turned back to her. 'Are you coming?'

'Is that wise, sir?'

'I don't know but I can't see another sergeant spare at the moment.'

Grace tried not to let her expression give away her alarm as she followed behind him. Surely her first possible murder investigation wasn't going to be on family soil?

FIVE

Grace wiped her sweaty palms discreetly on her trousers as Nick nudged the car up onto the pavement to park outside the crime scene. Situated on Leek Road, two miles from the city centre, Steele's Gym stood back from the road in a prime position. Once housing a preschool nursery, it was a single-storey building spread on an acre of land, with a car park to its right. According to Sam, the local authority register for business rates stated that Eddie Steele had been renting it since 2006. A large canvas banner hung on the wrought-iron railings at her side. 'No pain, no gain. All-in monthly passes only £40.' She doubted that would tempt anyone in today. They'd be more interested in what was going on outside in the car park.

'Good to go?' Nick asked her.

Grace looked back, unaware he had been watching her as she stared out of the window. 'I'm not sure I will ever be ready for this.'

'Just keep your calm. If they say anything, I'll handle it accordingly.'

She released her seat belt and got out of the car, joining DC Perry Wright who had parked in front of them. Grace had warmed to Sam but not so much to Perry. He had turned forty the year before; she'd learned he had been married to his wife, Lisa, for thirteen years and recently become a father to Alfie, who was three months old. Just like Nick, his blond hair was shaven close to his head to hide his receding hairline. Allie Shenton said he'd either be nice from the get-go as he was that type of person, or be aloof – not only because he'd known and worked with Allie for such a long time, but because he'd put in for the job of detective sergeant and Grace had beaten him to it.

Even though it was still early in the morning, sweat clung to her back. Despite her anxieties, it was too warm to be wearing the jacket to her trouser suit, but she didn't feel dressed without it, especially meeting new people. First appearances still counted in her eyes.

Across the main road, a crowd was already gathering in front of a row of terraced properties. As traffic zoomed by, three dogs sat patiently at their owners' feet, their morning outings either interrupted or lengthened. Two residents stood in their doorways holding mugs, chatting to themselves. Grace could almost hear them saying, 'Things like this don't happen on our doorstep.' It was the one thing she heard all the time, as if no one was allowed to bring ill repute to their part of the neighbourhood.

Her heels clicked on the pavement as she walked in silence with Nick and Perry towards the entrance gates. The crime scene had been cordoned off with police tape; all around them people worked. A police constable stood guarding the scene, writing down the names of people entering, checking IDs and pointing out where to go. There were several uniformed officers taking notes, and she saw one directing the traffic as it struggled to get past the row of police vehicles parked half on and off the kerb.

Ahead of them, she could see a small car with the logo of the local newspaper splashed across its side and wondered what their staff were like to work with. She'd prided herself in getting on well with the local newspaper's press team in Salford.

She, Nick and Perry each flashed their warrant cards. The crime scene tape was lifted and they dipped underneath it. They popped on white paper suits, latex gloves and covers over their footwear. Even though she was slim and toned, with a six-pack hidden underneath her shirt, the suit always made Grace feel as shapely as a hastily rolled snowman.

She tied back her long dark hair with a covered elastic band and placed a mask around her neck in readiness. Once she had it on, it would hide lips that had almost forgotten how to smile widely, but her eyes would still be seen. Grace knew you could tell so much by looking in people's eyes. Her own were brown and large, with long lashes that she accentuated with mascara and sculptured eyebrows. They were her best feature – when she was happy. For now, they were skittish, glancing around, trying to take everything in.

As Nick went off to speak to a uniformed officer, Grace took a deep breath, held her head high and walked forward. A white tent had been erected around the spot where the body lay. Forensic officers already in situ were suited and booted too.

'Do you get a lot of acid attacks in Stoke?' Grace asked Perry as they walked.

'Not many at all. I think the last one was some time last year.'

'And someone from the gym called this in, you say?'

Perry nodded his head in the direction of a man in his early twenties wearing a red tracksuit at the far end of the car park. He was giving details to a police constable, talking energetically and waving his hands.

'Trent Gibson. He was the first on shift. The gym opens

at seven and he found the body in the car park about ten minutes before.' Perry pointed to a black BMW where another forensic officer was going over it. 'That's Parker's car. Not sure why that wasn't burnt out to hide evidence. Doesn't make sense.'

'Well, it all seems to have been done for show, rather than someone trying to cover it up.' Grace turned back from checking out Gibson. 'I know we can't confirm the body until we have positive ID, but maybe our suspect thought it would prove who our victim was a little quicker?'

They reached the entrance to the tent and, after flicking the mask on, Grace stepped inside. She still put a hand to her mouth, trying to stop her instant gag reflex as her eyes fell on the seared face and hands of their victim. He was wearing gym wear, shorts and a short-sleeved T-shirt due to the weather being unseasonably warm. Splashes of accelerant had burnt holes in the material.

There were several people dotted around the crime scene. A forensic photographer was clicking away next to a man hunched over the body. His stooped position meant Grace couldn't see his frame, but she guessed him to be tall, perhaps early forties. He pushed up his glasses and smiled at her.

'Dave Barnett. Senior CSI, as I'm known as now since a nifty title change.'

'Grace Allendale.' She smiled back, even though he wouldn't be able to see it behind her mask. 'DS.'

'Yes, I know. Big boots to fill, but nice to meet you.'

'Do you have an approximate time of death yet?' Grace stooped down, repulsed but fascinated by the body at the same time. Even in her line of work, it never failed to amaze her what one human being was capable of doing to another.

'I'd say he died between ten p.m. and midnight last night. His face is a mess, but he has some quite distinctive tattoos on his biceps. He has recent dates and names of two people. Caleb and Mia.' Dave pointed at the body.

Perry gagged behind his mask and Grace hid a smirk. She already liked Dave Barnett.

'I'm not certain of cause of death yet, although it won't be because of the obvious.' Dave pointed to the body. 'But with the single stab wound to the chest as well, it looks like someone wanted to make sure he was dead.'

Having left the CSIs to do their job, Grace removed her mask and suit outside the tent. As she did so, she spotted a man waving for their attention. A leather satchel large enough to hold files or a laptop hung over his shoulder.

'Ah, come and meet Simon. Local press.' Perry placed the last of his protective gear into an evidence bag. 'What are you loitering round for?' he asked once he and Grace drew level with him.

'I wanted to know if you have anything for me?' the man responded, running his hand through blond, short, choppy hair as he caught Grace's eye. Close up, he reminded her of Callum Best, the celebrity. A cheeky-chappy sort who wouldn't look out of place if he came out with rhyming cockney slang or did a jig around a chimney up on a roof. He was dressed in a short-sleeved shirt with a navy tie that matched the colour of his trousers.

Perry shook his head. 'Nothing yet.' He looked at Grace. 'This is the legendary Simon Cole, senior crime reporter for the *Stoke News*.'

Simon laughed as he offered his hand to her and she shook it. 'Pleased to meet you.'

'Likewise.'

'Can you confirm it's Josh Parker?' he asked, looking at them both in turn.

'Where did you get that name from?' Perry narrowed his eyes.

'It's the word on da street.' Simon put on a voice and grinned. 'Is it true? Can you tell me?'

Grace shook her head.

'Can you confirm it's murder then?' Simon looked at her with pleading eyes.

'We're looking into all possibilities at the moment,' Grace replied.

Perry smirked.

'So you have nothing for me?' Simon glanced at Perry.

'No,' Perry said. 'You'll be the first to know when we do, though.'

Simon sighed. 'I suppose I'll go and talk to the public while I wait.'

Grace could see he was reluctant to leave. She guessed his reporter's nose was twitching, but his manner was warm, in contrast to that of a few of the journalists she'd dealt with over the years.

'How's everything going with Natalie?' Perry asked Simon. 'Things still bitter?'

'She's taking me for every penny.' Simon rolled his eyes. 'Which would be annoying if either of us had any decent money.'

'He got shafted for a younger model,' Perry explained to Grace.

'You make me sound like a car,' Simon protested.

'She walked all over him,' Perry added.

'I know, I know.' Simon nodded. 'I can't help being so nice.'

Grace saw how blue his eyes were as they crinkled up. Sincere too, which she didn't see very often.

'I'd best be off to do my job.' Simon pointed to the residents across the street.

Grace noticed him blushing and gave him a shy smile. She

turned to Perry once he'd gone. 'So, tattoos and the car make me feel confident Josh Parker is our victim, but we won't be allowed to release this information until we have a confirmed ID. Nick has gone to inform his wife, even though she can't see the body yet. For now, let's look at the CCTV footage and . . .' Grace stopped talking when she saw he wasn't listening. His eyes were trained over her shoulder.

A shiver of dread passed through her as she turned her head in the direction Perry was looking. Marching towards them were two men and a woman. The two men she recognised from Spice World the month before.

The woman shared the same hair and skin colouring as Grace. And, like Grace, she had long legs with a slim build.

'Well, well, well.' Eddie Steele was the first to speak, removing his sunglasses.

Grace swallowed as she brought herself tall to face her half-brothers and half-sister.

SIX

The situation was surreal. This was never how Grace had intended to meet her family. But then again, she hadn't expected the first murder case she worked on here in Stoke-on-Trent to be so close to home.

It was hard to speak in such close proximity to them. Although they had never met, Grace wondered if they knew as much about her as she knew about them. Her mum, Martha, had certainly suggested that. She had also told Grace that Eddie was two years older than her, that she was two months younger than Leon and had a half-sister three years younger. Their father, George, had been sleeping with both her mother and theirs at the same time, for a number of years, leading a double life.

Aware they were all looking at her, Grace stepped forward, but still she said nothing.

Eddie turned to Perry. 'I suppose you'll be wanting to speak to us?'

Perry nodded. 'We need to find out your whereabouts last night. General questions for now. This is DS Allendale.'

'Hello.' Grace held out her hand to Eddie. His grip was as firm as her own.

'Leon' – Eddie pointed to his brother – 'and Jade's our sister.'

Grace shook both their hands in quick succession, worrying in case any of them revealed they already knew of each other. The resemblance between her and Jade was so significant that she hoped Perry didn't notice. She could almost see her own eyes staring back at her.

But more than that, it was the way Jade stood: on her right foot to the detriment of her left, similar to something Grace always did. And the way she smiled, the full shape of her lips. She wondered what their mother looked like; was she similar to Grace's own? Martha Steele, née Benson, had been olive-skinned with dark brown hair and not an ounce of fat on her.

Grace took a deep breath and asserted herself once more. 'I believe DC Wright knows you all, so if I can get on with the questioning, we can do the formal things later.' She turned to Perry. 'Can you go and talk to Trent Gibson?'

Perry frowned, but she waved him away politely. She wasn't sure if the Steeles would blow her cover. On the one hand, it might be a good thing because then she wouldn't feel so deceitful. But then again, she could be removed from the case and she didn't want that either. 'Tread carefully' would have to be her motto for today.

She followed the siblings into a small and dimly lit hallway, its red carpeted flooring having seen better days. Walls were painted cream with the odd scuff mark. To the right was a door with a sign for toilets and changing rooms. Paint was peeling off the corner of the ceiling and the smell of artificial air-freshener lingered unpleasantly.

Grace looked around. She could see no security barriers, the kind accessed by a swipe card like the gym she used to be a member of in Salford, so there must be something else.

'Is there a signing-in book?' she asked.

'Inside the main building,' Eddie told her. 'We have lockers too. Things have a habit of going walkabout unless we put them away, if you catch my drift.' He pointed to a set of double swing doors. 'Be careful, the swing might come back and hit you,' he warned. 'Don't want to knock you out on your first visit.'

Grace forced a smile as he held the door open for her to walk through.

'We'll be saving that for the second time,' he muttered.

She turned to him, seeing no friendliness in his features. Up so close, her resemblance to him was uncanny. More noticeably, Grace could see how much he looked like George Steele as she remembered him from around the time she and her mother had left. Eddie must be about the same age as her father had been back then. It unnerved her: this was going to be harder than she had imagined.

Once through the doors, the room opened out into a large area. To one side was an array of gym equipment around the outer wall. On the other was a boxing ring with several punch-bags and weight benches around the side. Grace wondered why they weren't separated. If she was working out, she wouldn't want to see anyone punched to the floor, friendly or not. It would put her off completely.

'And you say you only have the one establishment in the city?' she asked Eddie.

'That's right.'

Walking inside Steele's Gym made Grace realise why they hadn't branched out across Stoke-on-Trent. Not everyone would like this set-up. It was intimidating, to say the least. Nick had mentioned that this wasn't its only selling point. She hoped she could find out more about what was going on behind the scenes.

Eddie showed her into a smaller room on the right of the

building. It had three doors leading off it. He pointed to the first on the left.

'Come through into the office and we can discuss things further.'

SEVEN

It was a tight fit to squeeze everyone in. The room held a desk and computer, a filing cabinet with paperwork piled on its top and a small settee squashed in front of an opaque-glass window. Leon and Jade sat down on that, while Eddie went behind the desk.

Grace cleared her throat as they all looked at her, once again waiting for her to speak first. The atmosphere was loaded, but she wanted everyone to know that today was about Josh Parker, not anyone else's grievances.

'First of all, let's get this over and done with,' she started. 'Any questions about why I am back are really none of anyone's business but my own. I'm sorry to hear of your father's death but I come here representing Staffordshire Police.'

'As if we're interested in anything that brings you here,' Eddie snapped. 'Your lot weren't in the slightest bit concerned when our father was murdered.'

'I doubt that is true,' she interjected, her tone firm, before turning to the matter in hand. 'Is there an overall manager or is it a joint effort?'

'It's a *family*-run business,' he said. 'Leon, alongside Josh, looks after the general running of the gym and the boxing club. Jade and our mum run Posh Gloss, and I oversee the finances and day-to-day running of everything. Has someone gone to tell Christa, Josh's wife?'

Grace nodded. 'We will need her to make a positive identification of the body. Can you take me through what would have happened at closing time yesterday?'

'Josh was on duty with two other trainers until the gym closed at ten p.m. He usually stays behind to do his own workout then, so my guess is he was in the building for about an hour.'

'Are your staff left to work alone?' Grace frowned. 'Haven't you heard of the lone worker policy?'

'You've seen the size of Josh Parker?' Eddie scoffed as he pointed to a photo on the wall behind them.

Grace turned to see a recent image of Eddie, his arms around their as-yet-unconfirmed victim, who was built like the proverbial brick house. From the photo, she plainly recognised him as one of the men she had seen at Spice World on the night out with her team last month. Parker was tanned with shorn hair, a huge smile revealing a gold tooth. He was wearing a tight black T-shirt that was clearly a size too small and showed every curve of a torso that Grace had to admit was impressive. An image of a cartoon character flashed in front of her eyes as she noted his square chin. And no, she wouldn't want to mess with him. Josh's killer must have some guts. Imagine if it had gone wrong.

'He was taken by surprise for someone to do that to him,' Eddie added. 'And it was outside the building, so don't come all high and mighty with the lone worker policy thing. We look after our staff here. We *always* look after our own.'

She pulled her shoulders up that little bit higher, trying not to show how intimidated she felt.

'So Mr Parker was the last one to leave the building?' Grace started her questioning again.

'We didn't murder him, if that's what you're implying,' Leon almost growled at her.

'Was Josh the last one in the building?' Grace repeated, ignoring his sarcasm.

'I expect so,' Eddie replied.

'We'll need access to any security footage you have, inside and out.'

'We have a camera that covers the reception area but not the gym itself.' Eddie went over to a machine, pulled out a CD and handed it to Grace. 'And outside we have a camera on each corner of the building, but it doesn't cover all of the car park at the back.'

Grace raised her eyebrows. It all seemed pretty convenient. And if their suspect knew this, he or she might have known where to carry out the attack with less likelihood of being seen.

'You mentioned a signing-in book,' she said. 'Can you get me a list of everyone who was in the building yesterday evening – say, from six p.m. onwards? Staff, customers and guests, please.'

Eddie sat forward. 'There'll be around a hundred people in here during that time. It's our busiest period.'

Leon whistled under his breath. 'That's a lot of people to question.' He folded his arms and stared at Grace.

Just as she'd thought when she'd first seen them the month before, Leon was so much like Eddie that he could pass as his twin. If it hadn't been for the faint two-inch scar visible to the side of his right eye, they might even have been able to use each other as alibis.

She had a feeling over the coming days she would get to know them regardless. Once the investigation was going at full steam, they would be sick of the sight of her and the rest of the team, who were probably already here by now.

Grace ignored Leon again, choosing to look at Jade who

34

hadn't said a word yet. She was crying, soft sobs and tears pouring down her face.

'Are you okay?' she asked.

Jade nodded. 'It's such a shock, that's all. I was only talking to him on Monday. It doesn't seem possible.' She blew her nose loudly.

'What time did you all leave last night?' Grace glanced at each one of them in turn.

'Half past six,' Eddie said.

'Did you go straight home?'

'Yes. My son can vouch for me. I took him to football training at seven.'

'I wasn't here yesterday,' Jade said.

Grace looked at Leon. 'What about you?' she asked when he didn't come forward with anything.

'I'd say about eightish.'

'I'd say be more specific.' Grace's voice was just as curt as his.

Leon sighed. 'It was about ten past eight.'

Grace nodded and then turned back to Eddie. 'I was also told that Josh was your right-hand man?'

Eddie's glare alarmed her slightly and her left eye began to twitch under the strain of it. But she didn't want to look away. She wanted to see if grief was washing over him. She was watching them all to see if their reactions were real or put on especially for her.

Eddie swallowed. 'He was my best friend. I'd known him since junior school.'

'You all knew him well, I presume?' Grace looked at the others.

'Yes,' Jade said before wiping her nose loudly.

'You might have known him too,' Leon taunted.

'I didn't go to your school. I would have remembered that.'

Embarrassed by the reference, Grace looked at her notepad again. 'Do you know of anyone who might have wanted to harm Josh?' she asked no one in particular.

'Probably half of Stoke at one time or another.' Leon folded his arms. 'But no one would have messed with him if they'd seen him before he was toast.'

'Leon!' Jade's sobs grew louder.

'Sorry.' Leon had the manners to bow his head for a moment. 'Bit of a bitch, though. Tough to lose him.'

The room dropped into silence again as they remembered their friend. Grace took the opportunity to get out her contact cards and hand them round.

'Is this for when we go out for a family meal?' Leon took one from her.

'Show some respect, Leon,' Eddie warned.

'I think I've given her enough of that already' – Leon folded his arms – 'so don't tell me what to do.'

Surprised by the reference to their connection to her, Grace was desperate to get out of there and rejoin her colleagues. But she had to have her say first.

'I'd really appreciate it if you didn't tell my colleagues how we know each other.' She paused for a moment. 'I think it's best that we investigate Josh's murder without any hindrance.'

'Better the devil you know, and all that?' Eddie smirked. Leon and Jade both opened their mouths to speak, but he held up a hand and shook his head.

'I'll find out who is overseeing the house-to-house enquiries and ask them to keep you informed of anything that comes up while we continue with our investigations,' Grace added. 'We'll be in touch shortly.'

Once outside the room, Grace breathed a sigh of relief. It had surprised her that they'd accepted her request to keep her identity to themselves, perhaps even given her reason for concern as to why. She would have expected them to stir things up, cause trouble for her straight away.

Yet even though she had felt intimidated by the encounter, a feeling of anticlimax washed over her. She'd wanted to meet them all for many years, despite her job and their reputation. Secretly, she'd hoped they'd be friendlier with her. In an ideal world, she might have got to know them, but today had shown that wasn't likely to happen.

There was one thing she had learned, though; from that meeting alone, she sensed that the Steele family were unnerved about something. Grace had seen the looks flicking between them. Were they trying to put up a united front that didn't exist? Or was it meeting her that had made them feel so uncomfortable?

She went to join Perry.

'We've just busted Parker's locker open,' he told her. 'There's the usual stuff in there – spare workout clothes, a towel, pair of trainers and some protein shakes. But we also found a leather bag full of sex toys, condoms, lubes, et cetera. And this.' He held up a key ring. Attached to it was a luggage label, a key and an electronic key fob. The numbers *171794* were written on the label in black pen.

'Playing away?'

'It's possible.' Perry paused. 'What did he mean back there?'

'Who?' Grace questioned.

'Eddie. When he said "Well, well, well"?'

'I've no idea,' she replied, spotting Nick returning. 'You?'

Perry shook his head. 'I just wondered, with it being a really strange remark.'

'It was,' Grace said quickly. 'I'll go and update Nick.' She walked away, hoping he wouldn't see the blush she could feel forming on her face.

EIGHT

Eddie pinched the bridge of his nose. He wanted to punch out, hit the wall, throw the desk across the room, anything to rid himself of the feeling in his chest. He wouldn't let his grief show in public, not even to his family. But Josh had been his friend since they were young boys and he trusted him more than he ever had any member of his family.

'What the hell went on here last night?' he yelled, slapping his hand down on the desk.

Jade visibly jumped. 'Don't look at me!' she pouted.

'I'm not. But someone knows something and I intend to find out who by the end of the day.'

'Ed, I'm sorry.' Leon walked round the desk to him and put a hand on his shoulder.

'Yeah, I'm sure you are.' Eddie shirked it off.

'What's that supposed to mean?'

'Well, there was never any love lost between the two of you. I also know what's been going on. Josh told me what you've been doing to make more money on the side. I was as pissed off with him getting involved as I am with you. It's stupid. And would you stop with the snivelling, Jade?' Eddie snapped.

Jade pulled herself upright. 'I have feelings!' she shouted. 'Josh was my friend too. I can't believe he's gone.'

'I can't believe someone would kill him at the gym.' Leon ran a hand through his hair. 'And what the hell is *she* doing turning up here?'

'Grace?' Eddie said, noting his brother had evaded his accusations. His informant at the police station had told him she was back. He hadn't been too pleased about it at the time, and had hoped their paths wouldn't cross so soon. He'd wanted to get a handle on her before deciding whether they needed to get her on side, to recruit her to their team.

'Yeah,' Leon responded. 'As a fed, she's a threat. As a person, she's not welcome at all.'

'I think she made it perfectly clear she didn't want anything to do with us,' Eddie reached for his phone. There were already seven messages waiting for him – news was getting around.

'I didn't get that impression,' Jade said. 'I think she was shy, maybe overwhelmed to meet us all in one go. Aren't either of you intrigued to see what she's like?'

'No, and you aren't going to find out either,' Eddie remarked. 'She isn't family and never will be.'

'But that's—' Jade began.

'But nothing.' Eddie glared her way. 'You'll do as you're told.'

Jade folded her arms and stuck out her chin. 'You might think you can still bully me – both of you – but you can't tell me what to do now that Dad isn't here. If I want to see my sister, then I will.'

'Tell me,' Leon mocked, 'why hasn't she been in touch before?'

Jade lowered her eyes momentarily. 'I don't know.'

'And why didn't *you* get in touch with her?'

'Because of Dad, and you.' Jade pointed at Eddie. 'You were always threatening – like you are now – exactly what you would do to me if I did. If it wasn't for that I would have got in touch with her years ago.'

'But that doesn't alter the fact that she never got in touch with you,' Leon scoffed.

'She probably hadn't wanted to while Dad was alive,' Jade said, adamant. 'But now he's gone and she's back in Stoke. Well, I think I might like to get to know her.'

'No,' Eddie said.

'You can't stop me.'

'You wouldn't have seen her if she hadn't come here this morning!'

'Like I said, I'm curious!' Jade leaned back and folded her arms.

'I don't want anyone to find out she's related to us, either,' Eddie stated.

'Fortunately, it doesn't seem like she is too keen to tell anyone,' Leon remarked. 'It was clear that Perry didn't know who she was. We could use that to our advantage.'

'No one finds out,' Eddie warned. 'I'll tell our mother the same when I see her later.'

'But—' Jade started.

'Stay away,' Eddie warned. 'She's blue and she can't be trusted.'

'I'd trust anyone over you, so I can't see why not.' Jade raised her voice. 'And losing Josh like that makes me realise how precious time is. If I want to see her, I will.'

'Who'd want to see you?' Leon sneered.

'Why do you always have to be so nasty?' With two strides Jade was out of the room, slamming the door behind her.

It was Eddie's turn to run a hand through his hair. '*Do* you know anything about this?'

Leon came to stand by his brother. 'No, I've told you that already.'

Eddie still didn't believe him. He clicked a file on the screen.

'We need to take a look at our security cameras to see what the cops will find on them.'

'Shouldn't we leave it to them?'

'We sort out our own business.' Eddie stretched up his arm, put a hand behind Leon's neck and pulled him down until they were eye level. 'If I find out you've had anything to do with this, you're on your own, brother or no brother, do you hear me?'

For once, Leon didn't try to resist his grip. Instead, he leaned on the desk with clenched fists, his eyes never leaving Eddie's. 'I hear you.'

'And the girls, Leon.' Eddie knew his brother would know exactly what he meant. 'It stops, right now. I'm not covering for you again, especially for something so exploitative. What were you thinking? What was *Josh* thinking?'

'Okay, okay!'

Eddie could mostly tell when Leon was lying, but he wasn't quite sure this time. His brother seemed sincere, but, then again, he'd been fooled by him before. 'I'll check the cameras.'

'I can do that.'

'I want it done properly.'

'I can do it properly!'

'And quickly.'

'Fine. Take control as usual.' Leon shook his head as he left the room too.

Once on his own, Eddie pulled up the backup camera footage on his computer. The police would be looking through what he had given them but he needed to see what was on there too. Starting from when the gym was closing, he watched to see if anyone slipped back in after going outside. It seemed impossible to think that just an hour later Josh would be dead.

There was a lull, he presumed, while Josh did his workout. The first time his friend came into view, it was 22.45. Eddie

41

watched as he checked over everything before setting the alarm and then leaving through the front entrance. From there he would head to the car park at the back of the building.

Eddie froze the frame and looked to see if he could see a shadow, an image, a shape that would suggest anyone was there. Purposely, their cameras didn't catch every angle of the car park, and lots of their members knew this. Josh had been on his own when he left the gym and locked up, but as Grace Allendale had insinuated earlier, it also showed that whoever had attacked him might have realised exactly where to do it. This could have been a very calculated kill.

He sat back in his chair and stared at the photo of him and Josh on the wall until he couldn't see through his watery eyes. Josh had been his stalwart. He was going to find out who had murdered his best friend and God help them when he got his hands on the bastard.

NINE

Visiting the families of the deceased wasn't a part of Grace's job that she enjoyed, but it always gave her a sense of the family dynamics. She'd worked on several cases in Manchester where spouses had feigned grief after having killed their loved ones and then tried to cover it up. It wasn't hard to spot. The cracks started to appear once the pressure mounted, mistakes were made, little white lies turned into inconsistencies.

But people could be manipulative, so Grace felt she needed to know everyone involved for that reason too. It was why she'd been the one to speak to the Steele family at the gym. She could have asked Perry to question them; she was his manager. For now, they were all persons of interest until any evidence came back. Which was also why Grace could understand Nick being keen for her to go to the victim's family home with him.

Josh Parker lived in the south of the city, on the southern edge of Stoke-on-Trent in an area called Meir Park, bordering Longton. Grace parked her car in a cul-de-sac of around twenty detached houses, surprised to see that he lived in such a nice area. Most of the gardens were tidy, lawns cut and looking healthy, flower beds and the odd tree a riot of autumnal colours.

'At least we know it is him because of his tattoos,' Nick sighed. 'Although we will need formal ID from Mrs Parker once the body is in the morgue.'

'Is there anything I need to know about Parker before we go in?' Grace asked Nick once the engine had been killed.

'He's married with two children. Five and eight, something like that.'

'Caleb and Mia? The names on his tattoos.'

Nick nodded. 'I think so. His wife is Christa, and despite her beauty she's a foul-mouthed layabout. Be prepared to be sworn at as she hates the police too.'

'Charming,' Grace muttered. 'What about work stuff?'

'He's always been with the Steeles doing something or other since he left school. Him and Eddie were as thick as thieves, literally. When the gym opened twelve years ago, Josh trained as an instructor.'

'Criminal record?'

'A bit for dealing and ABH in his teens, and a stretch for robbery in his early twenties, but he's stayed on the outside since, even though we know he isn't clean.'

'Oh?'

'Well, he mixes with the Steeles.'

'Ah.'

Nick smiled to acknowledge her discomfort. 'None of them have been trouble-free, but nothing really stuck for long. And they're all pretty pissed off that we haven't found out who murdered their father. I hate unsolved cases.' He unclipped his seat belt. 'I'm sure you've done your research on the family, but I'll be happy to go through anything with you at the station.'

At the front door, they showed their warrant cards. PC Warren introduced himself to Grace as the family liaison officer and showed them into a living room. He pointed to the garden through a large picture window.

'She doesn't want to speak to me,' he explained. 'Her mother is coming over, but she lives in Derby. She'll be here soon.'

'Shall I try, sir?' Grace wasn't certain she could get the woman to cooperate, but she would give it a go.

Nick nodded and she went outside, while he stayed indoors to chat with the officer.

Christa Parker was sitting at a table on the patio, dressed in black. She stayed seated but removed her sunglasses as Grace drew level with her. Grace tried hard not to stare: everything about the woman seemed false. Nails, hair, tan, lashes, lips. It had all been enhanced.

'Mind if I join you?' Grace asked tentatively.

'You still think it's him?'

'Yes.'

Nick had been true to his word about Christa. After sobbing, there was shouting, a string of expletives, in between smoking and stubbing out two cigarettes. Grace tried not to hear the swearing. She was used to it in her line of work, but when it was every other word, it became tedious and a little disrespectful, despite it being Christa's husband who had died.

'And you're certain Josh didn't mention anything unusual to you lately?' she asked. 'I'm sorry for the intrusive questions, but it will help if we know.'

Christa shook her head. 'He has many enemies – two scars from knife wounds from his early days as a bouncer. But no one would dare cross him now if they hadn't taken him by surprise. Someone must have been waiting for him. To throw acid on him and stab him when he was down? That's sick, and the sign of a coward.'

Grace said nothing, hoping Christa would fill the silence.

'Don't you have any clue who the bastard is?'

'We're making enquiries at the moment.'

'You mean you have no one?'

45

'It's very early into the investigation, Mrs Parker,' Grace explained.

'Not even anyone you want to question?'

'We'll be able to tell you more when we've gathered the evidence.'

Grace left when the swearing started up once more. She couldn't ask her to stop. The woman had to grieve the way she saw fit. As long as it wasn't being hurled at her, it didn't matter.

She could recall a few times when *she* had acted out of character when Matt died. She'd often gone into a ball of rage whenever anyone said she'd be best clearing his belongings out. It had taken her six months before she was able to do it, and even then the guilt had got to her. The sense of letting go of everything, its finality. Luckily, she'd had her mum around to help her through it. At least Christa Parker would have her mum there with her too.

When Matt had died, Grace's mum had been there for her. She didn't know what she would have done without her, and had been devastated when she too had passed away so soon after Matt. Since the age of twelve, Martha had looked out for her. Since she had been twenty-one, Matt had looked out for her. Now she had no one. So she could sympathise with Christa Parker, no matter how much she cursed.

Back on the road, Grace glanced across at Nick when they stopped as a set of traffic lights turned to red. 'Do you think this is a revenge killing?'

'We'll have to dig deeper to find out. Although, most of the criminals I'm familiar with wouldn't do anything on Steele land.'

'Too close for comfort?' Grace asked.

Nick nodded. 'George Steele's reputation died long before he did, but Eddie and Leon are known to use violence where necessary. Whoever did this would have known there'd be retaliation.'

'And even without the knife wound, throwing acid into someone's face takes guts. It can put the suspect in danger too, especially if they missed their target, so our killer could be deranged.' Grace glanced quickly at him before they moved off again. 'Not frightened to get hurt.'

'Or unaware of the risk.'

'Anyone spring to mind?'

'No, but I can't help thinking it's an inside job.'

Grace nodded. 'My thoughts exactly.'

TEN

By the time they got back to the office, it was nearing lunchtime. Grace had nipped into the nearby supermarket to grab something to eat. Once at her seat, she held up a bag of sugar-coated doughnuts.

'These will keep us going.' She smiled as eager hands reached out. 'Anything we should know, Sam?' she asked as she logged into her computer again.

'Yes, but I'm making coffee if we have snacks.' Sam raised her mug in the air. 'Anyone want one?'

Grace was unsure whether Sam was joking or not. She had asked for information and she expected to get it. She gave the older woman a look, and Sam sat down sheepishly before adding: 'The entrance to the side road the gym is situated on isn't covered by city CCTV or traffic cams. I've contacted their control room to see if we can get some footage sent over so that I can analyse whose cars were on the main road around the time of the murder.' Sam picked up a piece of paper and held it in the air. 'I've already got a list of registration numbers, which I've started on. It only covers the last hour of opening times, but it's a start.'

'Does anyone's name stick out?' Grace asked.

'Quite a few I know, but nothing that jumps off the page.'

'Great, thanks.' Grace nodded her approval. 'Someone needs to check the signing-in register too, see who came in and out and at what times – see if it tallies with statements.'

'I'm on to that,' Alex said. 'Although I suppose it's dependent on everyone actually signing in and out when they say they do, seeing as there are no cameras to back anything up.'

DC Alex Challinor was the final member of Grace's team. Alex had joined their office less than two years ago and, according to Allie, had rocked the boat immensely. He was married with teenage children and, at forty-five, was ten years older than Grace. He liked to think he had a look of Tom Hardy – she thought he had nothing of the sort – and policed with old-school tactics, which no one on the Major Crimes Team agreed with.

Even with the heads-up, Grace had tried not to take an instant dislike to him, but there was something about his mannerisms that made her suspicious. Still, she'd been fooled by people before; in her past job, some had put up a front of arrogance that she hadn't liked and then, after a few weeks working together, her opinion had changed when they had mellowed and got to know each other. So, for now, she was willing to keep an open mind.

'Indeed.' Grace nodded. 'Okay, Sam. Mine is one sugar please.'

Sam's smile was faint, making Grace realise that she *had* been joking when she said she was going to make coffee before giving Grace what she needed. The Stoke sense of humour was taking her a while to adapt to. Its residents were more self-deprecating than those where she'd come from. A very friendly folk, but sometimes she didn't know whether someone was kidding or not, so it was hard to join in.

She had also felt a need to assert herself during those early weeks, because if she became known as an easy boss, she'd never win over their respect.

Grace had only taken one bite into her sandwich before Nick was calling to her from the entrance to his office.

'Grace, can I have a word?'

Her shoulders drooped at his sombre tone. She stood up, quickly wiping her mouth and fingers with a napkin before walking across the room. Inside his office, Detective Chief Inspector Jenny Brindley was sitting in Nick's chair behind his desk. Jenny had been responsible for the Major Crimes Team for two years now, since the last DCI had retired. According to Allie, Jenny was one of the good people. She was fair, but she didn't like the bending of rules in the slightest. She never turned a blind eye and was definitely not old-school. She was more like brand-new shiny school – dotting the i's and crossing the t's to get a good job done. Grace much preferred those tactics, which was why she was immediately wondering what she had done wrong.

'Take a seat, Grace.' Nick pointed to a chair as he shut the door.

Grace did as she was told, nervous at the tension she could feel all around her. Nick sat down beside her.

Jenny leaned forward and clasped her hands together on the desk. 'It's come to my attention that you are involved in the Josh Parker case,' she said.

'I am, yes.' Grace's heart sank.

'And we are aware from your records that you are related to the Steele family.'

'We share the same father, but that's the only relevance.'

'Yes, we know that you've come clean to us about your connections.' She raised a hand when Grace was about to speak

50

again. 'I'm conscious that you don't have anything to do with them, and I understand you aired concerns before you arrived in Stoke, which is correct procedure.'

Grace felt herself holding her body stiff and tried to relax. It was like being in school again, getting grilled by a teacher. Not that she'd been told off too many times. She'd always been the quiet one in the class who didn't have many close friends, always handed in her homework on time and got awarded good grades.

'I think this is too sensitive for you and I'd prefer you to work on something else,' Jenny said.

'Oh, but—' Grace said.

'I think she'll do fine working it.' Nick sat forward to protest. 'Grace is good at her job, Jenny. From what I've seen so far, she's handled things with professionalism, respect and, I suppose, courage. It can't have been easy to roll up there and investigate the way she did, let alone run a team.'

Jenny smiled. 'I do like the faith you have in Grace, Nick.'

'It's not just me. You remember she did extremely well on the Caudwell case last year, which is why she came so highly recommended?'

The Caudwell case Nick was referring to was one Grace had found herself immersed in when she'd been first on call to visit a frantic woman whose estranged partner had turned up and wouldn't let go of their two-year-old son. The child was screaming to go to his mother and Craig Caudwell was threatening to harm him if things didn't go his way. In the end, it had been just him, Grace and little Henry in the room, but she had brought the child out in her own arms unharmed before negotiators were needed.

'Yes, I remember.' Jenny raised her eyebrows in mock surprise.

'She's a good worker. She's estranged from the Steeles and I don't think she should be removed from the case because of a slight connection.'

'It's not actually a *slight* connection,' Jenny stated.

Grace shuffled in her chair. They were talking as if she wasn't in the room.

'If we took every officer away from a case that they were related to someone on, we would have no one left to police anything,' Nick went on. 'Lots of officers have bad blood in their families. It's the reason why some of them join the force. But they still do an effective job.'

'And they are taken off cases when they involve direct family members,' Jenny remarked. 'It's a conflict of interest and can be open to corruption too.'

Grace thought it was time to speak out. 'With all due respect, Ma'am, I had no intentions of ever getting in touch with the Steele family. I was aware they were on my patch, I told you about it and I knew, with their connections, I would more than likely bump into them one day. But I handled the meeting professionally. I don't have any allegiance to them. I won't let anything interfere with my work.'

The room dropped into silence. Grace could almost hear the cogs working inside the DCI's head. She held her breath, waiting for her to speak again.

'Very well said, Grace.' Jenny nodded her approval. 'But it still doesn't change the fact that you are on a case with members of your family involved.'

'Which could work to our advantage,' Nick stressed.

Both women looked his way.

'We have someone who might get a little closer than normal.'

'Absolutely not.' Jenny shook her head. 'Look, I'm not happy about this, but realistically we are pulled all over the place at the moment, what with budget cuts and several officers on sick leave. You can continue to work on this for now, until another

DS becomes available. I do think your skills are best utilised on this, but when you visit Steele's Gym, I want you to take someone along. I don't want you to end up in court unable to defend yourself. Is that clear?'

'Yes, Ma'am.' Grace gulped under the woman's ferocious stare.

Jenny pointed at Nick and then to herself. 'We'll get it in the neck if you step out of line. Do you understand?'

Grace nodded. 'I won't let you down.'

'That's good to hear.' Jenny got up from her chair. 'I'll leave you to it.'

Once she'd gone, Grace blew out the breath she'd been holding and looked at Nick. 'I thought she was going to remove me.'

'She may very well have to,' Nick replied. 'But she's given us a bit of leeway for now.'

'It's risky though, isn't it?'

'I still think we could use your connection to our advantage.' Nick paused. 'Are you up for it, if we keep it between us? See what you can get from them that we can use?'

'But the DCI said—'

'What Jenny doesn't know won't hurt her, and it's on my head if it gets out.'

'I don't want to lose my job.' Grace wasn't so sure. 'I've only just got here.'

'Yes, yes, I know that.' Nick waved away her concern. 'I just think it will be good to get you close to them. We're under pressure following our failure to solve George Steele's murder. And because of that, Eddie and Leon are beginning to cause more and more issues in the city. I need someone to keep an eye on them.'

Even without getting into trouble, it had been weird seeing them all this morning. Grace didn't want to be associated with them in any way, but she knew how hard that was going to be with her curiosity fighting to find out more about them. So, if

53

she *was* going to be working close to them for the next few days, she might as well learn all she could, both on a professional and a personal level.

'I'll give it a shot.' She nodded.

'Great. Report anything back to me first. Keep it between us. And be careful.' Nick stood up. 'Team briefing is at six thirty. I'll need to do a press release before that, and then we can regroup and see where we are. If everyone on the list hasn't been contacted by then, you and the team can get on to it tonight.'

Grace nodded, knowing that it was going to be a long evening. 'We've made a start on gathering intel on Parker. He's obviously well known in the area and I'm catching up with what we have.'

'I'm sure your team can fill you in with everything necessary.' Nick nodded his head towards the door. 'Off you go, Sergeant.'

Grace left the room and sighed with relief. As she scuttled back to her chair, all eyes fell on her. For now, she was home and dry, but she would definitely have to watch her step gathering intel for Nick. There was no way she was going to be removed from this case.

ELEVEN

The day had gone so quickly that when Grace next looked up at the clock it was six p.m. The office was a buzz of activity after the press conference brought a deluge of calls. Hopefully something would come through for them. Alongside the evidence gathered and forensics they were waiting for, there had to be a clue to who killed Josh Parker.

She rested a hand on the back of her neck and moved her head from side to side. She still couldn't believe the first murder in her new job had been at Steele's Gym. God help her if they blabbed and her team found out who she was. It could open her up to all kinds of bribery accusations. But why would the Steeles keep it to themselves, unless they thought they could use it for their own benefit?

Grace had known a fair few bent cops in her years, so, in a way, she couldn't blame the DCI for thinking like that. But she was loyal to her colleagues and to the uniform, something they would only find out in time. If she had been working there longer than four weeks, people might have trusted her more. As it stood now, she'd have to work doubly hard at everything. Still, she was up for the challenge.

'What are Eddie and Leon like together?' she asked Perry, as she took a break from the list she was working her way down.

Perry leaned back in his chair as he spoke to her. 'From what I can gather, Leon seems to think he should be an equal to Eddie. But with Josh as Eddie's right-hand man, he's never stood a chance. I think he saw Parker as muscling in on his territory.'

'Like kids fighting over a girl,' she said.

'Pretty much. Leon thought Eddie gave Josh too much power. He obviously felt as if he was second rate. It was all childish. I'm not sure it's relevant though?'

'Oh?'

'This doesn't have the mark of anything Leon would do. I doubt he would leave a body to be found. And he's more into fast and furious if he does anything. He's known for using his fists to teach people lessons, not necessarily murder.'

'Most murders are born from attacks that go too far,' Sam said, as she looked over her notes in her notepad. 'Assaults that come from an argument when tempers are raised. And if he was known for murder, he'd be inside.'

Perry flicked an elastic band at her. 'You know what I mean, shortie.'

The band flew over Sam's head as Perry had intended. Sam rolled her eyes at him.

'What about the alarm codes?' Grace asked. 'Do we know who has access to the building?'

'There are five people.' Perry counted them off using his fingers. 'Eddie, Leon, Jade, Josh and Trent Gibson.'

Trent Gibson was the man in the red tracksuit who had reported finding Josh Parker that morning. He'd been inter- viewed and a record of his account taken. He'd been working at Steele's Gym for five years and had been on the alarm rota for the past two.

Grace nodded in recognition. 'So, do we know yet who was the last of them to leave the building, other than Josh? Did their times tally with what they told me?'

'Trent Gibson and Jade Steele weren't there that day. CCTV footage of the entrance and the car park we can see confirms this. Eddie left at six thirty. Leon was the last to see the victim.' Sam checked her notes. 'He left at 8.12 p.m. Cameras show both brothers leaving through the front entrance at those times, and then getting into their cars and driving away.'

Grace gnawed at her lip while she pondered. 'Do we have other ideas about what his death could be linked to, outside of the gym?'

'Apart from the ongoing investigations into racketeering, importing of illegal steroids and theft of anything they can lay their hands on, there's been a spate of cash-and-grabs increasing over the past few months. It's possible Josh was involved. Alex can tell you more about that.' Perry held up his hand as his colleague came back from a cigarette break. 'Grace wants to know about the cash-and-grabs.'

'Public being robbed at cash machines.' Alex perched on the end of Grace's desk. 'Either someone behind grabs their money after they've withdrawn it from the ATM, with force if necessary, or someone rides past on a scooter and grabs it.'

'What a pleasant bunch they are in Stoke,' Grace muttered. 'Almost the same as the lot I left back in Salford. So, you're saying that the Steeles run this operation?'

Perry shook his head. 'We think it's likely to be Trent Gibson. He'll be working for Leon, who doesn't get his hands dirty.'

'Oh!' Grace said. 'Does that put a different perspective on things?'

'Possibly.' Alex nodded. 'Of course, we don't have enough proof yet. But it seems likely Trent pays them a percentage of what his boys bring back. He also doesn't like anyone who thinks they can steal the money and not give him his fair cut. We've questioned two members from the boxing gym over the recent months after their parents complained they'd been beaten up, but they wouldn't press charges, and there wasn't enough for us to put forward to the CPS.'

'So how does Trent keep tabs on that?' Grace asked.

'Who knows? He doesn't act like he can count past how many fingers and toes he has,' Alex explained. 'We think his girlfriend might be the brains behind it.'

'Name of?'

'Clara Emery. She works at the gym too, on reception. We don't think Eddie has anything to do with it, and we reckon he'd be pissed off about it, in fact. He's always having to bail Leon out of trouble. But this is small fry compared to other things we hope to one day get them on once the evidence is stacked up. So, although we're looking into it, it's on the back burner.'

'They can't be making that much money from it.' Grace shook her head. 'Wouldn't their hit rate be so high that people would be on the lookout? And cameras on ATM machines would pick them up?'

'Not necessarily,' Alex said. 'Often, they watch where the money is put and then they steal bags, phones and wallets. Sometimes they're shifting larger things too. It's lucrative.'

'In a city this size?' Grace shook her head.

'You're a bit quick to dismiss our local knowledge, aren't you?' Perry raised his eyebrows in disbelief. 'You're doubting us already?'

'No, I was merely saying—'

'You want to learn about this patch then I suggest you listen to us. We've been here a long time before you. We know the people and what they get up to.'

'I wasn't suggesting otherwise, but—'

'If you're that *amazing*, Grace,' Perry butted in, 'you would have researched all this before you came here.'

'I don't *have* to know everything. That's why I manage a team, so that I can delegate.'

Silence fell amongst them.

'We're supposed to be on the same side,' she added. 'I'd appreciate it if you'd work with me, rather than against me.'

As Alex went back to his desk and all heads went down again, Grace held in her annoyance. Inside she was shaking, unaccustomed to raising her voice, but she had to show them she was boss. She wouldn't be walked over by Perry, nor anyone else for that matter.

TWELVE

Alone that evening in his office, while everyone else raised a glass to a fallen friend in the Windmill pub, Eddie rested his head on the desk and let out his emotion. Here on his own he felt he could. Once he got home, there would be questions from his wife, Georgina, who had come to the gym for most of the day until picking up Harry, their youngest son who was twelve, from school. Thankfully, Harry would be in bed when he did eventually get home, and sixteen-year-old Charlie would most likely be out with his friends, so the house would be quiet.

He leaned back in his chair and sipped at his whisky. It was the only one he'd have. He wasn't a drinker, not after he'd seen what it did to his father, and then Jade. *He* wanted to keep his wits about him rather than be taken by surprise by anyone. In his line of business there was always someone ready to pounce. This time it happened to be Josh who had suffered.

They'd managed to get back into certain parts of the building once the car park had been cordoned off, but the death of his friend meant that the gym had been shut, so their takings would be down. The gym membership was fine; most regulars paid monthly and the few who paid per visit wouldn't be worth mentioning. But it was more than that. He hadn't been able to do any of the regular behind-the-scenes stuff. There had been no money loaned, no stolen goods coming through the doors. Some of the boys had phoned to see what the score was, but he'd told them to steer clear. The blues being here was bad for trade in every respect. People would go elsewhere.

He cursed himself. What was he thinking? Josh was his friend. Business didn't matter at the moment, apart from keeping everything under wraps. He wiggled the mouse so the computer woke up again. The Facebook page for the gym had been alight with comments once news had begun to spread. Josh had been well liked, a brilliant instructor and motivator, as well as a valued member of staff. Eddie hadn't even begun to think of what he was going to do without him. It was too painful to contemplate.

He couldn't trust anyone the way he'd trusted Josh. He was the only one who knew what George had been like to live with. Eddie had put his trust in Josh and, to his knowledge, his friend had told no one what had been going on in the Steele house. Their bond had strengthened because of this.

And now he was left with an empty space to fill, in more ways than one. With Josh out of the equation, he knew that Leon would want to step up into his place. It wasn't possible; his brother was too hot-headed, and Eddie knew it was going to cause friction between them, but tough, he was used to it. Brother versus brother had been the norm since they were young, and their earlier years of hell would always be something that stayed between him and Leon.

Eddie scrolled through the messages that were still coming in. As well as his right-hand man, Josh had been a joker. Many would remember him for his sense of humour and his ability to play really silly practical jokes. Josh hadn't minded if anyone wanted to get him back either. He had always been game for a laugh.

He was also pretty big on YouTube, having his own channel and promoting Steele's Gym with his charisma as much as his advice. Eddie pressed on a video clip now, tears of anger welling in his eyes as he listened to Josh's voice. Seeing him racing around the screen as he threw right hooks at a punchbag, it was hard to think that he was dead.

He took another sip of whisky and gazed through the office window into the empty gym behind it. Rows and rows of exercise machines stood as if on duty. Not a murmur could be heard except from the hum of the drinks machine. The emergency lights were on, giving the whole place an eerie glow.

A noise startled him. He turned, standing quickly. It sounded like a door closing, but he knew he was in the building alone. He reached for the baseball bat he kept by the side of his desk and went out into the corridor. Stepping slowly along it, he made his way into the gym, glancing around in every corner.

After a few minutes, he realised it was nothing. There had been no door closing. It was probably the heating clicking on or something stupid like that, something that shouldn't have been enough to spook him.

Eddie went back to his office. There was crime scene tape across the side of the car park with no access, but was he risking it sitting here on his own? Was he next? Or had Josh's murder been a one-off? He thought of all his rivals. He had as many as Josh. Was it someone with a grievance?

Tomorrow he would start getting word out to see. Once the police were gone, he would be doing some investigating of his own. He was going to root out the bastard who had done that to his friend. He would cut his eyes out. He would burn him too. And there would probably be someone behind the person who had carried out the attack, paying them to do their dirty work. He was going to find out who was at the top of the tree.

One last mouthful and, with the drink gone, he threw the glass at the wall, taking great delight in the noise and the mess that it made. It was better than using his fists, which was what his father would have done.

THIRTEEN

Sleep was the last thing on Grace's mind as she arrived home just before midnight. She was famished, having only had time to eat a sandwich and the doughnuts throughout the day. She popped two slices of bread into the toaster and flicked on the kettle.

Well, the day hadn't gone as she had planned but she certainly hadn't thought of the date much. It hadn't even had time to infiltrate her thoughts. Meeting her half-siblings in that manner had been immensely awkward. She suspected Eddie and Leon were going to be trouble and go out of their way to stall things. Or maybe they would surprise her and work with her to solve the murder, and simply want to get the police off their backs as quick as possible. It seemed that had been the case after the murder of George Steele had gone unsolved. She would have expected them to be coming in for weekly updates until the suspect had been caught.

Still, it must have been a shock to find someone dead on their premises. And such a high-profile person too. Parker shared tips on personal training and had quite a large following on social media. His murder might not only affect the club revenue; the funeral would be huge and the attention brought to the gym would be massive. She could bet Eddie wouldn't like that.

She thought Leon, on the other hand, would lap it up. He seemed sharp, untouchable and a little ruthless. He tried to act as if he cared about Josh, but she could see it wasn't sincere. Whereas Jade, she thought, seemed to be the only one with real tears. Whether that was because she was not as insensitive as her brothers remained to be seen.

Perry had been pissy again today. She'd thought she was getting through to him, that he might ease off with the catty remarks and the undermining comments. She knew he missed working with Allie because he mentioned her all the time. *Allie did this* and *Allie did that*. Grace had to bite her tongue on several occasions.

She also knew he wanted to be in control, but she'd got the job, not him. She'd give him a few more days and if he hadn't changed his attitude she would have to talk to him about it. It wasn't something she would look forward to but she had to start as she meant to go on.

The toast popped up, burnt around the edges and hardly touched in the middle, but she slathered it with butter all the same. Coffee made, she went through to the living room and sank into a deep orange armchair. It had been Matt's favourite chair, so she hadn't been able to part with it; instead, she'd bought a clashing bright blue leather sofa to fit alongside it perfectly. Even though she had never really felt settled here on her own, the house had such a homely feel to it without her even trying. She'd only had to add dashes of colour to help, alongside cream painted walls and light wooden flooring.

She flicked on the television. Their investigation might get a small mention on Sky News. It would gather momentum soon, because of who their victim was.

She sat back and thought of the day. Although she would never admit it to anyone, when she'd met her half-siblings she wished she could have spoken more with them, to see what it had been like for them as children. Of course she would never share what had happened to her in great detail, but she would always wonder if it had happened to them too. Or had it stopped with her and her mum?

The news clip she was waiting for came on and she turned up the volume. She had seen it earlier, but it was always something she liked to keep abreast of as fresh clips came through. Flowers had started to appear along the perimeter railings of the gym when people started to hear the news, but since the press release had gone out, people had turned up in their droves. Now alongside them were teddy bears, cards, candles. A football strip from both of the city's football teams, which she bet didn't happen very often. In a weird way, the outpouring of grief for Parker had been good to see. A lot of murder victims went unnoticed.

Yet she'd heard a few rumours today of Josh's habit for hard knocks and doing whatever it took to get what he wanted. Perhaps they would find some good leads because of who he was. He must have had lots of loyal fans as well as enemies. Although his face was now damaged beyond recognition, he'd been exceptionally good-looking from what she had seen of his images everywhere, and he was a powerhouse of muscle underneath his clothes. She knew how many hours' training that would have taken and, even though it sounded strange, it was a shame to see all that hard work go to waste.

She wondered if the senior CSI guy – what was he called? – had worked out cause of death. Dave Barnett, that was it. She picked up a notepad and wrote down his name. So many people met in one day had made her face-blind and she hated forgetting people's names. In her line of work, you needed all the favours you could get; the last thing she wanted was to annoy someone because she couldn't remember the basics.

Exhausted, she went back through to the kitchen and loaded the dishwasher with its lone plate and mug. Then she thought better of it and washed them.

With one last glance at Matt's image at the bottom of the stairs, she checked the doors were locked, switched off the lights and set the burglar alarm. Going upstairs with its gentle beep in the background was reassuring but nowhere near as good as having someone coming to bed with you, to wrap their arms around you.

Grace had always been a loner, having only a handful of close friends growing up. It took her a long time to trust people, always having a guarded attitude. That way, she couldn't get hurt. It was obviously something to do with her childhood. Luckily, Matt had had the same kind of personality.

They had been an insular couple from the moment they had got together. They'd met at a bowling alley when she had been out with some of the girls from the station she'd been working out of and he'd been with a group of his friends. Her girls had been whooping and hollering and his group had started doing the same. After a lot of catcalling, they'd merged and she'd paired up with Matt. By the end of the evening, he'd invited her out for a drink and they'd been together ever since. They'd bought a house within two years and married a year later.

Things had been going great until the diagnosis. Sometimes they had laughed together but mostly there had been tears. It had been tough to go through, but she hadn't been the one dying so she had tried to keep their spirits raised. Matt had been determined not to give in until there had been no hope. He'd finally lost his faith when he had been admitted to the hospice. He'd been given weeks to live but had lasted only three more days. It was as if he knew that he wasn't going to see out the end of that month. And who could blame him? He'd been in so much pain, ending his life as a shadow of his former self. *Their* life together now gone.

After he'd passed away, Grace remembered the empty feeling she'd experienced going back to their home. Even so soon after his death, it was as if he had never lived there. An emotion she couldn't describe to anyone had washed over her – the grief, the anger, the fear, the relief; all mixed into one. Her work colleagues had rallied round, as too had her mum, but it hadn't been enough to keep the loneliness at bay. She'd stopped going out for a while, her job giving her the ultimate excuse to work long hours and have no time for socialising.

She paused halfway up the stairs, squeezing her eyes shut tightly so she couldn't see anything but coloured spots. She missed Matt so much, but she needed her sleep right now. She had to keep her head clear for the days ahead.

It was going to be emotional.

FOURTEEN

THURSDAY – DAY 3

The morning team briefing at eight thirty found over twenty people in a conference room that comfortably fitted only twelve. Grace had been lucky to bag a seat. Perry was standing behind her; Sam and Alex sat across from them; Nick was at the head of the table next to DCI Jenny Brindley. The rest were uniformed officers who had been drafted in to help.

'Welcome to Operation Wedgwood.' Jenny glanced around the room, waiting for someone to catch her eye. 'The Parker case. What's come in so far?'

Grace cleared her throat before speaking. 'There are lots of house-to-house calls to continue with today and Sam has been actioning anything against the ones yesterday. We still have a list of people to get through, those who were at the gym between six and ten p.m. when it closed. And after the appeal for people to come forward went out during the press release, we have a lot more to interview this morning.'

'What about his family? Friends? Acquaintances?' Nick glanced around the room. 'I know he must have a list a mile long of people that he knew, but are we making headway at all?'

'We ran through about fifty per cent of them yesterday,' Grace said. 'And we're planning on getting to the rest today. I'm sending my team across to the gym. We obviously can't use the car park yet, but they've been arranging to interview people at the same time to save them all coming here.' She pointed across the room to where a young man was sitting. 'PC Mick Higgins has been drafted in to help us for a few hours too.'

'At your service,' Mick beamed.

Grace tried not to laugh. His eyes were as wide as his smile, reminding her of how much she'd resembled an eager puppy when she had first started as a beat bobby. He was mid-twenties at a push, his auburn hair cut short, his baby face sprouting the makings of a beard – all the fashion at the moment, but not an accessory she was enamoured with. She couldn't understand the craze – give her a clean-shaven man any day.

Jenny nodded. 'Anything else?'

'We know Parker was on his own when he left the building,' Grace continued. 'You can clearly see him on the security camera coming outside.'

'So he was at his car before anything happened. But no sign of anyone else?'

'No, Ma'am.'

'There are fields at the back of the gym.' Mick chewed his bottom lip. 'Do we think our suspect could have escaped that way?'

'It's possible,' Grace acknowledged. 'I don't know the area as well as you guys, but I can see the canal towpath is a few minutes away on foot. It could take our suspect to any number of places where they could come out unnoticed.'

'Or there could have been a car parked nearby,' Perry suggested.

Nick nodded and turned to Alex. 'Can you get Grace familiar with George Steele's murder? Let's see if there are any similarities.'

'Will do.' Alex nodded.

Grace cleared her throat to speak out in protest, but Nick chose not to look at her and continued with the briefing. Once he'd brought everyone up to speed, he stood up to signal the meeting was drawing to an end.

'Preliminary PM results might be back for team briefing this evening.' He gave out a few more orders before clapping his hands. 'Right, people, you have your tasks. Go and do what you do best.'

When Grace returned to her desk, there was a jiffy bag in her in-tray, her name and the address of the station typed on a large white label. She leaned across and picked it up, wondering what it could be. Turning it over, she pulled on the red cotton that would open the seal. Seeing something wrapped in pink tissue paper, she popped her hand inside and drew out its contents. Unwrapping it revealed a Barbie doll: Moonlight Rose.

Grace frowned. She'd had the exact same doll when she was a girl. It had been a present from her father. She could specifically remember him saying that it was a rose for his rose. She shuddered at the thought. Who on earth would send her this?

Sam looked over Grace's shoulder as she walked past. 'A Barbie doll! Where's that come from?'

'I don't know. There's no note with it and the label isn't handwritten so I can't even hazard a guess.' Grace held on to the toy. 'I think it's someone's idea of a joke.'

'I loved my Barbie. Did you have one when you were young?'

'Yes. It was my favourite doll.'

'I got one for my fifth birthday. I think I took it to bed with me on that first night.' Sam giggled. 'Come to think of it, I think I took it to bed with me until I was about twelve.'

'Did you only have the one?' Grace asked.

'Yes. I didn't want any more. I remember my friend having several and I thought at the time it was greedy. How can you give attention to more than one thing at a time? They're collectors' items now, you know.' She clicked on to Google. 'That one has a sixty-quid price tag.'

'Maybe Ken will be delivered tomorrow,' Alex smirked, butting into the conversation.

'I'm surprised you know she had a beau!' Grace laughed.

'I have two older sisters. They used to nick my Action Man and hide him all the time.'

'You wuss! You let them girls walk all over you,' Sam teased.

As everyone took a few moments out to join in with the toy-related banter, Grace ran a hand around the inside of the envelope again, but there was nothing else inside it.

'Do you think it's anyone from your Manchester crew, winding you up?' Perry asked.

'I bet it is,' Grace said, but she felt strangely unnerved.

Would it be someone she knew? She wouldn't put it past any jokers at the station where she used to work, although they would probably have done something like this during her first week here. But how would they know about this doll? Could it be a coincidence?

She opened a desk drawer, placed the doll back into the envelope and popped it out of sight for now. When she looked up, Nick was beckoning her into his office.

'Can you go and see Kathleen Steele?' he asked as she got to him.

'Yes, sir. I'll take Perry with me,' Grace said.

'No, go alone – try and get her at home. Pry gently, if you know what I mean.'

Grace knew exactly what he meant. Go against their DCI's instructions. 'I don't think—' she started.

Nick put up his hand. 'It'll be fine. I'll square it if necessary.'

FIFTEEN

Then

She woke to the sound of screams and sat up quickly in bed.

'Mummy?' Pulling the covers back, she tiptoed across the carpet. When she reached the door, she hesitated. What if Daddy was so cross that he hit her again?

'Leave me alone!'

A bang. She jumped and almost ran back to hide under the covers, but there was another scream. She couldn't leave her mummy in the hands of a monster.

She opened the door. Another bang and the sound of breaking glass. She padded across the tiny hallway. The living room door was ajar so she peeped around the corner of the frame. Mummy and Daddy were on the floor. Daddy was on top of Mummy, but Daddy had his hands around Mummy's throat. Mummy was going red in the face.

'Mummy!' she screamed.

They both turned towards her, the room dropping into silence except for the sound of heavy breathing.

'Get back to bed.' Daddy pointed at her.

'You're hurting Mummy!'

'If you don't move by the time I count to three, it will be my hands around your neck.'

'Go back to bed, darling,' Mummy said. Her voice didn't sound like Mummy. It was all croaky and had a shake in it.

She shook her head.

Daddy got to his feet slowly. She froze as he clenched his fist and came towards the door. Then he slammed it shut in her face.

She ran back to her room. Because she knew what would happen next. Her plan hadn't worked. Grabbing her teddy bear, she crept into the wardrobe. She covered her ears with her hands to block out the sound of Mummy's screams. On and on they went.

'Don't hurt my mummy,' she sobbed.

She hated it inside the wardrobe. It was dark and things dangled over her and scared her. But it felt safer than being in bed.

And then it went quiet. She squeezed the teddy to her chest. She could hear Mummy crying too.

'Don't hurt her, George, please,' she begged. 'She's only six.'

'Get her in here.'

'No, let her be.'

There were bangs, as if someone had fallen. She heard Mummy groan. And then the bedroom door opened.

'I'll break every bone in your body if you don't come out from where you're hiding.'

Daddy's voice was so loud and scary. She held her breath, trying not to let him know where she was.

The wardrobe door was flung open. Daddy stood there. He had taken off his belt and wrapped it around his hand. She could see the buckle hanging down.

'Please don't hurt me, Daddy,' she cried.

He reached inside the wardrobe, grabbed a handful of her hair and pulled her to her feet.

'Come here, you little bitch.'

SIXTEEN

After dropping her team off at Steele's Gym, Grace headed for the north of the city. It was an address she hoped she'd never have to revisit and just the thought of it was enough to make her want to drive to the M6, the city's nearest motorway, and go anywhere instead.

Moreover, she wondered if maybe after her chat with the DCI she shouldn't be going to this address alone, but ultimately this wasn't Steele's Gym, and that was the only place she'd been explicitly warned about.

Brown Edge was a small village built on one of the south-westerly spurs of the Pennine Chain and looked particularly colourful now that autumn was creeping up on them. After she had passed fields and farms to get to the address in Woodhouse Lane, she pulled in at the side of the road and took a deep breath. Hardman House had been her childhood home. It wasn't a happy place. Even after this length of time away, there would still be ghosts of the past around, and in, every corner.

She got out of the car and walked up the driveway. Her footsteps were heavy, her heart beating as loud as a soldier's on a quick-march. The house was a pre-war detached with a double frontage and large bay windows. Years ago, her mum had told her that George had inherited it from his parents and hadn't spent any money on it so it had deteriorated, along with their marriage. The building itself was exactly as she remembered it, bar replacement windows and doors and a lick of paint here and there. The concrete on the driveway was old and breaking up, revealing pebble lakes that she walked around.

All at once, she remembered the places she used to hide: behind the bin store, the outhouse that led out to the garden, the attic with its winding staircase that George found hard to negotiate when he'd had a drink, the cupboard under the stairs – until he'd put a lock on it and used it to keep her in.

And the place where her nightmares had started.

She knocked briskly on the front door and took out her warrant card. A woman who appeared to be in her late fifties answered it. Her face was made-up as if it had been professionally done, her clothes immaculate. She pushed long tendrils of dark hair, flecks of grey apparent, behind her ears. She looked well, no clear signs of age interfering with her health. Her eyes reminded Grace of Jade, but her colouring was like Eddie and Leon's.

She almost bounced forward a step on heels as Grace held up her warrant card.

'Mrs Kathleen Steele? I'm DS Allendale and—'

'I know who you are,' the woman interrupted, smiling brightly. 'Come on through.'

Trying not to show surprise at Kathleen's over-friendly manner, Grace stepped inside the hallway, flinching as the door was closed behind her. It had always seemed dingy in her memories, but now it was light and airy. The wooden panels were still on the bottom half of the wall but the colour above them was a bright baby blue rather than the oppressive red she could remember.

She looked up to see the large opaque window above the stairs had been replaced with coloured glass, the image of a sunflower as bright as the sun coming through it. Yet even though the decor had most likely been changed several times since the night Grace and her mum had left, no one could erase the memories of those torturous years from within its walls.

If she stepped into the kitchen, which was the doorway at the far end of the hall, she would see George Steele holding her mother by her hair, a hand raised up ready to slap her. If she went into the dining room, she would see her mother flat out on the floor after he had hit her too hard and knocked her out. If she went upstairs to the family bathroom, she would see her curled up in a ball after he had assaulted her.

As she followed Kathleen Steele into the living room, a memory washed over her so vividly that fear gripped her insides and her stomach tightened. Blood rushed to her head and she had to sit down on the settee before her legs gave way.

'Are you all right?' Kathleen questioned. 'You've gone deathly pale. Would you like a drink?'

Grace could only nod, thankful for a few moments to regain her composure while she was alone. An image had come to her mind. George Steele coming at her with a knife. She'd had no recollection of it until then, but the memory was of her mum stepping in front of her to shield her. Was that where the scar on Martha's forearm had come from? Would George have killed her if her mum hadn't been there?

Kathleen came back into the room with a glass of water. Grace took it from her gratefully.

'I'm sorry to sit down uninvited,' she said. 'I don't know what came over me.'

'Oh, please don't apologise. I hope you're feeling better soon. At least your colour is returning. You gave me a fright.'

Grace sipped at the water for a moment before putting it

down on the coffee table. 'I wanted to ask you a few questions about Steele's Gym.'

'What would you like to know?'

'Just a few routine things, so that I can understand how it's run.'

Kathleen smiled. 'You mean that neither Eddie nor Leon are being of any use to you?'

Grace smiled. 'There was a little obstruction when I asked them anything. Do you have any say in the running of it?'

Kathleen sat down on the settee opposite. 'Not until recently. George would never let me work. He was a debt collector for some years – I'm sure you might know that already. But he was an alcoholic and the disease took over him eventually. He hardly went anywhere but the pub during his last year alive.' She paused for a moment. 'After he was murdered, Jade and I got to know each other better. I thought it would be good for us to work together on something, so we opened Posh Gloss, on a part-time basis. It's not terribly busy, but we get by; although mostly I'm in there on my own, or the receptionist, Clara, takes over.'

'Jade doesn't like doing nails?'

'My daughter doesn't like doing anything.' Kathleen sighed. 'Jade has always been a fragile soul. She's never been married but the last man she was with was hideous. She spent several years with him before he thankfully left her. She and my grand-daughter Megan have been living back in Stoke for about a year now, in their own house, but they spend a lot of time here with me since George was murdered. To tell you the truth, I like having them around; they each have a bedroom of their own here. The house is too big for me without him. We were married in 1996, just after you left, you know.'

Grace looked away fleetingly. It was awkward talking about it, but it was better out in the open. Kathleen had had an affair with her father. He had been married to her mother when her half-siblings were born. Kathleen had also lived with the beast. Even if she had no visible physical scars, Grace assumed she must have some mental ones. Grace did and she'd been a mere child.

Unless of course George Steele never laid a hand on Kathleen. And Grace couldn't ask her. It was none of her business.

'I didn't have it easy with George,' Kathleen said.

Grace jumped. It was almost as if the woman had read her mind.

'I bet he was as brutal to you and your mother as he was to me and my children?' Kathleen added.

Grace said nothing, then gave a small nod.

Kathleen looked at Grace, regret clear in her expression. 'I couldn't stop him,' she continued. 'But I couldn't leave with three children. I had no money, nowhere to go, so it was better to put up with it until the children were old enough to fend him off. And then it was too late for me.' She sighed dramatically. 'I only wish I had your mother's convictions. But George wore me down. Thankfully' – she swept her hand around the room – 'the house was put into my name, as George began to fear having anything in his own. Business sense, he called it, although he never made a will.' She half-smiled then. 'It did mean that when he died it was passed to me.' She paused. 'I hope you don't feel bitter that nothing was left to you.'

'Of course not!' Grace shook her head and refrained from saying what she was thinking. George Steele had ceased being any part of her life once they had moved to Manchester. If he *had* left her anything, she would have refused it.

'Eddie and Leon have never really seen eye to eye,' Kathleen added. 'You'd think they would, only a couple of years between them, but George made them rivals. It wasn't nice to witness.' She stopped as if thinking what to say next. Then, with a shake of her head, she continued. 'George Steele had a lot to answer for, but I'm afraid I had too. I should have found the courage that your mother did and left him years ago. He was a monster.'

Grace couldn't imagine how hard life had been for Kathleen, living in a house full of dread and fear, amongst so many family feuds.

She stayed for a few minutes more, asking basic questions about Kathleen's movements at the gym on the night Josh Parker was murdered, but she had got what she'd come for.

As she drove away, leaving all her demons in the house, she knew that everything she had witnessed yesterday at the gym had been a front. With what Kathleen Steele had just told her, it seemed that none of them really liked each other. But most families stuck together, and they didn't seem to be an exception.

SEVENTEEN

Kathleen watched as Grace reversed her car and drove out onto the lane. She stood in the window for a long time after the detective had gone, watching the leaves falling from the trees as they were taken away in the wind. Her shoulders drooped but her anger continued to rise. It had been such an effort to be pleasant to the bitch, but she had a reputation to uphold and if that meant being nice to her face, then, well, she'd have to do her best for the sake of appearances.

Because she hated Grace, and her mother, in equal measure. They had left her at the hands of George. She'd known about the girl and Martha Steele, long before they had moved to Manchester. If she was truthful, part of her had wanted them out of the equation so she could have George all to herself. But she hadn't realised how terrible things would get for her and the kids once they had gone.

If Martha Steele hadn't left with Grace, then maybe things would have been different. At the time, Kathleen had been fine living in her flat with the children, their father sleeping over two or three nights a week, even if it was a tight squeeze.

But George wanted them all to move in with him when he'd

found himself alone. On his own territory, he became even more predatory. And then he became obsessed with getting married. He'd managed to track Martha down and got her to agree to a quick divorce, on the grounds that he had committed adultery. To this day, she had no idea why he'd wanted to do that, rather than go and drag Martha back because his pride had been dented. Maybe it was all about saving face. Replacing Martha with Kathleen made it look as if it was George's choice to end his first marriage.

Kathleen hadn't wanted to marry George straight away. She would have preferred to see how things panned out. She'd always hoped that one day he would change, but like a lot of people whose lives were blighted by abusive partners, she had been taken in by sober George. Drunken George didn't give a stuff about anyone but himself. So she lived for the days of sober George.

He'd said he'd change if they moved in together on a permanent basis. But it was all lies. Living at the hands of a monster was not just degrading, it was debilitating. He had not only beaten her down with his hands, he had beaten her mentally. Saying she was never good enough, never able to leave because she didn't have anywhere to go, no one would want her. He'd given her no money, she had been dependent on him for everything. What did her children know about real hardship?

George had mellowed in his later years; he wasn't quite the bully he used to be, and Eddie and Leon had taken his place in the respectability chart. Since George had been murdered, things had improved drastically for everyone. There was no longer that sense of fear, and no anticipation that things could erupt at any time. Now Kathleen had to make sure her children didn't get into too much trouble instead.

It was a ceaseless battle. Half the time they never listened to her. They still blamed her for their suffering. How wrong they were when they said she could have got away from him.

Her shoulders drooped again, thinking of her daughter, and her granddaughter. It wasn't entirely Jade's fault, but she did play the victim card far too often. Although, to be fair, Kathleen didn't mind so much; Jade had all but left her to look after Posh Gloss since her last boyfriend had deserted her and she had moved back to Stoke, and it was Kathleen's first chance at running a business; during the past few months she'd found she'd really enjoyed it. Being around people was a joy compared to having to stay cooped up in the house all day, waiting for George to come home from wherever it was he'd been, figuring out what mood he was in as soon as he came through the door, as she had for so many years. And it was all because of Martha and her daughter.

So, despite putting on airs and graces, that woman coming to the house had annoyed her. What if Grace Allendale saw through her act and began to pry? There were secrets in their family, things no one was ever going to find out. She'd need to think what to do next, to keep everyone safe.

Now that George wasn't there, she would go to any lengths to protect them all. Nothing would come between her and her children. Not even the fact that Eddie had chosen not to include her in the meeting after Josh Parker had been found murdered on their premises. She was still angry they hadn't called for her to go in.

But she would protect them to the end, as any mother would. She always had done and she always would. Now would be no exception.

EIGHTEEN

On the third floor of St John's multi-storey car park, Jade Steele was waiting. She had a clear view of the door to the stairs through her rear-view mirror. She checked the clock on the dashboard: quarter past one. He was late. There were no new messages on her phone either. She would give him ten more minutes and then she would leave. Despite everything, he wasn't going to mess her around. It would be his loss more than hers.

Then the door opened. Jade admired his powerful stride, broad shoulders, head held high as he walked across towards her. He had a tiny look of her favourite actor about him, with his short dark hair and sexy come-to-bed eyes.

Alex glanced around furtively as he stopped at her car. A hand rested on the door handle, and she could almost hear him taking a deep breath before getting in.

'I thought you weren't coming.' Jade turned towards him with a pout.

'We'll have to be quick,' Alex told her. 'I can't stay long. I have work to do.'

She leaned across to him, bringing him into her embrace.

His lips crushed down on hers. His hand slipped inside her T-shirt, caressing her nipple through her bra, and she moaned.

Jade had got to know Alex during the investigation into her father's murder. She and Megan had moved to Stafford but had gone to stay at the family home for a few weeks. Alex had been cocksure whenever she'd chatted to him, enough to tempt her to join in with a bit of friendly banter. That had pretty quickly turned into flirting and they'd ended up in bed together. She knew it had been intentional on her part to get him there, but she hadn't expected it to continue. She'd assumed it had been a bit of fun for him. But when she moved back to Stoke permanently, she'd bumped into him again and he'd asked to see her.

At first, she'd sensed an ulterior motive for him too, but then she'd realised it could work both ways. It *was* fun. Whenever he rang her, she got to pick and choose if she wanted to see him. Alex was very much like Jade. He craved attention and loved to have his ego stroked, amongst other things. She could anger him in seconds with a few choice words; have him at her beck and call with others. Sometimes she let him take what he wanted; other times she needed something in return.

It had been a good partnership so far, one neither of them wanted out in the open. She was happy with the relationship though, especially the sex, which she'd missed. For now, she had what she needed. A good man in bed who didn't make demands of her every waking moment. It was perfect compared to what she'd been used to. Most of the men in her life had used her, manipulated her.

Most of the time she had been stupid enough to let them.

'We have to stop this for a while,' he said once they came up for air.

'You always say that but you never mean it.' She grasped the back of his neck and brought him to her, but he pushed her hands away gently.

'It's not safe after Josh Parker's murder.'

'No one can see us here.' Jade's smile was coy. She kissed him once more, feeling his resistance ebbing away. But then he stopped again.

'You do like what I do to you, don't you?' she questioned.

'Someone will notice if I'm gone too long.'

'How is Grace?'

'She's . . . coping.'

Her hand ran down his torso, her fingertips circling from side to side, until she found the buckle to his belt. 'Now, is there anything else I can do for you before you leave?'

'Not here there isn't!'

'Ah, well, suppose I'll have to take a rain check.' She licked her top lip and stared at him.

'You're such a tease.'

'Takes one to know one.'

As Alex got out of the car, Jade smiled to herself. She knew he didn't trust her; she didn't trust him either. Which made this a perfect arrangement for what she had in mind.

Grace could clearly remember the day she'd heard that George Steele had been murdered. She'd been in the station in Manchester and one of her colleagues had informed her. She'd told only those she'd had to about her connection to him; Grace found it hard to trust people, to get near to them at the best of times, so details like that were kept close to her chest.

She'd watched the investigation from afar, even when the leads had gone cold and the case remained unsolved. Strangely, she couldn't help wondering how his life had turned out, even though her overriding wish was that he'd suffered for what he'd put her and her mum through.

But it had done her a favour when it came to promotion. If George Steele had still been alive when Allie's job had become vacant, Grace would never have applied for it and perhaps been overlooked for further opportunities because of her reluctance to move areas. Even so, it still didn't sit right with her that his killer was at large, so she was keen for Alex to bring her up to speed now he was back from his lunch break.

Feeling nervous about slipping up, she took a discreet deep breath and wiped her sweaty palms before she wheeled over her chair and sat next to him. It was then she noticed the red tinge to his cheeks.

'Are you okay?' she asked.

'Yes, why?' Alex fiddled with the knot on his tie.

'You look a little flustered.'

'No, I'm fine.'

Grace let it go as he pointed to the screen.

'George Steele. Murdered fifteenth of March last year. How much do you know already?' Alex took a sip of coffee before looking back at her.

'Only bits I've read online and gleaned over the past couple of days,' Grace fibbed. 'Steele had been in and out of prison in his earlier years. Mostly evaded it afterwards.'

'His house stands on a fair plot; it was passed down to him by his parents. It's a short walk along a country lane from The Potter's, but he never arrived.' Alex sniggered. 'Or, more likely, he would have been staggering, knowing George Steele.'

Grace said nothing.

'Anyway, he was beaten around the head with a blunt instrument. We couldn't identify the murder weapon as there was so much damage done – it's something small, though. He was found lying on his back, but it looked like he'd tried to crawl away on all fours beforehand. I wonder when he realised his attacker wasn't going to stop. It seemed as if someone wanted to rid him of his features.'

Grace shuddered at the thought. 'So was he as mean as his reputation suggested?'

'He was a thug, by all accounts. If anyone crossed the line, he would certainly let them know he had found out. There were rumours that he did some damage to people himself.'

'You mean torture?'

Alex shrugged. 'I'm not entirely sure. I hear so many things in this job that it's hard to tell the truth from the lies.'

'Tell me about it.'

'He's supposed to have cut off a few fingers and removed some teeth, that kind of thing, although that sounds a bit too East End of London for me. But that all changed when someone beat him up a few years ago. He was a right mess, touch-and-go for a while; no one saw anything then either. It kinda knocked the steam out of him. I guess it made him feel vulnerable, and the more he drank, the more he became an easy target.'

'Where did you get this info?' Grace wondered why she hadn't heard any of this before.

'Jade Steele told me,' Alex explained. 'In general chit-chat while we were investigating. She was saying how he'd changed since that attack. How he stopped fighting but started drinking more.'

'What about Eddie and Leon?'

'Leon is a lot mouthier than Eddie, so ends up in more trouble,' Alex told her. 'I found Jade a bit dim, if I'm honest.'

'Really?' Grace wasn't so sure. She suspected Jade might be sharper than she let on.

'On the other hand, she can be very manipulative.'

'Oh?' Now Grace was intrigued.

'Just a hunch.'

Alex ran through everything he knew with her, but with no significant similarities between the two cases, Grace went back to her desk. There wasn't anything new she had learned about the case, but she had come away from the conversation with the distinct impression that Alex's word might not necessarily be trusted. How did he know that much about the Steeles that wasn't on file?

NINETEEN

It was half past two before Grace was able to think of getting a bite to eat. There was always a good choice of sandwiches in the canteen, but she needed fresh air today. And, away from the office, she could think.

It had been thirty hours since Josh Parker's body had been found, and the office was a hive of activity. They'd been checking out alibis for the time of the murder. Unless they were covering for each other, which would be hard to prove, all members of the Steele family had been at their respective homes with other family members.

Information was still being checked after it had come in from the press conference that had been televised yesterday. The death had been one of the front lead stories on the *Stoke News* for the past two days. Everything that could be done to raise awareness of the crime had, and would continue to be so. A few more officers had been drafted in to help out.

Some forensics had come back for Josh Parker. There were no traces of anyone else's DNA, nor had anything been found on the tarmac around the body or nearby. It was confusing, yet Grace liked this stage of the investigation: when evidence was being gathered and bits of information teased from people and pieced together, clue by clue, leading them to a suspect and arrest.

She had her head down against the rain as she crossed over Bethesda Street outside the city central library. Compared to the warmth of yesterday and the promised bright start that morning, it had been drizzling for the past hour, making everything seem grey and dismal.

'DS Allendale?'

She turned to see the reporter from the *Stoke News* rushing to catch up with her. Oh, no. What was his name?

'Hi there . . . Simon!' She remembered at the last moment.

He held up his hand as he caught up with her. 'Don't worry, I'm not going to quiz you about Josh Parker, although obviously I want to. Where are you off to? Mind if I walk with you?'

'Sure, but I was only going to Tesco. Nothing extravagant. I need a butty.'

'Do you have time to grab a coffee? Have you visited the Spitfire Cafe Bar in the Mitchell Arts Centre?' He pointed in the distance. 'It's on the way.'

Grace glanced at her watch. She didn't really have time. And although he was being friendly, she didn't want to give the impression she would be a pushover if he was after information. Having said that, he might be useful to her, knowing the town well.

'I promise it's all innocent and above board,' Simon said. 'Well, I might lie about that actually, on a personal level.'

Grace smiled. 'I don't have long, though.'

They walked in step along the pavement. Bethesda Street was on the outskirts of the Cultural Quarter that housed the city's Regent Theatre and Victoria Hall. The Potteries Museum and Art Gallery coming up further along the road.

'I remember visiting the museum as a child,' Grace told him. 'That mural above the entrance is amazing.'

'It depicts Stoke's industries in years gone by. Miners, potters, steelworks.' Simon pointed. 'If you look close, the cartwheel in the middle is half wheel, half semicircle of radiating hands.'

Grace looked and raised her eyebrows. 'Wow, I would never have noticed that.'

'You should spend an hour with our local historian, Fred Hughes. What that man doesn't know about Stoke-on-Trent isn't worth knowing.' Simon smiled. 'Haven't you been inside since you've got back?'

She shook her head.

'You must! You should check out the Staffordshire Hoard too. On your next lunch break.'

'You know they're a luxury! Who's that over there?'

Simon followed her eyes to where a bronze statue of a man sitting down reading a book was set on a large plinth.

'That's Stoke's famous author, Arnold Bennett. Didn't you learn about him at school?'

Grace cast her mind back. 'Vaguely.'

'The memorial was commissioned to commemorate the one hundred and fiftieth anniversary of his birth. It's so lifelike, I often wish I could sit on his knee and read the book he's holding up.'

Grace looked over as she drew level with the statue. Simon was right. He looked like an aristocrat, one leg crossed over the other and the book held high.

'Sorry, I sound like a walking encyclopaedia!' Simon baulked. 'Tell me, how are you settling in? Are you enjoying working with your colleagues?'

'Yes, I'm getting to know them.'

'They're not a bad bunch, on the whole.'

They continued on the pavement across to Broad Street. The Mitchell Arts Centre on the right was named after Reginald Mitchell, the designer of the Spitfire aeroplane, and had been opened by his family in his memory. After a revamp, the outside of the building had been created to look like the cockpit and side of the iconic plane. Grace thought it was a novel idea.

Inside, there were several vacant tables and they placed their order at the counter before settling down at one of them. Grace glanced across at Simon shyly, noting how similar in height and build he was to Matt. But that was where the similarity ended. Blue eyes to Matt's brown; Matt's darker hair to his blond. She did, however, feel the same warmth emanating from him.

'So, Simon, tell me about yourself,' she said before he could ask her.

'There's nothing to say really.' Simon sat back in the chair. 'I'm thirty-seven and quite a boring old fart. I've lived in Stoke all my life. Half the people I write about who've been in court went to my school. I studied journalism at Staffs Uni and got married too early to my childhood sweetheart. We have a daughter who is nearly sixteen. My wife is living in the marital property while I'm in a tiny starter home, which isn't bad because I don't have to listen to her nagging when I'm working long hours.' He sighed. 'Not a lot of that was in my life plan, but I do okay.'

'How long have you worked for the *Stoke News*?'

'Since I left uni.'

'You've never worked for anyone else?'

He shook his head. 'Does that make me boring?'

Grace shook hers too. 'It would make me the same. I've only ever been in the force since I left uni too. I take it you enjoy it?'

'Yes, fortunately I'm not one of the many stuck in a job I don't like. The hours can be a killer but the work is rewarding.' He put a hand to his mouth. 'I sound like I'm on an interview.'

Grace watched a slight blush appear on his cheeks and found she liked it.

'What about you?' he asked.

'Oh, I'm just as boring.' She paused. 'I was married, but I lost my husband to cancer two years ago.'

'I am *so* sorry.' Simon's eyes widened in horror. 'And there's me feeling miserable over the little things.'

'Don't be.' Grace waved away his comment but looked to the floor. Although she was used to sympathy, it was still hard to tell people she didn't know. She took a moment to compose herself before looking up again. 'So, what about Josh Parker?' She laughed to ease the tension between them. 'Easier to stay on neutral territory.'

Simon shrugged. 'I doubt I can tell you anything you don't know already about him.'

'And the Steeles?' Grace didn't want to push things, but she was curious too.

'Oh, *I* see. You only want me for my local knowledge! And there was me thinking you wouldn't want to talk to a journo for fear of me knowing all your secrets.'

A man brought over their drinks, setting them on the table between them.

Grace dipped her eyes, hoping her expression didn't give her inner thoughts away. Regardless of who he was, and of helping Nick out, she did want to know everything, even though her opinion of the family so far wasn't great. Eddie reminded her too much of George Steele, and Leon had made it perfectly clear he didn't want anything to do with her. Jade seemed to be playing the victim well, if Alex's thoughts were anything to go by. Even their mother, Kathleen, trying to keep the family together, was causing Grace to question her loyalty.

But it seemed unhealthy as well as unethical for her to get any closer. Plus, she didn't want to be taken from the case, so she was trying to keep her distance.

Their conversation changed to more ordinary stuff. After a while, Simon picked up his coffee cup and downed the last dregs. 'Right, I'd better go to see what's going on. It's court day – lots to report as usual.'

Grace stood up as he did. 'Thanks for the coffee. I think I might have found the perfect hideout for when I need a bit of thinking time.'

'Next time you're heading this way, give me a shout.' He handed her a card with his number on it. 'It was a pleasure keeping such lovely company.'

It was her turn to blush.

She followed him out and they chatted amiably as they made their way back to work. Leaving Simon at his office, she thought about him on the brief walk to hers. Grace had slept with two men since Matt's death; the first had been three dates over a week, the other a fling that had lasted two months. Neither had been fulfilling enough to take any further, nor had the few dates she'd had since. Bizarrely, she'd felt disloyal, letting someone else in. It was as if she was keeping secrets from the dead, which was stupid.

But she really liked Simon. He was fun to be around, and she felt quite at ease with him. It was something new.

She even hoped it might be the start of something good.

TWENTY

SATURDAY – DAY 5

Steele's Gym had reopened three days after Josh Parker's murder. At forty-nine, Dale Chapman prided himself on keeping fit and healthy. It had given him the upper hand on more than one occasion. Some of the fights he'd got into, he'd wondered why his wife hadn't asked more about the scratches that appeared on him every now and then. But so far, his seedy sideline was his dirty little secret.

Yet, even after a tough workout, Dale Chapman hadn't been able to rid himself of his stress. He'd thought a five-kilometre run followed by a weight-training session would have made him feel better, but it hadn't worked. He was always waiting for a hand to drop on his shoulder. He shouldn't have come really, but he was sick of putting off the inevitable. He had to get this mess sorted.

He'd almost broken the speed limit driving home. Who the hell did Leon Steele think he was, threatening him? Sure, he owed him money, but he was paying it back in other ways and Leon should be grateful that he'd got him the property to use.

Anger coursed through him, interspersed with fear. He was

trapped. Unable to pay the person blackmailing him, which was why he'd taken out the loan in the first place. He'd known it was a fool's game to take money from Leon, but he hadn't had a choice. Dale had to look after his own. If things got out, he would lose everything. Denying stuff was fine; there being tangible evidence was a whole new ball game. The Steele family were a law unto themselves.

He pulled into the driveway of his home, deadened the engine on his car and sat still for a moment. Despite the unhealthy yearnings he'd managed to keep from his family so far, Dale had done well for himself in Stoke, having set up his own electronics firm. Now he employed over seventy staff and had a top-class designer who was getting their business name known in far-off places.

The house he was sitting outside said he had made it. After trading up from a tiny two-up, two-down in a cheaper area of Stoke-on-Trent, he'd moved three times over the past twenty years, each one a larger property than the one before. He now lived in a five-bedroomed, individually designed home in a row of exclusive properties in Barlaston. He'd chosen the area due to its location only a few miles from the M6. He spent hours driving its length and breadth every week.

This one had not only cost an arm and leg to purchase, it had cost him his sanity, working to make ends meet for the mortgage. Thankfully, only the youngest son was at home now, having arrived fifteen years after the last.

When he finally got out of the car, the boom of music blaring from Oliver's bedroom made him sigh. He retrieved his gym bag from the rear seat of the car and closed the door. The alarm's lights broke into the darkness as two small beeps went off.

He took a few steps towards the front door. Had it been quieter, he might have heard the footfall behind him. A hand on his shoulder made him flinch and the hooded jumper that he'd slung over the top of the bag slid to the ground.

'What the hell are you doing here?' he said when he turned. 'I told you not to—'

But the words were lost, along with two teeth, as something heavy slammed into his mouth. His head reared to one side with the force, blood spurting out across the driveway. He didn't have time to react before something slammed into his face again. He dropped to his knees as it hit him for a third time. Dazed, he couldn't even help himself.

His attacker pushed him over, pinning him down as he writhed about in agony. By the time he was hit for the fourth time, he'd lost count. He no longer knew what was happening.

TWENTY-ONE

Grace was in the station car park. It had been four days since the murder of Josh Parker, and they'd had another late finish. It was nearly ten p.m. and she and Perry were the last to leave.

Despite the hour, all Grace needed right now was a dip in the bath and a glass of something chilled so she could have time to think away from the noise of the station. She had a head full of possibilities, links and queries, often finding her best theories at home when it was quiet. A snippet of information filtered through to fill in a missing link. A piece of the jigsaw slotted into place.

Before Grace had reached her car, a call came through from Nick.

'There's been another suspicious death. Can you join me?'

'Sure.' Grace waved to Perry, beckoning him over when she caught his eye.

'Anyone there with you?'

'Perry.'

'Bring him too.'

Grace jotted down the address. She was beginning to know

the city well already with its tight-knit roads and D-road, the Potteries Way and the long, long Leek Road.

'What's up?' Perry asked.

'Another murder. Your car or mine?'

'That's all we need.' Perry yawned loudly. 'And I was about to get a takeaway. Lisa won't be too impressed about spending another evening alo— Oh, sorry, I didn't think.'

Grace knew he thought he'd put his foot in it, forgetting that she spent most of her time alone. She waved his remark away. 'We'll take my car, and you can order something for her on the way. Blimey, there's a right nip in the air. It'll be Christmas in the blink of an eye.'

'I'm really looking forward to it this year. I'm down on the roster for my first one off in years.'

'Aw, your first as a family too.' Grace grinned, then rolled her eyes as her detective constable went all gooey-eyed on her. 'Did Alfie sleep any better last night?'

'He made three whole hours.'

'Ouch.'

One glance at Perry's face told her that everything was fine regardless. She was pleased that their relationship seemed to have improved slightly since their outburst in the office. Perry often talked to Sam about his wife and child, but not so much to Grace. She liked to think it was because he was sensitive to the fact that she had lost Matt, but she wasn't too sure he was just ignoring her. So it was good he was making an effort.

Barnaby Drive was lit up by lights from emergency service vehicles when they arrived on scene. Grace drew up outside number 8 just behind an ambulance.

'Anyone you know?' She turned to Perry as she killed the engine.

'Not on first hearing his name. Impressive house, though.'

Another ambulance near to the front door was parked, its

emergency siren and lights turned off. At Grace's estimate, there would be room to park at least five cars. After showing their warrant cards, she and Perry stepped under the crime scene tape, immediately hearing howls of grief from the house next door. She knew it was more than likely one of the family of the deceased that had vacated to there. The noise chilled Grace to the bone and she pushed back her emotions. She could deal with seeing anything by now, but the sounds of someone suffering got under her skin every time. She blocked it out as they dressed in forensic gear.

Nick briefed them both on what had happened and then they stepped inside the tent.

'Well, hello again,' Dave Barnett said. 'This is a nasty one, so be prepared if you want to see what's left of his face.'

Grace steeled herself as she stepped closer. Several teeth were scattered around in tiny pools of blood. She couldn't tell what colour the victim's hair had been because it was coated in the thick red substance. Where his face should have been was a mash of bone and mucus and pulp. It was her turn to almost vomit this time. She looked away for a moment to compose herself.

'That's brutal.' Perry held a hand to his mask.

'Yes, our suspect must be covered in blood,' Dave added. 'Your victim probably would have gone down easily after a couple of hits, I reckon. It was quite a frenzied attack. His wife found him. I've seen some sights, but this is one of the worst. I can't begin to imagine how that must have been. I doubt she'll sleep for weeks.'

'How cruel to do it right outside his home,' Grace acknowledged. 'It's rather personal, the same as the attack on Josh Parker. Like a hit, don't you think?'

'It's possible. Because he has a single stab wound to the chest too.'

Grace and Perry cursed in unison.

'Are you any further forward with the last murder?' Dave added.

'We're still gathering evidence.' Grace paused before saying what she was thinking. 'These knife attacks. Do you think they're symbolic? Maybe stabs to the heart? That would definitely be a more personal link.'

Dave nodded. 'It could be a possibility.'

Grace left Perry outside and went next door with Nick. As a detective constable, she had always found it daunting, but necessary, to go in to speak to relatives directly after a murder had happened. To be there as a detective sergeant was even more harrowing after such a brutal murder, but it was still something she saw as vital.

Dale Chapman's wife, Denise, was sitting at the kitchen table. A middle-aged woman, she had short brown hair that suited her long face. She played with a pair of red glasses in her hand, scrunched a tissue in the other. A young PC Grace hadn't seen before was sitting by her side.

Nick introduced them and pulled out a chair, sitting across from them both. Grace followed suit and sat next to him.

'We are so sorry for your loss, Mrs Chapman. Are you able to run me through everything, please?' Nick said. 'It's vital for us to understand what happened.'

'I saw the outside lights come on so I knew Dale had come home,' she began. 'But when I didn't see him after a few minutes, I came outside to investigate. Ralph spotted him first.'

'Ralph?' Nick questioned.

'Our dog. He's covered in Dale's blood!'

Grace glanced at Nick sideways, trying not to flinch.

'It was then that I saw him on the floor. He . . . he . . .' Denise broke down again. '*How* could someone be so barbaric?'

'Do you know why anyone would want to hurt your husband?' Nick continued.

'No! Dale was a kind man! No one would do *that* to him.' She retched and covered her mouth with her hand before running out of the room.

They let her go. Grace would need space if this had happened to her.

'Do we know who else was in the house . . .?' she asked the woman left sitting across from them. 'Sorry, we haven't met.'

'PC Maxine Wren. Their son, Oliver, ran upstairs as soon as we brought him round. The owners of the house let him use their bedroom to get away. They're both in the living room.'

'I'll go and talk to Oliver,' Grace told Nick.

Her footsteps were heavy as she went upstairs. No matter who was responsible or the reasons for such a brutal attack, the family would never be the same again.

As she took the stairs to the first floor, Grace could see that this was a family home. An array of photos and family portraits throughout the years were visible with every step she took. On the galleried landing, a bookcase held a mixture of crime thrillers, cooking manuals and Harry Potter books. There was a large teddy bear with a baseball cap sitting in a battered leather armchair next to it.

Her heart leapt into her mouth and she struggled to contain her emotions. There was never going to be a normal family home next door ever again.

She knocked on a door and waited. With no answer, she looked inside, but the bedroom was empty. She tried the next one to find a bathroom. At the third attempt, a teenager came to the door. He was taller than her, with dark gelled spiky hair and a wobble to his bottom lip.

'Hi, Oliver,' she said. 'I'm DS Grace Allendale. Could I come in for a moment?'

'I didn't see anything.' He stepped aside for her. 'I didn't hear anything either. I was listening to my music. He kept on telling me it was too loud but I . . . I . .' He broke down in tears, rushing into her arms.

Taken aback for a second, she froze. Then she wrapped him in her embrace, letting him grieve. These were going to be dark days for him. A death in the family was always hard. A murder was even worse. But this? This would be beyond comprehension.

Once he was ready to talk, they sat down on the bed.

'You have a brother and a sister, I was told?' She started with a simple question.

He nodded before sniffing loudly. 'James and Sarah.'

'Neither live at home now?'

'No, they're older than me. Both married. They'll be here soon.'

'Did you get on well with your dad?' she asked gently, noting that she'd want to check out his bedroom when she went back next door. Sometimes there would be the odd family memory Blu-Tacked around a mirror or propped up against a stack of books. It often gave her an insight into relationships and home life.

Oliver didn't speak for a moment, then shrugged. 'I didn't see him that much. He works long hours; most evenings and at the weekends he's playing golf or out for a drink.'

'Does your mum go with him?' Grace realised he was talking about his father in the present tense. 'For a drink?'

'Sometimes.'

'So did you know any of his friends?'

'Not very well.' He shook his head. 'I missed having him around, though. He was brilliant at *Grand Theft Auto*.'

Grace smiled. They chatted for a few minutes and it became clear he couldn't tell her anything else, so she left him and went back downstairs.

She found Nick outside in the driveway of next door, lights blazing behind him as more forensic officers arrived.

'Any luck?' he asked.

She shook her head. 'Poor kid is in shock. He doesn't want to come back to the house.'

Nick screwed up his face. 'Well, want to know where our victim was before he came home?'

Grace's chin rose. 'Go on.'

'He'd just done a workout at Steele's Gym.'

TWENTY-TWO

SUNDAY – DAY 6

The murder of Dale Chapman had warranted another late night. Grace had gone to bed at one thirty a.m. and was back in the station at half past seven. During the early hours, the Chapmans' house had been the scene of a full-scale search. Sam had gone straight over to the crime scene to view their security camera footage before sending over anything she thought valuable. Mrs Chapman and Oliver had remained out of the property until it had been swept for forensics.

The image of Chapman had looked familiar to Grace. She'd googled him that morning, read a few articles about his business and had a look around his website but come to the conclusion that she didn't know him.

Everyone assembled in the briefing room at half past eight. Even more officers had come on board. Now there were two murders they were looking to link, the DCI came into the meeting.

'Although the MOs are different, we're connecting this to Operation Wedgwood.' Jenny pointed to a photo on the white-board behind her. 'Victim number two. Dale Chapman. Aged forty-nine. Married with three children. Blunt force trauma to the head and face, resulting in death. And a single stab wound to the chest. We're obviously keeping an open mind right now, but Grace's theory of them both being stabbed in the heart as a symbol is a good one to follow up on.'

'Chapman lived on a quiet avenue, but all the gardens and driveways were open-plan,' Nick went on. 'It seems anyone can wander in off the road without too much trouble, although there could be more eyes on them, I suppose. A lot of the properties nearby have their own security cameras, so we'll be checking those today. On further inspection, we found one of the security lights broken. According to Mrs Chapman, she had no idea it was out.'

'The last place he visited was Steele's Gym,' Alex stated. 'He left there at 20.30 and was home twenty minutes later.'

Grace looked at the table briefly, hoping she wasn't blushing at the mention.

'Do you think someone is sending a message?' asked PC Mick Higgins, who had been drafted in to help them again.

'I don't know,' Alex said. 'It could be to the Steele family. Or the Parkers. What about the Woodmans?'

'The Woodmans?' Grace queried, wondering why she hadn't heard the name until now.

'The Woodmans are another of our crime families,' Perry enlightened her. 'Turf wars when they step out of line or go on each other's patches. Although they're not as big a name on the streets as the Steeles.'

'Well, Josh Parker I can understand,' Grace said, 'but what would the connection be to Dale Chapman? Have we any intel on him being connected to them in any way?'

Nick shook his head. 'Nothing. He's a well-respected businessman. Won some big local award last year. He's doing fine on all accounts. Where are we on forensics for Josh Parker?'

'Tests show there was no DNA found anywhere belonging to anyone else and so far we have nothing on any cameras,' Grace told everyone. 'Along with Sam, the CCTV analyst has gone through everything but there is nothing linking any cars to the gym for several hours. He is still analysing it though, and will let us know once he's done as much as he can.'

'If our suspect used a car, it's likely it can be pinpointed on the main road after the time of the murder,' Alex added. 'But we'd need a lead on the make, model or registration number. And we don't have any of those yet.'

'We're also going through his phone and financial records,' Perry added. 'Social media too. Nothing is obvious at the moment.'

Back at her desk, sustenance had arrived. Apparently, a hot breakfast was a Sunday morning ritual if they were working on a case. Usually there was no time to stop for food, so a meal first thing was the order of the day – literally.

Grace tucked into her bacon and cheese oatcakes with relish. Oatcakes in some places meant oat biscuits; nothing so fancy, but the Staffordshire Oatcake was a local delicacy, its recipe kept secret throughout the years. They were known all over the world, shipped out to faraway places too. In her opinion, they were best served hot, rolled up with cooked bacon and cheese, sausage and egg amongst other things inside it.

'Heavenly,' Grace said aloud. 'It's almost worth coming back to Stoke for,' she joked.

While she ate, Grace searched the computer database for what she could find out about the Woodmans. There were two brothers, both in their early fifties. Malcolm and Len had families of their own now, five boys and two girls between them ranging from early to late twenties. Two of the boys were in prison for GBH, and one had come out a short time ago and was now on probation. Grace wondered if this had anything to do with the recent attacks. Was someone trying to muscle in and warn the Steeles about something?

'What are you looking at?'

Grace looked up to see Perry standing next to her. She held up the piece of paper she had been doodling on. It was something similar to a five-year-old's masterpiece that they would show to a proud parent. There were bubbles, lines leading to them, lines crossed out, squiggles, names and arrows.

'I was trying to collate all the evidence we had,' she explained. 'Anything else linking the Steeles to the two murder victims, in the hope that they will all lead to one person.'

'And do they?'

'Not yet. Do you think the Woodmans are involved?'

'We know their family don't usually resort to this level of violence. They're petty thieves. They've done a bit of time for taking vehicles without consent, breaking and entering. But nothing along the lines of murder.'

Her phone went. It was Sam.

'I'm sending you an email with the camera footage attached from Dale Chapman's home. We have a figure dressed in dark clothes running from the scene.'

Grace quickly searched it out on the computer as Sam continued.

'We followed with the camera on to the street outside but lost sight. There are open fields across the way, so a number of possibilities. Our suspect could have vanished on foot. They could have gone into a house nearby. Or they were being picked up by an accomplice, or there was a vehicle parked close to drive away in.'

'You know the area better than I do,' Grace stated. 'Where would our suspect run to?'

'Into the dark and off camera? There could be lots of places.

It's possibly a local, someone who knew the area. Or maybe someone has been following Chapman for a while, checking out his moves.'

'From Steele's Gym?'

'That's possible too. Our suspect needed to know Chapman would come home around that time or else have to sit around waiting for him. Also, our suspect was careful to shield their face, keep their back to the lens as they left. My guess is whoever it was got away over those fields and we lost them. We've found a couple of shoe prints in the soil around the edge of the garden. We're going to match them up if we can, but from first impressions CSI reckon it's a common brand of trainer. The shoe size is relatively small. Size eight.'

'Could our suspect be a woman?'

'Impossible to tell,' Sam replied. 'But whoever it was has a slight frame.'

Grace pondered for a moment. 'So, basically, it could be anyone?'

TWENTY-THREE

When he heard about the murder of Dale Chapman from Alex Challinor that morning, Eddie shoved his chair across the room. Chapman had been a family friend for years. Eddie hadn't particularly warmed to him but he'd been a good customer of theirs, especially when Leon had started loaning him money.

The last time he'd seen Chapman was a week ago. Eddie had just come out of the gym when Dale was going in. They'd stopped for a chat, and there hadn't seemed to be anything wrong then.

He rang Leon but there was no answer. Jade came into his office as he disconnected the call.

'What are you doing here?' he asked. 'It's Sunday.'

'I couldn't sleep.'

'Hungover?' he sneered at her.

'No! I dropped Megan off at Freya's as they're catching the train to Birmingham. Then I heard about Dale Chapman. She had a text message from a friend of his son's.' She flopped down onto the settee. 'First Josh and now Dale? Why would anyone target him?'

'I don't know, but when I do find out who it is, I'm going to bring them down.' Eddie thumped the desk. 'No one messes with us like this. It's going to bring the cops here again. You haven't heard any talk lately?'

Jade flicked back her hair. 'I heard he had a fallout with Leon.'

'When?'

'Last week. Clara told me.'

Eddie remained deadpan. He'd heard that too. He'd have to look into that.

'Do you think we all might be in danger?' Jade asked.

'What do you mean?'

'Well, two people we know have been murdered. Both are members of our gym.'

Eddie shook his head. 'It's nothing personal.'

'Are you sure?'

'Yes. No one is out to get us. We're safe as houses in this city.'

A silence fell on the room as they each absorbed the news and its implications.

'I don't like this though,' Eddie said eventually. 'We'd better start asking our associates. There'll be rumours going around soon, once word gets out about Dale.'

'I'll keep my ears open,' Jade said.

'As long as you don't go blabbing about it.' Eddie sneered. 'You can't keep anything to yourself during pillow talk.'

'That's not fair!' Jade protested. 'A lot of my pillow talk, as you so smoothly call it, was to find out information for you and Leon.'

Eddie sat back in his chair and swayed from side to side. 'There's an idea.'

'Oh, no. I'm not doing any of that again.' Jade folded her arms. 'I'm not that teenager you could manipulate all those years ago. I'm a grown woman – a businesswoman at that.'

113

'You're also still a shrewd bitch that likes getting one over on someone.'

Jade glared at him. 'I'm not doing it!'

'I'm only asking you to listen out,' he chided. 'Just put some feelers out. See if anyone has any gossip.'

Jade stood firm for a moment and then dropped her arms to her sides. 'I'll see what I can find out, but I'm not making any promises. And you,' she said, pointing at him, 'and Leon need to do your bit too. As well as include me in more business stuff. I'm part of this family. Even more so now Dad is gone.'

'That's if Mother will allow you to be.'

At the mention of Kathleen, Jade turned and stormed out of the room. The slam of the door made Eddie clamp his teeth together. At least that would give Jade something to focus on, and keep her out of harm's way while he tried to figure out what to do next.

Grace went in to tell Nick about their latest findings. She caught him looking at his screen, hand on chin as he leaned on the desk with his elbow. He looked stressed, no doubt getting it from every side now there were two murders.

She wondered if she'd ever want to do an inspector's job, with all the added pressure. It was why she enjoyed her grade so much, so she could be more hands-on rather than behind a desk for most of the day.

Nick beckoned for her to sit down and Grace updated him.

'It's going to take an age to get to everyone,' she said. 'We now have over one hundred people in the gym on the two evenings the murders took place, even though at this stage it's a tenuous link.'

'And some of them you've already seen?'

'Yes. They're not going to take kindly to being questioned twice. We'll get there, though.'

'Seems all in hand.' Nick paused. 'How about you?'

Grace frowned at him.

'The Steele family. Everything okay? How have they been with you?'

'I haven't seen them for a few days, although I'm on my way to the gym shortly.'

'Who's going with you?'

'Perry.'

'Okay. I just wanted you to know that if you feel intimidated, or if they lean on you when they shouldn't, my door is always open.'

'I can handle them, sir. It's more my colleagues I'm worried about,' Grace said.

'They're not as slippery as the Steeles.'

Grace knew he was making a joke of the situation but she still didn't feel comfortable.

'You can't tell them now,' Nick said, almost as if he had read her mind. 'You'll lose their trust.'

'I'll lose it even more when they do find out, sir.' Grace sighed. 'They're bound to, sooner or later.'

'You worry too much.' Nick bowed his head and got back to his work. 'And less of the sir, it's Nick,' he added just as she was about to leave.

'Sorry, Nick.'

TWENTY-FOUR

Then

She hated her father. Why was he so cruel?

What kind of man ruled the house with the moods that he came in with when he'd been drinking? Her mum said he never worked a day in his life, but she knew he brought money in, so where did that come from? He must do something for it, unless he stole it. She couldn't see him doing that though. If he was stealing money all the time then he wouldn't be able to get so drunk. He'd have to keep his wits about him, be one step ahead of the people who were after him.

Her teacher said that bad people go to prison for a very long time. She wished that her dad would go to prison. Then she could be happy. It would be nice not to have to stay in her room for so long.

It would be nice not to be scared when he turned up. It would be nice not to be woken by her mum screaming at him to let her go, or for him not to hit her. She wished they could leave. They could live somewhere far away. She wouldn't mind if she didn't see her friends again and had to change schools. As long as they were safe and he didn't find them. They would be very happy without him. They could make noise, laugh and play. But not here, not when he kept telling her to stay in her room.

They shouldn't have to live like this.

Perhaps she should tell her teacher at school. Maybe she could help them. Although she knew she wouldn't dare. He didn't like anyone poking their nose in. She'd get in real trouble then. She would have to stay in her room a lot more.

She squeezed her eyes shut now, trying to imagine she was somewhere else. Anywhere but here.

TWENTY-FIVE

Grace pulled into the car park of Steele's Gym. Nick's words were still going around in her head. He didn't seem to be worried that there could potentially be another murder linked to her estranged family, never mind how her colleagues would feel if they found out who she was. She couldn't snap out of her discomfort, but equally knew she couldn't tell them herself. And she wanted to stay on this case now that she had started it.

She wasn't sure who her loyalty lay with in solving it though.

To judge by the lack of cars, the murders seemed to be keeping people away, despite the gym having reopened on Friday. Inside the reception area, Clara Emery sat behind a desk. She wore her blonde hair loose and nails painted vampire red. A silver stud over her left eye plus one in her top lip gave her a style of her own.

Even though Grace had met her briefly during the week, she still held up her warrant card. 'Is Eddie in? We need to speak to him.'

'I'll just see if he's free.' Clara picked up a phone.

'Free or not, I want to speak to him,' Grace muttered to Perry.

'He'll be with you in a moment,' Clara told them.

'Thanks.' Grace decided to do some digging while she waited. 'How is everyone feeling? It must have been a terrible shock on Wednesday. It was your boyfriend who found the body, right?'

'Yes.' Clara paused before continuing: 'Trent was a bit freaked by it. Said he couldn't get the image from his mind. He keeps screaming out in his sleep.'

'Do you live together?' Grace hoped her questioning sounded like small talk.

Clara shook her head. 'But he was with me when it happened. I told you that on Wednesday.'

Grace gave Clara a long stare before nodding. 'What can you tell me about Dale Chapman?'

'I didn't like him much. There was something about him that gave me the creeps.'

'Oh?' Grace encouraged her to continue, noting that Clara hadn't queried why she was asking and that she was talking about him in the past tense.

'He was one of those men who looked at you as if he was undressing you and didn't care if you realised.'

'Was he a regular here? Can you recall when you last saw him?'

'Last night.' Clara glanced around before telling them a very interesting nugget of information about an altercation Grace would be asking Eddie about.

After a while, when Eddie still hadn't arrived, Grace decided she was done with waiting. They went through to the gym. It was eleven a.m. She looked about as she walked, noting the T-shirts with the boxing club logos on them, the sense of safety in numbers. Packed with young boys sparring, testosterone levels as high as the noise. Apart from Clara, she was the only woman, but she didn't feel intimidated. The

119

average age of the clientele that morning must have been about seventeen.

'I'll go through to Eddie,' Grace told Perry. 'Have a word with some of the boys while I'm gone – see if anyone has any information for us.'

Eddie was sitting at his desk when she got to him. Grace sat down when he indicated for her to do so and he closed the door.

Just me and you, the gesture said.

'Sorry to keep you waiting. What can I do for you, *Sergeant*?' he asked.

'There's been another murder. Last night,' she told him.

'Yes, one of the boys in the boxing club told us it was Dale. His mum is friends with Dale's wife. It's worrying.'

For some reason, Grace wasn't buying that, but she kept her assumptions to herself. 'A bit close to home again?' she went on.

Eddie didn't take the bait. 'Have you found out any more information yet?' he asked. 'You say this happened last night? Do you know what time?'

'Within half an hour of him leaving here.'

Eddie sat forward. There was a short pause. 'You know that for certain, do you?'

She nodded. 'Mr Chapman signed out of the gym at eight thirty. We had a call from his wife at soon after nine. I was wondering if there had been anything happening here last night that might shed some light on it.'

'You mean you want to find evidence that someone followed him from here and beat him to death?' Eddie shook his head slowly in disbelief. 'And you think this because Josh Parker was murdered here too?'

'I'm not implying anything at the moment,' Grace stated. 'I'm merely asking you a few questions before we start talking to the rest of the staff. If you didn't see anything, then maybe they did.'

'I don't know what happened.'

'Just like you don't know what happened to Josh Parker. He was murdered, Mr Steele. On your premises.'

They stared at each other, like two hyenas ready to pounce. Grace waited for him to fill the silence.

'So because that happened here,' Eddie went on, 'and because Dale Chapman is one of our members, that means it's someone from my gym that murdered them both?'

'Not necessarily. But it could be someone that you know.'

'You think it was the same person?'

'It's a line of enquiry we are following.'

'Oh, I get it. You think this *someone* is out to get our family – by that, I mean *my* family. Not yours.'

'I was told by your receptionist that Dale had a falling-out with Leon yesterday,' she said, not taking the bait either. 'She remembers seeing them arguing. Is Leon around?'

'He isn't on shift until this afternoon.'

'I need to see him before then.'

'Why?'

'Is his address still the same one we have on record?'

'What is it with you, Grace?' he growled. 'Don't you believe your own family?'

'I want to talk to him.'

'If you think Leon has anything to do with the death of Dale Chapman then I assume you have evidence to bring him in for questioning?'

'I'm not about to bring him in.' Grace stood up, worried that Perry might come in at any moment.

Eddie stood up too, blocking her as she got to the door. 'You haven't been back in Stoke for two minutes and yet you're already causing me so much grief!'

'Only doing my job. You do want to find out who murdered your right-hand man, as well as one of your gym members?'

'Of course I do.'

He looked her up and down in a way that reminded her of their father doing the same when she was younger. It made her feel uncomfortable but more determined to stand her ground.

'You need to watch your back, Ms Detective,' he said. 'You never know who might be out to get you too.'

'Are you threatening me?' Grace glared at him.

Eddie held up his hands in mock surrender. 'I'm just saying it seems as if someone is out to get our family, so . . .' He let his words tail off purposely.

'But I'm not part of *your* family, and I haven't done anything to cause anyone to—'

'And you think I have?'

She pushed past him. 'We're on the same side here. *I* need to find out who has murdered two people in the space of a week: *you* want people to come to your gym. If anything else happens, we might have to close it until further notice and that will affect your—'

'You wouldn't do that.' He sniggered.

'Oh, please don't come with that one.' She pointed a finger at him. 'You're no more important to me than anyone I deal with on a daily basis. You're not getting any special treatment.'

'Maybe not from you.'

Her brow furrowed again. 'Excuse me?'

He pressed a finger to his lips. 'I'm saying no more.' He went to sit back at his desk. 'Close the door on the way out, will you?'

'I'll leave when I'm finished. I want to check Mr Chapman's locker – and the security camera footage please.' Grace wanted to tell him how obnoxious he was but decided it would be a waste of time. People like him didn't care anyway. He was only trying to intimidate her. 'Are you saying that someone is giving you information?' she continued.

'No, Sergeant.' Eddie shook his head in mock horror. 'Not at all. You must have misunderstood me.'

'Well, let me make myself very clear,' Grace replied. 'If I find out any police officer, of any rank, at my station is corrupt, then I will get him or her removed from the force. I have no time for moles.'

'Come on now, Grace.' Eddie's voice was jovial, almost taunting her with its cheerfulness. 'No need to take things so personal.' He paused, steepling his hands together. 'Speaking of which, you have two nephews who are dying to meet you. My wife is keen too, and I'm sure Kathleen would like to see you again. Any time you're free to call for Sunday lunch, it will be a pleasure.'

'I think I'll be pretty tied up for the next fifty years.' Grace opened the door to leave.

'Do your team know who you are yet?'

She stopped and turned back to him. It was a threat that he could follow through with at any time.

'It's none of their business,' she replied.

'Really?' Eddie scoffed. 'I wonder how they'll react when they realise they've been conned. I wouldn't like to be in your shoes.'

'I wouldn't like to be in *your* shoes if I find out that it was you who told them.'

She stared at him until he dropped his eyes. Then she left to find Perry.

Damn that man. It was so hard to tread the line between doing her job and keeping a civil tongue in her head. What was it with him and Leon that instantly had her back up?

'Any luck?' she asked Perry as she rejoined him.

Perry shook his head. 'No one heard or saw anything. I

would say the loyalty in there is pretty thorough. They don't even care if they get into trouble.'

'Let's check his locker before we go.'

There was nothing in it, except a towel hanging on the inside of the door and a washbag containing a few toiletries.

Back in her car, Grace pulled out of the car park, trying not to show Perry how rattled she was. Time to see if Leon Steele would be as unpleasant as his brother.

TWENTY-SIX

Clara Emery had been ecstatic when she'd got the job at Posh Gloss. She'd been working at Powder and Puff in Hanley for several years, learning the business as a junior and then a stylist. When a manager's job opened up, she'd assumed she would automatically get it, but it was advertised and that nasty bitch Michelle got it. She'd questioned the owner, Roberto, about it, saying she had worked tirelessly for him for years and thought he owed her, but all he'd done was say she could take care of the nail bar. At the time she had hated him for it, but jobs were hard to come by and she'd stuck it out.

When she'd been offered the position at Posh Gloss, she hadn't been able to contain herself when she'd given in her notice. Roberto had thought she'd never leave. He offered her more money to stay on, but she refused to back down. She would be getting a good salary working at Posh Gloss, even though she was working the reception too, and Kathleen Steele had told her there would be bonuses for the right person. It hadn't taken her long to work out what the bonuses were for. Kathleen wanted her to keep an eye on everyone, report back to her if she saw anything untoward, or anything she thought Kathleen should know about.

Clara was twenty-six and had met Trent Gibson shortly afterwards. He was two years older than her and seeing someone else at the time, but it hadn't stopped them flirting almost immediately. She had been sharing a bed with him a week later. He had a bad-boy charm about him that she idolised, and he was well in with the Steeles. Pretty soon so was she.

During the past year, she'd been sleeping with Leon and Trent in equal measure. Both knew about the other, although she'd always deny it. She knew they were using her, but she was using them. She could be devious too.

So she had a lot to thank Roberto for. Because her life had changed dramatically since the day he'd overlooked her, taken her for granted, and she loved every minute of it. The danger, the allure, the money. Nothing spelt all that out except being in with the Steele family. Leon was only a stepping stone to better things. She had her sights set on Eddie really.

She reached for her phone to send a message.

Job done.

Eddie cursed loudly. That stupid bitch Clara was going to get it in the neck for talking to the police. He'd told her to be helpful to them, keep them happy. That had meant not blabbing her mouth off, not arousing suspicion.

He jumped up and locked the door to the office. Alerted early enough, he'd searched Dale's locker this morning. He went over to the safe in the corner of the room. Reaching behind it, he pulled out a plastic bag. Inside it was an untraceable pay-as-you-go handset. It wasn't Dale's usual phone: Eddie had seen his smartphone plenty of times and had the number stored in his own too. This one had been hidden inside his washbag.

Knowing it was too risky to keep it there, Eddie slipped the phone into his pocket. He needed to get rid of it as soon as possible.

Next he called Leon.

'Where are you?'

'At home. Why?' his brother asked.

'Grace is coming to see you.'

'What does she want, did she say?'

'She wants to know where you were last night, and so do I. Dale Chapman is dead.'

'What the—'

'If you have anything to do with this, I'll break every bone in your body.' Eddie banged the palm of his hand down on the desk. 'I don't want the police here, not so soon after Josh.'

'Hey, slow down, bro. What happened to Dale?'

'Beaten to a pulp on the driveway of his home.'

'Fuck. Does he have cameras?'

Eddie realised he didn't know. Grace hadn't told him because he'd been so hell-bent on talking her down. 'I'm not sure. Look, she'll be over to your gaff soon. So make sure you get your alibi straight.'

'I haven't done anything! Although I need to stop her getting to Trudy before I do.' Trudy was Leon's wife. 'I didn't get home until midnight last night. I stopped by at Clara's.'

'You weren't on shift?'

'Trent's got a stag do next weekend. We swapped shifts, which is why I visited Clara when I finished.'

'I suggest you get your house in order, so to speak.'

He disconnected the call, annoyed by the effect Grace was having on him. Seeing her again had been a real shock, and it brought back painful memories of his father. He tried not to think about George on a regular basis. He had been such a bad influence in his life and his murder hadn't been unwelcome, despite his anger that the police still hadn't caught his killer.

He thought back to the first time he had seen his half-sister. He'd been fourteen and had been coming home from boxing practice. He and Josh had been fooling around, pretending to uppercut each other as they raced along the pavement. He loved his boxing sessions after school. They were the thing that kept him sane. He and Josh had just been in the ring and he was pumped up because he'd won three out of three fights.

He'd been telling Josh what a wuss he was and then he'd spotted George. He was sitting in McDonald's and he was laughing at something. Eddie saw him reach across the table for a woman's hand. She smiled back at him. There was something in her eyes that at the time he'd confused with love, but he now knew had been George's power over her.

There was a girl sitting next to the woman. She looked a couple of years younger than Eddie, about twelve. She was sipping on a strawberry milkshake. He wondered if George had bought it for her, and the Happy Meal box he could see next to it. George would never take them to McDonald's. He said they didn't deserve nice things. He said they had to earn them and so far they hadn't. Eddie hadn't really understood what he'd meant by this.

As he laughed again, George turned and looked out of the window and that's when Eddie had been spotted. He'd only been a few metres away on the pavement. George glared at him, and then his smile returned as he leaned over to the woman and kissed her. Not a peck on the cheek, but a lingering lips-on-lips kiss.

When he got home, Eddie knew he'd be in for it. George would make out he'd been watching him, following him, trying to catch him out. He ran up to his room.

All night he wondered if George was with her and the girl, or if he had gone to the pub, or out on another punching exercise to knock down one of his enemies. Eddie knew of his reputation. George should be good at fighting, the amount of practice he'd had dealing out punches to his family.

He had so many questions. Who was the woman and why was he seeing her? That hadn't been just a friendly kiss. They looked as if they were a couple. How long had he known her? Was that why he didn't live with Eddie's family? Did he live with *her* some of the time too? That wasn't fair on Mum after everything he put her through, put them all through. And the girl, who was she?

It had taken a while, but he'd clicked eventually. She had reminded him of someone, with her dark hair and eyes. She'd been huddled over her drink and then she'd put her head up and smiled at something George had said. It was then that he'd noticed the familiarity. She was the image of Jade.

It was past midnight when George had got home. Eddie had worked himself up into such a state that he was ready for him. How dare he make a fool out of their mum. How dare he play around behind her back.

The door to the bedroom opened and his father came into the room. He sat down on his bed.

'What did you see?' he asked.

'Nothing,' Eddie replied. Across the room, he noticed his brother pretending to be asleep, not wanting to be drawn into anything.

George sighed loudly. Then he grabbed Eddie's hair and pulled him across the bed.

'I said, what did you see?'

'Nothing!' Eddie cried. 'I saw nothing!'

'Best keep it that way. Because if I ever find out that you breathed a word about what you *didn't* see, then I will make you regret it in the most painful way I can think of. Have you got that?'

Eddie nodded fervently, tears pricking his eyes.

George pushed him and he fell heavily to the floor. As George made to leave the room, something snapped inside Eddie at last and he stood up.

'I wonder what your friends would say if they knew that you beat up your family,' he said. 'And going with another woman behind our mum's back? That's not manly either. That girl looks like Jade. Is she our—'

George's fist came at him before he could finish the sentence. Eddie's head reared to one side with the force. Blood poured down his face as vessels in his nose burst. A blast of pain like nothing he'd ever felt before exploded inside his head. George never usually went for the face. It was hard to hide the damage and deny any wrongdoing. Eddie would be off school for a fortnight with this. George would be in for it if anyone saw what he'd done.

He'd stood there holding his nose, blood coming through his fingers. 'You bastard,' he muttered under his breath.

He came towards him again. Eddie stepped away but George pulled his head back and grabbed the bridge of his nose, pinching hard.

Eddie didn't want his father to touch him but he needed to quell the bleeding. Once it was stopped, George released his grip and put his face down to his.

'Don't act all hard, son,' he said. 'You're not a man yet and from what I've seen you're a long way from it.'

And then he laughed.

Eddie drew his fist back and smashed it underneath George's jaw, just like the uppercuts he'd been practising with Josh earlier. He was aware he couldn't cause the damage his father did but he was sure as hell going to hurt him.

George put his hand to his chin where Eddie's fist had caught him and rubbed it. Eddie braced himself for what was coming next. What happened floored him, but there was no punch.

'Well, well, well,' his father smirked. 'It's about time.'

Eddie stood there, catching his breath.

'Maybe you are a man after all.' George's hand came towards Eddie and he tried not to cower. He placed it on his shoulder. 'I've wanted you to fight back for a good while now. I'm surprised it took you so long, but I'll put that down to having some kind of respect for your old man. But I'm warning you, don't ever hit me again.'

Now, in his office, Eddie brought up new camera footage on his computer. He had to be sure that Chapman wasn't followed as he left their establishment. It was the first thing the police would be checking.

Twenty minutes later, his conscience was clear. He had seen Chapman and his car leaving at 20.30. No one had got in the car with him. There had been fifteen cars left in the car park then and one by one he watched as their owners came back and drove away. No one had followed Dale Chapman outside. It didn't take into account the blind spot, but he would have seen a vehicle driving out of it if there had been one parked. Which meant that someone must have been waiting for Chapman at his own property.

He breathed a sigh of relief. For now, it seemed this murder wouldn't be linked to them after all. But clearly it couldn't be a coincidence that Chapman was a gym member, that he had been there before he died, that he had been arguing with Leon. And it had brought Grace to his door again, which was infuriating.

Eddie rubbed at his chin, deep in thought. Two people murdered and leading to their gym wasn't good. He needed to keep an eye on his brother and sister.

TWENTY-SEVEN

Grace parked outside Leon Steele's home, a little surprised to see it was only a few streets away from his brother's address. The house was a detached new-build with no more character than the dozen or so around it. She and Perry squeezed through two cars parked side by side in front of a double garage, a black Range Rover and a red Mini.

The front door opened as she got to it and Leon came out on to the step, making her realise that Eddie had most probably been in touch with him. Although she had assumed that would happen, it denied them the element of surprise.

She held up her warrant card, even though she knew it wasn't necessary. 'Can we have a few minutes, Mr Steele?'

'Come in,' he ushered, 'and Grace, please call me Leon.'

'It's DS Allendale.' She gritted her teeth.

Inside, Leon showed them through a large and bright hallway, marble tiles clicking under their feet, and into a kitchen with an island at its centre. It opened out into a huge breakfast room, the garden through the window showcasing a weeping willow tree in the middle of a large lawn.

A woman was sitting on a settee close to a set of French

doors. She stood up when she saw Grace, revealing pale wide-legged trousers and a jumper that slipped elegantly off her shoulder. Blonde hair trailed down her back and she smiled from a perfectly made-up face. Grace thought the shade of her ruby lipstick made her seem a bit drained, but it matched the colour of her nails as she held out a hand.

'This is my wife, Trudy,' Leon introduced. 'Perry, you know.'

'DC Wright,' Grace said.

'And this is DS Allendale – Grace.'

'Ah.' Trudy gave Grace the once-over. 'I've heard so much about *you* already.'

Grace didn't take kindly to the emphasis on the word 'you'. She realised that Perry was bound to have caught it too.

'What can we do for you?' Trudy asked.

'We're investigating a murder that took place last night.'

'Eddie has just rung,' Leon said. 'We couldn't believe it, could we, Trudy?'

Trudy shook her head. 'Not another one.'

Grace nodded. 'I wanted to check on your movements last night, Leon. What time you left the gym, what time you arrived home; did you go anywhere else in between?'

'That's outrageous!' Trudy piped up. 'You can't think Leon had anything to do with this murder!'

'We don't *think* anything, Mrs Steele,' Grace said. 'It's our job to investigate, so we never jump to conclusions. It's evidence that matters.'

'Relax, babe,' Leon told Trudy. 'There's nothing to worry about. If it helps matters by saying where I was, and gets the bastard who did this to Dale, then I'm happy to oblige. I don't have anything to hide. Do you think it's the same man who killed Josh?'

'We're keeping an open mind at the moment,' Grace replied.

'I left the gym just after nine p.m.,' Leon told them. 'Then I stopped off to see a friend and got home just before midnight.'

'A friend?'

'Graham Frost.'

It wasn't a name Grace was familiar with, but it seemed Trudy might be, as she straightened up beside her and glared at Leon. Perry seemed to know it too by the discreet look he gave her.

Grace frowned. 'Do you have a contact number for him?'

'You want to speak to him as well?' Leon sank back into the armchair. 'This is all a bit formal, isn't it?'

'We heard that you and Dale were seen arguing,' Perry joined in. 'Is that true?'

Leon pulled a face. 'We had a few words the week before last, that's all.'

'What about?' asked Grace.

'He was angry that the changing rooms were a bit messy after he'd finished his workout. I told him to mention it to the front desk, not me. He said I was above myself just because I was the manager. It was something and nothing. He apologised when I next saw him.'

'Which was?' Perry got out his notebook and pen.

'Last night, just before he left the boxing club.'

'Did you speak to him?'

'Yes, we had a chat about the Stoke match.'

'Did you sign out of the building?' Grace asked.

'Of course.' Leon nodded.

'We all do,' Trudy joined in, throwing Grace yet another icy look. 'For health and safety reasons.'

'You work there too?' Grace couldn't stop the cattiness from entering her voice.

Trudy glared at her. 'No, duck. I don't have to work. I have a good husband who provides for me while I take care of the house and our son. And don't you dare judge me! Especially knowing who your father was.'

'That's enough, Trudy!' Leon sat forward.

'Well, she needs to be put in her place.' Trudy looked at Perry. 'Has she told you yet?'

Grace blushed. 'I just need a phone number to corroborate what you say and I'll be on my way.'

Leon reached across the coffee table for his phone. He swiped a few times and then held the screen so she could see it.

Grace took the number down and stood up. 'I'll get this checked out and be back to you if necessary.'

Once they were on the driveway again, she breathed a sigh of relief, although she wasn't sure which was better. To be in the house, or outside now with Perry. Shit, he was bound to ask her what Trudy Steele had been referring to.

'I can't believe I said that to his wife,' she told him, to stop a silence dropping between them. 'I'm not usually that judgemental but she annoyed me.'

'She's a stuck-up cow who's never got her hands dirty, so don't worry about that.' Perry stopped abruptly. Behind them, there was shouting coming from the house.

'You'd better be telling the truth! If I find out you were with her again, I'll . . .'

Grace stopped too, but Trudy's voice was lost. They must have moved into another room or closed a door.

They carried on back to her car.

She got out her keys. 'Who is Graham Frost?'

'He's a ruse.' Perry opened the door after she switched off the alarm. 'He's used whenever anyone wants an alibi. Frost always says he is with whoever you want him to be with, for a price.'

'How convenient. What an idiot.' They got inside the car. 'Do you know who Leon is knocking off?'

'He's had lots of women on the side. I'm not sure who his latest one is.'

'Well, at least it explains his wife's bitterness over where Leon had been the night before.'

'Either way, the signing-in book shows Leon left at nine like he said, and if he does have an alibi, it will rule him out of the attack on Dale Chapman.'

Grace started the engine quickly to fill the silence. She could tell Perry was being short with her.

'So are you going to tell me or do I have to find out for myself?' he said eventually.

Grace wanted to tell him but the words wouldn't come. From the fury flashing across his face, it was clear he would never trust her once he found out anyway. She wished she could have been truthful from the start.

'I'm sorry, I can't.' Grace blew out the breath she'd been holding. 'I'm sworn to secrecy.'

'Like that, is it?' Perry scoffed. 'Well, don't blame me if I make my own assumptions.'

TWENTY-EIGHT

Perry didn't say another word on their way back to the station. He went straight into Nick's office on their return, closing the door behind him.

Grace flopped down at her desk and waited for the fallout. He'd obviously worked out who she was. It wouldn't have been hard, she admitted, but she wasn't heartened by the thought.

Nick's door opened and he shouted across the office.

'Grace, Sam, Alex. A word.'

Grace saw looks flick between her two DCs. Alex raised his eyebrows at her but she didn't speak. They followed her into the DI's office. Nick had put four chairs in a line. Her heart dropped as she spotted Perry's expression. But equally, Nick was just as fired up.

'Sit down, all of you.' He perched on his desk and folded his arms. 'What I say goes no further than this room.'

Grace kept her eyes fixed on a dot on the wall behind his head while Nick told them who she was. She heard Sam gasp and felt stung by it.

'You're a grass?' Alex sat forward in his chair. 'Really? You've been here over a month.'

'I am not a grass!' Grace protested.

'So what would you call yourself, then?' He shook his head in disgust.

'It was a management decision not to tell you all,' Nick informed them. 'Grace wanted to be honest from the start—'

'Yeah, right,' Perry interrupted.

'But we thought it was best for her not to say anything,' Nick continued.

'That's very gallant of her,' Alex joined in.

'I didn't want to come and work here under false pretences,' Grace explained. 'But I wanted the job.'

'*I* wanted the job!' Perry prodded his chest. 'And I'm far more entitled to it than you.'

'Why, because I'm a Steele?'

No one answered her. Grace noted that Sam hadn't said a word.

'Is that what's really bugging you?' Grace remarked. 'All of you?'

'You've all worked with Grace for a few weeks now,' Nick began, 'and—'

'We wouldn't have, had we known who she was,' Alex interrupted.

'Enough!' Nick's tone said nothing else was negotiable. 'What matters now is that we nail the person who has killed two men in the space of a week. We need to stick together as a team, and put our differences aside.'

Perry sneered at Nick.

'I said enough!' Nick reiterated. 'I don't think I have to tell you how childish you're behaving. This has nothing to do with Grace. And if I find out any of you have told anyone else who she is, then you'll not only be off this case, but you'll be out of my team. Do you understand?'

Three heads nodded.

'Good. Get back to work.'

Grace waited behind as they trooped out of the office. She groaned. 'I wanted to fit in here so much.'

'And you will. You'll just have to work at it.'

Nick sat behind his desk again. Realising she had been dismissed, Grace left the room. As she walked back to her seat, her skin burning with humiliation, she prayed she hadn't ruined her chances to be part of the team. She wasn't sure about Nick yet, felt uncomfortable about his work ethics, and all three of her DCs now had their heads down, clearly not wanting to make eye contact with her.

One thing was certain, her job had just got a whole lot harder.

That evening, Jade poured herself a large gin and tonic, slipped off her shoes and lay back on the sofa. All she'd heard for the last few days was Josh Parker this and Josh Parker that. Lots of people saying they would miss him and that he was a nice person. But it didn't wash with her. She'd known what Josh was really like, having grown up with him since she was a small child. He might be all smiley on his YouTube channel but he'd been a bully in real life.

Most people in the gym were scared to put a finger wrong in case he'd lash out at them. Any one of them could have reason to kill Josh. Indeed, a lot of the boys there didn't like to get on the wrong side of him. He could be quite cruel; his dark side had been ruthless at times. Jade couldn't even blame it on the steroids he pumped into his body. She'd known him way before he'd become addicted to them.

Eddie had been going ballistic for the past few days, with the police presence and then the *Stoke News* wanting interviews, as well as the TV van turning up. And now it was going to be all about Dale Chapman too. She'd hung around the gym today to see what people were talking about, mostly in reception, wanting to be close to the action.

She glanced at the clock on the wall and switched on the TV. The news would be on soon.

'Has it come on yet?' Kathleen asked as she came into the room.

'No. It won't be long, though.'

Kathleen handed her a plate and put a mug down on the coffee table. Jade hadn't wanted a meal but her mum had insisted on making her a sandwich. She hadn't felt hungry all day; didn't now either, but she took a bite anyway.

Jade lived in a small house she'd rented from the council when she and Megan had come back to Stoke a year ago. It was in a pleasant enough area on a nice estate but, now that Megan was getting more independent, Jade had started to spend more time at her mum's. It felt as if the house became lighter too, the threat of her father coming home drunk and disruptive no longer there.

Jade had also tried to cut down on her alcohol. Over the years, people who knew her had fallen by the wayside as they'd had to bail her out one too many times. She had a friend, Lorna, who had stuck by her through everything, but she couldn't stay with her. Jade and Lorna's husband, Tom, had never seen eye to eye, despite their daughters being so close.

Kathleen sat down beside her, crossing her legs elegantly. Jade couldn't remember a time she had seen her mother dressed down. Dad had insisted that she be presentable at all times. She'd heard him punish her on numerous occasions through the years, claiming she was dressed scruffily when she had been nothing of the sort, or not to his satisfaction, and she supposed it must be a force of habit. You'd think she'd want to slob out every now and then, like Jade did. Although, Jade noticed, Kathleen looked weary underneath her make-up. Bags under her eyes seemed more prominent than usual, shoulders drooping, body slumped forward as if she was worried about something.

'Are you okay?' Jade asked.

'Hmm? Oh, yes. I'm fine,' Kathleen replied. 'Although I could ask you the same. You look awfully pale.'

'Oh, I've just been feeling a bit sick lately. Nothing to worry about, I'm sure.'

'You should get some vitamins down you,' Kathleen soothed. 'What time is Megan due back?'

'She's on her way. I've just had a text message from her. Lorna is dropping her off.'

'Are you both staying over tonight?'

'Yes, if that's okay with you?'

'Of course. You know I enjoy your company.'

Jade smiled at her and then pointed at the screen. 'Here we go; here's our clip.'

Jade had first met Detective Inspector Nick Carter when her dad had been murdered. Now, there were about a dozen photographers in front of him, a few people holding phones close, recording the words as he spoke about Dale Chapman's brutal murder.

Grace stood behind him in the background, her expression sombre, hands grasped together in front. Her shoulders were high as if she was pulling herself up purposely. Was she pretending to be assertive? Was she tired but wanting to give the impression that she was coping? How Jade wished she could get to know her, see what made her tick. Maybe in time that would come.

'Is she still wearing a wedding ring?' Kathleen turned to her.

'Yes. I wonder if they had children before her husband died.'

Throughout the years, Eddie had kept an eye on Grace, keeping them up to date with whatever he thought relevant.

They all knew she had been married and her husband had died of cancer two years ago.

'Well, whatever, we need to keep her sweet,' Kathleen said.

'I suppose.'

When the camera panned round, it gave Jade a better look at Grace. Close to, the resemblance was uncanny. She and Grace had the same eyes, the same shape faces and chins, their builds were lean and willowy. Except that Grace had a determined streak about her that Jade would never have. She could bet no one had treated her badly over the years since she'd left.

'Would you like to get to know her?' Kathleen said, startling her from her daze.

'I'm not sure,' she replied, not wanting to give away that she did.

'I think you should.'

'Eddie won't like that,' Jade replied.

'Eddie isn't the boss of this family.'

Jade sniggered. Who was her mother trying to fool? But her thoughts turned back to Grace. Should she get to know her? Would it be fun? If she went to see Grace, it would be going against Eddie, but this could be her opportunity to get close. She liked the sound of that.

Without another thought, Jade reached in her bag for the contact card Grace had given her and sent a text message.

In the kitchen, Kathleen loaded the dishwasher and tried not to make too much noise. As usual, she kept all her emotions hidden. Her children thought she was cold, but it was a coping mechanism she'd perfected through the years. It hadn't been easy living with George. They might have suffered every now and then, but she had been hurt every day, every night, every minute he had been alive.

She'd always prayed that youth would conquer George's anger,

142

and her boys would lash out at him. They had in the end, but it had made her children insecure, nasty and uncontrollable. Eddie had a streak of his father about him, but Leon was much worse. Eddie fought against his dark side; Leon was content to let it show and use it to his advantage.

Jade had turned to alcohol, resulting in bad choices of men to hook up with. Kathleen's granddaughter, Megan, was the only thing Jade had ever produced of value. Megan was a light in a very dark world. Sixteen and beautiful, she had her whole life to look forward to. Kathleen only hoped she wouldn't go the same way as her mother. No one was getting their hands on her.

It was one of the reasons why she was keeping an eye on Jade. Now that George was no longer in control, she knew it wouldn't take much persuasion on her part to get them both to move in permanently. Jade could barely look after herself on a good day and Megan needed stability.

And now she'd got the chance to change things, she wasn't going to mess it up. She had been weak, but she could be strong now. To live her life how she wanted. To keep an eye on her family and what her boys were up to at the gym.

It had become second nature in the end to please George, to keep everything as he liked it, not to antagonise him. But she'd always known a day would come when she would be free of him, just as she had hoped for, wished for, planned for.

So she would bite her tongue and say nothing when Eddie thought he was the head of the family, telling Jade what to do. She had always been good at that.

TWENTY-NINE

Grace sat alone at her desk. It was eight p.m. and there was only her and Nick left working. It was what she preferred after all the glances and stares she'd received from her team that afternoon.

Her colleagues had been good in the scheme of things. They'd been working with other officers, and no one would have sensed an undercurrent. She wondered if they would ever have faith in her now. She wasn't sure she would trust anyone if they had tricked her the same way. But surely they must realise it wasn't her fault? She'd wanted to come to Stoke and that had been the only way she could do it.

Why had it been important to come home? Grace had thought about it a lot. It was perhaps to do with George Steele being murdered, meaning she would never have to face him again. Or could be because his murder remained unsolved and she'd wanted to look into why. Or maybe the truth, deep down, was that she was so lonely that she wanted to get to know some of her family. They couldn't all be criminals.

Grace Allendale, you are made of stronger stuff than this. Pull up your big-girl pants and get on with it.

Grace smiled to herself. She often heard Matt's voice in her head. Comforting her when she needed it. It was certainly good to hear it now, even if he was chastising her.

She was just finishing off going through some of the statements from the gym, seeing if she could spot any anomalies, when Nick appeared at the side of her desk, startling her.

'You shouldn't creep up on people like that.' She put a hand to her chest.

'I did shout across to you.' Nick nodded his head towards the door. 'Fancy a quick half?'

Grace couldn't think of anything she wanted less, but nodded all the same. If she said no, Nick would go and she would likely sit here alone for another couple of hours because she didn't want to go home to an empty house. Especially after the day she'd had.

They left the station and walked the two minutes to Chimneys, the local pub that everyone at the nick called their own. It was on the next street, situated behind their car park. A pottery kiln in the shape of a bottle had been opened up at its centre and a rectangular single-storey building had been attached to either side to form an L-shape. Its decor was old furniture and modern design intermingled to create a style of its own. Somehow it worked well.

They found a table and sat down. Grace looked behind her at a photo where a shire horse was being used to tow a cart full of earthenware through an open marketplace. Above her head was a shelf full of Wedgwood and Royal Doulton pottery, locked away behind glass panels.

'How are you feeling now?' Nick asked once they were settled.

'I've had better days.'

'I can imagine.'

They chatted about the cases and then sat in silence for a moment.

'Do you know why Allie left the Major Crimes Team, Grace?' Nick asked.

'I thought it was for a promotion?'

'It was and it wasn't. She said she needed a new start.'

'Yet she stayed in the city?'

'Once Stoke is in your blood, you can never leave. Surely you understand that now?'

Grace smiled, unsure if Nick was mocking her or not. Because no, she didn't understand.

'So she fancied a new role?'

'Not exactly. Allie had a sister who was raped and beaten, left for dead. She lived in a vegetative state for seventeen years.'

'How terrible!' Grace baulked.

'Three years ago, in the middle of another investigation, the attacker raped someone else and then came after Allie. She fought him off as he tried to kill her sister in hospital.'

Grace raised her eyebrows in shock. 'I had no idea. How is her sister now?'

'She died,' Nick said. 'Not because of the attack. She was on a life support machine anyway. Allie had to make the decision to turn it off. Nevertheless, I think she needed a break from working closely with people who knew all this happened.'

'Wow, that's tough,' Grace acknowledged. 'You'll still get to see her though, won't you?'

'Yeah, and she's great in the community. She'll do well in her new role. She'll get us some excellent intel.' He picked up his glass but put it down again. 'What I'm trying to say is perhaps the team are finding it difficult to adjust. They were very close to Allie, plus they understood her personal life.'

Grace fell silent for a while, her thoughts returning to Matt. She wondered if Allie was finding it as hard to move on as she was, or whether it had taken her less time. She hoped it was the latter. It was no fun being in limbo.

A few minutes later, Grace excused herself and went to the bathroom. She ran cold water over the inside of her wrists, aware how hot she was. It was great of Nick to take time out to chat to her, but she knew there was a hidden agenda. He wanted to see how much she had learned about the Steeles. She hoped he wouldn't be too disappointed when she had nothing to give to him.

Maybe it had something to do with loyalty. She felt unable to relax with the very people she needed to have her back. Teamwork was imperative in this job and yet she just didn't feel like a part of this one yet. At the moment she felt like the kid who was always left behind, that no one wanted on their side. That someone reluctantly had to have to make up their numbers when picking a team.

But it was entirely understandable. Perry, Sam and Alex all knew each other, regardless of who she was coming in and rocking the boat, plus she had upset the dynamics by taking Allie's job. No excuses, but it wouldn't be easy for them.

As she came out of the bathroom, into the lounge again, a new group of people had come in and were standing at the bar. Amongst them she recognised one of the faces. It was Simon. She smiled as he caught her eye and beckoned her over.

'Hey! How're things next door?' He glanced around the room, spotting Nick. 'Is this a social meet-up or a work thing?'

'Isn't it always a bit of both?' She found herself smiling. 'I don't think either of us will ever be off duty officially.'

He smiled too. After introducing her to his colleagues, he offered to buy her another drink.

'No, thanks. I'm going to head off home soon.'

'Pity. I was looking forward to more of your company.'

She blushed but didn't take her eyes from his. Up close, he was getting better looking every time she saw him. She noticed

147

the grey specks in his eyes, the clean and trimmed goatee beard he was sporting.

'I was wondering if you fancied grabbing a bite to eat one night?' he said, almost looking at the floor now. 'That is, after you're done with this case.'

She laughed inwardly. It was like being a teenager again, half wishing she had a friend to answer on her behalf.

She nodded. 'That would be great.'

He smiled again and raised his glass. 'It's a date then. Or rather a provisional date. I gave you a card, didn't I?' He patted down a couple of pockets on his jacket.

'Yes, I have your number.'

'Great!'

'Right, I'd better get back to Nick.'

She sat down and picked up the remainder of her drink. Hearing laughter, she glanced over to see Simon, talking with his hands to a rapturous audience. He looked so comfortable in his skin. He certainly appeared to be well-liked. He seemed nice without being intrusive, too over the top, too suggestive.

'I see you and Simon are getting friendly,' Nick acknowledged.

'What's that supposed to mean?' Her tone was defensive. Did he think she shouldn't be talking to him because he was a journalist?

Nick held up a hand. 'I just noticed you seemed happy around him.'

'More at ease with him,' she muttered. 'You lot are hard work when you gang up on me.'

'Gang up on you?' Nick laughed. 'Just because you come from Manchester?'

'Funny, ha ha.'

A message pinged into Grace's phone.

She retrieved it, hoping it wasn't anything to do with work.

It was and it wasn't. She covered it with her hand so that Nick couldn't see it. It was from Jade Steele.

Can you meet me? I have something to show you. Jade.

THIRTY

Perry parked in his drive and killed the engine. He'd been in Chimneys when he'd spotted Grace and Nick come in. He'd managed to give them the slip through the crowd, glad they hadn't noticed him. He didn't want to speak to either of them at the moment, unsure how he felt about Grace. Not because of who she was, but because she had kept it from them. Sure, she must have been under pressure, but she did have a mind of her own.

The light was on in the hallway when he got home, but it was dark in the living room. He closed the front door quietly and slipped off his shoes. Rather than throw his keys down as he would always have done in the past, he placed them quietly on the hall table. Then he padded through to the kitchen, trying not to make any sudden movements and noises.

Lisa was pacing the floor, her short blonde hair a little choppier than normal. Their son, Alfie, was wide awake in her arms.

'Hey.' He kissed her forehead and took the baby from her. 'How's he been?'

'Grumpy, like his father.' Lisa yawned. 'I'm warming his feed. Would you like a drink?'

'I'm not much for baby milk.' He grinned.

Lisa pulled a face at him as she busied herself making up the formula. Perry knew how upset she had been when Alfie wouldn't latch on to her when he'd been born. She'd struggled for a week and then given up. But it had been good for Perry as he'd been able to take turns feeding him too.

He decided not to have a drink. He needed to get some sleep.

'How's the case?' Lisa asked. 'I saw Grace on the news again. She's very pretty.'

There wasn't a hint of jealousy in her voice. Perry and Lisa had been married for thirteen years and Grace wasn't a threat to either of them. Their marriage was solid, despite the severe divorce statistics of being married to a cop.

'She's also George Steele's daughter,' he said.

Lisa stopped what she was doing. 'No way!'

Perry updated her with the day's events while Lisa gasped and held her mouth open.

'Will she be removed from the case now, do you think?' She squirted a few drops of milk on her forearm to test its heat.

'I really don't know. She should be.'

Perry bounced Alfie up and down in his arms. He'd thought Grace would be put on something else as soon as they had found out she was related to George Steele. Part of him had been ready to step up to the mark. It would have been great to have her as his deputy as she had a keen eye and a quick brain, but no, Nick had decided to leave her be for a while.

'That guy Josh Parker was a hunk.' Lisa put the bottle down and took Alfie from him.

'Hey!' He tried to look insulted.

'You know what I mean. Physique-wise. I can't imagine anyone ever getting the better of him. Someone must have nerves of steel.'

'Hmm.' Perry thought about that. 'That might literally be true if it turns out any of the family are involved.'

'What?' Lisa's brow furrowed in confusion.

'Nerves of steel. As in their surname being Steele.'

'Oh yes.' Lisa laughed. 'Do you have any leads?'

'No, not yet.'

'So, how is Grace dealing with it? You know, besides dropping that into conversation.'

'Just the same as I would.' His voice had an edge to it. Grace was doing fine, but he wanted her to fail. It should have been *his* first murder case as a sergeant. It didn't seem fair, especially now she had revealed her links to the family.

When Allie had left an opening, everyone had been sure he would get it. He'd felt pretty stupid when he'd found out he'd been unsuccessful. Even worse when it was someone from another force.

He missed being with Allie. He'd been working with her for so long that she was like family to him. She was only a few minutes away, in another part of the city centre, but it might as well be miles for the time that he didn't get to spend with her now. It had affected him more than he had let on to anyone when she had left their team. He couldn't trust Grace now, not like he had Allie.

Besides, everyone knew it was best to be promoted in-house rather than travel. He wanted to stay in Stoke now he had finally started a family. He couldn't expect Lisa to up and leave if anything else came up. Not with her network of support from her mum and sisters. So he'd either have to look outside of the Major Crimes Team to another division or stay as he was. He hadn't decided yet, mainly because he didn't want to leave the team he worked with. And murder was always interesting. There was never a dull day.

'I meant about your team knowing who she is.' Lisa glanced over at him. 'Look, I know you miss working with Allie, but you have to move on. Bring Grace round for tea.'

'After today? I don't think so!'

'Oh, come on. It wasn't her fault. You said Nick didn't want anyone to know.'

'We won't be finished with this case for some time yet.'

She gave him a stern look. 'I want to see what she's like.'

'Vet her, more like.'

Lisa nodded. 'She can't be as terrible as you're making out. Yes, she pipped you to the job, but you can't hold that against her.'

'I'm not.'

'You are.' She popped a bib over Alfie's head, wrestling his arms out of the way. 'Your son has the same stubborn streak. Invite her for tea on Thursday. If you're still busy with this case, you can change the night.'

Perry sighed. 'You're not going to let it rest, are you?'

Lisa shook her head. He kissed her on the forehead again.

'I'm going to grab a shower. Do you mind?'

'Not at all. You're on the midnight wake-up.'

Perry smirked. He might just get an hour's kip before then, if his mind would settle.

Most of the dead bodies he'd seen during his time at work had been as a result of beatings or stabbings. There had been a few domestics and the odd shotgun take-down, yet nothing as macabre as this one. Their work involved serious assaults and robberies, and the recent spate of cash-and-grabs Alex was looking into. Things like this didn't happen too often in Stoke-on-Trent, and they always kept him awake as he worked through everything.

The case fascinated him already, but if he'd voiced that to Lisa, she wouldn't understand. Two men murdered and stabbed in the heart. It took a warped individual to do that.

But, after the disclosure, did he trust Grace enough to work with her while they figured out who it was?

THIRTY-ONE

MONDAY – DAY 7

Grace sat at her desk, surrounded by her team but feeling very much on the periphery. The mood had been sombre since Nick's revelation, but they were all adults and so had got to work, their differences set aside for now. But Grace could still sense them simmering in the background.

At team briefing, Nick pointed out numerous pieces of information that had come in with regard to Josh Parker and Dale Chapman.

'Do we know what the weapon is yet?' Grace asked, sitting forward so she could see everyone.

'All we can tell for sure is that it was heavy and small – held in the hand,' Nick explained. 'It was used too many times on the victim to make a good impression in what was left of their head.'

From the corner of her eye, Grace saw Sam shudder at the image this brought up. It was almost too hard to imagine if they hadn't seen it.

'When Alex went over George Steele's case with me,' Grace said, 'it sounds possible that it could be the same type of weapon that was used to attack him too. Obviously we can't be certain, but the similarities are there because of the force used. What about a hand weight? Could that do so much damage?'

'It might very well do. Good work.' Nick nodded at both her and Alex in turn. 'This could be a potential lead. Let me know the minute you get anything from Dave Barnett.'

'I've been going through Dale Chapman's financial records from the Financial Forensic Unit,' Perry said. 'There are some interesting findings. His company was running well, but there are irregularities of large sums of money being taken out on a monthly basis. I can't find anything to suggest where it went. Cash transactions. One thousand pounds once a month for the past year. Then it stopped. His bank account now shows his money dried up.'

'Interesting.' Nick paused. 'Are there any accounts we don't know about that it was paid into?'

Perry shook his head. 'I can't find anything. There was a cash payment of five thousand going into a personal account a few months ago, but most of that has gone too. All drawn out a thousand pounds at a time. All in cash.'

'Drugs, maybe?' asked Alex. 'Steroids. Money borrowed from the Steeles?'

'If no money is going in, could he be paying someone to stay quiet about something he doesn't want anyone to find out about?' Grace suggested.

'Highly likely.' Perry pointed to the sheet of paper he'd brought with him. 'There are three payments to an online website, Dennings Toys. Turns out it sells sex products. That could give us a link to Josh Parker, with the bag of toys we found in his locker. I'm waiting on a phone call back from their accounts department.'

'So our victims could be more than just acquaintances at the gym?' Grace raised her eyebrows. 'Do we need to be looking into their sexual activities?'

'We can be discreet until Perry hears back about the email,' Nick said. 'Were there any irregularities with Josh Parker's finances?'

'No,' Perry told them. 'He had a regular salary paid in and payments going out, and there is twenty grand in a joint savings account with his wife.'

'Any more forensics we should know about?' Nick asked.

'We haven't found the knife, but the incision indicates it was the same size as the one used to stab Josh Parker. Confirmation will come through once the PM results are back.'

'Footwear.' Grace handed around photocopies of the shoeprint image found at Dale Chapman's crime scene. 'These have been identified as Adidas Originals ZX Flux – retail around fifty pounds. Very popular and widely available, so no help with that.'

'We need to be thinking who might be next if we don't get the bastard in time,' Nick said. 'But let's keep on the cross-referencing with our victims. It's great work and coming together.'

About to sit down at her desk, Grace glanced at her in-tray, her eyes flicking to a small jiffy bag that had landed there. She reached for it and opened it up. Inside was a tiny plastic Lego toy. A yellow dog. She frowned as she studied the envelope. Just like last time, there was a sticker with her name and the station address typed on it, and a local postage stamp. There was no return address. She popped the envelope in her drawer discreetly and, hiding the toy in her hand, went to show it to Nick. Even if there turned out to be no connection, she'd be better telling someone of it.

She rapped a knuckle on the door frame, walked in and closed the door behind her.

'I've had two toys delivered through the post, Nick.' She told him about the Barbie doll and placed the dog on his desk.

Nick glanced at her before picking the dog up to examine it. 'Did anyone else see it?'

'Not the second one.' Grace shook her head.

'Any thoughts?'

'It could be the Steeles warning me away from the job. I think these might be mine.' Grace took the toy from him. 'I left quite a few things behind when we fled from the house. Only the Steele family would know where to find them.'

'So what is their relevance?'

Grace shook her head. 'I don't know.'

Nick frowned, deep in thought. 'Let's keep this between us for now.'

'I'm not doing that again!' Grace's eyes widened in disbelief. 'My team will never trust me. And the DCI said that—'

'There are a lot of other things we have to get cracking with,' he interrupted.

'I don't feel comfortable about this, sir.'

'Grace.' Nick looked at her. 'Just trust me on this one for now. You and I know we have them, that's all that matters. If they need to be brought up, I'll figure out when.'

Feeling backed into a corner, Grace nodded and left the room. She walked across to her desk again, her cheeks burning as the pressure mounted.

What was going on with Nick? She had to question if he had her best interests at heart, or if he was out to get the Steeles no matter what the fallout would be for her.

THIRTY-TWO

Then

She couldn't believe she'd been given the doll. Dad had come home, laughing and merry, and handed it to her.

'Happy birthday, little 'un,' he said.

Her very own Barbie. She didn't have many toys, so this was a real treat. She threw her arms around her daddy's chest and squeezed him hard. 'Thank you, Daddy!'

She couldn't wait to take Moonlight Rose to school. At last she could join in with all the others, although she knew some of her classmates wouldn't be seen dead playing with dolls any more. But she didn't care about that.

She played with it all weekend. She never let it out of her sight. She even tucked it up in bed with her on Saturday night. She spent ages talking to it, telling it all about school, her friends and how much fun they were going to have together.

She didn't have a birthday party, not like most of her friends when they had reached the age of ten. But she didn't mind that. She was just happy with her doll. She'd wanted one for so long.

But everything changed on Sunday night. She was tucked up

in bed and woke to Daddy shouting. Suddenly the bedroom door opened and he stood in the doorway.

'You,' he pointed at her. 'You've been a naughty girl.'

'No, Daddy, I haven't.' She sat up and her doll fell to the floor. She saw him follow it with his eyes and she knew what he was going to do. She reached for it, but he pushed her hand away and grabbed it.

'Is this thing more important than your old man?' He put his face down close to hers.

'No, Daddy. I love you so much.' Instinctively, she put her arms around his neck and gave him a hug.

He pushed her away, staggering a step backwards. Then he laughed as he took her doll and clenched a fist around it. Then he pulled off its head.

'Please, Daddy, don't,' she cried. She couldn't help it, she knew he didn't like it when she talked back at him. Her tears wouldn't stop, even though he hated to see her cry. He said she was weak when she shed a tear.

The arms and legs came off next; he ripped it apart in a second. Then he threw the torso across the floor.

Her heart broke in two at the same time. All she'd wanted was to fit in at school and have something to be proud of.

Her tears were huge gulping sobs by now. She tried to silence them but she couldn't. She knew what would happen if she didn't. But they kept on coming. How could he be so cruel?

'Stop your whining.' He stood in front of her, his rage burning up.

'S-sorry,' she sobbed.

But it wasn't enough. He pulled the covers from the bed and grabbed her by the arm. To her protests, he marched her downstairs. She began to scream then.

'No, Daddy, please!' She kicked her legs out as he grabbed her by the waist and dragged her through the house. At the bottom

of the stairs, Mum was sitting in a heap. She got up and ran over to them.

'Leave her alone,' she sobbed, reaching out to her.

George sliced his free hand across her face and her mum stumbled back, hitting herself hard on the wall.

She tried to hold on to furniture, door frames, anything, as he pulled her out into the garden. 'Please! I'll be a good girl.'

He dragged her to the concrete sectional garage he used as a shed. Opening the door, he pushed her inside.

'Daddy, no!' She held on to his waist, but he wasn't listening.

'You're an insolent little bitch,' he said. 'You need to be taught a lesson.'

'I'll be good, Daddy! I promise!'

His hand cracked across her face and she cried out, holding on to it. It was enough time for him to open the door at the back of the garage and push her into the room that no one knew was there.

'No! Please, turn on the light!' she cried.

But the door closed behind her and she was plunged into darkness. Crying, she fumbled to the corner of the room and climbed onto the damp single bed. It was cold in there. Her teeth began to chatter. Her face was stinging where he had hit out. She was frightened, alone. But she was safe, thankful that it had been only the one slap that she'd received.

She pulled the grubby blanket around her shoulders and sobbed into the pillow. It would be morning soon and she could go to school. Get away from him. But she still wouldn't be able to play with her friends. Her doll, her lovely new Moonlight Rose that she had been so proud of yesterday, was ruined. Even if she could put it back together again, he wouldn't let her have it.

'I hate you,' she sobbed into her pillow. 'I hate you. I hate you. I hate you.'

THIRTY-THREE

The Quarter, a quirky cafe by day and bistro during the evening, had opened a couple of years ago. It was a perfect place for Grace to meet Jade Steele on her way into town. She'd received a phone call an hour earlier from Allie, who had a woman who wanted to talk to her. She'd arranged to meet at her office that afternoon, so she could head on up to see her straight after seeing Jade.

Piccadilly had a more relaxed atmosphere than a typical high street. Its pedestrianised walkway gave it a cafe-culture feel, a few independent retailers making up the remainder of the establishments.

The Quarter had a chic appeal to it, dressers full of crockery and mismatched chairs at tables, blending in seamlessly with a bar across one wall, mirrored glass behind it to give more sense of space. People were sitting at most of the tables, the scent of coffee and baking wafting to her every few seconds. It was somewhere Grace would definitely come back to for a meal one day, especially after eyeing the menu.

She ordered a cup of tea and took a table towards the back of the room, preferring not to be seen by anyone she knew.

Working meant she wasn't able to have the large glass of wine she needed to calm her nerves. She had felt strange when she'd received the text message from Jade. She'd tried to press her during a number of further messages this morning, but Jade had insisted they meet up. Away from the station, away from the gym.

A few minutes later, the door opened and Jade came in. Catching sight of Grace, she smiled and waved.

Grace eyed her half-sister surreptitiously as she strode across the room. She still hadn't got used to seeing someone who looked so similar to herself, although she wasn't sure she had ever oozed as much confidence and sex appeal. Jade had her hair tied up in a ponytail that swished behind her and a large black bag hung off her forearm. She was wearing a long necklace over a woollen dress.

'Grace.' Her smile widened. 'Thanks for coming. Can I get you another drink?'

Grace shook her head.

'Well, I am gasping for a cup of coffee. I won't be a minute.'

While she waited, Grace checked to see if any emails had come in. There was nothing new, certainly nothing that couldn't wait.

Jade was back in a moment and sat down across from her. Grace watched as she switched her phone to silent and laid it face down on the table.

'How's Stoke been treating you since you came back?' Jade asked, her smile warm and friendly as if they had known each other for ages.

'It's fine.' Grace wouldn't be drawn.

'It's all right, duck. That should be your answer.' Jade smiled. 'You need to speak the lingo now.'

Grace gave a faint smile in return.

Jade covered her hand with her mouth and retched.

'Are you okay?' Grace asked.

'Sorry, certain smells have a habit of doing that to me,' Jade explained. 'Morning sickness – although it comes at any time of day at the moment.'

'Oh! Congratulations.'

'Maybe. I haven't decided what to do about it yet. It's complicated.'

Grace sat back, unsure how to respond to that. How cruel life could be, that Jade could dismiss it, unsure whether she wanted to keep the child she was nurturing inside her, yet Grace had lost the chance to have one with Matt. Jade certainly couldn't be any further along than three or four months as she wasn't showing any signs.

She tried not to think of the time that she and Matt had discussed baby names and planned when to start a family. If he hadn't died of cancer, they might have had a child now. They were going to name it Morgan, girl or boy.

Jade leaned forward. 'Please don't say anything. I haven't told anyone yet. It's too early.'

Grace shook her head. She didn't have anyone to tell anyway.

'How are you settling in at the police station? I know most of your team through the investigation into my . . . George Steele's murder. I like Alex. He was nice to me.'

'You said you had something to show me?' Grace pressed to move things along.

'Yes, I do.' Jade nodded, and looked back to the entrance. 'And, here she is.'

The door opened and a teenage girl came in. Grace was taken aback. She walked across the room with as much confidence as Jade had done minutes earlier. It threw her.

'Sorry, I was on the phone talking to Freya. She was moaning about her dad again. I can't understand why he is so strict.' The girl pulled out a chair and sat down next to Jade. 'Did you order me a hot chocolate?'

'I did.' Jade held up a hand in Grace's direction. 'Megan, this is your Aunty Grace.'

As Megan gasped, Grace glared at Jade.

'I thought you two might like to meet.' Jade had a huge cheesy grin on her face.

For a moment, Grace couldn't speak. Then, realising how rude it must seem, and also how upset Megan might be if she didn't acknowledge her because she was so angry, she smiled.

'Well, hi, Megan. This is a surprise.'

'You're telling me!' Megan's voice was loud enough for a few diners to turn and look in their direction. 'What are you doing back in Stoke?'

Grace realised from that alone that Jade must have told Megan their history.

'She's going to find out who murdered Josh Parker and that other man, Dale Chapman,' Jade told her.

Megan frowned, then as the cogs worked in her head she raised her eyebrows in surprise again. 'You're a fed?' she asked.

Grace nodded. 'I'm a detective sergeant.'

'In Stoke?'

Grace nodded.

'Permanently?'

'Yes.'

Megan gnawed on her bottom lip. 'How long have you been back?'

'A few weeks now.'

Megan turned to her mum. 'You've known she's been here for a few weeks and you never said?'

'I only found out she was back last week!' Jade held her hands up.

'Why didn't you tell me then?'

'I'm telling you now, aren't I?'

Grace sat forward. 'Megan, I'm sorry that you didn't know

anything about meeting me today. I can assure you I didn't know either. I came here on your mum's request as she had something to show me and—'

'Ta-da!' Jade nodded her head in Megan's direction.

Grace sighed loudly. 'You have got to be kidding.'

'Hey!' Megan snapped.

'Sorry, I didn't mean anything by it.' Grace gave a weak smile.

'I wanted to show you your niece,' Jade defended. 'I know the boys are not keen on me meeting up with you, but I would love us to spend time getting to know one another.'

'I don't think right now is appropriate.' Grace stood and picked up her bag. What a fool she'd been: she'd assumed Jade had something to tell her about the case. 'I have to go.'

'But . . .' Jade's voice trailed off as she walked away.

'Real slick, Mum,' she heard Megan say. Grace would have laughed if she weren't so angry. It seemed Megan was very much like her.

But Jade should never have sprung that on either of them. If Grace was going to meet Megan, she would have wanted Megan to know before she came along too.

The more she'd learned about them, it seemed typical of the Steele family to only ever think of themselves and never about the effects their actions would have on people close to them.

She was out of The Quarter and marching away when she heard her name called.

'Grace, wait!' Jade ran after her.

'That was really insensitive.' Grace turned back. 'And unfair too.'

'I'm sorry.' Jade hung her head. 'I wasn't thinking. I thought you'd like to meet her.'

'You could have chosen a better way of doing things. Why didn't you tell me first?'

'Because you wouldn't have come, would you?'

'Well, you could at least have warned Megan.' Grace lowered her voice as a couple walking past glanced in their direction. 'It wasn't nice for her to find out that way.'

'She likes you. She's just told me.'

'She barely saw me.'

'You could always come back in.'

Grace shook her head. 'No, I can't.'

'I'm sorry,' Jade repeated, 'but I thought, well, you're a brilliant role model for Megan and I wanted her to see you as a strong individual. You've worked hard to get where you are and I think she could learn so much from you. She's strong too, much stronger than me.'

'That's not a good enough excuse.' Grace wanted to assert her authority, show Jade who was boss, but she didn't want to make a scene. How dare she put her on the spot like that! And what would Megan think of her now?

Instead, she left her there and continued walking up Piccadilly towards Stafford Street as she fumed.

She'd thought Jade had information, work information. But she had tricked her.

The whole meeting had been a waste of time.

THIRTY-FOUR

By the time Grace got to Stafford Street, her temper was cooling. She stopped outside the building that housed several council services and local offices, set above a stationer's. Allie and her team were in temporary offices on the third floor, until something more suitable came along.

Allie greeted her with a warm smile. She was a striking woman, tall, with long dark hair not dissimilar to her own. Her stride was confident, her manner friendly.

'Come on through.' Allie pointed to the tiniest of rooms in the corner of a large open-plan floor. 'It's not much to look at, but it's home for now.'

Allie brought Grace up to speed about the circumstances of the young woman who had asked to see her.

'She's eighteen and vulnerable,' she finished. 'As ever, she got mixed up with the wrong crowd.'

'Is she trustworthy?'

'She's never lied to me before, and she's someone I've tried to help on numerous occasions. She comes to me when she's in trouble or in need of advice, that kind of thing. I'm not a social worker, but it goes with the job, doesn't it? So I send her over to the support team at Striking Back upstairs if I can't help her myself. This morning, though, she told me she wanted to speak to the police about one of the murdered men, but she would only do it with me present.'

'Is she scared?'

'Petrified.' Allie picked up her notepad. 'She's in our interview room. It has a less formal feel to it, like a living room. We get a lot of our information through using this approach. Shall we go and see what she has to say?'

Regan Peters was sitting in an armchair as they went into the room. Her feet were curled up, shoes on the floor, revealing red chipped polish on her toenails. Her clothes looked clean, although a little big on her frame, Grace noted, but her long, lank hair was in need of a good wash. Her skin was pale, covered in spots and black rings around her eyes. The telltale life of a drug addict.

Grace and Allie sat down on the settee.

'Regan,' Allie said. 'This is Detective Sergeant Grace Allendale. She's here to listen to what you say, in the utmost confidence.'

Regan's eyes flitted between them both before fixating on the floor.

'Hi, Regan,' Grace said gently. 'Allie says you have something to tell me?'

'He raped me.'

Grace and Allie shared a look of horror.

'Who did, Regan?' Allie placed an encouraging hand on the young girl's arm.

'That dead man.' Regan looked up again. 'I saw him on the news.'

'What was his name? Can you remember?' Grace asked, aware she needed to tread carefully to find out. She had two dead men and a vulnerable girl who didn't trust the police and who could clam up at any time.

169

'Chapman, but he didn't call himself that.' Regan shook her head. 'He called himself Jenkinson.' She shuddered as she spoke the word.

'Can you tell me what happened?' Allie pressed as Regan began to look away again.

'I went to a few of his parties. I was paid two hundred pounds each time to be good to the men there. I was hungry and needed money for food.' She glanced at them momentarily. 'There were lots of young girls there to get the men in the mood, ply them with drink, whatever, and then there were a few of us who were paid to . . . entertain.'

'Who paid you?'

'A young woman.'

'Do you know her name?'

Regan shook her head. 'When I'd worked all night at the last one and everyone was leaving, she wasn't there. So I asked Jenkinson for it and he laughed at me. He said girls like me didn't deserve to be paid. He said they deserved to be treated badly. Then he locked the door and he . . . he raped me. He beat me, too. Left me bleeding everywhere.'

Grace cringed inwardly for Regan. No one deserved that. But, at the same time, this could give them another clue as to why Dale Chapman was murdered. And another name to look into.

'How many men were there?'

'About eight.'

'And did you have sex with all of them?'

Regan nodded.

Both Grace and Allie understood that Regan had only given consent because she thought she was going to be paid. But they also saw that while Regan had been used by eight men, she had been raped by another.

'When was the last party?' Grace continued.

170

'About four weeks ago.'

'And can you remember where the house was?'

Regan shook her head. 'It was in Hanford – off the main road. It was beautiful and had lots of bedrooms and a large driveway.'

'You can't remember the street name?' Allie asked.

Regan shook her head. 'I was taken there by him, Jenkinson. He took me home too, after he attacked me. He told me to tell no one, and if I mentioned the house or the party, I would get hurt.'

'Is that why you didn't report it?'

Regan nodded again. 'But I can tell you now, because he is dead. He can't do that to anyone else.' She started to cry and Allie rushed to comfort her.

Once she was settled again, they left the room, Allie promising to be back in a few minutes.

'That poor girl,' Grace fumed as they walked along the corridor. 'She must have gone through hell, the bastard.'

'I'll get her booked in with the rape crisis team and see if we can help her with anything else.' Allie paused. 'If you knew him as Chapman, I assume you've done the necessary checks. See if he has any property in the city under Jenkinson now. We need to find that house.' She covered her mouth with her hand. 'Sorry, I'm telling you how to do your job!'

Grace grinned. 'No apology needed!'

'I think I'll go and visit her mum too – see if she will be up to having her home again. She's trouble, but she is so lost. She has no one to turn to.'

Grace knew that one well. They were in the stairwell now and as she turned to leave she stopped. 'I . . . I hope you don't mind, but I heard what happened to your sister. I'm really sorry.'

'Thanks.' Allie nodded her appreciation. 'I heard you lost someone too. Your husband?'

171

'Yes. Cancer took him.'

'Oh, I'm sorry to hear that.' Allie touched her arm.

'It was two years ago now. I can remember telling everyone I was okay because I was tired of the sympathetic glances and the people who thought they understood me. They had no bloody idea what I went through. Did you ever get over losing her?'

Allie blew out a breath. 'It's hard to talk about really, but I guess you would know exactly how I feel. For now, I'm trying to move on with my life.'

'And how's that going?'

'Saying goodbye to my sister, *and* being the one who ended her life, was the worst but the best day. It ended years of suffering for her and waiting in agony for me and my husband. Karen was never going to get better. It's hard, with her not being around, but it's okay. I always used to think that I never spent enough time with her, what with working long hours and having the kind of job that required overtime at the drop of a hat, but when I thought about it, I did spend what I could with her.'

'I guess I'm still not used to being alone,' Grace sighed.

Allie nodded. 'You'll be fine, once you've settled in here and found your feet. You seem warm, Grace. I'm sure you'll fit in easily.'

Grace smiled too.

'I'm glad we're friends.' Allie pointed to the two of them.

'It's been good to talk to someone,' Grace admitted.

'So how about you and I go out for a drink one night, once this is over? Have a good old belly laugh, get lashed and then go on for a curry. What do you say?'

Grace nodded. 'Yes, I'd like that. Thanks.'

THIRTY-FIVE

If there was one thing Perry didn't like admitting to anyone, it was when his wife was right. But he had reflected on what Lisa had said about Grace. Perry wasn't sure he liked what his colleague had done regarding being economical with the truth, but he was pretty sure he would have done the same thing if it meant he had got the job.

He'd had such a great relationship with Allie Shenton that he had let it cloud his judgement of his new boss. The stuff with Grace's family didn't help, but underneath it all he could see someone who he could come to respect. He saw a fighter, a lone wolf who wanted to belong. She was making a mess of some things, but he'd done that even when he'd had a team around him and could go home and let off steam to Lisa.

Grace had no one, and she was embroiled in keeping secret something that she didn't want to, just because of her job. She shouldn't be on the case, but he could understand why Nick wanted her on it. And he'd rather have her than Alex any day of the week. Maybe he should cut her some slack.

He laughed inwardly. He must be going soft in his old age. Was it because he was a father now; had it mellowed him? Or was it because there was something he found vulnerable about Grace? Maybe first appearances could be deceptive.

'I'd be very careful of her, if I were you.' Alex nodded his head in the direction of the door where Grace had just come in.

'What makes you say that?' Perry glanced up from his computer.

'I've had word that she's bent.'

'You mean you've been talking to one of the boys at the gym again?'

'They're good informants.'

'They'll tell you anything!'

Alex shook his head. 'You'll be sorry you didn't heed my word once all this comes out.'

'Once all what comes out?'

'Her! We know she's been brought into our office to keep an eye on the Steeles, but she's also keeping an eye on us for them. She's working for both sides.'

Perry rolled his eyes. 'You really are an arse at times. Not everyone is out for what they can get, like you.'

'What's that supposed to mean?'

'Let's just say I've heard rumours too.'

In truth, Perry hadn't heard anything, but he wanted Alex to bite, see how guilty he was. There was clearly something bugging him about Grace that he didn't want to come out and say.

Alex's face dropped. 'You don't have a clue what's happening right under your nose.'

'Do you?'

'Yeah, I know stuff.'

'That you should be sharing?'

'Everything comes with a price.'

Perry straightened up. 'You're not being paid for—'

'Not me – her!' Alex raised his hands in mock surrender.

174

'I think I need a change of scenery,' Perry huffed. 'The air has gone quite stale in here.'

'Mark my words, she's trouble.'

Perry kept his opinion to himself. Even with the revelation about who Grace was related to, he knew there was less trouble in her than there was in Alex. He had never trusted him, and he wasn't about to start.

As Grace sat down at her desk, he studied her. She looked exhausted, and he wondered if she was having sleepless nights too. Even without Alfie to wake him, Perry was thinking of the case. But did it go deeper than that for Grace? She was trying to toe the line in so many ways.

She caught him looking at her. 'Everything okay, boss?' he asked.

She nodded. 'Yes, thanks. Just had a harrowing meeting with Allie.'

'Was it relevant?'

'Yes, I think so.'

Perry grabbed his mug. 'I'll make a brew and you can tell me all about it.'

As he collected everyone else's cups, he noticed Grace was holding in tears. He'd watched Allie do the same on several occasions, and didn't see it as a sign of weakness. Mostly it was compassion, or frustration. It couldn't be easy working through what she had this past week. He had to admire her for that alone.

Leon was in Clara's flat, taking a shower. He had been seeing her on the side for over a year now. Even though Trudy suspected he was having an affair, she hadn't found out anything concrete yet. After fifteen years of marriage, there was no doubt she was still a looker, if a little too plastic for his liking. Their relationship was okay, because she was a good wife in so many senses. She looked after him, his son and their home. They even had sex occasionally. But they both knew they'd been too young, too naive, and if she hadn't been pregnant at seventeen and kept the baby, they wouldn't be together now.

Jack was now fifteen; he'd leave school next year and join the family business, alongside Eddie's son, Charlie. Leon could already see the rivalry between the cousins building up. Trudy wasn't too pleased at the prospect of Jack joining them, but she couldn't complain. She hadn't worked a day in her life. No matter how the Steeles got their money, it had always been good enough for her to spend.

Leon had just been to the Windmill to gather with everyone else, paying his respects to Dale Chapman this time. Surprised not to see his brother there, he'd stayed a while to be social, but after half an hour, when Eddie still hadn't shown up, he'd left. There were so many people he knew that he didn't really want to see. Not wanting to go home so soon either, he'd rung Clara.

They hadn't spoken much, but he wondered how his brother would be feeling about Josh's death, especially now that Chapman was a goner too. Chapman wouldn't be missed, apart from the outstanding debt they stood to lose.

On the surface, Eddie seemed to be unaffected by it all, but Leon knew his brother was good at hiding his emotions. They all were, having learned to do that over the years. It was the same with loyalty in their family. They'd stuck together through childhood, the three of them, his brother and sister scared and relieved in equal parts when George's anger hadn't been directed at them. They all knew the game. They all knew the rules. They wanted to survive. In the morning they would examine wounds, cover up bruises, tend to cuts. Not bad for three children. But they had been used to it.

Leon hadn't wanted to grow up in that world, but he soon realised he didn't have a choice. Men used to have a go at him because of his father's reputation, so it was often better to get in there first. He'd always been in trouble at school over hitting other kids, and he never had a best friend like the one Eddie had found in Josh. His friends were few and far between.

Leon washed away the bad memories under the shower. He hadn't missed his father at all since his murder. In fact, it couldn't have come at a better time for him.

When he came out of the bathroom, a towel covering his modesty while he dried his hair with another, he noticed a clip about the murders on the news. Quickly, he searched out the TV remote and raised the sound, catching the last minute of the bulletin.

'If you have any further details, please contact the police on the number below.'

He sat on the edge of the bed, listening to the barrage of questions being fielded by the police. It was Nick Carter who had taken the conference. His father had had a few run-ins with the DI over the years. They'd grown up together on either side of the law. Carter had always wanted to nail George for something big, but George had been lucky not to get caught.

A muscle flickered in his cheek as he heard Josh's name mentioned again. He pressed his hand to it. He'd hated that bastard, for always taking over where he should have been. He'd even had to stop him from trying to muscle in on the parties. But at least his death had left him an empty place to jump into. Eddie wasn't going to be pleased, but Leon wasn't that kid he could push around any longer. It was his chance to step up, and he was going to take it.

He cast his mind back to one of his earlier memories of sibling rivalry. George had just arrived home. Leon had been woken by the sound of the front door slamming. Across the room, Eddie was sitting up.

A few minutes later, a commotion had started when he heard

his father lording it up with his mum. Eddie crept to stand behind the bedroom door, but Leon had stayed in his bed, not brave enough to leave the room. But every time he heard his mother cry out, he saved it deep in his memory, for when he was older. For when he could take George on. Eventually, he knew there would come a time when that would happen.

George was a bully. An evil, vile, despicable man.

A door opened and he wondered whose turn it would be tonight. Which door George would stop at. Would it be their room or Jade's?

George always went to the bathroom first. Once the chain flushed, the nightmare would begin. That night, the footfall stopped outside their door. Leon hid under the covers, hoping to feign sleep. Maybe George would move on. He didn't care who else he hurt instead.

The door opened and George stood in the doorway. Leon sat up, rubbing at his eyes as if he'd just woken up. George had a toy in his hand. It was an Action Man figure.

'Which of you jokers is playing with a doll?' George roared.

'It's not mine,' Eddie squeaked.

George took two strides across the room and grabbed Leon by the hair, pulling him to his feet and then throwing him onto the floor.

'Oi, arsehole, is this yours?' George asked him then.

Leon shook his head vehemently.

'Well, one of you is lying.' George was pointing at Eddie now. 'So I guess, as I'm tired tonight, it will be a punch for a punch. And you'd better make them good. If you don't do it right the first time, you'll get one from me. Is that clear?'

Silence.

'So, who's going to go first?'

'Me.' As Eddie had stood up and drew back his fist, the fear in his brother's eyes reflected in his own.

'Are you coming to bed or have I got dressed up like a whore for nothing?' A voice spoke behind him, jolting him back to the present. A hand grasped the bottom of his towel and pulled.

'I'm not in the mood, babe.' He kept a grip on the towel.

'But you asked to see me!'

Leon groaned. He'd called Clara up, thinking he might get rid of some of his tension. Usually, just the sight of her in a black basque and lace-topped stockings was enough to arouse him, but today it wasn't doing anything.

'It was a mistake to call you,' he said.

'I wish you wouldn't mess me around,' she muttered as she pushed past him.

He squeezed her roughly by the arm. 'Just remember who you're talking to.'

She glared at him in defiance and he felt himself harden at her response. He pushed her to the wall and pressed his lips to hers. She resisted at first, but then began to kiss him back and they moved to the bed. Leon moaned. He really shouldn't take his temper out on her. She was the one constant in his life that gave him pleasure, even though he knew he would discard her in an instant when the time was right.

Afterwards, they lay together.

'It's playing on your mind, isn't it, about the murders?' Clara said as she nestled into the crook of his arm.

'Wouldn't it play on yours?'

'I guess, but your secrets are safe with me.' She ran her fingers up and down his chest. 'It does leave things pretty neat for you, doesn't it?'

'What do you mean?'

'Well, I know how you've always wanted to be an equal to Eddie. Now's your chance.'

'What is wrong with you?' Leon sat up in bed, trying not to

push her to the floor. How dare she suggest he wasn't as good as Eddie.

'Nothing's wrong, babe,' Clara soothed. 'I just know how much you should have been top dog. Not Eddie, nor Josh – you. I just see a golden opportunity for you. One that you should take with both hands.'

He sat for a while before nodding, his temper calmed now. Clara was right, he was only trying to put up a smokescreen. The door *was* wide open for him now and he was going to step right in and take what was his, no matter what the consequences.

THIRTY-SIX

THURSDAY – DAY 10

Tom Davenport sat at the table in the kitchen. His wife Lorna had taken a call on her mobile and left the room to continue the conversation. Which was fine by him as he had enough to think about without her wittering on about something and nothing. Like having to tell her how he was about to lose his job.

It had taken him by surprise when he had been hauled into the office that morning. Although, in the back of his mind, Tom had realised what he was doing had consequences, that it might be only a matter of time before he was found out.

Despite that, he would have to go out that evening. Money might become tight, so he was going to see if he could find a way to bring in more.

'Who was that on the phone?' he asked Lorna as she came back through to the kitchen. 'Jade, by any chance?'

Lorna sighed. 'I can't help it if she needs someone to talk to.' She picked up plates from the dining table and took them over to the worktop. 'These murders are freaking her out. It's only natural she's worried.'

'Does she know anything else about them?'

'Not really.'

'Did she say if they were linked?'

'No. She thinks the police don't seem to have any clue who they are looking for.'

'Typical Jade.' Tom leaned back in his chair as she loaded the dishwasher. '*She* thinks she knows better than anyone else.'

'She's harmless,' Lorna defended her friend, closing the door of the machine with a bang. 'And let's face it, she has got a point. Someone should have been caught, or questioned, by now.'

'Someone could have been. The police might not be letting us know until they are sure. Jade doesn't know everything.'

Lorna set the machine to start. 'You're tetchy this evening, aren't you?'

'Am I?' Tom feigned surprise. Then he glanced at the clock. 'Freya should be back soon, it's nearing nine thirty.'

'She'll be home on time. I warned her before she went out.'

Tom stood up and stretched his arms in the air. 'I'd best be off myself or I'm going to be late.'

He searched out his car keys and phone and walked through the hall to the side door. Outside, the night was quiet as he got to his car. Then he heard his name being called. He listened, wondering if it had been his imagination.

There it was again, a voice he didn't recognise. It seemed to be coming from the back of the house. He walked around his car and into the open grassed area. It lit up as the security light picked him up.

There was someone in the garden.

Lorna Davenport sat in the living room, thankful she'd be able to relax in a few more minutes. Tom went to the golf club every Thursday evening for a drink with his friends. It was a time she always looked forward to, especially if Freya was in. It was quality time they had to themselves.

She picked up her mobile phone.

Where are you?

Freya's reply came back almost immediately.

I'm on my way. Will be there soon. Sorry. Is Dad in? x

No, he's gone out so we have a bit of peace and quiet :)

Yay! I'm running! x

How on earth was she going to keep Tom from finding out that Freya had defied her father and was still hanging around with her new boyfriend, Kyle? Her husband would go ballistic if he realised that Freya had gone against him. Lorna felt guilty for checking out her daughter's mobile phone before she'd gone out that afternoon, but at the age of sixteen she realised that Freya was capable of getting in a mess if she wasn't careful. Especially when her best friend was Megan Steele.

Settling down with her iPad, it was a few minutes before she realised that she hadn't heard the car start up, hadn't seen the headlights as Tom had reversed out of the drive. She stood up and went to the window. The gates were shut; usually he left them open until his return. Had he come back into the house without her knowing? She reached for the remote control and muted the TV.

She couldn't hear anything.

She got up from the chair, shouting his name as she opened the door to the kitchen. The room was empty, but the outside light was on, giving her a clear view of the driveway, garage and the garden. Was that someone bending over the ornamental pond?

Then she froze.

She wasn't sure that was her husband she could see.

'Tom?' She opened the back door and walked towards the pond. 'Tom, are you okay?'

A figure dressed in dark clothes and rolling down a balaclava lurched forward at her. She was pushed to one side, falling into the hedgerow that separated their drive from the next-door neighbour's, turning her ankle sharply.

Lorna tried to get up, but a fist cracked into her chin. By the time she had turned back, she was alone again.

She scrambled across the garden to the pond as quickly as she could, the pain from her ankle screaming at her. But all she could think of was getting to the heap that she could see on the lawn.

Goosebumps broke out over her skin as the cold air hit it, even more so when she could focus.

'Tom?'

He was lying on his back, his legs hanging out of the pond, his torso submerged. His outstretched arms were floating by his side. All around his head, the water was a darker colour, blood beginning to seep around his hair like a halo.

'Tom!' Lorna dropped to her knees and lifted his face, wiping water from his cheeks, his nose, his mouth. His eyes were closed, his limbs floppy.

'Speak to me.' She slapped at his cheek. 'Tom, wake up, wake up!'

THIRTY-SEVEN

Grace pulled into the car park of the supermarket. She was hoping she hadn't left it too late for flowers, but if so, she'd buy a larger box of chocolates. She popped a bottle each of red and white wine into her basket and a colourful toy that Alfie could play with.

By the time she'd got to the till, there were cupcakes alongside flowers in there too. Lisa could take them all; she was sure Perry would finish them.

Back in her car, her nerves started to show about where she was going next. She took a few deep breaths, hoping to calm herself. This was the first night off the team had had since the two murders had come in. Perry's wife, Lisa, had insisted that she cook for her, and she hadn't wanted to say no. Besides, she was curious to meet Lisa. Grace had questioned Sam discreetly and been informed that the couple had tried for a baby for several years. Sadly, Lisa had had three miscarriages before eventually giving birth to Alfie.

It would be a bittersweet moment for Grace. Although anxious about making a good impression with Lisa, their son Alfie would be a reminder of what she hadn't been able to achieve with Matt. It pained her to see couples with children happy and content, but she put on the brave face that was so often talked about. Tucked away her emotions, hid her pain. The British way of dealing with things.

She drove towards Baddeley Green. Perry's home was on a small estate built on the site that formerly housed one of Royal Doulton's plants, famed for its tableware and now collectable figurines the world over, which had closed in 2002. Deep down, she wanted Alfie to be asleep in his cot in his bedroom so that she wouldn't have to see him. Because she wouldn't be able to resist pressing his head against her chest, holding him to her, feeling him snuffling. And that would be upsetting.

But as soon as she walked up the path of the three-storey property, she could hear his screams. A harassed-looking Perry came to the door with the little boy in his arms.

'Sorry, he won't stop complaining,' he explained. 'We've been trying to get him down for the past hour.'

'Well, don't look at me,' she sympathised. 'I'm afraid I don't have the Midas baby touch. I do have wine though.'

'In that case, you'd better come in.'

They stepped into the hallway. A woman stood in the kitchen doorway wiping her hands on a towel. Lisa was in good shape considering she had given birth only a few months previously. There wasn't an ounce of baby fat on her tall, lithe figure. Her blonde hair was cut into a short, choppy style, her jeans and long-sleeved white T-shirt casual yet stylish. Her skin had caught a glow from the recent sunny spell. She looked very comfortable in her skin, if a little tired.

'Grace! How lovely to meet you at last.' Lisa gave her a wide smile, big blue eyes twinkling. 'I've heard so much about you.'

Grace laughed inwardly as Perry threw Lisa a glare.

'Nice to meet you too.' She lifted up her hand. 'I come with gifts.'

'Come on through,' she ushered. 'You can leave Grumpy Chops with his dad for a moment while we talk.'

Saved by screaming Alfie, Grace gave a half-smile to Perry and she went into the kitchen. It was minimalist, the way she liked it, and yet it felt inviting too. The modern white units looked fresh and new, with handleless doors and hidden nooks and crannies. She plonked her bag on the table, handed the flowers to Lisa and took out the wine.

'I don't know which to thank you for the most,' Lisa beamed. She handed Grace a wine glass. 'Are you driving?'

'Yes, just a spot for me, please.'

It took Perry another twenty minutes before he settled Alfie down, but after that the baby didn't make a peep. Inwardly, Grace sighed with relief. It meant she didn't get the chance to hold him and risk the maternal feelings she'd buried raising their head again.

'How can something so tiny make so much noise and mess?' Lisa sighed. 'I'm exhausted with it all.'

Grace could tell, but she also noticed contentment too. Envy tore through her and she pushed it down again.

They chatted a while over their meal and, for the first time since she had met him, Grace saw a different side to Perry. He might come across all hard man at work, but he was totally besotted by his wife and child. It was so good to see, even if it did bring a lump to her throat and emphasise her loneliness.

'How is the team treating you, Grace?' asked Lisa as she collected the dirty dishes before they moved on to dessert. 'I hope they're not being too hard on you?'

'Lisa!' Perry gave her a stern look.

'It's okay.' Grace smiled. 'I'm not sure anyone will ever trust me, but I'll give it my best shot.'

'Has Perry told you how much he misses Allie? I'm sure he had a crush on her.'

'You have no idea how far off the mark she is!' Perry shook his head. 'Allie was like a sister to me.'

Lisa laughed loudly, then glanced at the open door with a guilty expression. But Alfie never made a murmur. 'I'm joking, you big eejit.'

'It's a good job.'

'I like her too,' Grace joined in. 'She seems quite sincere whenever I've spoken to her.'

'Well, she can be quite hot-headed at times. Did she—'

Grace's phone went off. 'Nick. I'd better take this. Hello?' She raised her eyebrows. 'Right, I'll be there as soon as I can. Yes, I'm with him now.' She disconnected the call and looked at Perry. 'There's been another murder.'

'Address?' he asked.

'Endon. Leek New Road.'

'That will take us about five minutes to get to.' Perry stood up, shoving a piece of garlic bread in his mouth.

Lisa groaned. 'Well, I suppose that means more dessert for me.'

'Sorry, Lisa.' Grace wiped her mouth with her napkin. 'It was a lovely meal and it was great to meet you. And Alfie, if somewhat briefly!'

'Next time you can take him with you in a doggie bag.' Lisa laughed, then grimaced as she heard him stir. 'Go on, off with you. But be quiet.'

THIRTY-EIGHT

Grace could see emergency lights flashing in front as they pulled up as close as they could get to the large sprawling house. Set back from the main road in Endon, it boasted three floors, lights on at most of the windows, curtains open. At the side of the house was a driveway, leading to a double garage at the end of the garden, which could be accessed by a side rear door.

As they hurried up the drive, a woman in her mid-sixties, who had been standing on the step at the house next door, raced up to the dividing wall, followed by a man Grace assumed to be her husband.

'Is it true what Freya said?' she asked. 'That Tom is dead? That can't be right. I only saw him this morning.'

Grace stopped for a moment, knowing that the fact she couldn't comment on it would say much more than if she admitted it. 'Have the Davenports lived here long, Mrs . . .?'

'Proctor – Anne Proctor.' The woman had been joined by the man now. 'Yes, about fifteen years. That's about right, isn't it, Ray?'

Ray nodded. 'We've been here for nearing on twenty. They came just after Freya was born. They were so excited when they first moved in, even though the house was in terrible disrepair. But they put their mark on it over the years.'

'Did you get on well with them?'

'Yes,' Anne said. 'We didn't "neighbour" as such – we weren't in and out of each other's houses – but we always looked out for one another whenever we went on holiday. We could always borrow anything if necessary, and they were marvellous when Stanley died,' Anne added.

'Stanley?' Grace had one eye on the forensic team going in and out of the house.

'Our dog.'

'Right.' Grace nodded. 'So there has been no arguing lately, nothing untoward?' She raised her hand as looks of outrage shot across their faces. 'Sorry, I know it sounds intrusive but I have to ask. The sooner I can get a feel for them as a couple, the better.'

'You don't think Lorna had anything to do with this?' Anne shook her head vehemently.

'I haven't even been into the house yet, Mrs Proctor,' Grace said. 'But I do have to look at every angle. It's not always nice, but it enables me to do my job. You say you saw Tom this morning; when was the last time you saw Mrs Davenport?'

'I saw Lorna this afternoon as she went off to work.'

'Can you remember the time?'

'Half past one. She works at Morrisons in Leek. And, like I said, I saw Tom leaving this morning in his car, around eight thirty. He works – worked – at Staffordshire College, in Shelton. He was a lecturer there.'

'So nothing out of the ordinary? Just a usual day for them?' Anne nodded.

'Does Freya go off to school with Tom?'

'No, she leaves on her own. She walks. It's not far to Endon High School from here.'

'I can't believe he's dead.' Ray shook his head. 'He was such a nice man.'

Grace said nothing. What could she say? *Not everything is what it seems. You never know what goes on behind closed doors. Everyone has secrets.* She'd heard and used every cliché during her years in service.

Knowing she wasn't going to get anything else from them, she suited up before going into the house and through to the garden. Grace learned that the victim's wife had been attacked and as a result had been taken to hospital. Tom Davenport's body was still in situ, a white tent erected around it to hide it from prying eyes. Floodlights gave extra visibility to the scene.

As she stepped inside the tent, she caught sight of Dave Barnett. Nick was there too. He'd informed Grace that Dave had been in the middle of a family dinner when he'd been called away.

'It's another nasty one, isn't it?' Grace reached his side. 'Sorry to drag you away from the fun.'

'On the contrary.' Dave looked up at her and grinned. 'It's my Aunt Mabel's eightieth. Believe me, I would rather be at work. All those blue rinses, sherry and lavender smells.'

'Was the cause of death drowning?' Grace wanted to know.

'Not possible to say yet. But my guess is you're looking for the same killer of Josh Parker and Dale Chapman. I think Davenport was hit with the same or similar blunt instrument as Chapman. He then fell into the pond, where I believe he was held underwater to make sure he was dead.' He paused. 'And then he was stabbed in the heart.'

'Another one.' Grace shuddered.

After surveying the crime scene, she left the CSIs to it, cameras clicking away and evidence being marked up. She went into the house, where there were more officers in the kitchen, searching through the units and drawers.

'It's pretty busy around here, being on a main road,' Grace noted. 'Passing traffic would be a worry for an attacker, surely, even this late at night?'

'I suppose,' Nick glanced up at her, 'but it's dark enough for someone to slip away unnoticed. We'll set up an appeal to go out on the radio first thing in the morning. I'm going to need to take some advice on this. The press will have a field day if we get it wrong.' He sighed heavily. 'This is going to create pandemonium in the city regardless, but we need to be finding the connection and be thinking who the next victim might be. Three murders so close together is not good. We need to nail the bastard before the next one.'

'You say his wife found him?' Grace asked.

'Yes. She disturbed someone in the garden. She was pushed to one side and then punched in the face. Her ankle might be broken too. She's gone to A&E in an ambulance.'

She nodded. 'I'll take a quick look around.'

Grace always felt like a voyeur, looking through other people's belongings, part of their private lives, yet often it yielded a clue, a blueprint of the victim and how they lived. But here she found nothing except a family home. The living room was orderly; floral wallpaper on a feature wall and a settee made from squashy lilac cushions.

On a shelf by her side, she caught a glimpse of a family photo. Next to it another one, taken a few years apart if the young girl in it was anything to go by. A smiling Tom Davenport stared back at her from both. He hadn't changed much between the two images, still had that boyish charm about him. He seemed relaxed in both photos; Lorna Davenport was smiling too, as was their daughter.

On the surface, they appeared to be a happy family. How things can change so suddenly.

It was the same upstairs. Yet, even though she would keep an open mind, Grace believed they were looking for a killer from outside the family unit.

When she went back into the kitchen, Nick and Perry were standing in the middle of the room.

'You might want to see this. Uniform have just found it.' Nick held up a white greetings card that had been placed inside an evidence bag. On its front was a heart, broken in two, with three words printed underneath it.

I Miss You.

'They found that quickly.' Grace took the bag from him.

'He pulled out some papers and it fell to the ground,' Perry explained.

'The card is blank inside, but this was Sellotaped to it.' Nick handed her another evidence bag, with a piece of paper inside. It was a typed note.

Tom, please don't end things like this. I can't live without you. You are my life. I don't care if we have to hurt other people to be together. I just want to be with you. Please don't throw what we have away. We can work things out. I love you so much. X

Grace frowned. 'Where was it?'

'In the kitchen drawer. Second one down, shoved inside a gardening magazine.'

'Strange place to put something so personal,' Grace commented. 'Do you think our victim was having an affair?'

'If it weren't for the fact that we now have three male victims with stab wounds to the chest, it would give Lorna Davenport motive,' Perry said.

'But don't you find that a bit weird?' Grace questioned. 'If someone gave you a card like this, would you bring it into your home, where it could so easily be found?'

Perry shook his head. 'Nothing strikes me as odd nowadays.'

'There is a date on the magazine. It's pretty recent.'

Grace went outside. There was someone standing talking to Mr and Mrs Proctor. She waved when she recognised Simon and then removed her forensic clothing. As she walked towards him, his smile was welcoming.

'My favourite DS,' he said as she drew level with him. 'Got anything for me?'

'Now, you know I can't tell you anything yet.'

'It's worth a shot.'

Grace liked that he didn't push the issue. In his profession, there weren't many willing not to do so.

'How are you coping with it all?' he asked.

Now that question worried her. Was he asking for her thoughts on the case in an indirect manner, or was he genuinely concerned about her welfare? It was hard to call. Something she hoped she'd get used to in time. She wanted their professional relationship to stay just that, even if they might move on to be more than just friends outside of work. And it was something to look forward to, after all the recent darkness.

'Me? I'm fine.' She swept her hair behind her ear. 'We all have a job to do, I guess.'

'You'll contact me when you have something?' he questioned.

'Of course.'

Again his smile brightened up the night, but only briefly. For Grace, things in the case were escalating too quickly. Evidence wasn't back from Dale Chapman's murder yet, lots of pieces were missing from Josh Parker's, and now here they were again. Ten days – three murders. Three stab wounds in the chest. The heart.

Was someone working quickly for a reason? Or was their killer's rage escalating?

THIRTY-NINE

FRIDAY – DAY 11

The morning briefing was a hive of activity as every available body who could be assigned to their team piled in to listen. DCI Jenny Brindley sat at the back of the room.

Nick updated everyone about what had happened the night before, then turned to address the room on the plans. 'House-to-house started last night and we'll resume it this morning. We're also seeking any security camera footage nearby, or any witnesses that might have seen someone leaving the property.'

'Could our killer have legged it over the hedge and into next door's, maybe coming out a few houses down?' Perry questioned.

'It's possible,' Nick replied, 'and if so, it means our suspect is definitely agile.'

'And we're certain it's a he?' Grace asked. 'We don't have the evidence to back that up yet, do we?'

'No, but the punch to the face that Lorna Davenport suffered was one hell of a hit.'

'Not as hard as the hits the victims have taken,' Sam remarked.

'But like a trained boxer?' Grace suggested.

'Another possibility,' Nick concurred.

'Someone clearly knew that Tom Davenport was due to go out at that time of night,' Grace added.

'Or, like Dale Chapman's murderer, someone could have been lying in wait,' Alex remarked.

'Is there a link to Steele's Gym?' Grace asked. 'Is he a member?'

'Yes,' Nick said. 'But according to his wife, he hasn't been for a while. We'll obviously need to check that out, and see if he has a locker.'

A murmur went up around the room and Nick held up a hand for silence. 'The clear pattern is all our victims are male and all have been stabbed, so we need to figure out who the next target might be, see if we can forewarn people to be on their guard. We can cover some of this in the press conference this morning. I'm sure there will be lots of questions brought up after we go live with this.' He closed his notebook. 'Let's get some answers by the end of the day. Grace, a quick word?'

Grace waited with Nick until the room was empty again. 'Lorna Davenport left hospital last night and went to Jade Steele's home. Apparently they are good friends.'

Grace sighed. 'What are the odds?'

'Their daughters are best friends, and they know each other well.'

'All the same though – wouldn't you go to a family member before a friend?'

'We would – but who knows? She's staying there until her home has been cleared for forensics. I've spoken to Jenny about you staying on the case. I had to persuade her, but you're good to go at the moment.'

Grace nodded, trying not to show her relief too much. 'Thank you, sir.'

'There's a family liaison officer assigned, but I'd like you to visit Mrs Davenport after you've been to Staffs College. There's a Matthew Rushton who wants to speak to us first, and then you can go on your own to Jade's house.'

'Matthew Rushton?' Grace tried not to twitch at the sound of his first name. Matt had never liked being called by his full name. He'd always been known by his shortened version.

'He works there, student welfare,' Nick replied. 'See what you can find out.'

Grace nodded, her curiosity already piqued.

Grace left Nick recording the press conference with the DCI. She'd caught a glimpse of Simon as she'd passed the press room. He'd given her a discreet acknowledgement and she'd nodded back. No doubt his job was getting busier by the minute too. She mentally crossed her fingers that someone might phone in with some crucial information while she was out that morning.

Over recent years, Staffordshire College had been given a facelift and acquired new buildings. The surrounding streets were always busy during term times. Residents nearby often complained about the students, especially each autumn when the new term started and the quiet of the summer was gone again for another year. A few of them made far too much of a nuisance of themselves. But as well as some unruly behaviour, they brought a lot of business to the area, and a sense of excitement and growth.

Grace checked in at the main desk and, after a couple of minutes, spotted a man approaching her. He appeared to be in his late thirties, with brown jeans and a checked jacket and pale lemon shirt, open at the neck. His hair was longish but tidy, his fringe swept away.

'Matthew Rushton, Head of Student Welfare.' He held out his hand as she stepped forward.

'Staffordshire Police.'

Grace followed Matthew along a corridor and into a small

office. The walls held numerous certificates and a trophy for a basketball match in 2010 was resting precariously on a pile of folders. A photo of him with a woman, two children and a dog was visible on his desk, the angle showing more than she guessed he could see.

He sat down. 'Such dreadful news about Tom.' He shook his head in disbelief. 'Lorna rang me earlier. I can't believe she remembered to call us under the circumstances. But I'm afraid I wasn't quite truthful with her because of it.'

'I don't follow, Mr Rushton.' Grace settled into her seat, crossing one leg over the other.

'Tom has – had worked at the college for nearly five years. He was a brilliant lecturer, but I had to suspend him yesterday.'

'Oh?' Grace's chin went up.

Matthew coloured immediately. 'I thought he was a genuine all-round good guy, but there were complaints, rumours going round that he got more than friendly with some of the students last year.'

'Male or female?'

'Female. Apparently he's said to resemble an actor from *Emmerdale*.'

Grace nodded. Jeff Hordley. So that was who was niggling at her brain. In this job, she saw so many faces that she often wondered if she had met them or seen them on TV or in a film.

'Do you have names for me?' she asked, thinking of the greetings card.

'I was given two. Lucy and Stacey – I don't have surnames. I was about to look into it.'

'Can you get me a list together of all the students with those names, please? Current and past five years? Is that doable quickly?'

'Yes, certainly.' Matthew checked his watch. 'Would you like to talk to one of his groups while I see to it? Tom's lecture would have been covered by a stand-in anyway, but it's due to start in a few minutes. I expect the news is going around the students as we speak. I'm not going to mention that he'd been suspended, though. Or should I?'

'Difficult to call.' Grace stood up. 'Unless you have proof?'

'No, but you know how it works.' He shook his head. 'Any suspicions need to be looked into, hence the suspension.'

In the corridor outside, there were numerous young men and women walking around, a few mature students too. They passed through the crowds, down a flight of stairs and into a lecture room.

Twenty minutes later, Grace left the classroom. The students had been spoken to and given details of where to contact the police if they had any information. She had been pleased that, as they were leaving, Matthew had said there would be counselling for anyone who needed it. It was good to hear that the students' welfare was important.

Once on her own again, she was approached by a young woman, thick black hair flowing behind her. She looked seventeen at a push, but could probably pass for older thanks to heavy make-up. Deep foundation, black eyeliner and eyebrows and layers of mascara. Grace worried about today's teenagers growing up too quickly, but equally realised that she had been the same at that age.

'Do you know when the funeral is going to be?' the young woman asked.

Grace shook her head. 'I'm afraid it won't be for a while yet. We need to finish our enquiries before we can release the body back to the family.'

At the word 'body', the girl retched. She covered her mouth with her hand, the other resting on the wall as she tried not to throw up. Grace grabbed for a nearby chair and the girl sat down in it quickly.

'What's wrong?' she asked gently.

'I . . . I . .?'

'What's your name?'

'Charlotte Maidley.'

Charlotte looked up at Grace, make-up streaked in black lines down her cheeks.

'Is there something you want to tell me?'

The young woman burst into tears. 'He was a kind and gentle man.'

Grace waited for a few seconds, but she still wouldn't meet her eye. 'Is there someone you can talk to?' she tried.

Charlotte shook her head.

'What about the counsellor?'

'No!' Charlotte ran down the corridor away from her.

'I'd like to help,' Grace cried, but the girl had gone.

She searched out Matthew Rushton and told him about Charlotte. She also gave him her contact card in case anyone wanted to speak to her.

Once back in her car, she rang Nick to update him too. Then she sent a quick email to Sam, asking her to look into the list of names she was sending over from the college. They needed to cross-reference their intel for all three victims again.

She started the car but didn't move off straight away. Truth be told, she wasn't looking forward to her next visit, and now she had to be the bearer of more bad news. As well as her uncertainty as to how Jade Steele would react after their last meeting, she was reluctant to be the one to break Lorna Davenport's heart by telling her of her murdered husband's suspension.

FORTY

As she sped along the Potteries Way towards the address Nick had given her earlier, Grace tried to put herself into the shoes of the woman whose husband had been murdered. She could imagine how Lorna Davenport must have felt when she'd cradled her husband in her arms, knowing that he couldn't be saved, because she had done the same with Matt. Held him as he had taken his last breath. It was a heartbreaking moment – one you don't want to end even though there is nothing further to be done.

It seemed so cruel that Lorna would now have to learn of her husband's suspension. It was going to be hard to bring her up to speed with developments she might not be able to handle.

Jade Steele's house was in the middle of a large social housing estate off Scotia Road, Burslem. It was halfway down a narrow road, cars parked either side, making it difficult to get through. It seemed a very different set-up from that of her brothers and Grace immediately wondered why. She had no doubt that curtains would be twitching as soon as she parked up outside.

The front door was opened by PC Angela Stephens, the

family liaison officer who had been allocated. Jade was standing behind her.

'Lorna's taking a shower,' Angela told her. 'It's the first thing she wanted to do. She shouldn't be long.'

'Freya is with Megan in her bedroom,' Jade told Grace. 'They're welcome to stay here for as long as they need. We can move in with my mum. I decided it was best to keep Megan off school today too.' Jade wiped tears from her face. 'Would you like a cuppa?'

'Not for me, thanks. I have a few emails to catch up with.' Angela waggled her phone around. 'I'll be in the living room.'

Grace followed Jade through into the kitchen.

'Do you have anyone – any suspects in mind?' Jade asked. 'I mean, isn't it weird to have three murders so close together?'

Grace shook her head, wary of what she was saying and to whom she was speaking. 'We're gathering forensics at the moment. It's imperative the crime scene investigators do their job. I expect we'll know more soon.' She pointed to the kitchen table. 'Mind if I ask you a few questions?'

'Sure. So, tea?'

Grace nodded and glanced around the kitchen as she waited. It was a modest house, she assumed owned by the local authority. A typical layout for a compact three-bedroomed semi. The kitchen units looked new, pale sage doors underneath cream worktops. The noticeboard beside her was covered in photos of Megan, mostly with Freya by her side. A stash of lipsticks and mascaras sat atop a pile of teenage magazines on the table, a pair of slippers left by the side of a chair. It felt homely, but again she wondered about the difference between Jade and the other members of the Steele family. She'd seen Eddie's property on Google Street View; it was pretty much like Leon's. A large detached home. Did Jade choose to live frugally for a reason? Or had she squandered her money?

'How long have you and Lorna been friends?' Grace asked.

'We've known each other since we started at junior school. We were in the same classes, had Saturday jobs at British Home Stores, everything. Even Megan and Freya were born only two months apart. We were so happy they became best friends too.'

'Did you know Tom from school?'

Jade shook her head. 'I've known him since we were sixteen. He was one of Leon's friends.'

'What was he like?'

'I had a few dates with him first and, like you do at that age, we swapped boyfriends. I dumped my guy a few weeks after, but Lorna and Tom stayed together. He was one of life's good guys.' Jade moved to sit down at the kitchen table. 'He was settled with what he had. Happy with Lorna, and Freya. He's helped me out so much over the years too.' Her eyes brimmed with tears. 'I'm going to really miss him.'

'And you have no idea who would want to harm him?'

She shook her head. 'But I'll look after Lorna.'

'It's good that she has you. You seem really close.'

'We are. Of course we don't see eye to eye on every occasion, but she's always been very supportive to me.'

'Do you think they were having any problems as a couple?'

Jade smiled as she wiped at her eyes. 'No, they were so comfortable around each other. I suppose that's because they've been together so long.'

'Lorna never told you about any arguments?'

'Of course she did.' Jade took a sip from her tea. 'Tom wasn't a bad husband but he was quite controlling. He didn't hit her,' she hastened to add, 'nor force her to do anything she didn't want to do. All her needs were catered for, they lived a good life. So, yes, she'd sit right there where you are now and have a moan about him. But it was just that, letting off steam to someone. They loved each other. I wish I had a marriage like that.'

Grace smiled, thinking of Matt. She had been the envy of some of the officers she'd worked with. Matt had been understanding for the most part about her job and he helped out when she was at work – which was what she expected, but equally was refreshing when she talked to other colleagues who had partners who complained all the time.

'And how are you doing?' she asked Jade, wanting to change the subject quickly.

'Me? Oh, I'm fine, thanks. Morning sickness is a bitch, you know, but I'll cope.'

Grace gnawed at her bottom lip. She wanted to ask if Jade was going to keep the baby, surprised to find it still mattered to her if she didn't. But it wasn't any of her business.

'Look, I'm sorry about the other day,' Jade said, a look of embarrassment clear. 'It was silly, I know now. I messed up, but I wondered . . . could we try again sometime?'

Even though she was curious to get to know more about Jade, Grace didn't want to promise anything she couldn't commit to.

'Maybe, when I'm less busy,' she said.

Jade smiled. 'Great! I'll try not to make a tit of myself this time.'

Grace finished her drink and waited for Lorna to come downstairs. It had been okay seeing Jade again, talking to her in a civilised manner. She was glad she'd apologised for the meeting, and maybe it had been with all good intentions, if a little thoughtless. Grace would see how she felt when Jade next got in touch. Hopefully this case would be solved by then.

When Lorna came downstairs, Grace let her settle in the living room before going in to speak to her. She found her sitting on the settee, her foot bandaged and resting on a stool, but thankfully not broken. Her left eye was swollen and bruised, which indicated that their suspect might have thrown a punch with their right hand.

Grace took a few notes as they went through what had happened. It was heartbreaking to hear Lorna stop to cry every minute or so, but it was vital they did this as soon as possible. Lorna cried even more when Grace told her that Tom had been suspended and why.

'I can't take this in. He never told me last night!' She sat upright in a panic. 'This is all lies! Scandalous. Do they have any proof?'

'I'm afraid you'll need to take that up with the college, Mrs Davenport. I'm just trying to get a picture of Tom's last movements.'

'I want to be alone,' Lorna said. 'How long will it be, before we can go back to our home?'

'I'll let you know,' Grace said. 'I'm sorry, but we have to gather as much evidence as we can.'

'I'm not sure I even want to go back there really.' Lorna shuddered, her eyes brimming with tears again.

Grace blew out a breath as she left the room when they were finished. What a thing to have to go through. What was left of that poor family would be broken by the revelations.

FORTY-ONE

When Grace got back to the station, Sam beckoned her across before she made her way to her desk.

'We have camera footage of someone hanging around outside Tom Davenport's home after his murder,' Sam told her.

'Is it anyone we know?' Grace held her breath in anticipation.

'It sure is.' She pointed to the computer screen. 'This is Kyle Fisher. He's hidden behind fencing on the walkway opposite the Davenports' home; there for near on thirty minutes. I'm not sure if he is a watcher or if he is our man.'

'I've seen him before, at Steele's Gym.' Grace spoke with an excited tone. 'He was in the boxing ring.'

'Yes, he's one of our known troublemakers.'

'Good work, Sam,' Grace acknowledged. 'Let's bring him in.'

Kathleen had been busy stocktaking in Posh Gloss. As usual, if it had been left to Jade, nothing would have been ordered in. She wasn't sure she was ever going to get her daughter interested in the business. Jade would always cry off, not turn in, make a mess of something purposely. She had no go in her.

At least she had a valid excuse that morning. Kathleen had just finished a call with her and Jade had told her that the man killed last night had been Tom Davenport, and that she wouldn't be coming in.

To her right, Clara was painting a woman's nails. They were in the middle of a gossip fest about the recent murders.

'I can't believe the police haven't caught anyone yet,' Clara said, her head bent over as she brushed the varnish over the woman's nails. 'It smacks of incompetence, doesn't it, Maureen?'

'I was telling my Gordon exactly that last night.' Maureen nodded knowingly. 'It could be any one of us next if they don't catch him soon. It's not safe to go out at night!'

'I wonder who this one is?' Clara stopped for a moment before reaching for Maureen's other hand. 'Surely three men murdered in such a short space of time must have some similarities?'

'He's from Endon, it said on the radio.'

Kathleen didn't let on that she knew who they were talking about. She was just about to join in with the conversation when she heard raised voices. The noise sounded like it was coming from Eddie's office. Quickly, she walked towards it to see what was going on.

She was about to go in, but stopped when Eddie began to speak.

'This is the third person who can be linked to you. Do you have any idea who's behind this?'

'No, but when I get them—' Kathleen recognised Leon's voice, but Eddie interrupted his sentence.

'If this is to do with those parties—'

There was a bang, making Kathleen jump. It sounded like a hand being thumped on the desk.

'I'm as freaked about this as you are, Ed. I could be next, for all we know.'

Silence fell. Kathleen was just about to go in when they started talking again.

'Tom got suspended from work,' Leon said.

'What?'

'He rang me yesterday. Someone complained about him getting too close to the students.'

'For fuck's sake!' Another bang made Kathleen flinch. 'Why did you start them up again?'

'It was stupid, I know. But it was easy money.'

'It's tasteless, if you ask me.'

'I don't go with any of the girls!' Leon's voice rose.

'That's beside the point. The reason I wanted nothing to do with it was because I disliked what you were all doing.'

'Okay, okay! Well, I doubt there will be any more now.'

'How much did Dale owe us?' Eddie asked after a pause.

'Just shy of fifteen grand,' Leon replied. 'And if the cops find out that, we're going to be prime suspects!'

'And how exactly do you think they will find out, unless one of us tells them?'

'What about Grace?'

'What about her?'

'You need to warn her off. She's always creeping around. I don't like it.'

A pause.

'Does anyone else know what's going on?' Eddie said.

'Not to my knowledge.'

'So we stay calm, act normal if the cops come and question us. Get ringing around anyone who was at the last party. You need to sort this out, before one of *us* ends up dead.'

Kathleen gasped. What the hell had Tom Davenport been up to, to get suspended? What a stupid man to throw everything away, bring suspicion back to her family.

And what was all this about 'parties'?

As she heard movement, Kathleen scuttled off before anyone saw her.

FORTY-TWO

According to Sam, Kyle Fisher was eighteen, had been in juvenile detention twice for breaking and entering, and theft, and was a cocky little bastard heading for prison. One of three, he came from a stable family who hadn't been able to control him.

Before she went in to interview him, Grace spoke to a duty solicitor she hadn't met before. Mitchell Patrick introduced himself and she warmed to him instantly. His smile seemed genuine and he spoke about Kyle as if he was an adult rather than looking down on him because of his mannerisms, as some did.

Grace went into the interview room. Mitchell was sitting next to Kyle. She slid a chair out and sat down opposite.

Kyle's arms were folded, fingers on one hand revealing grubby, bitten-down nails. A pile of spots on his forehead and a few hairs sprouting on his chin that she assumed he was trying to pass off as a beard made him look younger than he was.

After going through the relevant details necessary to record the interview, Grace took out her notebook and started with her questioning.

'Kyle, can you tell me where you were last night in between the hours of eight p.m. and ten p.m.?'

'I was with my woman.'

'Your woman?' Grace raised her eyebrows. Kyle Fisher seemed barely a man himself.

'Yeah, I met her at seven and dropped her off about quarter to ten. Had some business to attend to.'

'Which was?'

He shrugged. 'This and that.'

'And where did you do your "this and that"?'

'Around.'

'So you dropped your girlfriend off. At home, was this?'

'Yeah.'

Grace waited for him to elaborate but was met with silence. She sighed inwardly.

'The address you dropped her off at – was it where she lived?'

'Yeah.'

'Which is?'

'Leek New Road.'

'That's an extremely long road, Kyle. What number?'

'Church View. It doesn't have a number. It's a monster of a house.'

Grace had started to write down the address but stopped and looked up. 'What's your girlfriend's name?'

'Freya Davenport.'

'You are aware that a man was found murdered in the back garden of this home?'

'Yeah. She told me her old man had been killed.' He folded his arms. 'But I had nothing to do with that.'

'Is that why you were hanging around outside the address after it happened?'

Kyle frowned.

'You were seen on camera across the road from the property, watching for over half an hour.'

'I wanted to know what was going on.'

'How long have you and Freya been together?' Grace asked next.

'Only for a few dates. I don't know her that well. She's not my type actually.'

'Oh?'

'She's a bit young.'

'How old are you? Seventeen?'

'Eighteen.'

'And you have lots of friends.' Grace smiled. 'I recognise you from Steele's Gym. Do a lot of sparring, do you?'

'I do a bit.'

'Good at it, are you?'

'Yeah, not bad.' His chest puffed out a little as she complimented him.

'Someone gave our victim's wife a right hook that nearly knocked her out. That wasn't one of your friends, was it? Perhaps slipped around the back of the property?'

'No.' Kyle threw her a filthy look.

'For all we know you could be in this together with some of your boxing mates. Someone attacks Mr Davenport, then you hang around afterwards to see if the coast is clear.'

'No!' Kyle shuffled in his seat. 'Look, if you must know I was dating Freya to get back at him! That bastard had been knocking my sister off.'

'You mean having an affair with her?' Grace probed.

'Yeah. Something happened and it was all over, but she was so upset she wouldn't tell anyone. Not even me. He's the same age as our dad – that's pervy, if you ask me. So I was seeing Freya to get back at him.'

'How exactly were you going to do that?'

'I . . . I was going to sleep with her and then dump her, like he did my sister. And then I was going to tell her what her dad had done.'

'That's hideous!'

'So is what her dad did to Lucy.'

'Your sister's name is Lucy?' Grace stopped writing again, excited at the revelation. They had only just started checking the names on the list from Staffordshire College.

'Yeah,' Kyle replied.

Grace needed to rule him out for certain now. 'Where were you last Tuesday evening between nine p.m. and eleven p.m.?'

'I was at home, with my mum and dad. We were binge-watching *The Walking Dead*.'

'And Saturday evening between eight and nine thirty p.m.?'

'I was in the pub. It was karaoke.'

'Did you sing?' Grace knew lots of people might have seen him if so.

'You couldn't get me off the mike.'

They would have to make sure his movements checked out but, if they did, Grace knew Kyle couldn't have murdered the first two men. Her gut instinct told her the same killer was responsible for this, which meant Sam had been right: if he was involved, he was just an onlooker. Forensics would likely confirm his statement once they were in, but as yet no one who couldn't be accounted for had been seen leaving any of the properties either side of the house.

But Kyle was the same frame and build as the person caught on camera running away from Dale Chapman's home, and Grace had seen him in the boxing club on Sunday morning. If Lucy was the same size and height as her brother, she too fit the description of the person caught on camera running away from Dale Chapman's home.

Grace needed to talk to Lucy Fisher, to see if she had sent

214

the note they'd found in the kitchen drawer. She could also quiz her on the parties.

'Does Lucy live at home with you and your parents?' Grace said.

'Yes.'

'I'll give you a lift. Do you have her number so I can contact her?'

'I don't know it off the top of my head but it's on my phone.'

Grace quickly went through everything with him again, writing it down so that he could check it over. Then she left the room and headed up the stairs two at a time.

FORTY-THREE

Tunstall, famously the birthplace of Robbie Williams, was the fourth largest of the six towns, in the north of the city. The Fisher family lived in a terraced house just off Greenbank Road where the former member of Take That and solo artist used to live.

Grace had taken her own car. Kyle got out almost before the wheels had stopped. It was clear he didn't want to be seen with her, even in an unmarked vehicle. She quickly followed him up the path.

Lucy Fisher was in the living room, sitting on the edge of the settee. She stood up when Grace entered. She was the same height and build as Kyle, with the same colour hair and features. There was such an uncanny likeness that Grace wondered if Lucy covered her blonde bob with a hood and wore no make-up, would anyone tell the difference between the two of them? It was worth noting.

'Hi, Lucy, I'm DS Allendale.' Grace flashed her warrant card.

Lucy burst into tears. 'I can't believe Tom is dead.'

'I'm sorry for your loss, but I'd like to ask you a few questions.'

Lucy's mum sat next to her. 'Take your time, duck,' she comforted.

Lucy looked up through watery eyes. 'I finished things with him because he was a pervert.'

'Can you tell me what happened, Lucy?' Grace sat down so she was eye level with her. 'Kyle says you've been really upset about something.'

Lucy looked up at her mum, almost for reassurance.

'It's okay,' Mrs Fisher said. 'Tell her what you told me.'

'I'd been seeing Tom for about two months. We used to meet after college had finished and sometimes, if we both had a spare session, I'd go to his office.'

'Did you have a sexual relationship with him?'

Lucy nodded. 'Not at first, though. I would go to his room for coffee and cakes. We'd play some music and talk. He was gentle and kind. Then one day it happened.'

'In his office?' Grace questioned.

'Yes.'

'So things were going good for you?' Grace couldn't see anything apart from a grown man who should have known better.

'Yes, until he invited me to that party.'

Grace's ears pricked up, instantly thinking of what Regan Peters had described. 'What kind of party?'

Lucy wiped at her face as more tears fell. 'I thought it was a house-warming do. Me and Tom had never been anywhere outside his office and I was excited when he invited me along. He wanted me to bring a female friend, so I would at least know someone as well as him, he said. But I decided to go alone. I wanted to spend time with Tom on my own.'

The room dropped into silence as Lucy struggled with her words.

'Kyle, please stop pacing!' Mrs Fisher said.

'I'm going to swing for someone if he hurt her,' he seethed, punching a fist into his open palm.

'He's dead, Kyle!' Lucy cried.

'What happened at the party, Lucy?' Grace asked.

'When I arrived, there were only a few girls. They were my age, maybe some younger, but they were all dressed in sexy dresses, high heels, lots of make-up. Some of them were really drunk. I was meeting Tom there so I went inside, trying to find him. As I went through the hall into the living room, this man grabbed me around the waist and pulled me towards him. He tried to kiss me but I struggled and got free. He slapped my bottom as I raced away.'

'Bastard,' Kyle raged.

'And then what?' Grace urged Lucy to continue.

'There were men everywhere; some of them staring at me. It was horrible and I couldn't find Tom for ages. And when I did see him, he was sitting in the conservatory, and there was another girl on his lap. He had his hand on her thigh and he was moving it up and down her leg. She was giggling at something he was saying.' She hung her head in shame for a moment. 'I was so shocked that I turned around and headed for the door. But another man stopped me, pushed me into the corner. I was terrified. He said he would pay me twenty pounds.' She glanced at her mum before speaking again. 'For a blow job! He thought I was a prostitute, Mum. I'm not that type of girl.'

Mrs Fisher took Lucy in her arms while she cried. Grace gave her a sympathetic look, understanding now why Lucy had been so reluctant to tell anyone what had happened. She could see she was upset, that the incident had brought back memories she was trying to forget, but Grace had to find out one more thing.

'What happened after that? How was Tom when you next saw him?'

'I avoided him, but he came after me. He wanted to know what was wrong, and when I told him, he said to stay away from him. He said he would deny anything I said if I told anyone about it. I . . . I made sure I was never alone with him again.'

'Why didn't you report it to someone at college?'

'I just wanted to forget it. I only had two weeks before I left anyway. I just put it down to me being stupid.'

'You weren't stupid at all!' Kyle shouted.

'Tom Davenport was a sexual predator,' Grace agreed. 'He was grooming you. It's not the first time he's done something like this by the sounds of things.' She waited. 'Lucy, I need to ask you one more thing. Can you remember where the house was? It would be really helpful for us if you can perhaps recall the area, or the street name, or what it looked like.'

'Seventeen Washington Place, Hanford. It's a big house set back along a private lane. You can't see it from the road.'

Lucy started to cry again then. Grace wound up their chat, asking where she was on the nights of the three murders and then getting her to write a few words. Grace had a photo of the greetings card sent to Tom Davenport stored on her phone. Lucy's writing didn't seem to match the words written on it. For now, she was satisfied with the answers.

She wanted to check out that address.

Before heading back to the station, Grace got on the phone to Sam, explaining what she had found out.

'Can you get on to the electoral roll and the city council to see who seventeen Washington Place belongs to, please?' she asked. 'Let's see if we can get in without a warrant first.'

By the time she got to her desk, Sam had the details she needed. 'The house is rented out, so the landlord is registered with the council,' she told her. 'I've just spoken to a Mr Vaughan

219

who rented out the property on a six-month lease to Mr Dale Jenkinson.'

Grace raised her eyebrows. 'That's the surname that Regan Peters mentioned.'

'He's not in the area but is happy that we visit the property. He's going to check the account the rent is being paid from too – there's no money coming out of Chapman's as we know, so someone else must be paying it.'

'Or Chapman has an account in the name of Jenkinson, which he must have had for years as everything needs ID nowadays to open anything. Or he has false documentation.'

'Mr Vaughan's certainly not happy that there may have been a crime committed on his premises,' Sam added. 'There's a key at his offices, but it won't be available until tomorrow as his staff have gone home.'

'Oh, I'm not sure that will be a problem,' Grace said.

In the evidence storeroom, Grace signed out the key that had been in Josh Parker's locker and took it back upstairs. Perry was just getting back from seeing Stacey Ridgeway. He went to speak, but she held up her hand.

'Update me on the way,' she told him. 'You and I are going on a mystery tour.'

FORTY-FOUR

'Stacey Ridgeway,' Perry said once he got in the car with Grace. 'She came up on the list that was sent over from the college. She finished there the year before last. I spoke to her after you called me. It seems Tom Davenport tried to groom her too. I asked if she had been to any parties. She said he'd invited her lots of times, tried to pressurise her into going to one, and when she wouldn't, he cooled things with her.'

'Obviously moving on to someone who would be a willing participant.'

'Yeah, the bastard.'

'I'll send uniform round to get a statement from her,' Grace said.

'So you think this house is going to be linked to all three victims?'

'Let's hope so. Lucy Fisher has alibis for the night in question, and the nights of the other two murders.'

'We also know Freya Davenport arrived home at 21.40, after Kyle dropped her off,' Perry said. 'An ambulance was despatched ten minutes before that. Her father had already been attacked. Traffic cams also confirmed Kyle Fisher's car on Leek New Road at the time of the murder, heading towards the Davenports' home.'

Grace sighed. 'Lucy said she didn't send a card to Tom Davenport either. There was no match with her handwriting. Do you think our killer planted it?'

'Another young girl he's knocking off?'

Grace shuddered. 'I hope not.'

It was nearing seven p.m. Washington Place was hard to find. It was situated up a small lane off a main road that you could easily miss if you didn't know it was there. Driving along it revealed numerous large properties.

Number seventeen was in darkness when they got there. There was a large wooden gate attached to a six-foot wall either side. After slipping on latex gloves, Grace took out the key ring from the evidence bag and pressed the key fob. The gates began to open.

'Pretty good hunch,' Perry said as she drove in.

Grace drew up beside a rambling house; she guessed it could have at least six bedrooms, with a one-acre garden at the front alone. A security light came on as she parked in front of a double garage.

Perry whistled. 'This must be worth at least half a million. It's huge!'

'A nice place for a party.' Grace turned to him before getting out of the car.

Outside, while the area was still lit up, Perry peered through a downstairs window. 'Doesn't look as if anything is out of place.'

Grace then tried the key in the front door. It opened to the sound of an alarm beeping, waiting to be turned off.

'And now for my second hunch. If I'm wrong, be prepared to cover your ears. There are six numbers on the luggage label. It starts with seventeen, the number of the property, so I'm thinking . . .' Grace pressed the last four numbers on the luggage label, 1794, into the keypad. The alarm was disarmed.

Perry grinned. 'I'm impressed.'

'I have a feeling we won't find anything inside, but if we do, we can backtrack.' Grace paused. 'We'll fetch the property keys from the landlord in the morning anyway. The main thing is we have been given permission to enter.'

Perry nodded as he got out gloves and popped them on. They walked through the large hallway, Grace's heels tapping on the marble-tiled floor.

A grand sweeping staircase took her to several bedrooms and bathroom upstairs, and a further two bedrooms in the attic. All were done in a high spec. It was a dream home, yet there were no clothes in the wardrobes, no dressing gowns hanging on doors. There were no books lying around, no toiletries in the bathrooms. Nothing looked out of place. It was as if the house was waiting to be lived in.

She joined Perry downstairs. He was looking in a large double fridge in a gigantic kitchen with a conservatory attached that was bigger than the downstairs of her whole house.

'Bottles of booze,' he said. 'No food in there, and none in the cupboards. All I can see is cleaning materials under the sink.'

'Someone's using it for parties,' she replied. 'And whoever it is has cleaned up well.'

Grace parked up outside her home and rubbed at her neck after switching off the engine. Another long day of sifting through information and intel, and trying to fathom out some answers. It was a good job at times that she didn't have a life outside of her work. Her rules, she knew: she was a police officer first and foremost. But there were still days she yearned to have some fun. Why should she be so hard on herself all the time? It's not as if anyone was there to tell her off.

She locked the car and stopped dead when she turned towards her house. On the doorstep was a jiffy bag. She hadn't ordered anything online lately; she hadn't even had time to browse on her iPad that week while watching trashy TV.

From a distance, it looked similar to the packages she'd found in her in-tray at work. Stupidly she glanced around, as if whoever had left it there would be observing her now. In her line of work, you always thought someone was watching you. It went with the territory, making it very difficult to realise when it was actually happening. A shiver rippled through her as she walked up to the front door.

The envelope was bigger than the previous ones and there was just her name typed on the label this time. There was no postage stamp, meaning it had been hand-delivered. Picking it up by its corner with her fingertips, she popped it under her arm and took it inside.

She stared at it in the kitchen while she made coffee and ate a slice of toast. She studied it, as if wishing its sender to give her a clue to its contents. Then she popped on a pair of latex gloves and opened it.

The significance hit her right between the eyes.

It was a Terry Pratchett book, the second in a trilogy. Grace had loved *Only You Can Save Mankind* and her mum had bought her *Johnny and the Dead* as soon as it had come out. An image so vivid came to her mind that she had to hold on to the worktop for fear of her legs giving way. She had been nine years old. George had found her reading this particular book and had pulled it from her hands. He'd torn out page after page as she'd cried at his feet, begging him not to. Then he had pushed it all into the fire and laughed, delighted that he had caused her so much pain.

When she was next locked in the garage, she had found a copy of the book hidden in the secret place that only she and her mum knew about. Mum used to leave her things to play with, sometimes a new toy, sometimes a bag of sweets or a comic. She had read the book several times over in the garage when she had been locked in there. She would never forget it.

Although the other toys were replicas, this looked like her original book. She flicked through the pages and, sure enough, she could see a few words written in pencil, notes she had made that she knew she could rub off so she wasn't spoiling the book. Even bending down the corner of the page was sacrilege to her. She'd been such a bookworm.

The book had been left in the garage when she had escaped with her mum, along with several of her belongings she hadn't taken with her. She pushed away the memories flooding back, at the same time realising it was a dead cert now that someone from her family had found her stash of secret toys in her hidden place. The Barbie doll, the yellow plastic dog and now the book.

Heart pounding, she went around the house, checking all the doors and windows were secure. Then she popped her phone on to charge before flopping down on the settee. If they could tap into her emotions like that, what else could they do? The book had been hand-delivered to her home address to make her feel insecure, and it had certainly worked. Someone must have been following her.

She went upstairs with a feeling of trepidation. From her bedroom window, she stared out into the night.

Was someone watching her now? She closed the curtains quickly to block out the thought.

Grace sat up in bed with a start. She flicked on the lamp at the side of her bed while she waited for her heart to slow down. It was three thirty in the morning. She hadn't dreamt about George

Steele for a long time. Her dreams had been filled with Matt, and occasionally her mum, who she missed dearly. She seemed to have blocked out her childhood from her nightmares, until now.

She flopped down again, squeezing her eyes shut to stop the tears. If she kept them closed, she could imagine her husband was there, lying next to her. She would feel safe that way. Nothing, or no one, could get to her.

In the distance, she heard a dog bark, a car driving past on the main road nearby. A radiator tapping. All things that usually comforted her, now they made her jump. Living alone, she realised how vulnerable she was if the Steele family wanted to come after her. Someone knew her address. Sure, it wasn't hard to follow her home and see, or even check records. People knew people. Any piece of information was available for a price.

Someone was playing with her, but why? Who had delivered the parcel to her door? Eddie, Leon or Jade? Or even Kathleen Steele? Or maybe it was someone else entirely. These were memories she had buried a long time ago. Why would anyone want to inflict pain on her?

At five a.m., she got up and ran, hoping to clear her mind, but it didn't work this time. As the treadmill went faster, Grace pumped her arms more. It meant she couldn't see the faded scar of a burn along the top of her arm. George had thrown a saucepan of boiling water across the room at her. There was another scar just below it. She'd got that when she tried to stop him as he'd been laying into Mum. She had lots of reminders like that over her body; some she'd covered with tattoos to stop her remembering.

She did a workout with weights but was pacing her kitchen at seven a.m., her mind not letting up.

She had things to sort out.

FORTY-FIVE

Then

She was playing happily in the kitchen when her mum rushed in.

'Quickly, run and hide. Your father is coming down the drive and he doesn't look very happy. I don't want you missing school again. I'm going to get into trouble.'

'But I can't leave you with him. He's so mean.'

'Please!' Her mum looked towards the door. 'Hurry!'

She ran out of the room, clutching her stomach as she did. She felt sick. She didn't want to leave her mum with him, but she had no choice.

Two months ago, he had broken her arm and she had got into big trouble. They'd had to go to the hospital and it was set in plaster. She had to tell the nurse a lie. That she had fallen over. Her mum said she was clumsy, but she wasn't. She didn't say anything though. She didn't want to get her mum in trouble too. If she had told them it was her father that had dragged her down the stairs by her arm and then twisted it up her back until she had screamed, her mum said she would be taken away. Sometimes she thought she wouldn't mind being taken away. But she didn't

227

say anything. Because she didn't want to go in a home with naughty children.

She only had time to run into the living room. The front door opened and she heard him shouting. Her mum screamed and then she heard a thud. He had hit her again. She just knew it. She had to go and help her.

But then the fear overtook her and she lifted the tablecloth and scrambled under the table.

Even though it was right under his nose, he hadn't found this secret hiding place yet. She closed her eyes tightly and covered her ears, but she could still hear him shouting. Her mum was trying her best to get him to be quiet and calm down.

She knew this would happen until he went to sleep. Then she could come out of her hiding place and help to clean up the mess he'd made. She'd have to be quiet, try not to wake him again.

One day she would get out of this house and she would never return. She hated it here. She hated him.

The door opened to the living room and she froze in terror. She pulled her knees towards her as she sat, hoping he wouldn't look under the table. He didn't; instead he sat down in the armchair.

She had to wait until she knew he was asleep until she dared come out. Finally, she heard him snoring. Slowly, she dared to lift up the tablecloth. He was out for the count but she still crawled across the room to the open doorway as quietly as she could. She held her breath, trying not to make a noise. Then, when she was out of the room, she ran into the kitchen.

'Mum!' she whispered. 'What has he done to you?'

'I'm fine.'

It was all she ever said to her. She wished they could leave right now.

Her mum was broken again. Why did he always do that to her?

FORTY-SIX

SATURDAY – DAY 12

There were only a handful of cars in the car park and no one on reception at Steele's Gym when Grace arrived at seven thirty a.m., half an hour after the gym opened. Even though it was early, she walked right through the quiet training area and into Eddie's office, hoping to see him before anyone else. He was sitting behind his desk, about to take a sip of something hot, but he put it down and raised his eyebrows at her instead.

'You're ruining my first coffee of the day.'

Grace slapped the book down on the desk. She placed the doll next to it and then the plastic dog, which she had fetched from her office.

'This stops now, do you hear me?' she said, her voice raspy with nerves. 'I will not be intimidated by any of your family, or anyone, for that matter. Playing stupid games and taking my time away from my work is not—'

'Whoa, slow down there, cowgirl.' Eddie held up a hand. 'Might you enlighten me on what the hell we are supposed to have done this time?'

'These toys. No one would know about them, except you and your family. I wanted to talk to you first.'

'What do you mean, only we would know?'

'I'm not going to spell it out to you. Just pack in the games or I will have you charged with wasting police time.'

Eddie pointed to the things she'd dropped on the desk. 'What have you brought those here for?'

'Don't tell me you haven't seen them before. You know perfectly well what their significance is.'

Eddie picked up the doll. 'I don't understand. What's the connection?' He reached for the book, but Grace snatched it away.

'This stops right now,' she repeated.

Eddie stood up. 'You think George let us have toys?' He shook his head. 'He didn't like us kids and would never buy us things. So I'm not sure how you think we would be connected to these, but you're barking up the wrong tree. Now, I have work to do, if you don't mind.'

His full height always intimidated her, even though she tried not to show it. She swallowed as he came closer, but he walked past her and opened the door.

'I'm not leaving until I have your word that this ends now.' She shook her head.

'I have no idea what you are talking about and I would be very careful who you are slinging allegations at.' He grabbed her by the arm.

She shrugged him off as he steered her out of the room, scowling as she walked away.

When she got into her car again, Grace took a moment to catch up with her thoughts. Eddie didn't seem to recognise any of the items, but he could be covering up for someone. And even though he didn't have a look of guilt about him, it had to be one of the Steeles.

* * *

Once Grace had left, Eddie sat back behind his desk and tried to work out the significance of the objects. He'd been telling the truth to Grace – he hadn't seen them before – but he knew they must have been planted by someone in his family.

Because now that Tom Davenport had been murdered, Eddie had worked out the connection to the Steeles. And that it could all be linked to the murder of his father.

He just needed to keep it from the police while he worked out what to do about it.

Grace hadn't planned to mention anything about the book being delivered to her home address, but when she got to work and sat down at her desk it didn't feel right keeping it to herself. She wished she could talk to her team, she needed to tell someone. So it made her feel deceitful, but she slipped into Nick's office.

They discussed what to do – Nick thinking it best to keep an open mind and let her look into it on the quiet. She hid her surprise, because she'd thought she'd be off the case for sure. After all, the Steeles were a family of interest, and essentially they were harassing her. It had certainly become more personal. But it was his call, she'd done what she'd thought was best.

She didn't, however, tell him she had called in to see Eddie.

She had just returned to her desk, when PC Higgins walked across to the team. 'I've been asked to bring these to you.' He placed several evidence bags on the table.

'Isn't that a handbag?' Grace pointed at one of them as she spotted a flash of black leather and what looked like a handle.

Mick nodded. 'It was found in the hedgerow of a house eight doors down from the Davenport home. The owners had been on holiday and only got back last night, so didn't notice it until this morning.'

'Stolen, perhaps?' Grace asked.

'It's possible, because whoever put it there didn't do a very good job. They left ID inside it.'

Perry flicked on a pair of gloves, pulled an evidence bag towards him and reached inside. There was a white T-shirt with a Staffordshire College logo on it.

'Women's, size ten,' he said, checking out the label.

Grace took out items from the other bags. A lot of make-up; a purse with money in it. An open pack of condoms. A teddy bear holding a heart.

And an ID card with a photo of the young woman she had met at the college yesterday.

FORTY-SEVEN

Grace was sitting across from Charlotte Maidley, in the same room she'd been in with Kyle Fisher the day before. As soon as they were ready, she ran through the necessary and then began to speak.

'I need to talk to you about Tom Davenport, Charlotte,' she said. 'In what capacity did you know him?'

The colour drained from the young woman's face. 'I . . . he was my lecturer at college.'

'Is that all? You can be truthful with me if there was more to your relationship.'

'We were seeing each other,' she whispered.

'How long for?'

'It started just before term ended in summer.'

'So, not long then,' Grace acknowledged. 'When was the last time you saw him?'

'The day he died. He wanted to see me urgently after my last lecture. We went to have a coffee. He was upset about something, but he wouldn't tell me what.' She frowned. 'And then he said he wouldn't be able to see me for a while.'

'Did he say why?'

'No,' Charlotte replied. 'I tried to get him to talk, but he wouldn't.'

'What time did you leave him?'

'It was just before six. My mum picks me up on her way home from work every evening.'

'Did you have any contact from him after that?'

Charlotte shook her head.

'Weren't you upset that he wanted to cool things between you?' Grace wanted to know.

'I didn't kill him!' Charlotte burst into tears.

'Don't be scared, Charlotte. I'm just asking questions for now. Did you try to contact him at all?'

'No. I didn't like to text him too much in case someone saw it.'

'Does anyone at the college know about your relationship?'

'We kept it quiet. He would have lost his job.'

Grace grimaced. He obviously hadn't told Charlotte about the allegations or the suspension.

'Did you ever see him outside the college?' she asked next.

'No, just in his office.'

'And you haven't told anyone about him either?'

Another shake of the head.

Grace took several pieces of paper from a folder and laid them out in front of her on the desk. She tapped the first image, of the greetings card.

'Do you recognise this?'

Charlotte leaned forward to study it. 'I didn't send it. What does it mean?'

'That's what we're trying to establish.'

'Well, it wasn't me.' She looked confused. 'But who else would miss him?'

Grace removed some further photos from the file, pointing to an image of a handbag. 'Is this yours?'

Charlotte nodded. 'It was stolen, from The Partridge, about a week ago. I went to the bathroom, came back to my chair and it had gone. I reported it to the staff, but there was nothing they could do. It's rife in there, I should have taken more notice of it.'

'You were alone?'

Charlotte shook her head. 'I was with two friends – Abbie and Harriet – but they didn't see anything. The Partridge is always full. Even at lunchtime, you have to push your way to the bar. Someone must have walked past and stolen it.'

'Do you have a T-shirt like this one?' Grace showed her another photo.

'Yes. It was in my bag. It was new. I'd only just bought it.'

'And is this yours?'

Charlotte sobbed when she saw the photo of the teddy bear carrying a red heart.

'Tom Davenport was murdered in his back garden and this bag was found eight houses down, hidden in the hedge.'

Charlotte shook her head. 'That doesn't make sense.'

Grace slid her notebook across to her and gave her a pen. 'Write something down. A couple of sentences will do.'

'Like what?'

'Anything. What's your favourite song at the moment? Write down a few words from a line of it.'

Charlotte wrote out a sentence and passed the notebook back to Grace. Grace compared the writing with the minimal letters on the note. She was no expert, but it didn't look similar. She took a deep breath. She didn't want to upset someone who was so young and vulnerable, but she had to question Charlotte further.

'Did Tom ever mention a party to you?'

Charlotte paused. 'He said he had a birthday coming up and that he was having a do at a friend's house.'

Grace nodded. 'Do you know anyone by the name of Lucy Fisher?'

'No.'

'This card could imply he was having an affair with someone else as well as you, that he'd told that person it was over and she, or he, wouldn't take no for an answer.'

'He?' Charlotte shook her head. 'He's definitely straight.'

Grace said nothing.

'I should know.' Charlotte sat forward.

'It could have been before he was seeing you.' Grace gave her a moment before carrying on. 'We found the card in the kitchen. Do you have a key to Tom's house?'

'No.'

'Have you ever visited his home?'

'No, never!' Charlotte cried. 'I had nothing to do with his death! I wouldn't do anything to hurt Tom!'

'So you don't have any idea why your bag would be found so close to his home after he was murdered?'

'No, I don't.' Charlotte began to sob uncontrollably then, putting her head down on the table.

Grace reached across to her. 'Is there anyone I can call for you?'

'I want my mum, but I can't tell her what I've done. She'll go mad when she finds out how old he is – was.'

'If she does, it will only be because she cares about you. Let me ring her and explain.'

Grace left the young woman with one of the PCs, her mind full of unanswered questions as she went back to her desk. Who the hell had written that note?

'Josh Parker had a key to seventeen Washington Place in his locker, along with a bag of sex toys,' Grace said to no one in particular as she sat down around her team. 'We have Dale

Chapman, who is a member of the gym – indeed, it was the last place he was seen alive. Regan Peters is claiming she was raped by Chapman at a party where she was paid to entertain, but unfortunately we have no evidence.'

'Chapman also ordered multiple sex toys and accessories from Dennings Toys,' added Perry.

'We now have Tom Davenport, who was suspended from his job the day before he was murdered,' Grace went on. 'There was nothing in his locker at the gym, but he has been linked to the same house by Lucy Fisher, who gave us the address in Washington Place.'

'So he was grooming Charlotte Maidley too,' Alex noted. 'He seemed to have frequented the parties, as well as recruited young women to take part in them.'

'At least we can take comfort in knowing that, even though their hearts will be breaking, Charlotte and Lucy both had a lucky escape,' Sam said, hoping to appease everyone.

Grace nodded. 'If drugs were readily available at the parties, either girl could have got hooked and involved more from then on too. At least we are on top of there being any more parties, for now.'

'Our killer could be one of the guests who attended the parties,' Perry suggested.

'Or one of the guests could be our killer's next victim.' Grace nodded. 'Our suspect could very well be one of the girls at the parties too.' She blew out the air in her mouth. 'How the hell do we find out who attended them without a list?'

FORTY-EIGHT

Jade stood in the shadows of the car park. She had been watching the door to the gym, waiting for Alex to come out. She wondered if his colleagues knew that he often called in to see Eddie or Leon. Alex clearly had no idea that she told her brothers everything she thought was relevant.

He came outside ten minutes later and she shouted his name, jogging over to catch up with him.

'Hi,' she beamed, leaning forward to kiss him.

He took a step back, glancing around. 'What are you doing?'

'Can't a girl kiss her fella?'

'Not here. Someone might see us.'

She grinned. She loved teasing him. 'What are *you* doing here?' she queried.

'I just called in to enquire about some sparring.' He started to walk towards his car.

'Really?' Jade grabbed him by the hand and pulled him behind the corner of the building out of sight. Pushing him up against the wall, her lips found his and she kissed him long and hard.

'It's early for a bit of fun, don't you think?' he said afterwards.

He couldn't speak any more, as her mouth bore down on his again. She teased him with her tongue, feeling his arousal against her. Somehow the threatening undertone of their kisses gathered momentum, his lips bearing down just as much.

Finally, she let him go.

'Alex,' she whispered, her eyes dark with lust. 'You're mine, you know that, don't you?'

He didn't speak.

'Alex?'

'What?' He was looking across the car park, watching someone get out of a 4x4, ducking out of the way.

'Are you embarrassed of me?' she pouted.

'No, but I'm a cop. I don't want to be seen hanging around here.'

'You could have just come to take down some particulars.' She laughed.

He clamped his hand over her mouth. 'Be quiet!'

She stayed still until he let her go. Then her head tilted up again, her mouth finding his lips with the flutter of gentle kisses. She stopped, looked up to see whether she had his attention. But his eyes were back on the car park, still afraid of getting seen.

She groaned.

'Aren't you bothered about these murders?' Alex asked her. 'You knew that guy, Tom Davenport, didn't you?'

'Yes, he was my friend's husband,' Jade said. 'Lorna is in pieces.'

'I just wondered if you'd heard anything about him, you know? Obviously someone was out to get him.'

'Or us.' Jade tutted. 'That's what you really mean, isn't it? Someone is trying to set up my family, and do I know who it might be.'

'No.' He glanced at her. 'Do Eddie and Leon think someone is after them, then?'

Jade glared at him.

'Sorry, the job gets in the way at times. Force of habit, I can't help it,' he said.

'I'm not a snitch.'

'I'm not asking you to be one. I'm just curious, that's all.' He checked his watch. 'I really have to go. I'm due in work.' He kissed her on the nose and turned to go.

Jade watched as he got into his car and left. She was certain Alex didn't know she knew that he was getting information for her brothers, but still, she didn't like him questioning her.

She'd let him think everything was okay, but it wasn't. He'd got nothing from her, but she hadn't been able to get anything out of him either. She'd wanted to ask more about Grace, but all he was after was stuff about Eddie and Leon.

He'd better not be using her to do just that.

Alex pulled out into the traffic and cursed under his breath. He didn't want anyone to see him with Jade, but neither did he want her brothers finding out he was hooking up with her every now and then. Eddie had been paying him money since George Steele had been murdered and Alex had been working on the case. He'd been after a way in with them for a while, desperate to earn more cash, and it had turned into a lucrative arrangement for him. When Allendale came back to Stoke, he thought the brothers had a right to know and the information had been appreciated. But if they found out he was seeing Jade as well, they might not be so welcoming. So he always checked to see if her car was there before going in. Jade must have come in after him. And either she didn't know anything, or she wasn't telling him everything.

He often wondered if she would do the dirty on him. Feed him dud information coming from Eddie or Leon, to catch him out, to see how loyal he was. If his intel was wrong, his colleagues would blame him. They would also start questioning where it had come from.

Christ, he didn't know who to trust. Paranoia. He didn't like it. He needed to get out of this situation. Being paid by her brothers in return for information was one thing, but having to sleep with Jade wasn't a great part of his plan. Originally, he had been attracted to her, but now there seemed no way to disentangle himself from the situation.

One thing was certain, he would have to watch his back.

FORTY-NINE

It never failed to amaze Grace how many green fields and how much tranquil scenery could be found a few miles in any direction of Hanley. She couldn't wait to have more time to start exploring some of it on foot, especially when the snow fell. Despite being told that the city's roads mostly came to a standstill if a centimetre of the white stuff dropped, she loved the cold weather.

The village of Bagnall was situated on the outskirts of Stoke-on-Trent, close to the neighbouring Staffordshire Moorlands. Grace was sitting in the car park of the Stafford Arms, an independently owned establishment that dated back to the sixteenth century. It was where Jade had chosen for them to meet. The website promised a picture-postcard pub with open fires and home-made cuisine.

Grace was glad it wasn't near to the police station. Even though she was on her own time, she still hoped no one saw her. Speaking of which, she cleared any important emails and then switched her phone on to silent. She would keep it in sight so that she could be alerted to anything that came in.

She got out of the car, the beeps of the alarm breaking

into the silence. The pub was on one side of a narrow lane, which framed a village green, with a further car park and a play area in its middle. For such a tiny place, it packed a lot into it.

Grace sniffed something delicious in the air as she stepped inside the doorway, greeted by a quintessential layout and a jovial atmosphere. People were milling around inside, lots of regulars amongst others coming to sample the local wares, she supposed. Her eyes scanned the room until they fell on Jade. She was sitting at the back, nursing a drink, and waved when she saw her.

The bar was busy as it was Saturday evening. Grace waited her turn to be served and then went to sit with Jade. As she drew level, she was shocked once again by their resemblance when they both had their hair down. She wondered if she would ever get used to eyes so similar to her own looking back at her.

'Have you been here long?' she asked as she slid into the seat.

Jade shook her head. 'Only a few minutes. You look tired. Another long day?'

'Yes.' Grace hoped she hadn't been brought here to be quizzed about work and the case.

But Jade picked up her orange juice and raised it in the air. 'To us,' she smiled.

Grace paused, then picked her drink up and did the same. 'To us.' The glasses clinked together.

They sat in silence for a few seconds and then both spoke at the same time.

'How's Lorna?' Grace asked after they had shared a false laugh.

'Broken, as you can imagine. I guess it's hard not to be able to arrange a funeral. Any news yet?'

Grace shook her head and took a sip from her drink. 'I must

admit that I was surprised she rang you when she found him. Doesn't she have any family nearby?'

'She did have parents and a sister, but they don't live local now.' Jade shrugged.

'How is Megan?'

'She's been upset too, but a real support for Freya. She sounds as if she's sixteen going on thirty.' They both smiled.

'She must make you very proud,' Grace added. 'She is beautiful.'

'And mouthy, as you know.' Jade sniggered. 'I'm still embarrassed that I thought you meeting her like that was a good idea. Maybe one day you'll be able to do it properly and enjoy it rather than have it forced upon you. That is, if you'd like to get to know her.'

'Maybe,' Grace volunteered. They sat in silence, watching as a group of people came into the bar and greeted others in a friendly but boisterous manner. It gave Grace time to wonder if she had done the right thing at all by coming to meet Jade. She couldn't think how to drop the toys into conversation without rousing suspicion and Jade not saying anything about them made her think that Eddie hadn't mentioned her visit to see him. Why would that be?

They began to chat about mundane things. Grace asked what it was like to have grown up in the city. Jade asked jokingly if her job was similar to *Line of Duty*. They both discussed their love of Vicky McClure as an actress, especially the recent role she'd played as DC Kate Fleming, and some of the other programmes she had been in.

Soon they were laughing, and it felt good. When an hour had passed, Grace ordered them coffee and, as the conversation turned to relationships, she found herself letting slip she was a widow.

'I'm so sorry for you.' Tears brimmed in Jade's eyes. 'I don't think I've ever been in love. Not *proper* head-over-heels love, like you. And if I did love someone in a fashion, it was never reciprocated.' She looked down at the table for a moment, as if to gather her thoughts. 'I was a wreck through my early years, got hooked on drink and drugs. Didn't care who I hurt as long as I was okay. I settled down a few times with different men, but they were all the same. They'd take their anger out on me.

'When I became pregnant with Megan, things got better for a while. But I soon slipped back to my old ways. It was when I was threatened by social services that my daughter would be removed from me because I couldn't look after her that I reached out to my mum. Megan was four then. I got a flat and was doing okay until I met Daniel. He treated me like shit, and the circle of violence started again.'

Grace had heard this tale before. So many people were emotionally and physically abused, made to feel they were worthless, until they didn't dare think of a life beyond the pain. She wanted to reach across the table and squeeze Jade's hand, but she resisted.

'And then I got help,' Jade explained, a proud smile forming. 'When George was murdered, we came to stay with Mum for a while and I got to know her properly for the first time ever. Found she wasn't as bad as I thought. She just wasn't strong enough to get away, I guess.'

Grace could understand that. It wasn't as easy as people who had never been in the situation thought. To be knocked down so low that you felt there was no alternative but to stay must be horrendous.

'I cleaned myself up and moved back to Stoke with Megan permanently,' Jade finished.

They talked a bit more in general, but the mood had turned melancholy as they both digested each other's histories.

Back in her car after they had said goodbye, Grace suddenly

became teary. How her mother had stayed with George Steele for all those years was beyond her. Even though he had abused her, Martha had been brave. Strong enough to cope with it until they could get away. Once again, Grace realised how much she had to thank her for, and how much she still missed her. At least they had managed to escape his evil clutches for the best part of their lives. Because if they hadn't, Grace might have become as mixed up as Jade.

She wasn't sure now if she should see her half-sister again, as it brought up so much excess baggage for them both. But she also realised how damaging it could be for Jade if she didn't. It would feel like Grace was rejecting her.

Even so, Grace had her own demons to deal with because of the way it had affected her as a child. George Steele had been a bastard. She was sure they would all be in agreement about that.

FIFTY

Elliott Woodman had been working overtime until ten p.m. at Deakin's Factory and needed sustenance before he went home to his girlfriend, Annie. He was also hoping to sweeten her up with a kebab and chips because he was going to be out a lot that weekend.

Elliott had met Annie when he was seventeen. Almost immediately, he'd fallen in love and wanted to settle down. But shortly afterwards, he'd been in court and sent to prison for twelve months for theft of motor vehicles. It was his third time locked up and this time he hadn't enjoyed it, didn't want to go back.

Elliott served six months of his sentence and Annie had written him a long letter every week, ensuring he missed her just as much as she missed him. On his release, he went round to her flat and moved in with her the same day.

He'd promised her he would stay on the straight and narrow and she'd become pregnant almost immediately. He was now the proud father of a six-week-old son, Ethan.

Annie was a great mother. They were young and capable of looking after a baby, but they were struggling for money. Elliott had held down his job for five months now. The pay was decent but it wasn't enough for all the added expense. There had been the top-of-the-range cot, pushchair, crib and all the clothes and accessories you could think of. His son wasn't going to want for anything. Ethan Woodman was going to get the best.

So Elliott couldn't afford not to work for Leon Steele. No one from his family knew, but he'd started going to the boxing club again on his release. He'd always admired Leon from afar. He found out he paid good money to fetch and carry, money Elliott couldn't turn down. Nor could his mate who had given him the tip-off.

He'd known that Annie worried about him going inside again, but he wanted to provide for his family. She hadn't been too happy last night when he'd told her he'd been doing some jobs for Leon, to bring some money in. Elliott knew he shouldn't, as the Woodmans didn't really mix with the Steeles, but his family were useless at making money.

Elliott's grandfather, Len, had been in prison with George Steele. They had fought to become top dog, neither of them winning outright, and ever since there had been a rivalry between the two families. The recent murders had been the talk of everyone. His family had been mentioned more than once, but Elliott knew it couldn't be any of them. They might be handy with their fists, but they weren't murderers. He was glad about it too.

Feeling hungry once he'd smelt his order in the car, he decided to eat his burger there and then. A dollop of tomato sauce dropped down his front. Cursing, he wiped at it but only made it worse. Annie would be mad at him for ruining another white T-shirt.

Afterwards, he screwed up the paper and put it on top of Annie's food. Then he set off again, turning the music up, banging a hand on the steering wheel in time as he negotiated the roads.

Minutes later, he pulled up outside his home. There were several blocks of flats in a small area, each having three storeys. They weren't much to look at, but some of them were being refurbished. He liked that they were near to the shops and pubs in Hanley.

They lived on the ground floor of Dane Walk, which was just as well now they had a pushchair. The stairwell had mostly stunk of piss when he'd first moved in, but once the tenant opposite had been evicted, things had improved. Annie had set their home up real smart. He was so proud of her and hoped one day to marry her.

A black 4x4 screeched to a halt a metre in front of him. He just had time to look up as blinding lights came at him.

'What the . . .'

Four men in balaclavas got out of the vehicle and raced towards him. Elliott scrambled to put the lock down on his door but was too late. He was dragged from the seat and out on to the tarmac.

He put up his hands in a vague hope of protecting himself, realising he couldn't take them all on. A kick to the face made him groan out loud. In fear of what was to come, he tried to curl up. Four pairs of boots and fists were bad enough, but when he spotted a baseball bat raised high, he knew he didn't stand a chance.

The first hit took two of his teeth with it. The second perforated his right eardrum. The third crashed onto his head as he tried to crawl away. In too much pain to defend himself, he sank to the floor.

The last thing he thought of before slipping into unconsciousness was Annie waiting inside the flat with Ethan. Beautiful Annie. Darling Annie.

She would be as mad as hell that he'd got himself into bother again.

FIFTY-ONE

Once home after seeing Jade, Grace closed the car door and went to retrieve her bag from the boot. A figure stepped out of the shadows and Grace jumped.

Eddie.

'What the hell are you doing here?' she snapped.

'We need to talk.' He grabbed her arm.

She tried to shrug him off. 'I'll scream if I have to.'

'Don't be so melodramatic. I'm not going to hurt you.'

They stopped at his car.

'Get in,' he demanded.

'I don't think so!' she countered.

Eddie opened the passenger door. 'I only want to talk, sort some things out.'

With a sigh, Grace climbed inside. She might as well find out what he wanted, and there was no way she was letting him into her home. That was her sacred place, away from the Steeles. And nor did she want to chance him being too much like his father. His looks still startled her at times, memories rushing back about George Steele raising a hand to her behind closed doors.

Eddie got into the driver's seat and turned to her. For the

first time since she'd met him, she could sense his anxiety.

'These murders. I need to know what we're up against.' He paused. 'Is there anything you can tell me?'

She glared at him. 'Nothing more than the general public know.'

'Don't give me that crap. I know they've all been stabbed in the heart.'

Grace couldn't hold in her fury and she banged a clenched fist on her thigh. Where had he heard that? Who the hell at her station was giving out classified intel?

'Who told you that?' she demanded to know.

'It's true, isn't it?'

'I'm not going to confirm anything for you.'

Eddie threw her an icy stare. There was silence in the car before he spoke again. 'I need someone I can trust at the station.'

Grace laughed, and then her mouth dropped open. 'You're serious?'

'Yes.'

'You think you're untouchable, don't you? If I have to pull you in, then I will.'

'How much?'

'*What?*' Grace couldn't keep the disgust from her voice.

'I can pay you – weekly if you like. All you need to do is keep us in the loop about what's happening – you know, anything that may be detrimental to us. We can also look after you, see no harm comes to you. After all, no one will touch a Steele.'

'I'm not listening to any more of this rubbish.' Grace reached for the door handle.

The central locking clicked down, trapping her inside the car.

'Don't think I won't arrest you for obstructing an officer,' she said firmly. 'Let me out.'

'I'll release you when I'm good and ready.' Eddie shook his head. 'You are one stubborn cow.'

'Have you really not worked out that I can't stand you, or your precious family?'

'Oh, that cuts me to the bone, Gracie.'

'It's Grace.' She turned her head sharply. 'No one ever calls me Gracie. It's always plain and simple Grace.'

'Yeah, yeah.' Eddie started up the engine. 'You need to think about what I said.'

'Whatever you want me to do, it's not going to happen,' she repeated. 'I'm not for sale and I never will be.'

'A certain someone at your station always gives me what I want.' He turned to her. 'Ah, you thought I was joking before, did you?'

Grace wasn't about to admit to him that she'd had doubts about one of her colleagues already.

Eddie shrugged. 'I'll leave that for you to work out. All I want you to do is think about the offer I'm making. I need someone else on the inside, and you and me could be good working together. Let's call it a family partnership.'

'Over my dead body.' Grace glared at him. 'I know what you've done in the past. I don't doubt that you've been involved in lots of things we've yet to find out about as well. I could never condone that. And I won't allow you to dictate to me either.'

'You do the maths, little sister.' Eddie released the locks on the doors. 'Things are going to continue the way they are with or without your blessing. You need to think about where your loyalties lie. Is it better to be protected, or live with the fear of attack?'

'I'll tell you again, no one threatens me.' She glared at him. 'I have the law on my side.'

Grace hid the tremble of her hands from him as she got out of the car. Eddie had gone before she had time to put her key in the front door. Once inside, she slid across the bolts and turned all the lights on downstairs.

In the kitchen, she took a bottle of water and drank from it quickly, gasping for air as she did so. That man had some nerve turning up at her home. Why would he think she would ever take bribes from him? She had never been corrupt and that wasn't about to change. And what did he mean by someone in the station?

She flopped into a chair. She wouldn't be going to sleep anytime soon, adrenaline was pumping around inside her.

But she would get to the bottom of things, because she wouldn't be working for Eddie Steele, or anyone else on the wrong side of the law. She might feel vulnerable at times, but she was strong. And that was the side of her that Eddie Steele would always see.

Grace was halfway through a run on her treadmill, having been unsuccessful in getting to sleep for three hours. It was now two a.m. She pushed the speed up to the maximum she could manage, wanting to punish herself, to stop her from thinking too much.

Who in her team would be a grass? Was it Alex? Well, she still didn't trust him and she obviously had her suspicions but nothing concrete. Sam? No, despite her being quiet at first, she was coming around now and joining in conversations with Grace. So was Perry. They both seemed to be getting used to life without Allie Shenton by their side.

Being threatened by Eddie had upset Grace more than she liked. If he knew her address, it could have been him that delivered the toys.

A sob stuck in her throat and she coughed it away, slowing the machine a little. This was when she missed Matt most. At the end of the day, she would come home, exhausted but exhilarated at the chance of getting a conviction. She would talk things through with him, brainstorm the details she could share.

Two heads were always better than one. She would sleep on something he had mentioned and her brain would go to work on it. In the morning, she'd often had more answers, joined a few more dots.

She'd told him what she knew about George Steele, about what he'd done to her and her mum, and explained about the Steele family. Now, she only had herself to listen to, no one else to talk with, and sometimes that was dangerous. She had to be careful not to get too emotionally involved with Jade, but she was a link to her family, and her past.

If Matt was here, he would have told her what to do about the Steeles. He would have grounded her, chastised her if necessary, surrounded her with his love. The feelings of overwhelming loss still came back to her when she thought she couldn't cope with what life was throwing at her. Of course, she was used to being on her own, but it didn't stop her from aching to be with Matt again; of what could have been – what *would* have been if there had been more time.

There was no doubt she had put him on a pedestal on occasions. Not everything had been perfect between them. Sometimes he'd hated her job. His work as a graphic designer had been mainly home-based, so he'd spent a lot of time in a spare room they had converted into an office. She'd often said this was the advantage they had over other couples. If he'd had set hours in an office, they would have been ships passing in the night, they might never have seen each other.

But everything had worked for them.

She wondered if meeting Simon had perhaps started this off. She'd seen him again that afternoon. He'd been walking past the car park as she had been getting into her car and she'd gone out to chat to him. It was just general chit-chat. Nice stuff, still talking about meeting up when they weren't too busy.

The treadmill came to a halt as the workout finished.

She reached for Matt's hoodie and wrapped herself in it. Then she picked up her weights. She would do a few curls, exhaust herself, try to clear her mind. It might make her sleep.

Tomorrow was going to be an early start and another long day.

FIFTY-TWO

Then

'Come on, you know you like orange juice,' George said, bringing the glass up to her lips. 'I want you to drink it all down.'

She did as she was told, spilling it out of her mouth in her haste. Quickly, she wiped at her chin where it had dripped, hoping he wouldn't tell her off for being messy.

But he didn't. He just smiled at her.

'That's right,' he encouraged. He filled the glass again. 'A little more.'

She didn't want any more, could feel her tummy complaining about all the liquid, but she couldn't refuse to drink it. So she drank that quickly too.

'I'll be back soon. If you're good, I might have a treat for you.'

She frowned. What did he mean by that? She was always good!

A few minutes after she had been left alone, she began to feel drowsy and lay back on the bed, covering herself with the blanket. She hoped she wouldn't have to stay here too long. She was still in her school uniform. He'd come to her as soon as she had got home.

When the door opened twenty minutes later, she saw her father standing in the doorway, but there was someone behind him. Another man. They both came into the room.

She sat up hurriedly. The room began to spin. Were there two men or four? She couldn't quite make it out.

What was happening to her?

'I don't . . . I don't feel well,' she slurred.

'Come out from under there. We want to see you,' her father said.

She flopped back onto the bed.

In frustration, George grabbed the cover and threw it to the floor.

'How old is she?'

Was that someone else's voice? Her eyes refused to focus, the room spinning violently this time. She was afraid she was going to be sick. He wouldn't like that!

'Twelve,' George answered. 'She looks young. Especially in that uniform.'

There was someone else there. She tried to focus, could only see a flash of red hair. Hands came at her. She slapped them away, but they grabbed her, holding her arms above her head.

Someone sat on her legs. A hand ran up her thigh, over her stomach, her breasts. She squirmed.

'Yeah, she'll do,' the stranger's voice said after a moment. 'As long as she's compliant.'

'Don't worry. I have plenty more orange juice, to start with.'

Laughter rang in her ears as she was left alone again. She tried to sit up once more, but the room span out of control this time. Had there been something in the orange juice? Was she drunk?

This time she vomited all over the threadbare rug. The smell was ghastly, but not as bad as the cheap aftershave that was lingering in the air.

FIFTY-THREE

SUNDAY – DAY 13

After less than two hours' sleep, Grace woke to a phone call. It was Nick telling her about an attack the night before.

'His name is Elliott Woodman. Can you go to the hospital and speak to his parents? Find out what went down?'

'Me?' She sat up in bed. 'Can't one of the others do it?' She had never pulled rank before and felt uncomfortable doing it, but even so. It was a DC's job.

'I want you to go.'

'But it isn't connected to our case.'

'Exactly.'

She paused. 'So, you're taking me off Operation Wedgwood?'

'Of course not. I'm just letting people think I am.'

Grace ran a hand through her hair in frustration. 'I get that, but I want to work with my team.'

'No questions, Grace. Just keep your mind on Operation Wedgwood but look as if you are working on the Woodman case.'

Grace disconnected the call and swore loudly.

* * *

Before she went to visit Elliott Woodman, Grace stopped off at the scene of the crime. She walked around the area, talking to a few people who were rubbernecking, and getting to know Elliott's background before she met his family.

She stayed for a while before heading off to the Royal Stoke Hospital in Hartshill. The hospital wing that the High Dependency Unit was located in was a new block that had been recently finished. The building, with its efficient self-service log-in centre and its state-of-the-art computers, could be a challenge to negotiate, but at least there was someone there to assist people. She asked for directions at the reception and then followed signs to the visitors' area of HDU.

There had been so many hospital visits with Matt that she'd lost count. She recalled walking along corridors like this one, alone and frightened, visiting him or leaving him. Not knowing what to expect. Always dreading the worst; sometimes getting it, sometimes not.

After sanitising her hands, she pushed on the door. The room was eerily quiet. Grace glanced around. There were people sitting together in three separate groups. A nurse in a blue uniform sat behind a hatch in the wall. Grace crossed over to it and held up her warrant card.

'I'm looking for the family of Elliott Woodman.'

'Over here,' a man said.

Grace turned. It was the larger group of the three, a couple in their mid-fifties and a teenage girl. A young baby was sleeping in a car seat on the floor next to them.

'DS Allendale.' She held up her warrant card again. 'Mind if I sit down, or would you rather go somewhere else?'

'Here is fine,' said the older woman.

'I'm sorry to hear about Elliott's attack. We'll do our very best to get to the bottom of who did this to him,' she told them. 'How is he?'

'It's touch-and-go for the next twenty-four hours. He has swelling to the brain,' the man replied. 'His skull is fractured in two places, so is his jaw, and his eye socket is smashed. Whoever did this to him set out to harm him good and proper.'

'Are you his father?'

'Grandfather, Len Woodman.' He pointed to the woman across the way. 'She's his grandmother, Helen. That's his girl-friend, Annie.' He pointed to the woman in her late teens. 'His dad has gone home for an hour after being here all night.'

'Have you any idea why he was attacked?' Grace sat down next to him. 'Can you think of someone who might have done this to Elliott?'

'No. He's not long been out of prison – got into a bit of bother – but no one would dare touch my boys unless they wanted to deal with me afterwards. When I find out who it is, I'm going to . . .' He seemed to remember where he was, and who she was, as his words faded out.

Grace leaned forward, closer to the young woman. 'Annie,' she said. 'Is there anything you can tell me about Elliott that would help me understand why this happened to him?'

Annie shook her head, tears dripping down her face. She wiped at them furiously.

'Nothing's been going on lately that you've been worried about? Did Elliott say anything was on his mind?'

'He's been hanging around with Kyle Fisher,' she said. *That name again.* 'I've told him not to because he's trouble. But he didn't see him last night because he was at work till ten.'

A nurse came over to them. 'We can allow visitors for a few minutes. Only two at a time.'

The women stood up. Once they had gone, Grace turned back to Len. 'Why not run me through it all again? Elliott finished his shift at ten last night. You know this for certain?'

He nodded.

Grace gave him time to compose himself as he struggled to keep his tears at bay.

'He's a bit of a lad, but Elliott doted on baby Ethan.' Len looked down at the little boy who was asleep at his feet. 'Annie said he'd rung her when his shift finished, to say he couldn't wait to see her. He was getting something to eat and asked her if she wanted anything. He said he'd bring her some chips.'

'And that was what time?'

'Ten fifteen. It's only a twenty-minute drive from the factory to his home. They must have been waiting for him.' He shook his head. 'Whoever did this will be dead by the time I've finished with him.' He took a deep breath. 'Sorry. I've never seen injuries like them. I bet the Steeles had something to do with it.'

Grace felt herself go cold despite the oppressive heat of the room. 'Why do you say that?'

'Our families have never got on. I bet they think we're involved in these murders.'

'We can't be certain of anything at this early stage, Mr Woodman, but do you think this could be a retaliation for something?' she enquired gently.

He shrugged a shoulder and looked at the floor. Grace could feel him shutting down.

He paused, then looked up at her. 'I don't know what's going on at the moment, but my family are not involved. Someone did this to my Elliott and you need to find out who.'

'We'll do our very best, Mr Woodman,' Grace replied. 'You have my word.'

Moments later, Annie and Mrs Woodman came rushing back to them, having been ushered from the ward. More staff raced past them, running in the opposite direction.

'All the buzzers went off on the machines and they made us come out here while they worked on him,' Annie sobbed. 'I think his heart has stopped.'

FIFTY-FOUR

Back from hospital, Grace was catching up with her team when her desk phone rang and she was summoned by the DCI. With a heavy sigh, she made her way upstairs.

The high-ranking officers were all situated on the floor above the incident room. It was the first time she had been upstairs. Jenny's office was half the size of their meeting room, a table that sat eight at its far end. The large TV on the wall was tuned into a news channel, its sound on mute. The wall was adorned with certificates and photos of Jenny at various points in her career.

Nick was seated at the table, instantly making Grace assume she was in trouble.

'Come, sit down.' Jenny pointed to a chair and then sat down too. 'What's going on with you, Grace?'

'Ma'am?'

'Did I or did I not specifically ask you to stay away from the Steele family or else risk coming off this case completely?'

Grace wasn't going to give anything away without knowing what she was getting the blame for. It could be any number of things, given the past few days.

'I'm not entirely sure what you mean,' she offered.

Jenny slid a piece of glossy paper towards her.

Grace took it, embarrassment flooding through her. It was a photo of her and Eddie, sitting in his car. It had been taken last night while he was outside her house. She closed her eyes momentarily before looking back at Jenny.

'I . . . I was off duty, Ma'am.'

Jenny raised her eyebrows. 'And that's supposed to make a difference?'

'I haven't done anything wrong, have I?' She glanced at Nick, hoping he would back her up. He said nothing, but at least he was shaking his head. 'He's not a suspect.'

'What if he is involved in the attack on Elliott Woodman?' Jenny said.

Ah. Now she understood. If it was found that Eddie was involved in any way, it would give him an alibi. It would also raise questions about Grace herself too.

'So?' Jenny pressed.

'He was waiting for me last night when I got home. Rather than make a scene, I got into his car and we had a chat.'

'About what?'

'Jade wants to meet up with me,' she lied, hoping the blush she could feel rising on her cheeks wasn't about to give her away. It was the first thing she had thought of, worried that if she mentioned Eddie was trying to turn her that she would make Jenny even more suspicious of her. 'She's trying to get the family together so we can all be introduced properly,' she added. 'I said no, of course.'

'Why didn't Jade ask you that herself?' Jenny quizzed.

'I don't know.'

'So maybe she didn't want to meet up with you. Maybe this was Eddie Steele getting someone to take the photo of you and him together.'

'*Do* you think he's a suspect?' Grace was confused.

'It's possible anyone could be at this moment in time!'

Grace ran a hand through her hair. 'Can I ask you where you got this from, Ma'am?'

Jenny looked at her. 'It doesn't matter.'

'It matters very much to me.' Grace couldn't help herself.

'Was whoever took this photo following Eddie Steele?' Nick finally joined in. 'Or was someone following Grace?'

Jenny didn't answer the question. 'All I'm concerned with is that you are following protocol.' She turned to Grace. 'I told you that I would remove you from the case if you got too close and—'

'He was waiting for me! I didn't go chasing after him.'

'Not this time. But I don't want Operation Wedgwood jeopardised because of your actions.'

'I'm not a criminal!' Grace shouted, losing control.

'That's good to hear!' Jenny raised her voice too.

Grace's cheeks reddened, shocked at herself for speaking out against a senior officer. She took a moment to calm herself before speaking again.

'Am I being watched, Ma'am?' she wanted to know.

'Of course not,' Jenny replied. 'But you should realise that nothing gets past me. You would do well to remember that.'

'I must reiterate that he came to me,' Grace insisted.

'*I* will be watching you from now on, Grace. That will be all.' Jenny's tone was firm. It meant there would be no more questioning.

Grace stood up and left the room, trying to keep her anger inside. What the hell was going on in this station? First she was accused of being a mole, and now someone was out to set her up by taking photographs. And why wouldn't Jenny divulge where it had come from? Why the secrecy?

She would never trust the Steele family. They wouldn't look after her unless she joined them, and that wasn't an option. But she was realising she could trust no one here either, not even her own team, and especially not higher management. Nick hadn't stuck up for her in that meeting, he'd just let her take the rap.

Whoever had passed on the information to Jenny was out to get her. It was time she started watching her back and did some digging of her own.

Nick stayed in the room with Jenny when Grace left. He had to make his feelings known, having stayed on the periphery for too long. But Jenny beat him to it.

'I told you what would happen, Nick,' she snapped once Grace was out of hearing range. 'She is no longer working on the case.'

'I trust her.' Nick sat forward. 'Without her, we would be nowhere.'

'We have three murder victims and no leads! I don't see that as getting very far.'

'You know what I mean,' Nick stressed. 'Look, I told Grace to get close to the Steele family. I thought it would help if we had someone on the inside.'

'After I specifically told you not to?' Jenny shook her head in despair. 'It's not a good example to set.'

'I'm willing to take the rap if things go too far.'

She tapped a finger on the photograph. 'I think it's beyond that now!'

Nick picked it up and studied it. 'How did you get it?'

'It was hand-delivered – posted by an anonymous source through the *Stoke News* letter box.'

Nick raised his eyebrows. 'And you never thought to tell me first?'

'Since you went against my instructions and left Grace to her own devices, why should I?'

Nick couldn't understand her petulance. Surely, as their DCI, Jenny should want to tell them what was happening?

'Can we see on camera who it was?' he questioned.

She shook her head. 'A figure in a hoodie. Who else would it be?'

'I'll follow up on it – see if we can track—'

'We don't have the manpower for that. We have three dead men in the morgue.'

There was a pause while they regrouped their thoughts.

'Grace is good at what she does, Jenny,' Nick tried again. 'Getting under people's skin, it's her speciality.'

'Aren't you forgetting who is in charge here?' she barked.

'No, Ma'am. But if you won't trust my judgement, then I won't trust yours either,' Nick retorted.

'It will be on your head when all this goes wrong.'

'It's a chance I'm willing to take.'

Jenny paused for a moment and then shook her head. 'I know Grace is good at what she does, and I know we are thin on the ground, but it's too risky.'

'You've just been arguing we have three murdered men!'

'I know that too, but we also have protocol – she's been left to her own devices for far too long as it is.'

'They are not her immediate family – they are estranged!' Nick protested. 'It would be different if she'd been in regular contact with them, but she hadn't met any of them. Nor had she seen George Steele since she was twelve. That's twenty-three years! You can't call that family!'

Jenny gnawed at her bottom lip. She shook her head once more.

Nick got to his feet abruptly and left the room before he said something he might regret.

FIFTY-FIVE

Feeling pushed from pillar to post, Grace had been at her desk for a few minutes when Sam beckoned her over to the large TV on the wall. She pointed to the screen.

'Ford Fiesta there belongs to Elliott Woodman. He leaves the car park at Deakin's Factory, Goldenhill, at ten p.m.' She pressed a button on the remote control to fast-forward the footage. 'He stops off at Percy's kebab house on High Lane, Burslem.' She pressed the remote again. 'Here he is getting back into his car and driving away. Check out the black 4x4 behind him.'

'It's a Range Rover Sport, isn't it?' Grace asked, never taking her eyes away from the screen.

'Yes. It stays with him for a while, then Elliott parks up outside his home.'

Grace recognised the scene she had visited earlier, outside the flat that Elliott Woodman shared with his girlfriend, Annie.

'The next part is gruesome,' Sam warned before pressing the play button again.

Grace watched the vehicle pull up beside the Ford Fiesta. She gasped in horror as four figures got out and set upon Elliott

Woodman. It wasn't easy viewing as they pummelled him to the ground. There was one clear ringleader who wouldn't stop, not until the others had dragged him away.

'I want those bastards,' she whispered. 'We need to get the images enhanced.'

'Already on it. I'm just going through the footage following the 4x4 afterwards. The driver is still covered up with a balaclava. The back windows are blacked out, so are the front, but they don't seem to be above the legal limit.'

'Who's the Range Rover registered to?' Grace asked, already bracing herself for the answer she knew she'd get.

Sam paused. 'Leon Steele.'

Grace grimaced; so much for staying away from the family. 'Okay, let's bring him in.'

'Do you want me to come with you?' Perry said from behind them. Alex was standing next to him.

Grace jumped. She hadn't heard them come over.

'Yes, thanks, I do.' A bit of tension fell away from her. She didn't know who to trust right now, but it was imperative that she pushed her feelings to one side. She didn't want to arrest Leon without the backup of her team. For now, her investigation into who was out to get her would have to wait.

Nick came back on to the floor. 'I've just had a call from the hospital,' he told them. 'Elliott Woodman didn't make it.'

Grace's shoulders drooped and she kicked out at a chair.

'We're going to get lynched by the press,' Alex remarked then turned to Grace. 'Unless you can smooth this over with your friend, Simon, Sarge.'

'Shut up, Alex,' Perry warned.

Grace ignored Alex while she explained to Nick that they were bringing Leon Steele in.

Nick nodded. 'Sam, can you start setting everything up here?'

'Will do, sir.'

Grace grabbed her coat from the back of her chair. 'Let's get the bastard.'

Leon Steele had been in custody with his solicitor for twenty minutes when Grace and Nick headed downstairs.

'Are you sure it's the right thing for me to sit in with you for this?' she asked. They were at the door to the interview room. 'I don't want to get you in any bother.'

'It's my call.'

Grace nodded her appreciation. She wanted to hear what Leon had to say, see what had happened, but she wasn't sure she'd be able to sit quietly while she waited for answers to Nick's questions.

'That poor kid had everything to live for,' she said. 'And this just puts more pressure on our resources.'

Before they went in, Nick placed a hand on Grace's forearm. 'Try and stay calm,' he told her.

She swallowed to clear her already dry throat.

Leon was sitting down, his solicitor next to him writing away. Grace hadn't met the woman before, but on first impressions she seemed affable as they gave each other a faint smile. In her late thirties, she couldn't help but think the solicitor was more masculine than she'd expect Leon to go for, with short cropped hair and a cheap black suit. Then, pulling herself up for making assumptions, Grace supposed she'd be the best that money could buy regardless.

Much to her annoyance, Leon looked relaxed as she sat down across from them.

Once they were all seated, Nick began the proceedings.

'Can you tell me where you were during the hours of 21.00 and midnight last night?' he started.

'You've arrested me for the assault on Elliott Woodman. I don't have anything to do with that.'

'I'm afraid Elliott Woodman died this morning of his injuries.'

Leon's eyes widened, and his shoulders sagged. 'Ah, I'm sorry to hear that. He was a good kid. I liked him a lot.'

Nick slid an image across the desk. 'Is this your vehicle?'

Leon looked at it. 'Yes.'

He slid another one over. 'This is the same vehicle going into Dane Walk. Seconds later, Elliott Woodman was attacked.' Nick flicked open the laptop.

Leon watched the footage retrieved from city CCTV. He banged his fist on the table before looking away in disgust.

Nick slid another image across the desk. 'This is your vehicle driving off down Dane Walk.' He tapped the photo. 'And this is Elliott Woodman lying beaten up on the floor. Someone either followed him home or was waiting for him, in your car, and now he's dead.'

'I wasn't in my vehicle then,' Leon answered, 'if that's what you're getting at.'

'You're saying someone else was driving?' Nick questioned.

'That's obvious.' Leon's face was poker straight. 'Unless someone has cloned my plates.'

'Would someone do that?' Nick asked.

'It's possible.' Leon stayed deadpan. 'To set me up.'

'So who had your vehicle?'

'I have no idea. I parked it up in the gym car park and left it there. I didn't even know it had gone missing.'

'You want us to believe that you weren't in the car?' Grace couldn't hold back any longer.

'I've just said I wasn't.' Leon sighed.

'Do you think the Woodmans are muscling in on your patch?' Grace asked. 'Or maybe you assume one of them is responsible for the recent spate of murders? Perhaps you wanted to send them a message that they need to stop by attacking one of their own? Only someone went too far?'

'You really know nothing about loyalty, do you, Grace?' Leon shook his head.

'It's DS Allendale to you.'

She glanced at Nick, who gave her a small nod she took as permission to continue.

'I don't need to be loyal to anyone but myself,' she continued. 'You should try that, rather than be told what to do all the time.'

'You are some character.' He glared at Grace. 'But you are definitely not a Steele. Steeles look after their own.'

'Someone is dead, Leon!' Grace reiterated. 'I don't have any loyalties where murder is concerned. When there has been a crime committed, I don't care about anything but getting the suspect off the street and behind bars.'

'Then you'd better get out there and *look* for a suspect,' Leon stressed. 'Yes, that's my car, but I wasn't driving it. Someone's setting me up.'

'How convenient. Who was driving it if you weren't?'

'I don't know.'

'Because . . .' Grace pushed.

'Look, I know where you're going with this, but I do have an alibi. A watertight one.'

'Would that be a Mr Frost, by any chance?' Grace scoffed. 'Goes by the name of Graham, to his friends?'

Leon stared at her. 'I was on the 21.40 train from London Euston.'

Grace froze. If this was true, it would be confirmed by CCTV, meaning he did indeed have an alibi. But why hadn't he said so at the beginning of the interview?

'Go on,' Nick said.

'I got into Stoke Station just after eleven p.m. and then I took a taxi back home. Trent Gibson was going to give me a lift into work when I rang him. He didn't pick up so I had to get a taxi.' He folded his arms. 'My car had been parked at the gym because Jade had given me a lift to the station yesterday.'

'Why not leave your car at the station car park?' Nick asked. 'It seems strange that you would take your car to the gym, to leave it sitting there all day, then get a lift to the station and a taxi home?'

'Molloroy Motors picked it up and brought it back. It was in for a service and valet. I thought I'd have it done while I was in London.'

'So you have no idea who would have been in your vehicle?' Nick said.

'I don't.' Leon stared at them both in turn. 'But I do want to know which bastard is trying to set me up by using it.'

FIFTY-SIX

It took all of Grace's strength not to slam the door as she left the interview room and headed back to the office.

'That man!' Grace told Sam what Leon had told them. 'We've impounded his car for now. He might be able to prove he wasn't driving the vehicle, but that's not to say that he hadn't conveniently set all this up while he was in London so that he had an alibi.'

'He's involved somehow. It all sounds a bit too convenient,' Perry said as he walked past and sat back at his desk.

Grace nodded, still annoyed at her behaviour in the interview with Leon. She had let him wind her up. He had shown her up in front of Nick. Leon had known all along he wasn't in the vehicle.

'Can you check in with Molloroy Motors?' she asked Perry. 'See if the service took place, where the vehicle went and who was driving it. Phone records of Leon Steele need examining and cross-referencing too, and camera footage needs checking from Steele's Gym again. Any luck with the images, Sam?'

'Still looking through them, Sarge.'

'There has to be a link somewhere. Elliott uses the boxing

273

club – I saw him there. Let's hope at least one of the guys who was in the vehicle is a known associate of the Steeles. We know there is no stab wound, so it's not directly linked to Operation Wedgwood. So we keep looking, at everything. Double-check, triple-check!'

Grace got her head down again. This was personal now. This wasn't about her family. This was about the death of a young boy. She had seen the video footage. The murder of Elliott Woodman was weighing heavily on her mind.

After he was released, Leon got a taxi to Molloroy Motors. He stormed across the forecourt and into the garage where several men were working. He grabbed the first one he came to and punched him in the stomach.

'Who took my car?' he shouted.

The man doubled over. 'I don't know!'

'Don't tell me you didn't see anything!'

Kenny Webb came out to see what the fuss was all about. Kenny was the proprietor of the garage and also acted as a caretaker for some of his friends who were locked up. He was looking after the six branches of Car Wash City that belonged to local criminal, Terry Ryder. Ryder had been in prison for the murder of his wife since 2011. Kenny had also been associated with the Steele family for years.

'Who gave you the order to set me up?' Leon threw him against the wall, his forearm across his chest to stop him moving. He raised his fist in the air. 'You'd better start talking.'

'I didn't see anything! We did what you wanted and we took the car back!'

'Who did you leave the key fob with?'

'Some woman on the reception!'

No one was talking, no matter how hard he threatened.

'I need wheels until I can get mine back,' he said eventually.

Kenny threw him a set of keys and pointed at a car. 'I've only got a hatchback.'

Leon cursed but took the car anyway. When he arrived at the gym, Eddie wasn't in his office, so he pulled up the camera footage from the day before. It showed that his vehicle had been brought back mid-afternoon and parked at the rear of the car park. So it might not have been anyone from the garage after all.

He pressed fast-forward to later in the evening and watched as it was driven out at 20.45. He froze the frame and zoomed in, but he couldn't see inside the car. There had been no sign of anyone walking to or from the vehicle where the camera spanned the area, which meant someone must have entered through the back of the car park purposely.

He fast forwarded once more until his vehicle appeared again, around 23.00. A figure got out and disappeared behind the vehicle. He zoomed in again but still couldn't tell who it was. But it all led to someone doing the dirty on him.

Eddie came in when Leon was still checking it over.

'I'm going to swing for that bitch if she hauls me in like that again,' he told his brother. 'She's had me in an interview for two hours!'

'Who?'

'Fucking Grace! I've just been arrested in connection with Elliott Woodman's murder. He's dead, did you know?'

Eddie groaned. 'I hadn't heard. When did this happen?'

'Earlier. They told me when I got arrested.' Leon paced the room. 'This is way too close to home. I'm not hanging around waiting for someone else to die.' He unfolded his arms and rested his hands on the window ledge. 'I'm going out there today. Heads are going to roll for this. Elliott was a good kid.'

'Was he working for you?' Eddie asked.

'Only as a runner. He'd deliver things for me, nothing too

heavy. He didn't want to end up back inside again. But he wasn't working for me last night.'

'And you expect me to believe that?'

'Yes, I do!'

'You got him killed!'

'Oh, come on,' Leon scoffed. 'You make it sound as if we are the mafia.'

'He's a Woodman! His family will screw us over if they think we are involved. Why were you so friendly with him anyway?'

'I felt sorry for him.' Leon turned to Eddie. 'He reminded me of myself when I was a kid.'

'*We're* family, and that means *we* stick together. The Woodmans need to look after their own.'

'I'm telling you, I wasn't involved. He's one of my best boys.' Leon showed him the security footage and pointed to a figure. 'Who does this look like to you?'

Eddie leaned in closer and studied the image on the screen. 'It could be anyone. It's not very clear – nothing distinguishable. Who do you think it is?'

'I have no clue.'

'Want me to contact Alex?'

'I don't like him.' Leon shook his head. 'You should have got Grace on side to do that by now. I don't like her either, but she should be working for us.'

Eddie snarled. 'She's not easy to turn.'

'If she doesn't come around soon, there's ways of making her.'

'I can handle her,' Eddie said.

'You haven't made a great job of convincing her so far!' Leon shook his head. 'She needs persuading. A good slap or two will change her mind.'

'I told you to leave her to me,' Eddie warned. 'I don't want you manhandling her.'

'After the way I've been treated this morning?' Leon stood and squared up to his brother. He prodded himself in the chest. '*I'm* the victim here. She's trying to set me up for murder.'

Eddie paused. 'Were you involved?' he asked again.

'I was in London!' Leon shouted. 'This isn't a coincidence. Whoever attacked Elliott wanted me to take the rap for it.'

'I don't see how—'

'This had better not be Jade's fault.' Leon glared at his brother as he was about to leave. 'I hope what happened isn't about to come and bite us on the arse.'

'It's not Jade I'm worried about,' Eddie said, then without warning, he punched Leon full in the face. 'They know about the house!' he yelled.

Leon pushed his brother away. He threw a punch back, but Eddie blocked it and landed one in Leon's stomach.

He doubled over.

His temper spent, Eddie caught his breath.

'I've had some of the younger boys following Grace on their scooters.'

'She'll find nothing. The property is cleaned after every party.'

'You don't get it, do you?' Eddie seethed. 'It doesn't matter if they don't find anything. The fact is they are on to you. I'm not bailing you out again.'

The door opened and Kathleen appeared. 'What's wrong with you two? I can hear you from the salon!'

Eddie glared at Leon before glancing at his mum sheepishly.

'Luckily, there aren't any clients in,' she said. 'What's going on?'

'Nothing,' Eddie said.

Kathleen looked at Leon.

'Nothing.' Leon wiped blood from his lip.

'You're shouting about nothing?'

Still they remained quiet.

'I suggest you two calm down.' Kathleen spoke to them as if they were children. 'And if whoever is attacking these men is linked to our family, surely one of you has an ounce of brain to sort it out!'

Once she'd left, Eddie sat down. Leon flopped back in his chair. The fight had gone from both of them but the worry was still there.

'Who is out to get you, Leon?' Eddie asked him again. 'Have you heard anything?'

'I told you. I have no idea.'

'Well, let's get ringing around. Start with our lads in the boxing club, get them to spread the message round that we are after anyone who knows anything. And people need to know I wasn't involved. This is your mess, not mine. Offer a reward for information. We need to sort this ourselves, before one of *us* ends up dead.'

FIFTY-SEVEN

As she was working on Elliott Woodman's murder, Grace had spent the rest of the afternoon talking to witnesses who had or hadn't heard anything the night before. She drew a blank after three visits and went back to the station.

While she'd been out, she had tasked Perry with visiting all three of Operation Wedgwood's victims' wives to see if they knew anything about the property in Washington Drive. It was sad that these men were abusing young women, but their wives did seem oblivious to it. Grace didn't blame them for not knowing about their husbands' activities. People could be deceitful. She was sure the house was a clue, but it had been cleaned thoroughly, leaving little for forensics.

Grace had also tasked Alex with checking the women's alibis again, and also seeing if they knew each other at all. It would be ludicrous to suggest that they had each murdered their husbands, but every eventuality needed to be looked into. Nothing could be ruled out.

Perry had then questioned a few of the neighbours in Washington Drive. As the house was so far back along the lane, no one had heard anything, but a couple said they had seen a black 4x4 coming and going. Grace's first thought had been that it could have been Dale Chapman's. Now she wondered if it might have belonged to Leon Steele.

Leon tried to keep his speed down as he drove around Potteries Way, heading to Limekiln Bank. The events of the day kept running through his mind. When Elliott had recently joined the boxing club with Kyle, the two of them had reminded him of Eddie and Josh at first, thick as thieves, and it had hurt. Once Josh had come on the scene when Leon had been twelve, Eddie had never had time for his little brother. Leon had grown up lonely, choosing to fight to make people be his friends. He'd scare people into wanting to hang around with him.

But Leon had found a soft spot for Elliott, and when Elliott had ended up inside for ABH, Leon had felt responsible for some reason. He'd looked after his girlfriend, given her money for things for the baby. He'd told her not to say anything, and to this day Elliott had never given him the impression that she had. Later, when the fuss had all died down, he would draw out some money and take it to her.

But first he had a job to do.

He parked on the street and banged on the door to Clara's flat. When she opened it, looking bewildered at his expression, he grabbed her by the wrist and pulled her towards him.

'Who did you give my key to when my motor was returned?'

'Stop it!' she cried. 'You're hurting me.'

'Was it Trent?'

'It was in my bag! And then I gave it to Trent this morning, to give to you when he picked you up.'

'I haven't seen him. I got collared by the police.' Leon thought for a moment. Even if Trent had the key now, that didn't mean it had been with Clara all that time.

'You'd better be telling the truth,' he warned.

'I am.' Clara tried to push his arm away. 'I don't understand. What's going on?'

Leon released her. They moved through to the living room and he told her what had happened.

She sat down abruptly. 'Did the police say anything about who they think it might be?'

'Of course they didn't,' Leon snapped. 'Because they think *I* had something to do with his murder.'

'And did you?' she asked, frowning.

'No, I did not!'

'So it must be routine stuff then. Although' – she paused – 'did they say whether or not his murder was connected to the others? It's all gone quiet on who they are looking for. I'm scared to go out alone in case I'm bumped off.'

'Why would you be next?' Leon rolled his eyes.

'Has it escaped your attention that you're connected to all three men via Washington Place?'

'Don't be stupid. Of course it hasn't.'

'Well, I can be linked to them too. We could both be on a hit list for all you know.'

'This has nothing to do with you.' Leon rubbed at his aching neck. 'Someone wanted me out of the picture, knew when I was out of town.'

It had played on his mind after he'd spoken to Eddie. He'd been on the monthly run to check on their suppliers in London. Who had known he would be out of the city? Eddie, for certain. Jade had dropped him at the station yesterday. His mum had been in the car too.

He glanced at Clara. She had known as well. Would she play him? Frustration tore through him. He couldn't trust anyone.

'I can't think straight here.' He marched to the front door.

Clara raced after him, held on to his arm. 'Please stay! Just a little while longer.'

He pushed her away. 'There are things I need to do.'

'Wait! We need to sort out the books!'

Leon opened the door and left her on the step. Then he went back to her, grabbing her roughly by the arm.

'If this is anything to do with you, I'm going to swing for you,' he seethed.

'I swear, I don't know anything!' Clara cried.

Leon let go and pushed her away. He glanced around as he walked back to the car, to see if anyone was following him, but he couldn't spot anything.

Once Leon had gone, Clara didn't know what to do with herself. She didn't like this now. Her plan to get in with the Steeles was crumbling around her and she had a feeling she was heading for a big fall.

Why was the lure of the bad boy always her downfall? First it was Trent continually asking her for alibis, then it was Eddie asking her to lie to the police. Recently, it had been Leon who had got her involved in the parties.

She rang Eddie. He would sort everything, make sure nothing came back to her. There was too much at stake for him if she got caught by the police. She could say so much.

'What are you ringing me for?' he demanded.

'I need to see you. I think I'm in trouble. I think *we're* in trouble!'

'What's going on?'

Clara told Eddie about her conversation with Leon. 'I'm worried that he'll land me in trouble with the police and I—'

'My family are more important than you. You're on your own if you've made a mess of things.'

'But Eddie, I did what you asked and—'

The line went dead.

Clara swallowed her fear. She didn't want the police to find out what else she'd been up to as well as the parties. It was too risky to continue anyway.

Boy, she *was* in deep trouble.

FIFTY-EIGHT

Eddie pulled up on the driveway of the place he hated so much. He hardly ever set foot inside Hardman House now; instantly, memories came flooding back of his father's funeral. Everyone had gathered at the house to await the arrival of the hearse. He remembered his mother walking into the church behind George's coffin. He remembered the three of them walking behind, all with families of their own. He would never know what the others were thinking, but he'd wanted to push the coffin into the grave as soon as possible, to get rid of George and his legacy. It didn't matter to him that his father's murder was unsolved. In fact, it was much better that it hadn't been.

Not many people had come back to the house afterwards, which he wasn't sure was out of respect for what happened to George or the fact that everyone felt more comfortable at The Potter's, his local pub.

Kathleen was at the door as he got out of his car. She welcomed him inside and he followed her into the sitting room.

'What's so important that you couldn't see me at work?' He came inside. 'Or even talk to me over the phone?'

'What was all that shouting about with your brother earlier?' Kathleen came back with a question of her own.

'I told you. It was nothing I can't sort out.'

'But I overheard you talking about parties, at some house.' Kathleen paused. 'I hope it isn't—'

'Whatever it was, it's not going to be happening again.' He frowned. 'You called me here about that?'

'No.' Kathleen sat down on the settee and patted the cushion next to her. 'I'm worried about Jade. I think she is up to something.'

He sat down. 'Like what?'

'I don't know, but it involves the police.'

'You mean she's seeing Grace?' Eddie shook his head. 'I told her not to. I knew she'd get too attached.'

'It isn't Grace.'

Kathleen reached for her phone and brought up a photo. 'Do you recognise him?'

Eddie studied the image he was shown. 'That's Alex Challinor.'

'I saw Jade with him at the gym.'

'Doing what?'

'Just talking. They seemed to be having words, though. I asked her who he was, but she got angry and told me it was none of my business. I hope she isn't falling for him. He's the one on our books, isn't he?'

Eddie nodded, knowing how much his mother loathed him keeping things from her. 'And he'd better not be playing one of us against the other for more money.'

'She has been splashing out lately. I know she's bought Megan a new iPad – although she told me she'd bought it cheap from someone from the gym. It's one of those large ones, a Pro or something. I've seen her in a few new clothes too.' Kathleen gnawed on her bottom lip. 'She won't say anything, will she?'

'She knows not to.' Eddie's voice was stern.

'But she could get us all into serious trouble.' Kathleen got up and paced the room. 'Can you tell her to stay away from him, and Grace?'

'I will. But you need to calm down.'

'She could ruin everything.' She paced some more.

'You're always looking out for yourself.' He pouted.

'That's not true!' Kathleen laid a hand on his arm. 'You know how horrific it was, for us all, when your father was alive. Please don't let the truth get out now. It would devastate us.'

'Have you forgotten what he did?' Eddie stood up.

'I have scars that mean I will never forget.' Kathleen's hand moved to his face and she looked at Eddie with so much love that a lump formed in his throat. 'We're family,' she added. 'We have to stick together.'

Eddie nodded. He loved his mum as much as he despised her. None of them deserved what they had got from George Steele.

'Leave it with me,' he told her.

Driving home in his car, Eddie stopped at traffic lights and banged a fist on the steering wheel. Did Alex Challinor really think he could pull the wool over his eyes, use his sister to get what he wanted? Well, he could do that too.

He wouldn't be taken for a fool by anyone.

Once Eddie had gone, Kathleen went to bed. Jade and Megan were staying over at Lorna's house, now that the police had cleared it of forensics. It wasn't what she'd wanted, but she wasn't going to beg Jade to stay with her.

She tossed and turned, trying to sleep. She had always looked after her family the best she could, but even with George gone they were still falling apart. Now she relied more than ever on Eddie to help her, even though he treated her like a second-class citizen, as if she wasn't capable of keeping anything to herself. But she had her life to thank him for many times over.

Almost at once, memories flooded back of one night in particular when he'd been ten years old. She had been asleep in bed and heard the front door bang shut. She'd frozen, wondering what George's mood would be like. Would he be drunk and angry? Or would she get the nice happy George that showed himself every now and then?

He'd bounded into their bedroom, the door crashing into the wall behind it. She'd sat up quickly, turning on the lamp at the side of the bed.

'Did you have a good evening?' she asked.

'What do you think?' He yanked off the covers and threw them to the floor. 'I was attacked by some thick bastard who is going to get the wrath of me when I next see him. Do you know what I'm going to do to him? I'm going to put my hands around his neck and squeeze real hard.'

He grabbed her ankles and pulled her down the bed. Hating the feel of him, she prayed he would be quick tonight. Sometimes it took him forever if he had brewer's droop. Others it was fast and furious and she would be left bruised for days to come.

But this time it wasn't sex he was after. His hands went around her neck as he mistook her for someone else.

He squeezed hard. 'When I find out who it is, they are going to wish they'd never been born.' Spittle flew from his mouth.

'Stop!' Spots came before her eyes and her chest tightened as she struggled to breathe. 'George, stop!'

'I'll tear his eyes out and rip his teeth out one by one.' George squeezed harder. 'No one makes a fool out of me.'

Kathleen couldn't speak. His weight bore down on her as he straddled her chest. She pawed at his hands with her own, her arms thrashing around as she tried to hurt him in some way. Stop him, take him out of his trance.

One arm went limp, and her mind flipped forward to the three children she had let down. She was going to leave them with this monster.

The monster who had ruined her life because she had been weak and unable to stand up to him.

The monster who had ruined their lives too, through no fault of their own.

But he would be the monster who would go to jail for her murder. That was a comforting thought as she closed her eyes.

She must have been seconds away from death when she heard footsteps behind her. The weight on her chest increased but the hands around her neck let go of their grip.

She gasped and coughed, trying to fill her lungs up with air again too quickly as George fell to one side and she scrambled from underneath him. She sat on the edge of the bed as the room came back into focus.

Eddie was standing in front of her, a hard-backed book in his hand.

Leon was cowering in the doorway, too scared to come into the room. Jade stood behind him.

'Are you okay?' Eddie asked, a tremor in his voice.

'Yes, I'm fine. Go back to bed, all of you.'

'But, Mum,' Leon cried. 'I heard—'

'It's fine, honey. Daddy's a bit drunk, that's all. Take your sister with you.'

Leon and Jade padded away, but Eddie remained by her side.

'He's going to kill you one day,' he said quietly, tears in his eyes.

Kathleen couldn't speak. Eddie had seen and heard way too much for his years. All the children had.

'I won't let that happen,' Kathleen replied.

Behind them, George snored in a drunken stupor. She looked up at her eldest son, regret clear in her face. Her children shouldn't have to see this, but what could she do? She had no choice but to stay. Besides, George wouldn't remember any of it in the morning.

But they always would. Every one of them.

Now, Kathleen sat up in bed and began to cry. She rarely showed her emotions, wanting to be strong, but in private she never held back. George Steele had a lot to answer for – and he was still wrecking her family.

She couldn't have that any longer.

FIFTY-NINE

It was nine p.m. when Grace finished for the day. At last, things were beginning to piece together. They'd received lots of calls from the public after Elliott Woodman's death, and there had been several sightings of four youths running along Leek Road and into Leonard Avenue minutes after Leon Steele's car had been returned to the gym car park.

Her phone rang as she was getting to her car. Simon's name flashed up on the screen.

'Hi.' She held the handset between her shoulder and chin as she searched for her keys. 'Sorry I haven't had time to speak to you today. It's been a tad busy again.'

'I'm only just finishing for the night too. I rang on the off-chance you haven't eaten and might want to grab a takeaway?'

'Ooh, yes, I'm starving.' The words were out of her mouth before she had time to think about them. Really, sleep was what she needed most. There would be another early start in the morning and she wanted to have a bit of downtime to put her mind to work. But remembering the twinkle in his eye that she kept seeing made her stomach roll for more than just food.

'Excellent. What do you fancy?' he asked.

'Something quick. Fish and chips?'

'Right. Tell me your address and I'll be with you soon.'

Half an hour later, they were full to bursting. They'd eaten on trays on their laps in the living room, amiably chatting about anything and nothing. For once it was great not to talk about work.

'Nice place you have here,' Simon said, glancing around.

'Thanks, it's not much but it's beginning to feel like home.'

'Do you ever get lonely?'

The air began to crackle with electricity, or at least that's what it felt like to Grace. She was sitting a metre away from him, yet it was almost as if she could feel his warmth.

'Of course I do,' she admitted. 'But I like my own company too.' She laughed. 'Which is good, considering the job I do. There aren't many men who will put up with the hours I work. Don't divorce statistics say that one in two marriages fail now anyway?'

'Whoa, I was only thinking about dating each other,' Simon joked. 'You've married me off again!'

'Oh, I—' Grace blushed. She hadn't realised he was talking about them. She thought he'd been asking in general. But then again, had she?

'Coffee?'

She got to her feet quickly and reached for his tray.

'Please.' He smiled as he passed it to her. 'White, one sugar.'

Grace went through to the kitchen and popped the dishes into the dishwasher. Two plates for the first time since she'd moved in. She grinned. It was nice having Simon here. She needed to get in touch with the rules of dating though. She'd had no idea he was flirting with her.

'Need a hand?'

She jumped when she realised he was right behind her. When she turned around, there was something about the way he looked at her – they reached out and kissed each other at the same time. First it was tentative, but then it became more passionate. She wrapped her arms around his body, ran her fingers through his hair.

His mouth trailed tiny kisses down from her lips to her neck and she shuddered at his touch. She urged him to find her lips again. His hand slipped inside her top and a soft moan escaped her.

With no hesitation, she tugged at the bottom of his shirt, freeing it from his trousers. He undid the cuffs and pulled it over his head, throwing it to the floor. Then he took the bottom of her top and pulled it up and over her head. He threw that to the floor too, smiling shyly.

They moved back into the living room and dropped onto the settee. Once his hands found the button on her trousers, she took it as her cue to shimmy out of them, while he did the same with his own. She wanted him to feel her, to be inside her, to make her come alive again.

'Wow, I had no idea you were harbouring all those tattoos!' Simon laughed and pointed to his forearm. 'I only have a tribal band and that hurt like hell so I didn't get any more.'

Hearing him say that had a sobering effect. The first one she'd had inked was a small half-moon and three stars on her right shoulder. It had led to almost one a year since and now she had ten over various parts of her body that mostly couldn't be seen unless she was naked.

The tattoos reminded her of who she was, even the ones she'd had done to cover scars of the past.

Simon didn't know the truth about her. She couldn't move forward until she'd told him, but she was wary in case he thought she'd tricked him purposely.

'I can't.' She put her hand over his.

He stopped and sat up. 'Oh,' he replied.

'I'm sorry. It's not your fault. I . . . I just . . . it's complicated.'

'It's okay.' Simon reached for his trousers eventually. 'You don't have to explain.'

'But I do!' She touched his arm.

He turned to her after he'd pulled on his shirt. 'Haven't you slept with anyone since?'

Realising he thought she'd stopped because of Matt, she hated herself, but she played along with it.

'I've had a couple of quick flings.' She watched him recoil. 'What's wrong with that?'

'Nothing. I was just wondering how you've gone without regular sex for that long. It's okay when you're married to fall out of love and not want it, but—'

'My marriage ended when Matt died, not because we fell out of love. There's a massive difference there,' she retorted, standing up quickly.

'Sorry, that came out wrong. I was talking about myself actually.' Simon stood up too. 'But don't you miss the intimacy? I know I do.'

'If you're only after me for my body' – she pointed to the door – 'then you can leave right now.' She stopped and broke out into a shy smile. 'I'm sorry. I . . . I guess I wanted this to mean something. I don't want to rush into anything we'll both regret.'

'I wouldn't have regretted it.'

He dared to take her hand and she stepped closer to him. Put her arms around his waist. Thankful when she felt his arms around her, she breathed in his scent, pushing back the tears that were threatening to fall again. She wanted him to feel familiar. She wanted him to be someone she cared about. But she was so afraid he wouldn't want to know her after he learned she hadn't been honest with him.

'Simon, I . . .' But the words wouldn't come.

'I'd better go.' He spoke into her hair. 'Before I can't stop myself again.'

Once alone, Grace closed the door and the house felt empty. She ran a hand through her hair and pulled on it as she glanced at herself in the hall mirror. Her skin was flushed, her eyes shining. But her mind was in turmoil. An image of Matt flashed up in front of her and tears welled in her eyes. Why had she used him as an excuse? Was it because she felt something for Simon, that she wanted a relationship with him to work so badly? She really did like him.

She groaned. She would be so embarrassed when she next saw him. But surely that was better than him being angry, feeling let down once he found out the truth?

'Well, you certainly cocked that up, Allendale,' she muttered. 'What a bloody mess.'

SIXTY

MONDAY – DAY 14

Directly after team briefing, Grace walked across Hanley from the police station up to Stafford Street. Even though she was on the Elliott Woodman case, she wanted to speak to Allie about personal things.

It was nearly two weeks since Josh Parker's murder and she and her team had worked flat out without any days off. It was usual practice in a case like this – long hours, all leave cancelled – and she could see how it was wearing everyone down. But what she did love, and admire, was the steely determination they all had to catch the killer before there was another victim.

Her phone went off. She'd missed a call from Simon, so he'd sent a message.

Can we talk about something personal? Are you free now?

She popped her phone back into her pocket, her cheeks burning as she recalled the embarrassing incident the night before. She'd had another restless sleep, another run and a weight workout before she'd finally dropped off for an hour around five a.m.

She certainly wasn't ready to speak to him about what had happened yet.

It wasn't long before she was sitting in the reception and spotted Allie walking towards her. Allie had taken one look at her troubled face and shown Grace through into her office where they could speak in private.

'I don't really have anyone to talk to,' Grace began, 'and I . . . I'm in trouble. I think someone is out to get me.' She took a deep breath and told Allie the connection she had to the Steele family, including what had happened yesterday with her DCI. It felt good to have someone to confide in, even if she shouldn't.

Allie wasn't as surprised as Grace had expected her to be though.

'I kind of know who you are already,' she grimaced.

'Perry?' Grace might have guessed.

'It was Sam, actually,' Allie admitted. 'She rang me after she found out, wanted to chat about her feelings. Fair play for you to coming back to Stoke though.'

Grace's smile was faint. She wanted to hear more about Sam, but she could tell Allie had loyalty to her old team and she admired her for that.

'I'm wondering if you have any idea who might be causing trouble,' she went on.

Allie leaned forward in her chair. 'Well, I know my team well and I doubt it would be any of them. Alex is a bit of a snake, but even so. Then again, I haven't been there since you started. How have you felt working amongst them? Have there been any bad vibes?'

'I've made a few mistakes,' Grace admitted. 'And I know this probably sounds stupid to you, but I'm not sure I trust Nick. What's he really like, Allie?'

'You mean did *I* trust him when he was my boss?'

'Yes.'

'Absolutely.' She nodded. 'I've never had a problem with him, always found him fair, even when I went over the top at times. He can be a bit full on, though, if he knows of a weakness he can exploit.'

Grace sat for a moment. That made sense.

'I just wondered if you could think of anyone who would work in the Steeles' pocket, or be on their payroll?' she asked. 'I know it's not hard to find out my address if someone follows me, but it's spooked me out that someone could be watching me.'

'Would you like me to have a word with any of them? Air your concerns?' Allie suggested.

'Thanks all the same.' Grace shook her head. 'But I have to do this myself, don't I?'

Feeling a little better after chatting with Allie, Grace was back at her desk when another text message came in from Simon.

Sorry about the article in the paper today. I want you to know I had nothing to do with it.

She froze. What did he mean? Quickly, she went online and typed in the website address for the *Stoke News*. The first link on the homepage was about their case, but there, in a large header further down the article, was her name, revealing her to be the daughter of George Steele.

Humiliation gripped her insides. That must have been why Simon was trying to contact her earlier. Shit, why didn't she take his call instead of thinking it was about last night! At least she could have forewarned everyone.

But then another thought crossed her mind.

Someone *must* be out to get her.

Nick marched across the room and threw a copy of the newspaper down in the middle of their desks.

'I've just had this handed to me. How the hell did they get this information?' He looked around the room.

'I have no idea,' Grace said, flustered. 'I'll check with the press office.'

Alex stretched across for the paper, scanned the words and then scowled at her. 'This is your journo friend, Simon's, doing, isn't it?'

'You can't put the blame on someone without proof,' she snapped.

'I bet he's being paid by the Steeles too.'

Grace held back her anger, staring at Alex until he caught her eye again. 'You think *I'm* a mole?'

'I always knew that you're working for them. It's way too much of a coincidence you coming back to Stoke once George Steele was murdered. Which one of them is paying you?' he replied.

'Which one of them is paying *you*?' she hit back.

'You two, my office, now!' Nick shouted. The room dropped into silence as everyone stopped what they were doing to rubberneck.

Nick slammed the door behind them as they stood in front of his desk. 'What is your problem?' he cried. 'We're in the middle of a murder investigation and you're at each other's throats when you should be working together.'

Alex folded his arms and glared at Grace. 'I think she's leaking information.'

'On what grounds?'

'Call it a professional hunch,' he said.

'This is actually quite childish of you,' Grace reacted.

'No, no, I'm really keen on hearing him out.' Nick leaned back on his desk. 'Go ahead, Alex.'

Alex shook his head.

'You must have something, surely?'

'She's a mole,' Alex insisted. 'I know it, even if you don't.'

'Enough of this crap. Get back to your desk. We have work to do,' Nick barked.

They stood up and made for the door.

'Hang on a minute, Grace.'

Grace turned back to Nick, wondering what else she had done wrong.

'Just keep your temper in check,' he told her. 'I know he's an idiot but don't let him bring out the child in you.'

'Sir?'

'Take a break. Calm down and then we'll have a recap. I'm not sure I can salvage this mess, though. Do you know who told the press?'

'No.'

'You didn't slip up?' His voice was kind rather than accusatory.

'I'm sure I didn't.'

It was unusually quiet outside Nick's office when Grace stepped out, only the sound of a phone ringing and the murmur of a lower-than-normal conversation.

'You need to figure out where your loyalties lie,' Alex said, his tone hushed as she got to her desk.

Grace walked away, but she turned back again just before he sat down.

'Do you know something?' Her voice was quiet too. 'When I first started working here, people warned me that you were a smart-arse, but I gave you the benefit of the doubt. I like to form my own opinions. But now I realise that you are a dick through and through.'

Alex grabbed her arm as she moved off. 'Don't speak to me like that.'

'Someone in this office is ratting us out,' Grace stared at him pointedly, 'and I'm going to find out who it is.' She pulled her arm away from him and marched away.

SIXTY-ONE

Grace left the incident room and took refuge in the only place she knew she could get a bit of peace. The ladies' bathroom was empty. She went into a cubicle and sat down on the toilet. Who the hell did Alex think he was? She had never grassed up another cop, she had never taken a bribe and she never would. He should know her better than that by now.

More to the point, who had given that stuff to the *Stoke News*? And why hadn't Simon tried harder to warn her? She would at least have been prepared. She could have had time to think exactly who would be feeding that kind of thing to the press.

Hearing the door outside go, she stood up, flushed the toilet and went out to wash her hands. Sam was waiting for her.

'Don't let him get to you,' she said. 'I know it's hard because he's an idiot.'

'I never believed people when they said he was so nasty.'

'You're right. He's just a dick, but he'll calm down soon.'

'I've been here for over a month!'

'I'm not saying how he acts is okay.' Sam leaned on the wall as Grace dried her hands.

'Have you any idea how hard it is for me?' Grace broke. 'I'm trying to settle into a new job, something that I've never done before, and I'm clearly not doing it as well as I should be. I've moved back to a place where bad memories come flashing at me with everything I do. I've come face-to-face with an estranged family who are known in Stoke for criminal activities; with the unsolved murder of my father hanging over me. Alex makes me feel really crap with his put-downs and I'm trying so hard to fit in. Now, I'll be off the case for sure.'

Sam placed a hand gently on Grace's forearm after the outburst.

Grace gathered herself together again and gave out a loud sigh. 'Sorry. You shouldn't have to hear all that.'

'Never heard a thing.' Sam grinned, then her smile dropped. 'You have been hard to get to know.' She paused. 'You're very guarded. I get that, because of the family thing, but you need to trust us. We're on your side.'

Grace felt tears prick at her eyes and blinked profusely. Sam was right. She shouldn't let her suspicions affect her judgement.

'I'm going to grab a cup of watery tea from the canteen.' Sam checked her watch. 'Do you want to join me?'

Grace smiled but shook her head. 'Thanks for the offer, but there's someone I need to see first.'

Jade sat across from Bethesda Police Station on level three of the multi-storey car park, as near to her usual spot as possible. She knew Alex would be mad with her, but what the hell.

The door opened and he strode across, fists shoved in his jeans, his jacket flapping in his haste.

She snorted. He didn't look happy. Good, let him have a taste of his own medicine. She got out of the vehicle, the floor empty of people at the moment.

'I've been waiting for ages,' she whined as she leaned on the side of the car, arms folded.

'If you hadn't threatened that you'd come over and ask for me, I wouldn't be here. What do you want?'

'To see you.'

'I don't have time for this,' he told her.

'Has something happened? You look pissed off.'

'It's that – that stupid woman.'

'Grace?' Jade frowned. 'Has she found out about us?'

'Never mind that. Have you seen the *Stoke News*?'

'What does it say?'

'That she's your bloody sister.'

'No!' Jade had to stop herself from laughing out loud.

'Someone is leaking information to the press.' He glared at her. 'Is it you?'

'No, it isn't!'

'Well, it must be Eddie or Leon, then. It's got to be one of you. Because they think it's me and it isn't.' Alex ran a hand through his hair and paced in front of her. 'People are getting suspicious.'

Jade frowned. 'Of me and you?'

'Of everything!' he said. 'It has to stop.'

'We've kept it quiet so far.'

'If your family find out, I'll be in for it. I can't afford to lose their cut.'

'So it's okay for you to lose me?' Jade huffed. 'You're not dumping me. I won't allow it.'

'We have no choice. We have to cool it for a while. Besides, I've done what you asked.'

'No!' She leaned forward and put her arms around his neck. 'I need you.'

He took hold of her hands and pulled them down to her side before pushing her away gently.

'It's too risky. Grace is a shrewd bitch. She has her suspicions.'

Jade's hackles went up. 'She's not giving you the come-on, is she?'

'Of course not!' Alex shook his head in dismay. 'She's just getting too close to the truth.'

'Then stop her.'

'I can't. She's on to me. This could be my job on the line.' Alex paced in front of her. 'You have to leave me alone.'

'No!' she shouted.

The lift doors opened and a woman with a pushchair came out on to their floor. Alex took the opportunity to walk away from Jade.

'Where are you going?' she demanded.

'Back to work, while I still have a job.'

'You can't.'

'Stop hassling me!'

Jade reached for his arm, but he shrugged her hand away. 'Alex, please!'

He pointed at them both. 'This, you and me, is no longer part of the bargain.'

Tears welled in Jade's eyes, but she wasn't upset. They were tears of anger. He wasn't walking away from her. She ran across the floor and blocked the door to the stairwell.

'Move out of my way!' he told her.

'I'm not going anywhere!' Jade's voice echoed across the floor. The woman with the pushchair stopped what she was doing and looked over.

Alex grabbed her arm and pulled her to one side. 'You stay away from me! Do you hear?'

Jade followed him, screaming at him as he jogged down the steps.

'You'll regret this!'

'You don't own me.' Alex scowled but continued on his way.

'Just remember how much I know about you!' Jade shouted after him.

SIXTY-TWO

Then

She spent so much time on her own locked in the garage, but she never got used to it. She had a lot of thinking time, sitting in the dark with her knees brought up to her chest. Back against the wall so that she could see who came in through the door.

She never knew how long she would be in there. Sometimes the hours dragged, sometimes it seemed like minutes if she managed to get some sleep.

Things were going around and around in her head. Why did he lock her up all the time? It wasn't as if she was ever naughty. She always did as she was told, her childhood gone because she'd been so scared to enjoy it.

At twelve, she was turning into a woman. Her father had noticed. She'd heard him and a man talking about her outside the room.

The door opened and she sat up quickly.

'Hi,' a man smiled as he walked towards her.

She swallowed. It was the man who had come before. He looked the same age as her father.

He held out a bag to her. 'Here, take it. It's for you.'

Inside there was a bottle of cola, a packet of crisps and a tube of sweets. She glanced up at him.

He reached inside, opened the bottle and gave it to her. 'Go on, enjoy.'

She took the drink from him. He opened the crisps for her and handed them to her after taking one for himself.

'Go on now. I don't bite.'

He sat with her while she had her treat. He didn't speak, just stroked her hair every now and then. She inched away from him until, suddenly, she couldn't move. It wasn't long before she began to feel unable to respond at all.

His advances became more obvious.

'Your father owes me money. He suggested that he could pay off his debt in other ways.' He rested his hand on her thigh, moving it higher.

She couldn't flinch at his touch, yet she wanted to scream out. But she managed to whimper as she smelt that cheap aftershave again.

'Hush, hush,' he whispered, putting a finger to her lips before parting them.

SIXTY-THREE

Downstairs at the back of the building, Grace pushed on the door with so much force it almost came back at her. She crossed Bethesda Street in the direction of the *Stoke News* building. Waiting in the reception area calmed her a little bit but, as soon as she saw Simon, her temper heated again.

They left through the front entrance and walked to the side of the building.

'I tried to warn you earlier,' he began as she marched in front of him. 'I rang you and then I sent you a message.'

'I didn't have time to reply.' She slowed, unwilling to admit her error of judgement. 'Who was your source?'

Simon shook his head. 'I can't tell you.'

'You can't tell me, or you won't?'

'That's rich, coming from you after the secret you've been keeping.'

'Oh, come on,' Grace cried. 'That was the reason I stopped last night. I was afraid this would ruin things.'

'Well, it didn't help finding out from someone else.'

'Thanks a million for your support,' she said. 'Did I bruise your ego that much?'

'Wait a minute. You think this has anything to do with what happened between us?' Simon sounded shocked. 'You've got some nerve.'

'No, I – sorry. I'm angry.' Grace looked across the street for a moment, watching people walk on by oblivious to her life falling apart. 'I can't think straight when I have my whole team accusing me of being a liar.'

'We had no choice,' he replied. 'We had sensitive information.'

'And you didn't think to go to Nick when you couldn't get through to me? I don't buy that, not from you.'

From the corner of her eye, Grace saw Alex coming out of the multi-storey car park. She frowned when she spotted Jade Steele running towards him, reaching her hands up to touch his face. There was an exchange of words before Alex pulled away and walked off.

Anger boiled in Grace, but she couldn't let Simon see her reaction. Alex would have to wait. She turned her attention back to Simon as he began to talk again.

'My boss is the news editor for crime,' he said. 'I tried to stop him running with it but he wouldn't hear of it. And you should see the emails and comments arriving daily about the serial killer. People are outraged. They think you're not doing enough, that there's going to be another murder before anyone is caught. He thinks the public had a right to know you were on the case.'

'Why? To make it look as if I'm in on it?'

Simon shrugged.

Grace could understand their logic, but it was still wrong. She stepped out of the way for a woman walking past before moving back to him.

'This might set things back. And if that happens, it'll be on your head.'

'That's a bit unfair.' Simon pouted.

'Unfair is when people turn against you because they think you've been put there as a mole for a criminal family. Because stuff has been leaked to the press! I've worked hard on this case and now your – your secret informant – has ruined it.'

'If I knew who it was, I would tell you. Trust me!'

A car screeched out of the car park and they both turned to look. Jade Steele was behind the wheel.

Grace thought of the scene she'd just witnessed between Jade and Alex. 'I really don't know who to trust any more.'

Nick beckoned Grace into his office as soon as she hit her desk. She kept her scream deep within as she made her way across the floor.

'I can't keep you on this now, you know that, don't you? You're to have no more contact with the Steeles.'

'That's impossible.' Grace shook her head. 'Absolutely not, sir.'

'I beg your pardon?' Nick gave her a warning glance.

'I said no. You knew it was a conflict of interest and that I would struggle with my team to fit in, not to mention my stress levels going through the roof as I've been trying to keep everything together. You wanted me to stay on the Steeles' case during this investigation so that I could infiltrate the family to find out information for you. Now it's running deeper than Steele's Gym, I think I'm entitled to stay on it.'

'Why is it so important to you?'

'Because I want to find this killer!'

'Is that all?'

'Should there be anything else?' Grace scowled, although she realised what he meant. There was more to this but she wasn't going to mention how she felt to him. 'I want to be seen bringing them down if they are involved,' she continued. 'And I have to get people's trust too.'

'But the public know who you are,' Nick replied.

'They won't care as long as we charge someone! It's hardly front-page news, is it? So what if I'm related to them?'

'It's against protocol.'

Grace folded her arms. 'I'm not leaving this investigation. You need me on it.'

Nick raised his eyebrows. 'Don't flatter yourself.'

'I'm not.' Grace had never been more serious. 'I want to arrest this bastard as much as you do, as well as sort out what's been going on in Washington Place. So, do what you do best, keep Jenny off my back and I'll do the rest.'

Nick stood open-mouthed.

'Please,' Grace added, remembering her manners.

Nick shook his head, but there was a faint smile on his face. 'I'm glad you're on our side. I wouldn't like to mess with you if not.'

'I just want justice for everyone, sir – Nick. More importantly, for those girls. We don't know how many of them are out there. If we ask for them to come forward, how many will? And how many will we never find out about because they are too scared to speak out?'

There was a pause. Grace wondered if she had gone too far. She had never been this outspoken before. She stared at her boss, willing him to agree.

'One day, Grace.' Nick nodded. 'Jenny is out of the office tomorrow, so I can keep things away from her until then. But you had better clean up.'

Grace nodded too and left his office.

Back at her desk, she sighed heavily, almost wanting to rest her head in her hands and hide away again. All around her, people were surreptitiously glancing her way. Had she ruined her chances of ever putting down roots here?

Maybe she shouldn't have come back.

310

She'd have to put in for a transfer if things didn't improve. She'd give them time first. Six months was enough. If she hadn't fitted in by then, she would move on. Perhaps go back to Manchester, not necessarily with her tail between her legs. Maybe she had belonged there more than she'd realised.

At least there she had friends, even if they were only work colleagues. She had someone to go for a drink with, someone to chat to about last night's TV. She could have more if she made an effort.

Yes, she would give it six months. But she was not coming off this case.

SIXTY-FOUR

Grace kept her head down at the start of the evening team briefing. She wasn't sure if anyone wanted to be in the same room as her right now, but no one, not even her, had any choice. There was work to be done.

'Right, listen up, everyone,' Nick told them as he came into the room and stood at the head of the table. 'There's been a lot of things happening lately and I am pissed off with this team not rallying around one of our own. Grace acts on *my* command and is doing a bloody brilliant job, so if any of you have any complaints, then I suggest you take them up with me. I want you all to stop grumbling and work together. We are not kids any more – the bickering stops right now.' He banged the palm of his hand on the table. 'We have three deaths, and a fourth that could possibly be linked, and no suspects. I think that needs to take precedence, don't you?'

Nick took a few seconds for his words to sink into the deathly silence that followed. As a result, there were a few red faces but, ten minutes in, his words had united them again. Grace felt relieved. They needed to concentrate on the case now, to ensure the residents of the city felt safe and had faith in them.

The team chatted through all the events, brainstorming, trying to put pieces of evidence together. It was good, reassuring.

Finally, after two further hours at her desk, Grace was done. She wondered if Simon might be in Chimneys. She couldn't face texting him and perhaps having to wait for a reply. Having time to think had made her realise how harsh she had been on him that afternoon. It wasn't his fault that his editor had run with a piece of private intel, and he *had* tried to warn her.

She was at her car when Alex appeared by her side. He grabbed her forcefully by the arm.

'I want a word with you,' he said, then marched her to the side of the building. She tried to shake him off but he pushed her into an alcove out of the way of prying eyes. Behind him she could see the side of their station, the city library and the Smithfield buildings. But no one would be able to see her.

'Get your hands off me!' She tried to pull her arm away but he held on to it.

'Keep your nose out of my business.' His eyes were dark, an ugly scowl on his face. 'You're messing in something that's beyond your capabilities.'

'What are you up to, Alex?'

'It's nothing to do with you.'

'It is when it involves the Steeles. You need to stay away from them. They don't have any loyalty.'

'Like you, you mean?' Alex sneered. 'We all know where your allegiance lies. Opening your legs for that journalist. I've seen you, creeping around with him.'

'Have you been following me?' Grace stood tall and looked him in the eye but he didn't answer her question. Her heart was racing, the traffic noise from the nearby Potteries Way fighting to be heard over it. 'Were you meeting Jade Steele earlier?' she asked then.

'You mean *your* sister?' he sneered. 'She's nothing like you, thank God.'

'What's that supposed to mean?'

'She seems extremely loyal.'

Grace wouldn't bite. 'What did she want?'

'I didn't meet her.'

'Oh?' She frowned. 'That's funny, because I saw her car leaving a minute or so after you walked past.'

Alex had the nerve to shrug. 'I didn't see her.'

'So what were you doing in the multi-storey car park?' For now, she didn't mention that she had seen them together.

'Just grabbing a bit of fresh air.'

Grace leaned in close. 'Don't take me for a fool. I'll find out if you have been seeing her, and then I'll want to know why. If she is your informant you only have to say, but then again, you would have said that a long time ago. But you didn't, did you? Just like you never said that you knew who I was when I first arrived. It was you who told the Steele family I was working in Stoke, wasn't it?'

Alex shrugged again.

'Answer my question!'

'You're a lone wolf, Grace. Just like me.'

'I am *nothing* like you.' Grace rebuked his insinuation. 'The Steeles won't protect you when all this goes pear-shaped.'

'Eddie has my back.'

'So you *are* involved with them! You're a bigger fool than I'd originally had you down for.'

Alex grabbed the collar of her jacket either side of her neck and pulled her close to him. 'What I have going on with Eddie is not going to change just because you've come back on the scene. He'll look out for me because I look out for him. And his family.'

Grace tried not to show her distaste. 'All you're concerned about is one-upmanship.'

'Exactly!' He pushed her into the wall. 'You're too stupid to see what's right under your own nose.'

She pushed him back. 'Get away from me!'

'Everyone thinks this case is too personal for you,' Alex went on. 'We're all thinking you're involved somehow, so it's only a matter of time before you're booted out of Stoke. And I'll still be here.'

'I won't ever be tarred with the same brush as you,' she sneered.

Alex moved closer again. Grace balled her hand in a fist and got ready with her knee.

'I'm warning you.' Sweat glistened from his forehead. 'You breathe a word of this to anyone and you're a goner.'

'And *I'm* warning you. They may be watching me, but I'm watching them too. I'm also watching you.'

After a few tense seconds, she pushed him away again. This time he left her alone. Minutes later, she heard him screech out of the car park.

Grace got into her car, hands shaking as she caught her breath. That bastard! Who the hell did he think he was? No one threatened her like that and got away with it. His cards were well and truly marked.

Leon drew up in Clara's street and went into the back garden of her flat. He reached up to the top of the outbuilding, pushing aside a plastic cover that hid a spare key. Then he let himself into her home. He'd made sure Clara and Trent were both at the gym before he'd left, but still he checked the rooms to be sure he was alone. When he was satisfied, he went into the bedroom. Now that Tom had been murdered, he needed to clean up everywhere, and everything. It was all getting too real now. There were too many clues.

Lifting up the bedside cabinet, he placed it on its side on

the bed. Taped to the underneath was a small black notebook. He shoved it in the pocket of his jeans and replaced the cabinet and the items on top. He'd yet to find out where Dale's phone had gone. He knew the police hadn't found it, unless Alex wasn't telling him everything, and the number had been out of service when he rang it.

Once outside again, he drew level with the vehicle he'd taken from Molloroy Motors. A message came in to his phone and he fished it out of his pocket. He frowned when he saw who it was from. Then he heard his name being called as a figure dressed in black ran at him.

Before he could respond, something was sprayed into his face. He dropped his phone as his eyes began to sting. Pepper spray; he'd been sprayed twice before by the police so recognised its effects.

As his eyes burned, he scrunched them shut to try to stop the pain. The first smash across the head with a heavy object knocked him to his knees. With the second, he dropped to all fours. Immediately, he was pulled up. He tried to resist but, dazed and unable to see, all he could do was lunge with a fist that missed its target.

The car door was opened. As he stumbled around with his eyes still closed, he was almost guided into the back seat. Helpless to resist, he tried to sit up, kicking out with his feet. His assailant straddled him, hitting him again and again.

'Stop!' Fear tore through him as he realised that this had happened to Josh, that he had been left impaired purposely.

That this could be the killer.

He tried to push his assailant away. 'Leave me alone!'

A knife was plunged into his chest.

SIXTY-FIVE

At home, Grace parked in the drive of her house and switched off the engine, her hands still shaking from her altercation with Alex. She reached for her phone to call Nick, but then decided she'd be better putting her thoughts into order first. She was about to accuse a member of his staff of taking money in return for confidential information.

Yes, it would be best kept until the morning when she would be calmer. She needed to state her case in a professional not emotional way. After all, it would be Alex's word against her own.

She took a shower, thinking that this had to be the worst day in her career so far. She'd been outed in the press, had a run-in with her boss, knew her team would never trust her, and the final straw was being accosted by that idiot. How dare he threaten her.

Ten minutes later, the doorbell rang. Upstairs in her bedroom, she crossed to the bay window and looked down on to the driveway. It gave her a full view of the front door.

Simon.

She couldn't hide her surprise when she opened the door.

He pointed at her dressing gown and wet hair. 'I'm not interrupting anything, am I?'

'No.' Grace held the door open for him. 'I've not long been in. Help yourself to a coffee while I get dressed.'

She went back upstairs as he headed into the kitchen. Wondering what to put on, she rummaged through her clothes for something . . . something . . . what? She hadn't got a clue what he'd come to say after her outburst earlier. She ran a comb through her wet hair, popped on jeans and a jumper, added a dash of lipstick, a quick spray of perfume and went downstairs.

In the kitchen, Simon had made a coffee for her too.

'I rang Perry this evening,' he told her once they were seated in the living room.

Grace looked up. That wasn't what she'd been expecting.

'And what did he say to you?' she asked.

He paused for a moment. 'He thinks you're struggling.'

'Oh, that's big of him to tell me!'

'Not with the job,' he added quickly. 'With the whole thing of coming back to Stoke, spying on your family, keeping everything secret. He says Nick has pushed you too far. He says you should talk to him and Sam more.'

She raised her eyebrows inquisitively. 'So why aren't either of them here now?'

'I told him I would come instead.' He smiled. 'I guess your luck ran out,' he joked.

Grace smiled faintly, glad of it. She didn't want to fight with Simon. She didn't want to fight with anyone, she had nothing left to give. More than anything, she realised she wanted someone on her side.

'When you heard who I was, did you ever think that I was working for the Steeles?' she wanted to know.

He nodded. 'It's played on my mind today. But that's why I'm here now, because once I'd had time to think about it, I'm

318

sure you're better than that. I also thought maybe you'd been placed here undercover to infiltrate your family and see what information you could find out.'

She snorted. 'Even if the force *would* allow it, I doubt anyone would have thought the Steeles warranted that much attention.' She waited for Simon to look at her. Unsure what to say, she apologised again.

'I'm not interested in that any more.' Simon shrugged. 'Sure I was hurt when I found out, but really I can't say I blame you for not wanting to tell anyone.'

'I *did* want to,' Grace acknowledged, 'but I was warned not to.'

'It couldn't have been easy; living with George Steele, I mean. And correct me if I'm wrong, but isn't Leon the same age as you?'

'Yes. George was having an affair at the same time he was married to my mother – well, it was more of a double life really. Eddie was born first, two years before me, and I came along two months after Leon. Finally, there was Jade. But we never met, until recently.'

Grace sat back in her chair. It felt good to have someone to talk to.

'We were all damaged kids,' she continued. 'Once my mum and I left Stoke-on-Trent it didn't taken long for George to find us, but apparently all he'd wanted was a quick divorce. I found out that he'd moved his other family into the home we'd shared with him, and later he married the woman he'd been seeing at the same time as my mum.'

'Double trouble.' Simon laughed awkwardly at his attempt at humour.

Grace couldn't smile. 'George had been a bastard to Mum. Before we left, I can remember lots of times he'd come home and beat her up – the nights when he hadn't been with Kathleen

Steele wherever she lived, I presumed. Sometimes Mum could barely walk the next day. Other times he wouldn't mark her, but he would punish her enough that she wouldn't be able to go out to work.' Grace fought with her emotions as her eyes welled up.

'We hardly had any money. If he hadn't been left that awful house, I'm certain we would have become homeless. Mum worked a full-time shift and often did extra hours cleaning in the local pub to make ends meet. George would never give her money and if she did have some stashed away, he would take it and spend it getting drunk.'

'But you got away.' Simon's voice was soft as he came to sit beside her and put a hand over hers. 'That's some story, and it makes all the difference to hear it.'

'Why?'

'Because it shows me what a loyal person you are.'

She raised her eyebrows. 'I didn't have any choice at the time.'

'Maybe not, but you were still brave to go through all that and not come out as damaged as the Steele siblings.'

They sat in silence then. Grace scrunched her eyes shut to block out the pain.

'It's late.' Simon stood up and held out his hand. 'I should go.'

Grace took it and stood up too. She smiled at him. 'Thanks for listening. Does this mean we are friends again?'

Simon nodded and kissed her lightly on the cheek before leaving.

Grace closed the door behind him and headed off to bed. She was glad they had cleared the air. Tomorrow was going to be a challenging day all round, especially with Nick beginning to crack under the strain, and she was desperate for a good night's sleep.

But, as usual, her mind wouldn't allow it. Who had leaked

the information to the press about her background? She thought back to Eddie's suggestion that he had someone on the inside. He also knew that their three victims had all been stabbed in the heart.

Then there was seeing Alex and Jade both at the car park earlier. They must have been meeting, but why?

Not to mention Alex's accusations and threats.

The more she thought about it, the more she realised there could only be one logical solution. Her gut instinct had been right.

It had to be Alex who was leaking information about her and the case.

SIXTY-SIX

TUESDAY – DAY 15

Grace had just finished a run on her treadmill and begun to make toast when her phone rang. She groaned, hoping it wasn't someone telling her there had been another murder, not when she had a feeling they were closing in.

But it wasn't anyone from work. It was Jade. Grace sighed as she slid her finger over the screen to take the call. This had better be important at seven thirty of a morning.

'I . . . can I meet you?' Jade's voice broke. 'I need to talk to you.'

'I'm not sure I will be free today, Jade. I'm really busy at work right now.' Grace heard sobbing down the phone. 'Are you all right?'

'I need someone to talk to, and I – I have to tell someone.'

'What's wrong?' The toaster threw out her breakfast and she grabbed the first slice to butter.

'I want to make a complaint about another officer.'

'In relation to the ongoing murder investigation?' Grace stopped, knife in mid-air.

'No, it's about an assault. DC Alex Challinor raped me.'

Grace gasped. She wanted to ask Jade if she was certain of the allegation before she put it out there, but she didn't want to seem disrespectful. She might have her doubts about trusting Jade, but as a rule she would hear anyone out before making a judgement. Imagine if Jade *had* been raped and she hadn't believed her.

'I wasn't going to say anything because I know how difficult it would be to prove,' Jade went on.

'That mustn't stop you coming forward. We have a specialist team.'

'Who would believe me over the word of a police officer?'

'We would listen to both sides of the story,' she stated.

During her career, Grace had known a lot of women who hadn't wanted to press charges after coming forward. Even if charges could go to the Crown Prosecution Service without their testimony, if they had enough evidence to pursue a charge, it still required a lot of work to prove. She hated it, but it was true.

'You have to come into the station,' Grace said. 'Are you able to talk about it while I arrange for a special victims' officer to see to you too?'

'I only want to talk to you.'

'You can, for now. But afterwards, I have to pass it on. I'm not qualified to deal with your needs.'

Jade burst into tears. 'I knew I should never have told you.'

Toast forgotten, Grace sat down at the kitchen table. 'You should, and it was very brave of you to do so. Can you tell me what happened?'

'I've been seeing him for a few months and when he got rough with me during sex, I told him to stop and he didn't. Afterwards, he apologised and said it would never happen again.'

'And did it?'

Jade nodded. 'Several times.'

'Is . . .?' Grace paused, realising it was none of her business.

'Yes,' Jade replied. 'It's his baby.'

Grace grimaced.

'I . . . I love him, Grace, and I thought in time he might change, get to love me too. But I realise now he's using me,' Jade went on. 'That's why he does what he does. I've been a fool. And it was so hard to keep from Megan – and my family.'

'The pregnancy?'

'No, the fact that I was seeing him at all. He's a fed. You know how our family feel about them. Keep up, Grace!'

Grace frowned, shocked at the change in Jade. One moment she had been crying, the next she was as mad as hell. She had never heard her like this.

'Can you meet me at the station?' she asked. 'I need to book you in to see someone.'

'I can't.'

'It's a serious allegation, Jade, and—'

'You don't believe me!'

'I didn't mean that!'

'Forget I ever said anything.'

'I can't do that now.'

'You're all the same, you people!'

Why was Jade telling her this only now? Had Alex done something to upset her yesterday? Was that why she'd seen her screeching out of the car park?

The line went dead.

'Jade? Shit!'

Nick wasn't at his desk when Grace arrived at the station, but Sam was and she had been hard at work. Grace was so thankful to have her on the team. The woman was one of the best unofficial CCTV and intelligence analysers she had ever worked with. Meticulous down to a fault, Sam didn't mind the hours lost watching for one- or two-second clips that could turn a whole case on its head. Just like she was about to do now.

'Have you had any sleep?' Grace asked her DC.

'A little. Craig has man flu: he's been snoring all night so I couldn't sleep. I came in at six; he's taking Emily to breakfast club.' She took a sip from her coffee. 'Something was bugging me about a tip-off I had after the press conference yesterday, so I went a bit wider with the search.' She paused the TV image. 'Watch,' she instructed. 'This is shortly after the time of the attack on Elliott Woodman.'

Grace stood by her side. An image came on the screen of four young men walking along Victoria Road, Fenton. One of them had a distinctive hoodie on.

'That's the boxing club logo!' Grace almost squealed, recognising the pattern and colour straight away.

Sam nodded, then pressed play again.

Grace watched one of the figures drop something into a passing bin. She turned, mouth wide open. 'Gloves! Did we get them?'

Sam nodded. 'Uniform have just brought them in.' She handed her an evidence bag. 'They don't seem to belong to the ringleader and, of course, we could wait to get forensic evidence. Or . . .' She pressed fast-forward on the remote again, stopping after a few seconds, where she freeze-framed something for Grace to see.

Grace stepped closer to look, and then grinned. Sam had found an image of the four men. Three had hoodies drawn real close to hide their faces, but one hadn't. Grace pointed to the one she recognised.

'Trent Gibson!'

Sam gave a little bow.

'You beauty!' Grace beamed. 'I'll get on to uniform, see if they can bring him in. If not, we'll nab him ourselves.' Behind her, she spotted Perry coming in. 'I need a quick word with you both in private, before Alex arrives.'

SIXTY-SEVEN

After she had contacted control room and a patrol car had been sent to collect Trent Gibson, Grace was sitting with Perry and Sam in the staff canteen. She explained what had happened the night before.

'I know I haven't earned your trust, but I wanted to tell you before I told Nick,' she finished. 'To make sure I'm doing the right thing. My head is on the line for so much stuff at the moment that, even though I know Alex's behaviour was wrong, I feel I need proof.'

'Have you told anyone else?' Perry asked.

Grace shook her head.

'I think you're right to let Nick decide,' Sam said. 'If Alex has been feeding the Steeles – anyone for that matter – with intel, then he deserves to go.'

Grace looked across the canteen. 'But what happens if it backfires? It's my word against his and I—'

'I'll come with you,' Perry offered.

'Me too,' Sam said.

Grace blew out the breath she had been holding and nodded. 'Okay.'

They went downstairs and back on to their floor. Alex was at his desk now. Grace walked past him, head held high, with the rest of her team behind her.

Nick sat quietly through everything she told him. Occasionally, he shook his head. Most of the time, he scowled.

'You know I'll need to speak to him,' he said once Grace had finished. 'It's a serious allegation. It will have to be looked into.'

'Yes, sir. I do.' Grace swallowed.

Nick stood up, went to the door and beckoned Alex into the office.

'What's up, boss?' Alex glanced sheepishly at them all in turn.

While Nick spoke, Grace watched for Alex's reaction.

'That's ridiculous!' He glared at Grace. 'You're lying.'

'I'm not the liar here,' she insisted.

'I'm telling you, she's making it up!' Alex pointed at Grace.

'So you didn't attack her last night?' Nick wanted to know.

'Of course not! We might have had words, but I didn't hurt her if that's what you're suggesting.' Alex looked at everyone else in turn. 'I can't believe you'll take her word over mine. She's been here five minutes!'

'And you've been underhand before,' Nick replied. 'She hasn't.'

Alex lowered his head momentarily.

'Why the hell would you get involved with the Steeles?' Nick shouted.

'I haven't!'

The air in the room was loaded as each one of them remained quiet.

'She's lying,' Alex repeated.

'Why would she do that?' Nick asked again.

'To take the scent off herself!'

Grace couldn't keep quiet any longer. Alex had tried to bully and ridicule her in equal measure. It was time some home truths came out.

'Is Jade Steele making up her pregnancy too?' Grace spoke quietly.

'For fuck's sake,' Perry muttered.

Alex baulked. 'She never told me about that.'

'Is it yours?' Nick demanded.

'How the hell would I know?'

'Okay, I'll rephrase myself. Could it be yours?'

Alex stalled long enough for them to make their own opinions, his cheeks turning a deep red in seconds. Perry lunged at him, a fist in the air. Grace stopped it as Sam pulled him away.

'Hey, cool it!' Nick said, arms raised. 'How long have you been seeing her?' he addressed Alex.

'Not long. I've been trying to get information out of her.'

'None that you have come forward with?'

Alex shook his head. 'She's not been very forthcoming, but I'm working on it.'

'How much information have you used against Grace?' Perry's fist clenched and unclenched at his side. 'You had us thinking it was her who was ratting us out!' He shrugged off Sam, reassuring them both he was calm.

'Was it you who sent the photo to the *Stoke News*?' Grace wanted to know.

Alex frowned. 'What photo?'

'Oh, come on!' Grace cried.

'I don't know what you're talking about!'

'So, what did you learn during pillow talk?' Perry pinched the bridge of his nose, unable to look at Alex.

Grace glanced at him, wondering if he was doing something with his hands rather than punch out again. She knew she wanted to.

Nick's face was the darkest Grace had seen it. 'Give me your warrant card.' He held out his hand.

'You can't suspend me!' Alex cried.

'I need to take advice, but for now, just get out of my sight. Wait for someone to call you before you come back here.'

Alex turned in disbelief. Then he pointed a finger in Grace's face. 'I'm not finished with you yet.' He shoulder-barged her as he left the room.

Nick shook his head. 'Let's get back to work and crack on while Jenny is out of the office. I can keep this from her for now.'

Grace waited behind, and closed the door when Perry and Sam had left the room. 'I need to tell you something else. I didn't want to say it in front of everyone.' She told him about Jade's allegations that morning.

'What the hell has he got himself involved in?' Nick groaned and rested his head in his hands. 'Do you believe her?'

'I don't want to sound disrespectful to anyone who has been raped,' Grace replied, 'but I don't know what to believe. There's something about Jade that doesn't sit right. I'm wondering if she's bitter because things have cooled between them and she's left carrying his child.'

'Christ, if so, there's his job gone. It was on the line anyway.' He thought for a moment. 'Let's get a rape crisis referral for Jade Steele, just to be sure. A special victims' officer might not be available to visit today, but at least we can try to do something.'

She nodded, and then paused. 'You mentioned something underhand he'd done before?'

'He's on a yellow warning for cajoling with a witness. It was more hearsay, but a complaint came in that alleged he tried to get them to withdraw their statement. Of course, he denied it.'

Grace pulled a face. 'He deserves to lose his job.'

'I'll need to bring him back in if he's left the building, speak to him under caution and get his side of things.' Nick nodded. 'Thanks for telling me.'

Grace turned to leave. 'Are you certain I'm okay working this?' She wanted to know she had his back. Nick would be in as much trouble as her if Jenny got wind of what was happening.

'I trust you, Grace.'

'Thank you, Nick.'

Outside, Grace spotted Mick coming towards them, waving for her attention. She opened the door.

'Trent Gibson has been booked into custody,' he told her. 'But someone else has handed himself in.'

'Let me guess,' Grace said. 'Kyle Fisher.'

Mick nodded. 'He wants to talk to you.'

SIXTY-EIGHT

It was the second time in three days Eddie found himself back at Hardman House. He'd tried Jade's home first, but when he found it empty, he'd wondered if she would be here. His mum said she seemed to be spending a lot of time here lately.

Knowing Kathleen was at work in Posh Gloss, he used his key to get in. Sure enough, Jade was in the kitchen when he went in. One look at her face and he knew she was running scared. He grabbed her roughly by the arm as she stepped back from him.

'I've just had a call from Alex,' he told her. 'What's your game?'

'What do you mean?' There was a shake to her voice.

'You've accused him of raping you! What's going on?'

'I haven't done that at all!'

'Don't insult my intelligence!' He stepped towards her, hands raised. 'He told me you were pregnant.'

'He's lying! Please don't hit me!'

Jade screamed so loud that Eddie froze. Images of his mother came back at him and he put his hand down immediately. He had never hit a woman, nor would he start now.

But Jade made him so angry. He could never work out when she was lying or telling the truth. She had become so adept at fooling people.

'I haven't done anything,' she cried.

Eddie leaned on the worktop and looked out of the kitchen window. For the life of him, he couldn't think why Jade would want to spend time here. Well, there was one reason, which was clearly proving its influence. Kathleen.

'I told you last week to back off.' He turned to his sister. 'You need to stop what you are doing – you're going to get found out. I can't protect you then.'

'I don't need protecting.' Jade pointed at her chest. 'I can look after myself. I always have and I always will.'

'No, you haven't! Look what a mess you've made of your life. You've played the victim for too long. It's time you woke up to what you're doing, got some help and looked after Megan. Where is she today? Is she at school?'

Jade shrugged.

'Have you spoken to her?'

'She texted me. She's staying with Freya.'

'Is that wise? Lorna has enough to contend with at the moment.'

'Freya needs Megan.'

'Megan needs you!' Eddie grasped her shoulders. 'She needs a mother to look after her. Don't you want her to have a stable relationship with you, and with men, so they won't use her?'

'Yes, I do.' Jade burst into tears. 'But I don't know how to be a good mother.'

Eddie took her into his arms while she sobbed. She was such a liability, but this wasn't all her fault. Jade had never had a mother as a role model. She had been made into what she was by their father. How Eddie wished he'd been able to stop him and his friends when they were younger. But by the time he found out what was going on, it was already too late.

'I love you, Jade,' he spoke into her hair. 'But you need to get a grip.'

He felt her nod against his chest.

'You promise me?'

'I promise,' she sniffed.

Eddie left the house. His phone rang as he got to his car. It was Trudy.

'Have you seen Leon this morning?'

'No, why?' Eddie replied.

'He didn't come home last night. Ed, I'm worried about him after all these murders.'

'Let me make some calls and I'll get back to you.'

Eddie cursed after he'd disconnected the call. When did he become his brother and sister's keeper? It was like being a parent looking out for Jade and Leon at times. Even so, Leon missing was a huge worry.

He tried his brother's phone but got no reply either. Although there was one place that Trudy wouldn't have tried. He searched for Clara's number and rang her.

But she hadn't seen or heard from Leon either.

Where the hell was he?

Grace was sitting across from Kyle Fisher in an interview room. He was holding back tears, his right eye sporting a large black bruise.

'You wanted to speak to me about something, Kyle?' she said. 'Does it concern Elliott Woodman?'

Kyle chewed his bottom lip and then nodded. 'He wasn't supposed to die. We were only told to give him a warning beating.'

Grace frowned. 'Who is "we"?'

334

'I'm not saying any names.'

'That's okay. Did you enjoy your takeaway?'

Kyle squirmed in his seat but said nothing.

'We can see four people on CCTV, after you got something to eat on Victoria Road. We've identified one of them as Trent Gibson. Is this correct?' Grace raised her eyebrows at him.

Eventually, Kyle nodded.

'Who told you to beat him up?'

He shook his head at this. 'I'd be dead by the end of the day.'

Grace wanted to tell him that this was Stoke-on-Trent, not the East End of London, but after what she had witnessed over the past few days, she decided against it. The boy was scared. She needed to keep him onside.

'So, the warning beating,' she said. 'Did you know it was going to be Elliott Woodman?'

'No! I swear I didn't. I couldn't even warn Elliott either. It was too late.'

'What went wrong?' Grace asked.

'Gibson got too rough. We tried to stop him but he kept on hitting Elliott with a bat.' Kyle thumped a curled-up fist into the palm of his hand. 'It was as if he became possessed. So I told him last night I wouldn't be doing any more jobs. That's what he did to me afterwards.' He pointed to the bruise around his right eye. 'I'm not doing time for him. I played my part, but I wasn't a murderer. Elliott was my mate. I tried to stop him!'

'You still took part.' Grace leaned forward. The tears in his eyes were falling now. He was just a kid, mixed up in something that had got out of hand. But he would still have to answer for his actions. He could have walked away. He could have said no. Peer pressure had won again.

'How much were you paid?' she asked next.

'One hundred quid each.'

'You and . . .'

Still he said nothing.

'You're willing to go to jail for Elliott's murder?' Grace couldn't hide the disgust in her voice.

'There was no mention of murder. We were only going to give him a beating!'

'Who paid Trent?' Grace demanded.

'No one.' Kyle shook his head. 'He paid us.'

Grace couldn't be certain he was telling the truth. The things she'd learned about the Steele family over the past fortnight made her think they were involved. She knew Kyle was scared of something – or someone. She took out her notepad and flicked through to a blank page.

'How did you get your money? Your payout for doing Elliott over.'

'Gibson gave it to us. I haven't spent it. It's in my bedroom.' He glanced up, the glimpse of the boy inside the man creeping through now he knew there was no going back. 'I wish I hadn't got involved. I'm having nightmares thinking about the state his head was left in.'

'An innocent young man was murdered. I hope those visions stay with you for the rest of your life.' Grace pressed him, part of her strategy to get him to give in and tell her who else was involved. 'How you could do that to one of your own, I can't imagine. You clearly have no morals.'

'I was scared!'

'It will be far more scary where you are off to. Who was with you, Kyle?' She pointed to the image with the four of them. 'Who are the other two?'

Kyle said nothing.

'Tell me who they are!'

Kyle's voice cracked as he spoke. 'Craig Dellaway and Robert Stockton.'

Grace wrote down both names. She let Kyle sit for a moment before gathering her paperwork, signifying the interview was over.

SIXTY-NINE

Nick thought it best that Grace interview Trent Gibson, so she grabbed a quick cuppa while she updated the team. After their showdown, Alex had left the building. Nick had been trying to contact him on his mobile, to get him to come back to the station. So far his efforts had proved futile. Officers had been sent to his home address to bring him in. She wouldn't put it past him doing a runner, although that would be pointless too.

When she explained the circumstances behind Alex's absence, after a shocked silence, anger erupted from his colleagues. Grace couldn't blame any of them and was grateful she managed to appease them, getting their minds back on the job for now.

In the interview room again, she lifted the lid to her laptop and showed Trent the images they had captured from CCTV.

'Do you recognise yourself on here?' she asked.

Trent sat forward and studied them. He looked up through long eyelashes.

'Naw, I don't know any of them.'

'Not even this one?' Grace pointed to another image.

Trent shook his head.

'It clearly shows you, Trent. You're saying you weren't on Victoria Road at ten p.m. on Saturday night?'

Trent shook his head again. 'That image doesn't prove anything except that I had something to eat with my mates.'

'Okay.' Grace produced an evidence bag containing a pair of black gloves. 'Do you recognise these?'

Trent glanced sideways at the duty solicitor before turning back. 'No comment,' he replied.

Grace shrugged. 'Ah, well. I'll get them processed and you can go back to your cell. I'm sure they'll have some DNA on them, maybe blood from Elliott's vicious attack. The clothes we'll be seizing from your flat might have too. Then it won't look good when we do find it and you haven't cooperated with us. In fact, it's going to make you seem extremely devious when you've denied it's you in the image and it's plain that it *is* you. I doubt a judge will like that once you're thrown in front of one.'

'You Steeles are all the same. You're trying to set me up!'

'I am not a Steele.' Grace tried to stay calm.

'You could have fooled me,' Trent muttered. 'The Steele women are all stronger than they look.'

'Elliott Woodman was beaten to death. I'm only interested in his killer.' Grace watched him flinch at her last word. 'Was it Leon Steele who paid you?'

Trent looked straight ahead at the wall behind her. 'No comment.'

'You do know we have camera footage of Leon getting off the train at Stoke Station? The train from London? So he couldn't have committed the murder.'

'That doesn't prove anything. He could have got on the stop before.'

'It was a straight-through train from Euston. It takes just over an hour and a half. He has a solid alibi. It wasn't him.'

'No comment.'

'Who was it, Trent?'

Trent glared at her. 'I want to speak to my brief – alone.'

And then it dawned on her. She had been so busy focusing on the Steele brothers that she hadn't been able to see what was staring at her.

'You were trying to set Leon Steele up!' she cried.

'No comment.' Trent squirmed in his seat.

'I get it now. With him going away for the murder of Elliott Woodman, and Josh Parker gone too, it would mean you could work next to Eddie. Fancy yourself as a hard man, did you?'

Trent wouldn't even look at her as she continued.

'But now that Leon can prove he wasn't in Stoke at the time of the murder, your plan has backfired.' Grace shook her head slowly. 'I wouldn't like to be you when everyone finds out what you've done, especially the Steele family. You'll have one hell of a black mark against your name.'

Still Trent said nothing.

'You'd be better off going inside! Although actually, come to think of it, someone is bound to find out what happened. Cons don't like betrayals.'

After a few more attempts to get him to admit what he'd done, Grace closed her notebook. 'If you're not going to talk, there's nothing further I can do for you,' she told him. 'You'll be returned to your cell until we have the evidence we require. I suggest you use the time wisely to have a word with Mr Patrick here. A confession will work much more in your favour. As soon as word gets out, we can't protect you if you don't play ball.'

She was almost at the door when she heard him speak.

'It was me.'

She turned to see Trent holding his head in his hands. 'I killed Elliott.'

Back at her desk, Grace sat down with a sigh. It was great that they'd got a confession for Elliott Woodman's murder, yet she couldn't help but feel unhappy about it.

'Why do they let themselves get dragged into such atrocities?' she sighed.

Perry looked up at her. 'Who really knows?'

Grace took a mouthful from a full mug of coffee, grimacing when she discovered it was cold. She checked her mobile, suddenly remembering the handset having vibrated in her pocket while she was interviewing Trent Gibson. Dialling voice-mail now, it was a message from Eddie.

I can't find Leon. His wife hasn't seen him since last night. He's not answering his phone from either of us and he hasn't shown up for work. I've rung everywhere I think he might be and no one has seen him. I'm worried about him. Call me back. Please.

SEVENTY

Grace's blood ran cold as her thoughts jumbled together, something that Trent had said in the interview about strong women had set her thinking. She raced over to Nick's office to find Sam and Perry already with him.

'I've been tearing through the numbers on Gibson's phones with the tech team,' Sam said before she could speak. 'Clara Emery's phone number is on there obviously, as they're a couple; it's also on Leon Steele's phone, but that makes sense as they both work at the gym. So, could be something or nothing, but Chapman's is there too, under Jonathan this time – and there is a list of other numbers we have no names for but which appear on all three phones. The tech team are looking at them now. It's just a hunch, but I wonder if she's been involved in the parties – perhaps stocking up, cleaning, getting the girls there. After all, she works for the Steeles.'

Grace thought back to the young woman Regan Peters had mentioned who had paid her as she quickly scanned down the list.

'There's a number that they've all rung too, but it's unavailable,'

342

Sam added. 'It's a pay-as-you-go option, and untraceable. Out of service.'

'Good work,' Nick said. 'Bring Emery in for questioning.'

Grace nodded. 'I'll also apply for warrants to search both hers and Gibson's flats. But she's not top priority right now.' She played Eddie's message on speaker.

'Listen up!' Nick ushered them all into the meeting room where they could see the whiteboard.

'Nick, can I run something past everyone?'

When he nodded, Grace stood in front of them. She took a deep breath and began, hoping she had the trust of her team. Several officers working with them came to listen too.

'Let's take the victims in order.' She pointed to the first photo on the whiteboard beside her. 'Josh Parker. According to quite a few women we spoke to, plus statements from the public, he was handy with his fists, not just on men but on men. We also have reason to believe he was involved in organising the parties at Washington Place.' She pointed to another photo. 'Dale Chapman – also known as Dale Jenkinson. We think he was being blackmailed for something. We also believe he raped Regan Peters at one of the parties.

'Victim number three.' She pointed to the image of Tom Davenport. 'He didn't really have a lot to do with Steele's Gym, which threw us off a little, but through interviewing several young women, we've found he's part of a ring of men who are luring young girls to these parties. We also know he was having an affair with at least one of his students at the college. So, we see a connection between all three victims: the parties.

'Victim number four – Elliot Woodman. We thought it was one of the Steele clan attacking a rival family in revenge for the first murders, but I think we were wrong-footed. After interviewing Gibson, it seems he was setting up Leon Steele for the murder of Elliott Woodman so that he could muscle in with Eddie and be his right-hand man. But it backfired on him. So, what if that murder was a red herring?'

People began to glance at each other as things started to click into place.

'Let's go back to one of our original ideas,' Grace continued. 'Footwear, smallish size – shoe prints found at the homes of Dale Chapman and Tom Davenport were a match.' She used her fingers to count off. 'Images of a slight and nimble figure running away from Dale Chapman's murder scene. A blunt object used to attack them. Identical knife wounds. And then there's another victim, one not on the board: George Steele.'

Before anyone could interject, Grace opened a laptop that was on the desk, pressed a few keys and brought up an image of a pair of purple neoprene-grip hand weights. She turned the screen round to face everyone.

'This is something people can use during walking or aerobic exercise, shaped to be held easily in their hand. Look at it – isn't it similar to a knuckleduster? Especially if it was held the wrong way round, so the weight was at the front.' She demonstrated by balling her hand into a fist and rubbing her knuckles. 'Imagine how hard a punch could be administered then, even if the person throwing it was smaller than the victim – a woman, for example?'

'It would put some force behind it,' Sam agreed.

'You think the link is to a female who attended one of the parties?' Perry questioned animatedly as he caught her drift.

'No.' Grace glanced around the room while she took another deep breath, emotion threatening to spill over at the discomfort of what she was about to voice. 'But I do think it has something to do with the parties. I think they've been happening on and off for years. Whether or not the Steeles are running them now remains to be seen. But I think one of the

Steeles set them up: George Steele. George had the necessary contacts to start something like this. What if the person who killed George is now targeting other men involved?'

'Kathleen Steele had plenty of motive to kill George. She was a victim of continual domestic abuse. However, Kathleen doesn't have motive or links to the other three victims. But Jade Steele does.'

Murmurs spread amongst them and Grace held up her hand.

'Jade Steele told me she'd had a fling with Josh Parker in her early teens and had left him because he was too violent. Maybe she found out about the parties too. I wonder if it was Jade who was blackmailing Chapman – Jenkinson, whatever his name is – about his involvement in them? It would ruin his reputation if it got out. He'd pay a lot of money for that, I reckon.'

Nick was up on his feet and at her side.

'Jade mentioned she'd had a few dates with Tom Davenport. She also told me he was a lovely man and she got on well with him, but that was probably a lie to throw me off her scent. And Lorna is Jade's friend.'

'Do you think she got worried for Megan Steele, hanging around with Freya Davenport?' asked Sam.

'Yes.' Grace went over to the whiteboard. She pointed to where the name of her half-sister was written in capital letters. 'Jade Steele has the upper hand because every one of our victims knew her. She could get close without rousing suspicion before attacking them. And let's face it, everyone thinks she's dizzy; the weakling, the underdog.' Grace thought back to Jade's allegations about Alex. 'And now Leon Steele has gone missing . . . I don't think Kathleen would kill her own son, not even to protect her daughter.' Grace looked around the room at them all. 'Which again leaves Jade.'

'If Leon is involved with the parties, Jade might be planning on killing him next – if he isn't dead already.' Nick snapped his fingers. 'I want all available units out there looking for both of them. Let's bring her in now!'

'She called me earlier, wanting to see me. I think I know where she'll be.' Grace took a deep breath. 'I think she wants to lead me back home.'

SEVENTY-ONE

Kathleen had been in Posh Gloss when the police had arrived and asked Clara to accompany them to the station for questioning. Then, hearing from Eddie that Leon was missing, she'd locked up the salon and driven straight home.

So many thoughts were running through her mind as she negotiated the traffic: how this was all getting out of hand now; how she couldn't protect her family any more.

As she turned into the driveway, she noticed Jade's car in front of the door. She parked next to it and rushed inside.

'Jade?' she shouted.

'I'm upstairs.'

Kathleen hurried up to her. She found her in a dressing gown, her hair wet.

'You haven't just got up, have you?' she asked. 'It's nearly midday.'

'Of course not.' Jade rubbed at her hair with a towel. 'You're home early.'

'I tried to call you. No one can find Leon.' Kathleen's voice faltered.

'Oh, sorry, I must have missed your call when I was under

the water.' Jade glanced at her mobile she'd thrown down on the bed.

'Have you seen him, or spoken to him today?'

'Not since yesterday at work. Why?'

'I'm worried about him. What if someone has hurt him and he's—'

'You shouldn't be concerned with him,' Jade screamed. 'You should have helped me!'

It took Kathleen by surprise and she flinched.

'What do you mean?' It was then she noticed the clothes in a pile behind Jade. A pair of jeans with wet patches deep red in colour. A pale blue jumper covered with speckles of blood. 'What's that?'

'I cut myself this morning.' Jade looked at her sheepishly.

'Where? That's a lot of blood. Are you all right?'

'Of course I am. Don't start worrying about me now.'

Kathleen paled. 'You haven't done anything to Leon, have you?'

'Why would you care? You're not interested in anyone but yourself!' Jade pulled on jeans and a jumper as she spoke.

'Tell me, Jade.' Kathleen pointed to the clothes. 'What have you done?'

'I've finished your precious son off.' Jade sat on the bed and slipped on a pair of boots. 'You do realise he started those parties up again?'

'What parties?'

'Oh, come off it, you knew all about them.'

'No, I . . .' Kathleen stopped, all at once putting the pieces together. 'I didn't know. I swear!'

'I wasn't having anyone suffering what I went through as a child. He deserved what he got!'

'Leon wasn't involved with the girls. He was just taking the money!'

348

Jade shook her head. 'Oh, what do you know!'

'I heard him talking to Eddie. He didn't like what had happened and said he was stopping the parties now.'

'Only because the police have cottoned on to him.'

'No, it's not like—'

'Save your breath, Mother. He's gone now. They're all gone. I finished them *all* off.'

Kathleen went cold, goosebumps breaking out all over her skin. Surely, no – not again. She wouldn't be able to protect Jade if this was true.

'Wait a minute!' Her eyes bulged as Jade's words sunk in. '*You* killed all those men?'

Jade raised her eyebrows. 'You sound surprised? As if I don't have it in me.'

'No, that's not what—'

'I know what people think about me, but they're wrong.' A snarl crossed Jade's face as she stood up and crossed the room towards her. 'I told you years ago that I would get Jenkinson back for what he did to me. When I heard about those sex parties starting up, well, I began to think about *all* of the men who had let me down. Who used me, abused me, and then moved on to other victims to do the same.' She slammed a fist into an open palm at each point. 'I wasn't even thirteen, the first time Dale raped me. Remember that?'

'Oh, Jade,' Kathleen began.

'I told you it was happening and you said not to say anything.'

'It wasn't like that,' she insisted. 'If you'd told anyone, things would have been much worse!'

'Dale got my trust, you see,' Jade continued as if she wasn't there. 'He used Rohypnol at first, and then, for kicks, there were no drugs at all. He said I would be better after being worn in. All I can remember was being sore, and bleeding afterwards. Not being able to walk properly. And you did nothing!'

349

'I was weak,' Kathleen tried to explain. 'Your father and his friends were too powerful for me. George used me too, to pay off his debts. I was trapped as well.' She hesitated, as if trying to find the right words. 'I'm sorry – I should have done more. But it doesn't mean you have to keep killing people! You need to finish this. It's got out of hand! You can't keep on—'

'I can do whatever I want.'

The phone on the bed began to ring. Grace's name flashed up on the screen. They both saw it.

'The police could have worked out what you've done! Jade, please.' Kathleen took hold of her arm. 'You have to tell me where Leon is.'

Jade shrugged it away. 'Let go of me.'

'You need help! We can sort out something for you. Don't worry about Megan. She can come and stay with me until you feel better.'

It was as if the light went out of Jade's eyes at the mention of her daughter. Kathleen had hoped it would appease her, make her realise that Megan would be well cared for. But it seemed to have the opposite effect.

'You are not having my daughter!' Jade screeched.

'But it's for the best, don't you see?'

'She's not for sale!'

Kathleen paled. 'I didn't mean I was going to—'

Seeing the look on Jade's face, she stepped back, moving towards the door as Jade lunged at her. She ran out to the landing heading for the stairs. The front door was open. She must have forgotten to close it in her haste to find Jade. If she could get down the stairs and into her car, she might be able to escape.

Before she could get a hand to the banister, Jade pushed her hard in the back. Kathleen flew forward, losing her footing, and fell head first down the stairs. Her shoulder connected with the wall, and she landed with a nauseating thud on the ground floor. Her right leg crumpled beneath her.

'You should have protected me!' Jade screamed behind her.

Grace drove to Hardman House in a convoy, emergency sirens on full pelt and lights flashing as they rushed to the scene. Jade wasn't answering her phone, so patrol cars had been sent to her home address, as well as to Steele's Gym.

Perry turned to her as she negotiated a corner sharply. 'What would be her motive to attack Leon? Could he really be involved in those parties?'

It didn't sit right with Grace. 'I'm not sure,' she replied.

'Do you believe he harmed Jade as a child?'

'Not sexually, but perhaps in other ways.'

'So Leon missing means what?'

'I think he's probably dead.' Grace took a gulp of breath as emotion rushed through her at the thought. She glanced at Perry as she negotiated the road. 'We have to stop her from killing anyone else. We need to find Kathleen Steele – and Jade's daughter, Megan. Eddie too. She could go after any one of them.'

They were at the house.

'The front door is open.' Grace brought the car to a halt in the driveway.

They scrambled out, flicking out batons and, with caution, went inside. Kathleen Steele was lying at the bottom of the stairs, her leg at a peculiar angle underneath her. Blood trickled down her face from a cut to the head.

Jade was stooping over her mother. She froze for a second when she saw them.

'Stop. Police!' Grace shouted.

But Jade ran down the hallway away from them. Grace went after her, Nick and Perry close behind. She could hear Sam already on her radio calling for an ambulance for Kathleen.

'Jade! Stop.'

Jade was in the back garden by the time they ran through the kitchen. Grace could remember running through the garden as a small child, but had she been running away from George Steele? Or had she been happy, roaming freely? Had she ever been happy at this house?

But then her mum appeared in the memory and she was in front of her and she was laughing. And she knew it was a happy memory. It was what she needed.

Come on, Grace, you can do this.

Grace pointed towards the garage. All the time, she tried not to think of her childhood. The fear of going down the path, dragged to that place, of being shut in that room. Seeing it now reminded her of everything George had put her through; how much she had suffered at the hands of the man who had fathered her.

She pushed aside these thoughts as she raced forward. Nick was already heading into the garage. Grace followed him inside, Perry behind her.

Palpitations shot through her and she tried desperately to control her breathing as her fingers began to tingle.

Breathe, Grace.

This had been the place in her nightmares. She prayed the only thing that had gone on in there since she'd left was kids being locked up. Nothing else, please, nothing else.

Inside, the side walls were lined with shelving units filled with rusty tools, boxes of screws and nails, paint tins, DIY paraphernalia. The remnants of yesteryears, the smell of musty air. Light flooded through a gap in the roof, but everywhere else remained dark.

'Where is she?' Nick asked, trying to see in the darkness. 'Is there a light anywhere?'

Grace remembered where the switch was and pressed it

352

down. The single bulb was dim, but at least it illuminated the space a little.

'Can you remember this?' Perry whispered as they stepped forward cautiously again.

'Yes, this was the workshop. She'll be in there.' Grace pointed to the back. 'There's hidden access.'

They inched forward. Nick found the door and pushed it open, the smell of faeces flooding the air. As their eyes grew accustomed to the dark again, they focused on what they could see.

Grace struggled not to throw up. There was the single bed that she had slept on many nights as a child. A naked man was bound to the headboard by each wrist, his feet held together with tape that was then stretched down to the bottom of the bed and secured. Blood covered his face, his head lolling to one side. Around his mouth was tied a scarf. He groaned loudly, pulling at the binding on his wrists.

When he turned towards them, Grace gasped. It wasn't Leon. It was Alex.

SEVENTY-TWO

Jade stood beside Alex, a knife in her hand. Dried blood covered most of the blade.

'You have no right to be in here!' she screamed.

Nick stepped inside, Grace beside him. She put her hands out in front, eyes flitting around the room.

'Whatever Alex did to you, you don't have to worry about him any more,' Grace said.

'Get everyone out of my room!'

'I can't do that, Jade,' Nick spoke slowly. 'Unless you put down the knife.'

'I only want to talk to my sister.'

'Then put the knife down.'

'No!' Jade began to wail.

Grace knew by now the place would be surrounded. They just needed to calm Jade down enough to arrest her. Then they could ask her about Leon. It was too risky to mention his name yet. Jade was irrational enough to fly at any of them with that knife. They had all seen first-hand what she was capable of. And if they could move out of the way of the blade, they might be able to take her down, but what if she lunged at Alex? He

354

wasn't able to defend himself. It was too dark in there to risk that.

'Did you like the toys I sent to you?' Jade asked.

Her laughter chilled Grace to the bone, but she nodded her head.

'Pretty neat that Alex delivered them, huh? Did it bring back terrible memories?'

Grace nodded again. This seemed to make Jade happy and she laughed once more.

'I always had hand-me-downs. Yours or my brothers'. I hardly ever had anything of my own. Daddy didn't like me enough.'

'George was a horrible man and you didn't deserve what happened to you, Jade,' Grace said softly.

'Don't come all preachy on me. And where were you, Grace? Because when you left, he turned on me.'

'I'm . . . I'm sorry.' Grace's tone was gentle. 'But you weren't the only daughter he hurt.'

'You never had to meet Mr Jenkinson though, did you?' Jade had a tear running down the side of her face.

Grace glanced at Nick, wondering when to make her move.

'Jade,' Nick said, 'don't you think you—'

'Shut the fuck up!' Jade's eyes almost popped out of their sockets as she screeched. 'This is family business. If you don't listen to me' – she pointed the knife at Alex – 'then I will stab him in the heart and it will be your fault.'

'No more violence, please!' Grace stepped forward with her hands held out in front of her.

Jade lunged at her with the knife. Grace shifted to one side, losing her footing and falling to the floor. She rolled, landing with a thump against the wall. Pain erupted inside her head as it connected with the leg of a workbench.

'Now look what you made me do!' Jade ran towards the bed with the knife raised in the air.

Nick rushed towards her, his baton elevated, but Grace jumped to her feet and brought Jade down with a rugby tackle. The knife clattered across the floor while she held on to her feet. Jade struggled and kicked out, the heel of her boot smashing into Grace's cheekbone.

As Grace's grip loosened momentarily, Jade scrambled away from them. But Perry and Nick pulled Jade back to the floor and Grace quickly straddled her torso to keep her down. She pushed Jade's face into the ground. Jade wriggled underneath her as Grace got out her cuffs and put them around her wrists. She snapped them shut with satisfaction. They had got her.

'Jade Steele, I'm arresting you for the murder of Josh Parker, Dale Chapman, Tom Davenport and George Steele, for the assault on Kathleen Steele and Alex Challinor, and in connection with the disappearance of Leon Steele,' Grace said. 'You do not have to say anything. But it may harm your defence if you do not mention when questioned something which you later rely on in court. Anything you do say may be given in evidence. Now, get up.'

'You have to let me go, Grace,' Jade said as they caught their breath.

'Where is Leon? What have you done with him?'

Jade gave Grace a half-smile. 'We could have been close if that bastard hadn't done what he did to us. Will you come and see me in prison?'

Grace stayed quiet.

'Will you, Gracie? I'll be scared on my own.' Jade looked over her shoulder as she was marched away. 'Please! I need something to look forward to. Don't leave me, Grace! Please!'

Grace held on to the door frame to stop her legs from giving way as everything came rushing back to her.

SEVENTY-THREE

Then

'Here,' George said to her, handing her a bag. 'I've bought you a nice dress and some new shoes. Try them on for me.'

She took the bag from him, looking inside to find a number of items. She pulled out a checked pinafore. There was a white blouse, sandals and ankle socks too. She hadn't worn ankle socks in a good while.

There was something else. She pulled out two pieces of red ribbon and a teddy bear.

'I want you to tie your hair up in bunches,' he said. 'Then we're going out. Bring the teddy with you. I'll be back in ten minutes.'

'Where are we going, Daddy?' she asked.

'Somewhere special. Now, hurry. We don't want to be late.'

Once he had left the room, she dressed quickly. Everything was in the bag. There were even white knickers and a vest. She hadn't worn a vest in ages, but she put it on anyway.

Her hair was difficult to tie up, but she did her best. She was sitting on her bed waiting for him when he got back and stood up as soon as he came in.

'Let me look at you.' He was in front of her, nodding. 'Yes, that will do. Come on then, follow me.'

It took them about ten minutes to get to their destination. She wasn't familiar with the house they stopped at but, as he drove along its gravelled driveway, she noticed it was huge, extremely elegant and she eyed it with awe.

But when she got out of the car, something told her she shouldn't go inside and her feet refused to move.

'Go on.' George shoved her hard in the back. 'And remember, you need to do what you're told and behave yourself for these gentlemen. You show me up and you're for it, do you hear me, Jade?'

SEVENTY-FOUR

As the medics rushed in to attend to Alex, Grace found herself unable to move. Tears were on her face as she realised that Jade had not been truthful about everything that had happened to her. If she had, then maybe Grace might have been able to stop her earlier. The toys had been sent to tease her, but they were also a cry for help, to be found out, to be stopped. Everyone, including Grace herself, had thought they'd been sent by the family to taunt her. Why hadn't she acted sooner?

Luckily for Grace, her experience with her father and all it had entailed had ended the minute she had been removed from the property. For Jade, the nightmare was still continuing.

She glanced around the room, the smell overwhelming her. The darkness engulfing her, the memories in every corner coming out to get her. This had been her hell. She could remember the sting of his hand, the roar of his voice, the tears of frustration when she hadn't done anything to deserve the treatment she got.

But most of all she remembered the mother who had been brave enough to lead them both to safety. She'd been asleep in this room that night and she'd been woken by a noise. She recalled the lock being undone on the door and the light coming on. She'd pulled herself up the bed and into the corner of the room, her back to the wall.

'Grace?' her mum whispered. 'Grace, come quickly.'

Grace ran across the room.

'We don't have too much time.'

She put on the shoes Mum handed to her, and then Mum helped her with her coat too. By her side were two suitcases.

'Are we leaving?' she whispered.

'Yes, but we must be quiet. We don't want to wake him before we're gone.'

They got to the front door and Mum turned to her. 'I'm so sorry, Grace,' she said, tears pouring down her face. 'I've let you down by being here too long, but now I have enough money and courage to find a way without him. I just wish you hadn't suffered too.'

Grace didn't say anything but hugged her mum tightly. 'I love you, Mum,' she whispered.

'I love you too, Grace.' She took her hand. 'Are you ready?'

'Ready.'

Mum pulled back the lock. Grace half expected her father to be standing at the other side of the door as it was opened. She imagined the grip of his hand on her hair and the thud of her back hitting the wall, just like it had done earlier, before he'd almost thrown her in the garage. But there was no one there.

They both went out, closing the door quietly behind them, and rushed down the path. They ran for a few minutes, out of their road and around the corner. There was a car waiting for them, a taxi. She heard her mum sob as they ran towards it.

Once they were inside it and on their way, Mum held her close and ran a hand over her hair. 'I want you to remember this moment, Grace. This is where our lives there end and our new futures – brighter futures – begin.'

'Are you okay?' Perry asked, coming over to her.

'I will be.' Grace nodded, her eyes misting over with tears.

'This is so bleak. I don't know how anyone can get over anything like this.'

'Maybe they don't.' Grace blew out a breath before speaking again. 'The night before we left for good, George brought home a man. He said he'd taken a shine to me and I remember hearing him arguing with my mum. She seemed so scared.'

'He didn't—'

'No.' She shook her head vehemently. 'It took another ten years before she told me George was in debt and the man was willing to take me to his bed for a few nights and the debt would be clear. George had agreed. That could have been Chapman. I was twelve years old.'

Perry put an arm around her shoulders. She could see his face darkening as she spoke.

'That was the reason why we left so quickly,' she said. 'George was going to sell me for his own needs. Jade must have found out that the parties had started up again, and it tipped her over the edge.'

On a shelving unit was a hand weight similar to the image she had brought up online. A purple covering was stained with a darker substance. Grace pointed at it.

Perry drew her close as she burst into tears.

SEVENTY-FIVE

Grace sat in the interview room beside Nick. The duty solicitor was Mitchell Patrick. Sitting next to him, Jade was playing with her hair, flicking a portion of it over and around her index finger. Her eyes looked wild as she stared at Grace, her smile manic.

The interview was started. The plan was for Nick to lead, and Grace to help when necessary. If Jade would only speak to Grace, and she could get her talking, then Nick would stay quiet. Upstairs, the team were watching on video link, ready at the drop of a hat to go and find Leon, if they could get his location from Jade. Dead or alive, they had to find him.

'Jade, can you tell me where your brother Leon is?' Nick started. 'It's imperative we find him, see if he is all right, as no one has seen him since—'

'I'm not speaking to you,' Jade interrupted. 'I will only speak to Gracie.'

'I have to stay here, Jade,' Nick said. 'We can't conduct this interview without two officers.'

'Liar!'

'Where were you on the night of Tuesday—'

'I was in bed with Graham Frost,' Jade cut in again. 'Everyone's favourite alibi.'

As Jade's laughter filled the room, Grace shuddered inwardly. It chilled her when Jade's eyes landed on her again.

'I won't speak to anyone but Grace,' she demanded.

'I'm here.' Grace sat forward. 'You can tell me anything.'

'Like what?'

'Well, apart from knowing where Leon is, and if he's safe, I'd like to know how you are.'

Jade stopped playing with her hair and glared at her. 'You don't care about me. You've never cared. No one has.'

Grace let her speak. She wasn't sure whether to appease her, agree with her, or disagree with her, say that she was loved. She wasn't sure because she really didn't know.

'Would you like to talk to me about it?' she offered.

'Sure.' Jade leaned forward. 'But if I start telling you what happened, then you are going to listen to all of it, and it's not nice to hear. Are you sure?'

Grace wanted to say no. She didn't want to hear anything that would bring back memories for her too, but she nodded. This was all about finding Leon now. She had to remember the rapport she had built with Jade previously. And she had to ask the question that they all wanted to know.

'Yes, I'm sure.' Grace nodded. 'Go right back to the beginning for me, from the moment that you killed your father.'

The room dropped into silence. Nick glanced at Grace surreptitiously as Jade gnawed at her bottom lip.

'I thought all the pain would stop when I killed him,' Jade confessed.

'Who?' Grace wanted a name.

'Our father, Grace.'

'George Steele?' she pressed.

'Yes! Keep up.'

As she and Jade stared at each other afterwards, Grace could imagine her team upstairs, punching the air but wanting to stay quiet to listen to every word Jade said. This was clearly just the beginning.

'He started it all,' Jade added. 'He locked me in the garage, brought a man to abuse me when I was twelve years old and then, when that wasn't enough, he took me to a house so other men could abuse me too. He wasn't content to whore me out to just the one once I got used to it.'

Grace tried not to flinch at Jade's words; they were hard to hear.

'While he was around, Megan wasn't safe, was she?' Grace continued.

'No. And even more so since they'd started the parties up again. I was damaged goods at sixteen and didn't have to go to any more. But when I realised they were still happening, I thought I would put a stop to them by killing Daddy.' She smiled. 'It was the first time I ever felt powerful, you know? Daddy used to make the boys fight each other all the time. He had nicknames for them, rather than call them by their first names. Little Runt was what he used to call Leon. Eddie was known as Twatface. How cruel was that? Daddy said it was to toughen them up, make them hard so they could continue with the career he had made for them.'

Grace hadn't heard any of this and wondered what kick George Steele got out of it, what had started the regime off in the first place. Had his parents abused him as a young boy? Would she ever find out if so?

'And Leon?' she queried. 'Did you attack him?'

'Don't interrupt, Gracie.' Jade glared at her. 'As well as set the boys on to each other, George used to make them beat me up too. It was always Leon who hit me the hardest. Eddie used to look out for me, but Leon was just plain old mean.'

Silence again as Grace struggled to speak.

'Where is Leon, Jade?' Nick asked, his tone gentle.

'Do you know all the dead have secrets?' Jade looked at him, almost as if she had forgotten he was there until that moment. 'Josh was my first love but he treated me really bad. He beat me up, when all I wanted was to be loved.'

'Did he like young girls too?'

'I didn't think so, but I didn't actually realise he was involved in the parties until I overheard him and Leon talking one night. Josh was saying how they were bringing in easy money, but Leon was arguing that the girls were young and naive. Josh told him not to worry, that they would be looked after. It wasn't hard to work out what was going on from that. I bet there would have been some older women there, but they were using them girls, I'm sure of it. Because *I* was told I would be looked after all those years ago and look what happened to me!'

'So you got your revenge by throwing acid in his face?' Grace had to know why.

'Not exactly. Have you seen the size of him?' Jade's eyes flitted between them. 'I needed to make sure he would go down, because killing him would cause such mayhem, as well as bring attention to that bloody gym. I watched him writhe around on the floor, heard his screams. He deserved everything he got.

'He was always going on about the things that he had done. The image he'd created of himself was pathetic. He had to have the most expensive car, the best job, the prettiest woman on his arm, even though he was married. He thought he was top man and could muscle his way into everything. He wasn't. He used to beat me, make me cry, make me *beg* for him to love me, and he knew what I'd gone through as a child. I hope he rots in hell for what he did.'

'How did you get away, after you'd killed him?' Grace asked as Jade took a breath.

'I slipped out of the back of the gym car park, over the fence and into the field behind.' Jade used her fingers on the desk to indicate her walking. 'It was quiet. Josh had stopped screaming once I'd stabbed him. I ran to the canal towpath. There were so many places I could go from there.' Jade laughed again, turning to Grace. 'I couldn't believe how calm I was when I threw the acid at him. And when he recognised me just before, pure gold!'

There was silence in the room again. It was hard to take it in; what Jade was saying was so cold. Grace knew they needed to ask about Leon, but she also knew they weren't going to get anything from Jade until she was ready. So they would let her confess to everything first, to get to what they wanted.

SEVENTY-SIX

'We need to take a break,' said Mitchell, checking his watch and sitting forward.

'I'm fine!' Jade roared, making him sit back again. 'Chapman – number three! Just like the last time, I was a ninja in the dark. It's a good job I'm fit though, as I had to run for my life after killing Dale. I was covered in blood. All those years of pent-up frustration and taking those beatings had made me capable of that. He had gone down so easy with that first hit. The look on his face had been priceless. I mean, me making him feel like that!'

Jade's eyes were wide with delight, as if she was proud of herself.

'I never thought it would be such a frenzied attack,' she went on. 'After killing Josh with the knife, I'd planned on doing that to the others. I hit Dale a few times with the weight to get the upper hand, but that wasn't enough. It felt so good to just hit him and hit him and hit him.' Jade banged her hand down on the desk, making everyone jump. 'I had to stop myself from throwing up when I looked at where his face had been.'

Grace tried not to retch too.

'Once I'd caught my breath, I got out my knife.' Jade made a stabbing notion in the air. 'I plunged it into his heart, just like he'd once stabbed a knife through mine and ruined my chances to have a normal life. Then I leapt off him. I knew there were cameras on me, so I'd been careful to shield my face, keep my back to the lens as I took his brains out. It was a good job Megan was staying at my mum's that night, I can tell you! There was blood all over me and my clothes! But I'd planned for this. I had brought more clothes just in case this happened. So I got rid of the bloodstained ones quickly.'

'How?'

'I just threw them in the bin!' She giggled. 'It was collection day. I hid everything inside a black plastic bag and put other rubbish on top of it. It was easy-peasy.'

Grace sat back in resignation as she worked out the missing links. The real reason why the attack on Chapman had been so vicious. The money being paid out from his account. The age Jade would have given birth to her daughter.

'Dale Chapman is Megan's father,' Grace said quietly.

Jade nodded vehemently. 'Can you imagine that getting out? Of course, he always denied it. So I made him pay me – a thousand a month. I hated seeing him at the gym, but at least I had something I wanted from him now, so it made it more bearable. Then he refused to give me any more. Well, I wasn't having that. He was rich. He wouldn't miss it. But I needed it.'

'And Tom Davenport?' Grace queried. 'You told me that you liked him. That wasn't true, was it?'

'All lies, Gracie. You are so gullible,' Jade sneered. 'You thought I was pregnant by that loser, Alex, too.' She shook her head. 'I don't think so.'

Grace kept her face straight. It probably wouldn't be the last time she'd find out that Jade had tricked her.

'He didn't rape you, did he?'

'Of course not,' Jade told her. 'Besides, there is no baby.' She laughed. 'Everyone thinks he's been using me, but it's the other way round. He was good in bed, I'll give him that, and we had so much fun sharing our knowledge.' She huffed. 'But in the end he rejected me, like everyone else did. And so he had to pay for that.'

'Tom Davenport, Jade?' Grace wanted to keep her on point.

'When I found out about Washington Place, and that the parties were still going on, I had to do something!'

'How did you find out about the house?'

'I saw him with a young girl one night and followed him – it was him that led me there. I couldn't believe it when I saw Josh and Leon's cars parked in the driveway. That's when I realised what was going on. So I kept an eye on things for a while. When Tom finished with that girl, he started knocking off another one at the college he worked at. I thought Lorna deserved better than that. And she needed to know what he was like.'

'So you left the card at his house.'

Jade nodded.

'And you stole Charlotte Maidley's bag. Why did you try and set someone else up?'

'You were too *good*, Grace. You were catching up with me quicker than I had intended. I wanted to have some fun first.'

'And Tom?'

'I hid in their garden. We argued and I hit out at him. Tom lost his footing and fell backwards into the pond.'

'He was alive when he hit the water,' Grace said.

'Oh, I knew that. I could see his head had come up, so I forced it under again. I watched him for a few seconds, and then I stabbed him.'

Grace couldn't believe how heartless she was. She had certainly fooled a lot of people.

'But then Lorna came out,' she said.

'Yes! I had to get past her, so I pulled down my balaclava before she saw it was me. And then I hit her and pushed her. I was so sorry she got hurt. But, don't you see, I did my best friend a favour! I saw Megan and Freya's names in that black book, and I wasn't letting them do that. They weren't getting my daughter too.'

'Black book?' Grace wondered if this would be vital evidence as to who had been at the parties.

'It was in Clara's handbag. Leon had it on him the last time I saw him. You'll see it soon.'

Grace pushed down her emotions. She felt like kicking out at something, anything to get rid of the pain. Jade had used her. She hadn't wanted to get to know her at all. Grace had been foolish – and it hurt.

'Is Leon alive, Jade?' Nick joined in once more.

Jade stared at him.

'Did you . . .' Grace stumbled. 'Did you kill him too?'

'A stab to the heart,' Jade said. 'I didn't beat him too much though. There wasn't time.'

A sob escaped Grace. 'Are we looking for a body?'

Jade smiled slowly.

Tears formed in Grace's eyes and she let them fall. 'Please, Jade, you have to tell me where I can find him.'

'Don't cry, Gracie.' Jade reached across the table and stroked the back of her hand.

Grace sat forward and put her hand over Jade's. 'I have to know.'

They stared at each other, Grace willing her silently to tell her where he was.

'Please,' she repeated, more tears rolling down her cheeks.

Jade's eyes were watery too. 'Don't cry.'

'Then tell me where he is.'

A loaded silence dropped on the room. Grace never took her eyes from her half-sister.

'Please, Jade!'

'He and Eddie bought a terraced property in Redmond Street, Bradeley,' Jade admitted, finally. 'Number twenty-two. They're doing it up to rent out.'

Grace snatched her hand away from Jade and was out of her chair in a flash.

'Where are you going?' Jade cried after her. 'Hey! Grace!'

Nick followed Grace out of the room called her back as she was about to tear up the corridor.

'Excellent work in there,' he told her. 'But I think you'll be better staying at the station. We'll go and get Leon.'

Grace shook her head. 'No, sir. I have to be there.'

'You're too emotional right now.'

'You think?' She wiped at her cheeks, took a deep breath and smiled. 'Played her at her own game in there. These are crocodile tears.'

SEVENTY-SEVEN

With lights blazing once more, Perry raced across town in a squad car to the address Jade had given Grace. There were several cars behind them and a small police van, every available officer having been on standby.

'Come on!' He banged his hand on the horn at slow traffic. 'Move out of my way!'

'We're too late, anyway,' Grace said, failing to keep the emotion from her voice. 'She will have killed him.'

'You're so sure?'

'Yes. She's cold and calculating. She sucked me in. I can't believe how much I fell for it.'

'You shouldn't beat yourself up about it. Jade had us all fooled.'

Grace disagreed. 'I should have known better.'

'Why? Because she's your sister?' Perry shook his head as he raced across three roundabouts in quick succession in Smallthorne. 'I know it says "Wonder Woman" on your mug but you don't have to live up to its reputation. How would you know?'

'She gave me clues, which I missed.'

'The toys? They wouldn't have led us to her. She was clever to hide her trail, I'll give her that.'

They pulled up in Redmond Street, a row of terraced houses whose doors opened out on to the pavement. The officer from the car behind brandished the enforcer, known as the big red key. Grace banged on the door of number twenty-two.

'Police!' Grace glanced through the window, thick netting hiding clear visibility. But through the intricate lace pattern, she could see into the room. It was unfurnished, bare plaster and floorboards. There was a cement mixer in the middle of the floor, building materials by the side.

She flicked her fingers before snapping on latex gloves. 'Break it down,' she commanded.

The door went in after two bashes.

'Police!' they all shouted as they headed inside.

As rooms downstairs were cleared, Grace and Perry headed upstairs, uniform hot on their tail. But there was no sign of Leon.

Officers were already in the yard, a tiny three metres squared. A sectional garage that could be reached from the entry behind the property took up the rest of the room. Grace gasped – was it coincidence that he was in a garage similar to the one at Hardman House, their childhood home?

Perry opened the side door. Inside was a red hatchback. Grace's stomach gave an almighty lurch as she saw there was someone in the car. A man was slouched, half covered by a blanket. His face was a bloody mess, but she recognised the style of his hair, the two-inch scar just visible to the side of his right eye.

'Leon!' Grace shouted as she opened the rear passenger door. She thought he might have flopped out, but he didn't move.

Perry was round the other side of the car, pulling away the blanket. Leon's feet and hands were secured together with plastic ties, similar to the handcuffs they often used.

Was he dead? She couldn't bring herself to check his pulse, didn't want to find out. Knew she had to.

In the distance, she could hear the sounds of an ambulance. She felt around his neck. Nothing. But then . . .

'There's a pulse,' she cried. 'It's faint, but he's alive!'

SEVENTY-EIGHT

Going back to her childhood home and facing all her demons in one fell swoop had drained Grace completely. But after an investigation as big as this one, there was always so much paperwork to do.

So she was at her desk by half past seven, even after working late the night before. All the evidence needed to be collated for the Crown Prosecution Service. Even without a confession, all procedures had to be meticulously checked to ensure they hadn't messed up gathering crucial evidence that a lawyer would rip apart. Everything had to be in its rightful place so that Jade Steele could be found guilty by a jury. Jade was due in front of the judge that morning. She'd obviously be put on remand. Grace wondered if she would plead not guilty by way of insanity. Either way, she was facing a long time without her freedom.

Grace still didn't know what she thought of that. She couldn't understand yet how she should feel. She wanted to be a police officer, uphold the law, but learning all those things about Jade, and what had happened to her, Eddie and Leon when they were children, made her feel guilty. She had got away, they hadn't.

If her mum hadn't had the strength and courage to up and leave, how different things could have been for her. At least Grace had Martha's determination and grit, and not her father's devious nature and past.

Was she sad that Jade had killed George Steele? It was certainly bittersweet because it triggered so many more murders, but it had allowed Grace to come back to Stoke-on-Trent. The city had got under her skin. She wasn't going to leave again. She liked its diversity, its culture, its beating heart. But she wanted to look out for Jade too. She would keep an eye on her, although she wouldn't let anyone else know.

Kathleen Steele had come away from the fall with a broken leg and a few cuts and bruises, but nothing serious. She'd been released from hospital last night. Megan had gone to stay with Eddie and his family. Grace wondered if she would stay there or go to live with Kathleen while Jade was on remand. No doubt the house would go back to the council once the rent stopped being paid, and the house was unoccupied.

Clara Emery's interview had been enlightening. After checking all the calls and texts on Trent Gibson's phone, and some subtle questioning, she'd confessed to delivering the photographs and tipping off the *Stoke News*, which everyone had assumed had been down to Alex. It seemed as though she was everyone's go-between. Although she couldn't prove it, and Clara wouldn't admit to it, Grace wondered if Clara had been asked by Eddie to take and deliver the photos to put some heat on to her. Either way, Clara was now on charges to pervert the course of justice, and her flat and Trent Gibson's were being searched.

The black book had been found in the back pocket of Leon's jeans. They had scoured it, but technically there wasn't anything they could do with it. The book was full of names, but mostly first names – no addresses next to them, no emails, no mobile numbers. Grace assumed it had been kept that way deliberately because of its operation.

When questioned briefly late last night in hospital, Leon had denied having anything to do with Washington Place. They had nothing to place him there either. They had nothing to place anyone there, but they would question Leon further when he was fit to be interviewed properly. The investigation into the parties had been passed on to the Sexual Exploitation Team for further investigations. Regan Peters was helping them with enquiries. She and Allie had offered to be around for her whenever she needed them.

'Morning,' Sam said as she came to her desk and sat down.

'Hey. Did you manage to get any sleep?'

'Like a baby. I was exhausted.' She smiled. 'Your cheek doesn't seem as puffy today.'

Grace's hand moved to where Jade had kicked out at her. It was still a little tender and bruised, but she had hidden it well with make-up.

'All I can say is I'm glad she wasn't wearing heels.'

Sam smiled and then picked up her mug. 'Want a brew?'

Grace nodded and watched her colleague walk down the office towards their cramped kitchen. She herself had got up during the early hours of the morning and fired up the treadmill, blasting out a quick three miles, hoping it would get rid of the pent-up stress. She'd had to stop several minutes in because she couldn't see for her tears. In the end, she'd given into it and poured out her sorrow. It hadn't eased everything, but it had been cathartic.

Now, it was good to get back to normality. Routine – hot drinks, banter, paperwork. Lots of paperwork. She'd better make a start.

Laughter rang out in the room. She looked up and across the open-plan office that she had come to call home. Grace breathed in the ambience. It was so good to hear. Everyone in this type of role needed to let off steam somehow. The day-to-day jobs that officers were sent to, the things they had to deal with, was it any wonder people were stressed?

Alex's empty seat caught her eye, but she didn't want to think about him. He'd been checked over at the hospital and released a few hours later. He'd cracked after his ordeal with Jade, and everything had come out. How he had been asked by Jade to mess around with Grace and used to find out what was going on during the investigation. However, he denied taking money from Eddie and Leon Steele in return for intel. Of course, everything would be looked into further, and they needed to see if they could gather evidence before approaching Eddie and Leon. Grace didn't know whether she would look forward to that or not.

She was glad now that she had come to Stoke – no matter how hard the past three weeks might make the future for her. She was up for it, ready for whatever the people of Stoke-on-Trent threw at her. And she was ready to string the Steeles up for whatever part they played in anything. *She* would do that. She and her team. Her first role as detective sergeant and the case had been solved. She just prayed the next one wasn't so close to home.

'Morning, boss,' Perry said as he arrived at his desk. He put down the cake tin he'd brought with him. 'Lisa made these.'

'Cakes!' Sam got back to her desk, lifted the lid and oohed.

'Mine is the one with the marshmallows on the top.' Perry pointed out the one he wanted.

'Which one is mine?' Grace asked.

'The one with the star on, of course.' Perry sat down at his desk and switched on his computer.

'I hope there isn't one for Alex,' Sam said. 'Can't say I'll miss him.'

'I don't expect *anyone* will miss him,' Perry agreed.

'Aw, I was actually getting to like the insensitive soul,' Grace grinned.

Perry looked at Grace after a moment. 'So how are you doing?'

'I'm good.' She smiled, realising he was talking about her outburst after Jade had been arrested. 'Thanks.'

'And Eddie?'

'Eddie?' She frowned, unsure what he was getting at.

'Does he still want you to be on his team?'

Grace baulked. How did he know that?

'Allie rang me. She gave me a right bollocking; told me to be kind to you.'

Grace blushed. It seemed she did have friends, after all.

Perry grinned and then his face turned all serious. 'I can't imagine what you went through as a child, but after what you did to get a conviction, I'll always have your back in the job.'

'Me too,' Sam said, smiling at her.

Grace smiled too. It was good to hear at last.

SEVENTY-NINE

Grace left the station early that night and drove through the city traffic to Steele's Gym. After a day of monotony following the recent excitement, her mind had had time to be still, which had given her breathing space.

It was business as usual by the looks of the full car park at six p.m. Life went on, no matter what. It didn't surprise her to see no one manning the reception desk. She marched in and through the gym. She wasn't going to knock on the office door to announce her arrival. Instead, she was going to walk right in.

But she did take a deep breath first.

'You have some nerve coming here,' Eddie growled.

His harsh tone didn't shock her any more.

'How is Leon?'

'He's doing okay.'

'That's good to hear. And Kathleen?'

'Coping. Look, quit with the happy family chatter. What is it that you really want?'

'We need to talk.'

'I've got nothing to say to you.'

'I have plenty to say to you.' She leaned on his desk. 'Did you know what Dale Chapman had done to Jade?'

'Not until years later,' he confessed. 'She never told us he was Megan's father either.'

'You had no idea?' Grace found that hard to believe.

'You have to understand, it was survival of the fittest.' Eddie looked pained. 'We didn't want to know what was going on in case we got dragged into it as well. He locked us up too, in the cupboard under the stairs. I still have a fear of enclosed spaces.'

Grace gulped. George had done that to her before starting to use the garage.

'As far as we knew though, she was just being imprisoned,' Eddie went on. 'That's what Kathleen told us too. I wish I'd done more to help her, and I'll never forgive myself for that.'

'Is that why you lied for your sister?'

Now his face was poker straight.

'You all knew that it was Jade who killed your father, didn't you?'

'Our father.'

'I repeat, *your* father. And answer my question.'

'No comment.' Eddie sat back in his chair.

'It's why none of you pushed the matter when the case went unsolved, isn't it?'

'You have a mighty fine imagination, Grace.'

'Sadly, I can't prove any of that.' Grace didn't rise to the bait. 'But I will be keeping an eye on you. This is my city now – my home – and I want whatever you're doing to stop.'

Eddie smirked. 'You're having a laugh, aren't you?'

'Do you see a smile?' She made a circle around her face with her index finger.

'There really is no Steele in you,' Eddie said snidely.

'Good, because I never want to be a Steele!'

Eddie came from behind his desk. He walked towards her, stopping a few inches away from her face.

He held up his hand. It seemed more of a peace offering than a threat, but she was still wary.

'The offer to join us is still open,' he said.

'Not negotiable.' She pointed a finger in his face. 'I have your cards marked.'

As she turned and left the room, the silence was palpable.

Once she'd closed the door, she marched out of the building. The sky had darkened, but her mood had stayed optimistic. Yet, only when she got into her car did she breathe freely again. Eddie still reminded her of their father, but he didn't scare her as much because of it any more.

She'd let him think things were equal between them, but one thing couldn't be more certain. As a person, she might not be strong enough to stand up to him. But as a police officer, she always would be.

EIGHTY

Grace got out of her car and walked towards the garden of remembrance. In front of her was peace and serenity, overlooked by an autumnal sun that had brought with it a fresh but cheery day. No matter how many times she came here, she always ended up with a lump in her throat. She supposed it was to be expected, but this visit was a necessity, a trip in between her usual ones to her mum's grave and Matt's final resting place.

Matt had been cremated, so thankfully she hadn't felt as if she was leaving him behind when she'd returned to Stoke. He hadn't wanted to be buried. He didn't want to give her, nor his family, the burden of having to come and visit, tend to a grave and replace dying flowers. So, at his parents' home, they had planted a bush in his memory.

Grace realised now that she missed his family. She'd always got on with his sister, Steph, and his younger brother, Benjamin, but being the loner that she was, once Matt was no longer there, it had seemed awkward. She'd let visits between them get longer and longer. It had been easier to deal with.

She turned and headed down a pathway, hedges either side that led to a large circle of lawn, benches dotted around its circumference. Flowers were blooming, leaves dropping and the sense of peace she felt overwhelmed her. She sat down: there would be no tears today.

Matt would have been so proud of her, cracking her first case as a detective sergeant. He would have been pleased how she had handled things, despite the mistakes she had made. She missed him so much, every day, but she was ready to move on now.

She hummed a little to herself and then smiled when she realised the tune. 'Pretty Amazing Grace' would always remind her of Matt, and the life they had shared, even if it had been cut short. He used to sing the song to her all the time, and she hadn't been able to listen to it since.

She got out her phone and looked up the song, sung by Neil Diamond. Digging out her earphones, she listened to it, its words of peace and love and hope surrounding her with the same.

It had been two long years without him, yet it wasn't hard for her to imagine he was sitting by the side of her now, or to feel her husband's hand as it rested on the top of hers.

'I want you to know that although I'm moving on, you will always have a place in my heart that will never be open to anyone else,' she whispered. She put a hand to her chest. 'Right here. But I . . . I think you would have liked the man who's walking towards me now.'

Simon said he'd give her time alone before joining her. He'd done the same during the week. Even though they had seen each other at work, he'd sent her text messages – chatty how-are-you types, nothing more committed. They'd talked and she'd invited him to visit with her today.

'Hey you,' he said as he joined her.

A hand went through his hair, something she had noticed he did when he was nervous.

'Hey yourself.' She looked at him, feeling an instant blush come to her skin.

'So, what do we do now?' Simon asked after they had sat in silence for a few minutes.

'I think you should take me out.' She nodded. 'On a proper date. Make me laugh, make me *feel* again.'

The smile he gave her could have lit up any city at night. 'I can certainly try,' he replied.

She returned the smile shyly. A brighter future, that's what she needed. She had to let someone in or else face being lonely for the rest of her life. It might not lead to anything, but it could take her some way on the journey to finding happiness again.

She had to give her and Simon a chance. There was no need to be lonely any more.

The wind blew her hair and it whipped across her face. Finally, she felt able to say goodbye to her husband. Or au revoir, for now.

With Simon by her side, she turned and walked out of the garden the way she had come. She didn't look back.

She didn't feel burdened with the grief of it all any more. This is what Matt would have wanted. And this is what she wanted too. Her home for now was in Stoke-on-Trent. Let the Steeles do their worst. She was made from stronger stuff than them.

She was an Allendale.

AUTHOR NOTE

To all my fellow Stokies, my apologies if you don't gel with any of the Stoke references that I've changed throughout the book. Obviously, writing about local things such as *The Sentinel*, Hanley Police Station and Staffordshire University would make it a little too close to home, and I wasn't comfortable leaving everything authentic, so I took a leaf out of Arnold Bennett's 'book' and changed some things slightly. However, there were no oatcakes harmed in the process.

TICK TOCK

Is time running out for Grace and her team?

Mel Sherratt returns with a thrilling new book
April 2019